KOKORO

A NOVEL

The very best of Japanese fiction and nonfiction now in English translation.

THE LIBRARY OF JAPAN

The Library of Japan is an unprecedented attempt to collect the best of Japanese fiction and nonfiction, in good modern translation, for presentation to a western audience. Produced under the aegis of the Japan-U.S. Conference on Cultural and Educational Exchange, its 30 volumes are designed to make Americans aware of a fascinating literary treasure trove, much of it not hitherto available in English. Co-chaired by Daniel J. Boorstin, historian and former Librarian of Congress, and Frank B. Gibney, Vice Chairman of Encyclopaedia Britannica's Board of Editors and author of numerous works on Japan and the Far East, the editorial board includes scholars and editors from both countries. Despite their academic sponsorship the books in the series are designed specifically for the general reader, to make Americans aware of the remarkable social and cultural underpinnings of modern Japan. The first volumes, spanning the past 150 years, make their own statement about Japan's self-modernization and its eminence as a world cultural as well as economic force.

Kokoro
A NOVEL

AND SELECTED ESSAYS

Natsume Sōseki

Translated by
Edwin McClellan

Essays translated by
Jay Rubin

Preface and Foreword to Essays by
Jay Rubin

MADISON BOOKS
Lanham • New York • London

Madison Books
4720 Boston Way
Lanham, Maryland 20706

3 Henrietta Street
London WC2E 8LU England

Distributed by National Book Network

Co-published by arrangement with the
Pacific Basin Institute

The paper used in this publication meets the minimum
requirements of American National Standard for
Information Sciences—Permanence of Paper for
Printed Library Materials, ANSI Z39.48–1984.♾™
Manufactured in the United States of America.

The Library of Japan Edition First Published
February 1992.

Library of Congress Cataloging-in-Publication Data

Natsume, Sōseki, 1867-1916.
[Kokoro.   English]
Kokoro a novel and selected essays / Natsume Sōseki ;
translated by Edwin McClellan, essays translated by
Jay Rubin.
p.   cm.— (Library of Japan)
Includes bibliographical references.
1. Natsume, Sōseki, 1867-1916—Translations into
English.   I. McClellan, Edwin, 1925-   .
II. Title.   III. Series.
PL812.A8A26   1992
895.6'342—dc20   91-33241 CIP

ISBN 0–8191–8248–6 (cloth, alk. paper)

British Cataloging in Publication Information Available

Partial funding provided by The Japan Foundation and
the Japan–United States Friendship Commission.

CONTENTS

TRANSLATOR'S NOTE

Sōseki wrote *Kokoro* in 1914, two years before his death and two years after the death of Emperor Meiji. The emperor's death marked the end of an era that had begun in 1868 and that meant so much to Japanese like the first narrator's father and, perhaps in a different way, to Sensei, the second narrator in the novel. "On the night of the Imperial Funeral I sat in my study and listened to the booming of the cannon," writes Sensei. "To me, it sounded like the last lament for the passing of an age."

General Nogi, whose death is also mentioned, was the general who led the costly attack on Port Arthur during the Russo-Japanese War (1904–1905). He committed ritual suicide on the day of the emperor's funeral. One ostensible reason for this—the one given in the novel and seemingly accepted by Sensei—was that in the civil strife known as the Seinan War (1877), in which Nogi served as a regimental commander in the Imperial Army, his regiment had lost its standard to the enemy in battle and, in atonement for the disgrace, he killed himself years later when his emperor was dead.

Lafcadio Hearn, who taught English literature at the Imperial University of Tokyo before Sōseki, defines "*kokoro*" as the "heart of things." It is as good a definition in English of the elusive word as any I know.

Edwin McClellan
New Haven, 1991

PREFACE

Histories of modern Japanese literature present a melange of schools, movements, groups, and splinter groups, but they always give the novelist Natsume Sōseki (1867–1916) a chapter of his own. Sōseki towers over the latter part of the Meiji Period (1868–1912) and the first years of Taishō (1912–1926) as if he had attained artistic and intellectual heights that separated him permanently from his contemporaries. And now he stares out at his countrymen from the site of his ultimate lone enshrinement: the face of the thousand-yen bill.

Sōseki was very much a man of his times, however. Like other Meiji writers—Ōgai, Tōson, Katai, Doppo, Ichiyō, Shōyō, Roan, Kōyō, Rohan—he took a two-character literary name that linked him with the early poets; it is as "Sōseki," rather than by his given name, Kinnosuke, that he was and is known to his countrymen. And although he is invariably labeled an "antinaturalist," his writings shared much thematically and stylistically with the novels of the school that dominated the literary scene after the Russo-Japanese War of 1904–1905, when Sōseki first started to publish. He clearly saw himself as aligned with the new generation of writers who were questioning traditional values, and he spoke out in defense of the naturalists when government agencies strove to diminish their impact.

Central to the literary project of the naturalists and of Sōseki—and what made them all appear deeply suspicious to members of the establishment—was their exploration of the self. In neither case, however, do we see a simple affirmation of the independent self in opposition to family or nation, for, having found the self, the writers quickly realized that this modern entity brought with it the pain of isolation.

In a passage well known to students of the Japanese language, the critic Nakamura Mitsuo speaks of the "paradoxical pride" felt by Meiji intellectuals "in living in doubt and disillusionment."[1] They were proud of their accomplishment in having discovered their separate identities, and miserable at being cut off from the enfolding communities that had once provided them assurances of continuity and belonging.

If these themes—rebellion, generational conflict, self-discovery, loneliness—sound somewhat adolescent, then perhaps the late Meiji period can be seen as a time of national adolescence. And if Sōseki was the writer who articulated these problems of his time with the greatest clarity and forcefulness, then we may be justified in seeing him as an artist of the stature of a Dostoevsky, whose deep sensitivity to his age and nation yielded works that transcend both.

Each new generation of Japanese readers rediscovers Sōseki. And Western readers who discover Sōseki find in him not an exotic curiosity but a modern intellect doing battle in familiar territory. This is especially true in the case of *Kokoro* (1914), the twelfth of the fourteen novels that Sōseki published between 1905 and 1916. The novel can be read with a minimum of background information and commentary. Its simple cast of characters requires no list of dramatis personae. But for readers who wish to explore the ideas and events that lay behind Sōseki's work, it is presented here along with two of his best-known lectures, "The Civilization of Modern-day Japan" (1911) and "My Individualism" (1914).

Note

1. Nakamura Mitsuo, *Nihon no kindai shōsetsu* (Iwanami shoten, 1954), p. 137.

SENSEI AND I

I always called him "Sensei."[1] I shall therefore refer to him simply as "Sensei," and not by his real name. It is not because I consider it more discreet, but it is because I find it more natural that I do so. Whenever the memory of him comes back to me now, I find that I think of him as "Sensei" still. And with pen in hand, I cannot bring myself to write of him in any other way.

It was at Kamakura, during the summer holidays, that I first met Sensei. I was then a very young student. I went there at the insistence of a friend of mine, who had gone to Kamakura to swim. We were not together for long. It had taken me a few days to get together enough money to cover the necessary expenses, and it was only three days after my arrival that my friend received a telegram from home demanding his return. His mother, the telegram explained, was ill. My friend, however, did not believe this. For some time his parents had been trying to persuade him, much against his will, to marry a certain girl. According to our modern outlook, he was really too young to marry. Moreover, he was not in the least fond of the

---

1. The English word "teacher" which comes closest in meaning to the Japanese word *sensei* is not satisfactory here. The French word *maître* would express better what is meant by *sensei*.

girl. It was in order to avoid an unpleasant situation that instead of going home, as he normally would have done, he had gone to the resort near Tokyo to spend his holidays. He showed me the telegram, and asked me what he should do. I did not know what to tell him. It was, however, clear that if his mother was truly ill, he should go home. And so he decided to leave after all. I, who had taken so much trouble to join my friend, was left alone.

There were many days left before the beginning of term, and I was free either to stay in Kamakura or to go home. I decided to stay. My friend was from a wealthy family in the Central Provinces, and had no financial worries. But being a young student, his standard of living was much the same as my own. I was therefore not obliged, when I found myself alone, to change my lodgings.

My inn was in a rather out-of-the-way district of Kamakura, and if one wished to indulge in such fashionable pastimes as playing billiards and eating ice cream, one had to walk a long way across rice fields. If one went by rickshaw, it cost twenty sen. Remote as the district was, however, many rich families had built their villas there. It was quite near the sea also, which was convenient for swimmers such as myself.

I walked to the sea every day, between thatched cottages that were old and smoke-blackened. The beach was always crowded with men and women, and at times the sea, like a public bath, would be covered with a mass of black heads. I never ceased to wonder how so many city holiday-makers could squeeze themselves into so small a town. Alone in this noisy and happy crowd, I managed to enjoy myself, dozing on the beach or splashing about in the water.

It was in the midst of this confusion that I found Sensei. In those days, there were two tea houses on the beach. For no particular reason, I had come to patronize one of them. Unlike those people with their great villas in the Hase area who had their own bathing huts, we in our part of the beach were obliged to make use of these tea houses which served also as communal changing rooms. In them the bathers would drink tea, rest, have their bathing suits rinsed, wash the salt from their bodies, and leave their hats and sunshades for safekeeping. I owned no bathing suit to change into, but I was afraid of being robbed, and so I regularly left my things in the tea house before going into the water.

*

Sensei had just taken his clothes off and was about to go for a swim when I first laid eyes on him in the tea house. I had already had my swim, and was letting the wind blow gently on my wet body. Between us, there were numerous black heads moving about. I was in a relaxed frame of mind, and there was such a crowd on the beach that I should never have noticed him had he not been accompanied by a Westerner.

The Westerner, with his extremely pale skin, had already attracted my attention when I approached the tea house. He was standing with folded arms, facing the sea; carelessly thrown down on the stool by his side was a Japanese summer dress which he had been wearing. He had on him only a pair of drawers such as we were accustomed to wear. I found this particularly strange. Two days previously I had gone to Yuigahama and, sitting on top of a small dune close to the rear entance of a Western-style hotel, I had whiled away the time watching the Westerners bathe. All of them had their torsos, arms, and thighs well-covered. The women especially seemed overly modest. Most of them were wearing brightly colored rubber caps which could be seen bobbing conspicuously amongst the waves. After having observed such a scene, it was natural that I should think this Westerner, who stood so lightly clad in our midst, quite extraordinary.

As I watched, he turned his head to the side and spoke a few words to a Japanese, who happened to be bending down to pick up a small towel which he had dropped on the sand. The Japanese then tied the towel around his head, and immediately began to walk towards the sea. This man was Sensei.

From sheer curiosity, I stood and watched the two men walk side by side towards the sea. They strode determinedly into the water and, making their way through the noisy crowd, finally reached a quieter and deeper part of the sea. Then they began to swim out, and did not stop until their heads had almost disappeared from my sight. They turned around and swam straight back to the beach. At the tea house, they dried themselves without washing the salt off with fresh water from the well and, quickly donning their clothes, they walked away.

After their departure, I sat down, and lighting a cigarette, I began idly to wonder about Sensei. I could not help feeling that I had seen him somewhere before, but failed to recollect where or when I had met him.

I was a bored young man then, and for lack of anything better to do, I went to the tea house the following day at exactly the same hour, hoping to see Sensei again. This time, he arrived without the Westerner, wearing a straw hat. After carefully placing his spectacles on a nearby table and then tying his hand towel around his head, he once more walked quickly down the beach. And when I saw him wading through the same noisy crowd, and then swim out all alone, I was suddenly overcome with the desire to follow him. I splashed through the shallow water until I was far enough out, and then began to swim towards Sensei. Contrary to my expectation, however, he made his way back to the beach in a sort of arc, rather than in a straight line. I was further disappointed when I returned, dripping wet, to the tea house: he had already dressed, and was on his way out.

*

I saw Sensei again the next day, when I went to the beach at the same hour; and again on the following day. But no opportunity arose for a conversation, or even a casual greeting, between us. His attitude, besides, seemed somewhat unsociable. He would arrive punctually at the usual hour, and depart as punctually after his swim. He was always aloof and, no matter how gay the crowd around him might be, he seemed totally indifferent to his surroundings. The Westerner, with whom he had first come, never showed himself again. Sensei was always alone.

One day, however, after his usual swim, Sensei was about to put on his summer dress which he had left on the bench, when he noticed that the dress, for some reason, was covered with sand, As he was shaking his dress, I saw his spectacles, which had been lying beneath it, fall to the ground. He seemed not to miss them until he had finished tying his belt. When he began suddenly to look for them, I approached, and bending down, I picked up his spectacles from under the bench. "Thank you," he said, as I handed them to him.

The next day, I followed Sensei into the sea, and swam after him. When we had gone more than a couple of hundred yards out, Sensei turned and spoke to me. The sea stretched, wide and blue, all around us, and there seemed to be no one near us. The bright sun shone on the

5

water and the mountains, as far as the eye could see. My whole body seemed to be filled with a sense of freedom and joy, and I splashed about wildly in the sea. Sensei had stopped moving, and was floating quietly on his back. I then imitated him. The dazzling blue of the sky beat against my face, and I felt as though little, bright darts were being thrown into my eyes. And I cried out, "What fun this is!"

After a while, Sensei moved to an upright position and said, "Shall we go back?" I, who was young and hardy wanted very much to stay. But I answered willingly enough, "Yes, let us go back." And we returned to the shore together.

That was the beginning of our friendship. But I did not yet know where Sensei lived.

It was, I think, on the afternoon of the third day following our swim together that Sensei, when we met at the tea house, suddenly asked me, "Do you intend to stay in Kamakura long?" I had really no idea how much longer I would be in Kamakura, so I said, "I don't know." I then saw that Sensei was grinning, and I suddenly became embarrassed. I could not help blurting out, "And you, Sensei?" It was then that I began to call him "Sensei."

That evening, I visited Sensei at his lodgings. He was not staying at an ordinary inn, but had his rooms in a mansion-like building within the grounds of a large temple. I saw that he had no ties of any kind with the other people staying there. He smiled wryly at the way I persisted in addressing him as "Sensei," and I found myself explaining that it was my habit to so address my elders. I asked him about the Westerner, and he told me that his friend was no longer in Kamakura. His friend, I was told, was somewhat eccentric. He spoke to me of other things concerning the Westerner too, and then remarked that it was strange that he, who had so few acquaintances among his fellow Japanese, should have become intimate with a foreigner. Finally, before leaving, I said to Sensei that I felt I had met him somewhere before but that I could not remember where or when. I was young, and as I said this I hoped, and indeed expected, that he would confess to the same feeling. But after pondering awhile, Sensei said to me, "I cannot remember ever having met you before. Are you not mistaken?" And I was filled with a new and deep sense of disappointment.

*

I returned to Tokyo at the end of the month. Sensei had left the resort long before me. As we were taking leave of each other, I had asked him, "Would it be all right if I visited you at your home now and then?" And he had answered quite simply, "Yes, of course." I had been under the impression that we were intimate friends, and had somehow expected a warmer reply. My self-confidence, I remember, was rather shaken then.

Often, during my association with Sensei, I was disappointed in this way. Sometimes, Sensei seemed to know that I had been hurt, and sometimes, he seemed not to know. But no matter how often I experienced such trifling disappointments, I never felt any desire to part from Sensei. Indeed, each time I suffered a rebuff, I wished more than ever to push our friendship further. I thought that with greater intimacy, I would perhaps find in him those things that I looked for. I was very young, it is true. But I think that I would not have behaved quite so simply towards others. I did not understand then why it was that I should behave thus towards Sensei only. But now, when Sensei is dead, I am beginning to understand. It was not that Sensei disliked me at first. His curt and cold ways were not designed to express his dislike of me, but they were meant rather as a warning to me that I would not want him as a friend. It was because he despised himself that he refused to accept openheartedly the intimacy of others. I feel great pity for him.

I intended of course to visit Sensei when I returned to Tokyo. There were still two weeks left before the beginning of lectures, and I thought I would visit him during that time. A few days after my return, however, I began to feel less inclined to do so. The atmosphere of the great city affected me a great deal, bringing back memories. Every time I saw a student in the streets, I found myself awaiting the coming of the new academic year with a feeling of hope and tense excitement. For a while, I forgot all about Sensei.

A month or so after the start of lectures, I became more relaxed. At the same time, I began to walk about the streets discontentedly, and to look around my room with a feeling that something was lacking in my life. I began to think of Sensei, and I found that I wanted to see him again.

The first time I went to his home, Sensei was out. I remember that I went again the following Sunday. It was a lovely day, and the sky was so blue that I was filled with a sense of well-being. Again, he was not at home. In Kamakura, Sensei had told me that he spent most of his time at home; indeed, he had even told me that he disliked to go out. Remembering this, I felt an unreasonable resentment at having twice failed to find him. I therefore hesitated in the front hall, staring at the maid who had informed me of her master's absence. She seemed to remember that I had called before and left my card. Asking me to wait, she went away. A lady then appeared, whom I took to be the mistress of the house. She was beautiful.

Very courteously, she told me of Sensei's whereabouts. I learned that every month, on the same day, it was Sensei's custom to take flowers to a certain grave in the cemetery at Zōshigaya. "He left here," said the lady regretfully, "hardly more than ten minutes ago." I thanked her and left. Before I had gone very far towards the busier part of town, I decided that it would be a pleasant walk to Zōshigaya. Besides, I might meet Sensei, I thought. I turned around and started to walk in the direction of Zōshigaya.

From the left side of a field I entered the cemetery and proceeded along a broad avenue bordered on each side by maple trees. There was a tea house at the end of the avenue, and I saw coming out of it someone that looked like Sensei. I walked towards him until I could see the sunlight reflected on the frame of his spectacles. Then, suddenly, I cried out aloud, "Sensei!" Sensei stopped, and saw me. "How in the world . . . ?" he said. Then again, "How in the world . . . ?" His words, repeated, seemed to have a strange echo-like effect in the stillness of the afternoon. I did not know what to say.

"Did you follow me? How . . . ?"

He seemed quite relaxed as he stood there, and his voice was calm. But there was on his face a strangely clouded expression.

I explained to Sensei how I happened to be there.

"Did my wife tell you whose grave I was visiting?"

"Oh, no."

"Well, I suppose there was no reason why she should. After all, she met you today for the first time. No, of course not, there was no need for her to tell you."

At last, he appeared satisfied. But I could not understand the reason for his remarks.

We walked between tombstones on our way out. Next to those with inscriptions such as "Isabella So-and-so . . ."

and "Login, Servant of God," were those with Buddhist
inscriptions such as "All living things bear within themselves the essence of Buddha." There was one tombstone,
I remember, on which was written, "Minister Plenipoten-
tiary So-and-so." I stopped before one that was particularly small and, pointing at the three Chinese characters
on it, I asked Sensei, "How does one read that?"

"I presume they are meant to be read as 'Andrew'," said
Sensei, smiling stiffly.

Sensei did not seem to find the way in which different
customs were reflected in the tombstones amusing or
ironical, as I did. Silently, he listened to me for a while as
I chattered on, pointing to this tombstone and that. But
finally he turned to me and said, "You have never thought
seriously of the reality of death, have you?" I became
silent. Sensei said no more.

Towards the end of the cemetery, there stood a gingko
tree, so large that it almost hid the sky from view. Sensei
looked up at the tree and said, "In a little while, it will be
beautiful here. The tree will be a mass of yellow, and the
ground will be buried beneath a golden carpet of fallen
leaves." Every month, I learned, Sensei made a point of
walking by the tree at least once.

Not far from us in the cemetery, a man was leveling off
a piece of rough ground. He stopped and, resting on his
hoe, he watched us. Turning to our left, we soon reached
the main road.

Having no particular destination in mind, I continued to
walk along with Sensei. Sensei was less talkative than
usual. I felt no acute embarrassment, however, and I
strolled unconcernedly by his side.

"Are you going straight home?"

"Yes. There is nothing else I particularly want to do
now."

Silently, we walked downhill towards the south.

Again I broke the silence. "Is your family burial ground there?" I asked.

"No."

"Whose grave is it, then? Some relation of yours perhaps?"

"No."

Sensei would say no more about it. I decided to mention the matter no further. But after he had walked a hundred yards or so, Sensei suddenly reopened the conversation.

"A friend of mine happens to be buried there."

"And you visit his grave every month?"

"Yes."

Sensei told me no more that day.

*

After that day, I began to visit Sensei at regular intervals. I found him always at home. And the more I visited Sensei, the more eager I became to see him again.

Despite this, however, there was no great change in Sensei's manner towards me. He was always quiet. At times, he seemed so quiet that I thought him rather lonely. I felt from the start his strangely unapproachable quality. Yet, at the same time, there was within me an irresistible desire to become close to Sensei. Perhaps I was the only one who felt thus towards him. Some might say that I was being foolish and naïve. But even now, I feel a certain pride and happiness in the fact that my intuitive fondness for Sensei was later shown to have not been in vain. A man capable of love, or I should say rather a man who was by nature incapable of not loving; but a man who could not wholeheartedly accept the love of another—such a one was Sensei.

As I have already said, Sensei was always quiet. Moreover, he seemed to be at peace with himself. But sometimes I would notice a shadow cross his face. True, like the shadow of a bird outside the window, it would quickly disappear. The first time I noticed it was at the cemetery at Zōshigaya, when I suddenly spoke to him. I remember that I felt then, though only for a passing moment, a strange weight on my heart. Soon after, the memory of that moment faded away. One evening, however, towards the end of the Indian summer, it was unexpectedly brought back to my mind.

As I was talking to Sensei, I happened for some reason to think of the great gingko tree that he had pointed out to me. And I remembered that his monthly visit to the grave was only three days away. Thinking that it would fall on the day when my lectures ended at noon, and that I should be relatively free, I turned to Sensei and said:

"Sensei, I wonder if the gingko tree at Zōshigaya has lost all its leaves by now?"

"I doubt that it will be quite bare yet."

Sensei was watching me carefully. I said quickly:

"May I accompany you, when you next visit the grave? I should like to take a walk around there with you."

"I go to visit a grave, not for a walk, you know."

"But surely, we can go for a walk at the same time?"

Sensei was silent for a while, then said, "Believe me, visiting the grave is for me a truly serious matter." He seemed quite determined to distinguish between his pilgrimage to the grave and an ordinary walk. I began to wonder whether he was making this excuse because he did not wish me to accompany him. I remember that I thought him oddly childish at the time. I became more forward.

"Well, then," I said, "please allow me to accompany you as a fellow visitor to the grave." I really did think

Sensei's attitude rather unreasonable. A shadow crossed his brow, and his eyes shone strangely. I cannot say whether it was annoyance or dislike or fear that I saw in his expression. But whatever it was, there was beneath it, I felt, a gnawing anxiety. And I was suddenly reminded of the way he looked that day at Zōshigaya when I called to him.

"I cannot tell you why," Sensei said to me, "but for a very good reason I wish to go to that grave alone. Even my wife, you see, has never come with me."

I thought his behavior very strange. But I did not visit Sensei with the purpose of studying him. And I decided to think no more about it. My attitude towards Sensei then is one of those things that I remember with a certain amount of pride. Because of it, I believe, we were able to become so close to each other. Had I been curious in an impersonal and analytical way, the bond between us would surely not have lasted. I was, of course, not aware of all this at the time. I hate to think what might have happened had I acted differently. Even in his relationship with me, he was in constant dread of being coldly analyzed.

I began to visit Sensei two or even three times a month. One day, seeing that my visits were becoming more and more frequent, Sensei suddenly said to me:

"Why should you want to spend so much time with a person like me?"

"Why? I don't think there's any particular reason . . . Am I a nuisance, sir?"

"I did not say that."

Indeed, he never seemed to regard me as a nuisance. I was aware that the number of his acquaintances was rather limited. As for those who had been in the same class with him at the university, I knew there were no more than two or three in Tokyo. Sometimes, I would find at his house students who were from the same part of the country as Sensei, but it seemed to me that none of them were as close to him as I was.

"I am a lonely man," Sensei said. "And so I am glad that you come to see me. But I am also a melancholy man, and so I asked you why you should wish to visit me so often."

"But why should you want to ask?"

Sensei did not answer me. Instead, he looked at me and said, "How old are you?"

The conversation seemed to me to be rather purposeless. Without pursuing it any further, I left. Four days later, I was back again at his house. As soon as Sensei appeared, he began to laugh.

"You're back again," he said.

"Yes, I'm back," I said, and I laughed with him.

Had anyone else spoken in such a way to me, I think I should have been annoyed. With Sensei, it was somehow different. Far from being annoyed, I was happy.

"I am a lonely man," he said again that evening. "And is it not possible that you are also a lonely person? But I am an older man, and I can live with my loneliness, quietly. You are young, and it must be difficult to accept your loneliness. You must sometimes want to fight it."

"But I am not at all lonely."

"Youth is the loneliest time of all. Otherwise why should you come so often to my house?"

Sensei continued: "But surely, when you are with me, you cannot rid yourself of your loneliness. I have not it in me to help you forget it. You will have to look elsewhere for the consolation you seek. And soon, you will find that you no longer want to visit me."

As he said this, Sensei smiled sadly.

*

Fortunately, Sensei was mistaken. Inexperienced as I was then, I could not even understand the obvious significance of Sensei's remarks. I continued to see Sensei as before. And before long, I found myself dining at his house occasionally. As a result, I was obliged to speak to Sensei's wife also.

Like any other young man, I was not indifferent to women. But being young and my experience of the world being what it was, I had so far not had any opportunity to form any friendship with a woman. My interest in women had been limited to glances thrown at those who were completely unknown to me. The first time I met Sensei's wife in the front hall, I thought her beautiful. And each time I saw her after that, I was similarly impressed by her beauty. But I felt, at first, that there was nothing of any interest that I could speak to her about.

Rather than to say that she possessed no special qualities worthy of note, it would perhaps be more correct to say that she had never been given an opportunity to show them. My feeling was always that she was little more than a necessary part of Sensei's household. And it would seem that she regarded me, albeit with goodwill, simply as a student who came to talk with her husband. Apart from Sensei, there was no bond of sympathy between us. My memory of the early part of our acquaintance, then, consists of nothing more than the impression of her beauty.

One evening, I was invited by Sensei to join him in a cup of saké. Sensei's wife came to serve us. Sensei seemed more cheerful than usual. Offering his empty cup, he said to his wife, "You have some too."

"No, I don't really . . . ," she began to say, then accepted the cup somewhat unwillingly. Frowning slightly, she raised to her lips the cup that I had half-filled for her. A conversation then followed between her and Sensei.

"This is so unusual," she said. "You hardly ever ask me to drink saké."

"That's because you don't like saké. But it does you good to drink occasionally. This will cheer you up."

"It certainly will not. It makes me feel uncomfortable. You, however, seem to have become quite gay. And you haven't had much."

"Yes, sometimes it seems to cheer me up. But you know, it doesn't always."

"And how do you feel tonight?"

"Oh, tonight I feel good."

'Then from now on, you should drink—just a little— every evening."

"That, I cannot do."

"Please do. Then you will stop being melancholy."

Apart from them, there was only the maid in the house. Every time I went there, the house seemed to be absolutely quiet. I never heard the sound of laughter there, and sometimes it seemed almost as if Sensei and I were the only people in it.

"It would be so nice if we had children," Sensei's wife said to me. "Yes, wouldn't it?" I answered. But I could feel no real sympathy for her. At my age, children seemed an unnecessary nuisance.

"Would you like it if we adopted a child?"

"An adopted child? Oh no," she said, and looked at me.

"But we'll never have one of our own, you know," said Sensei.

Sensei's wife was silent.

"Why not?" I asked.

"Divine punishment," Sensei answered, and laughed rather loudly.

*

Sensei and his wife seemed to me to be a fond enough couple. Not being a member of the family, I could not of course know how they truly felt towards each other. But whenever I was with Sensei, and if he happened to want anything, instead of the maid, he would call his wife. (The lady's name was Shizu). "Shizu," Sensei would call, turning towards the door. The tone of his voice, when he did so, always sounded gentle to me. And her manner, when she appeared, seemed always willing and obedient. And whenever they kindly invited me to dinner, and I had occasion to see them together at the table, my pleasant impression of their feelings towards each other would be confirmed.

Sometimes, Sensei would take his wife to a concert or to the theatre. Also, I remember that they went away together for a week's holiday at least two or three times during the period I knew them. I still have with me a postcard that they sent me from Hakone. And I remember that the time they went to Nikkō, I received from them a letter with a maple leaf enclosed.

There was, however, one incident that marred my general impression of their married life. One day, I was standing as usual in their front hall, and was about to announce myself. I heard voices coming from the living room. An argument, rather than an ordinary conversation, seemed to be taking place. The living-room was immediately adjoining the front hall, and I could hear well enough to know that it was a quarrel, and that one of the voices, which was raised now and then, belonged to Sensei. The other voice was lower in tone than Sensei's, and I could not be sure whose it was. But I was almost certain that it was his wife's. She seemed to be weeping. I stood there for a short while, not knowing what to do. Then I left, and returned to my lodgings.

A dreadful anxiety filled my heart. I tried to read, but found that I could not concentrate. An hour later, I heard Sensei calling from beneath my window. Surprised, I looked out. "Let us go for a walk," he said. I looked at my watch and saw that it was past eight o'clock. I had not bothered to change my clothes when I returned. I left my room immediately.

That evening, Sensei and I drank beer together. Sensei was not a heavy drinker. He was not the sort of person to go on drinking if a reasonable amount did not have any cheering effect on him.

"It just won't work this evening," Sensei said, with a wry smile.

"Can't you feel gay?" I asked, feeling sorry for him.

I could not forget what had happened earlier that day. It bothered me terribly, like a fish bone in my throat. I could not decide whether I should tell him about it or not. Sensei noticed my anxiety.

"There seems to be something the matter with you this evening," he said. "To tell you the truth, I am not my usual self either. Have you noticed?"

I could not say anything in reply.

"As a matter of fact, I quarreled with my wife a short while ago. And I allowed myself to become stupidly excited."

"But why did you . . . ?" I began, but could not bring myself to say "quarrel."

"You see, sometimes my wife misunderstands me. And when I tell her so, she refuses to listen. That is why today, for instance, I unwittingly lost my temper."

18

"In what way does she misunderstand you, Sensei?"

Sensei did not answer my question. He said:

"If I were the sort of person she thinks I am, I would not suffer so."

How he suffered, my imagination then could not conceive.

On our way back, we walked for a while in silence. Then he began to speak again.

"I did a terrible thing. I should not have left home in such a fit of temper. My wife must be worried about me. When we think about it, women are unfortunate creatures. My wife, for instance, has no one in this world but me to depend upon."

He was silent for a while. He seemed not to expect a reply from me. He then continued:

"Of course, my last remark would lead one to suppose that the husband is self-reliant. Which is laughable. Tell me, how do I appear to you? Do you think me a strong or a weak person?"

"Somewhere in-between," I answered. My reply, it would seem, was a little unexpected. He became silent again, and we continued our walk.

The road leading to Sensei's house passed very near my own lodgings. When we reached the corner of my street and I was about to bid him goodnight, I began to feel that it would somehow be heartless to leave him then and there. "Shall I walk you home?" I said. He made a quick, negative gesture with his hand.

"You had better go home. It's late. I must go home too. For my wife's sake . . ."

"For my wife's sake . . ."; these last words of Sensei's strangely warmed my heart. Because of them I was able to enjoy an untroubled sleep that night. And for a long time after, those words stayed with me: "For my wife's sake . . ."

I knew then that the disagreement which had occurred between them was not very serious. I continued to visit them regularly, and I could see that it had been an exceptional occurrence. Moreover, he took me into his confidence one day and said:

"In all the world, I know only one woman. No woman but my wife moves me as a woman. And my wife regards me as the only man for her. From this point of view, we should be the happiest of couples."

I cannot remember clearly why it was that he took the trouble of telling me this. But I do remember that his manner at the time was serious, and that he was calm. What struck me then as being odd was his last remark: ". . . we should be the happiest of couples." Why "should be"? Why did he not say, "We *are* the happiest of couples"? Was Sensei indeed happy? I could not but wonder. But very soon, I brushed aside my doubts concerning Sensei's happiness.

One day, for the first time since I met her, I had a good talk with Sensei's wife. I had previously asked Sensei to discuss a book with me, and he had kindly invited me to visit him that day for that purpose. I arrived at nine o'clock in the morning, as arranged. I found Sensei out. A friend of his, I learned, was sailing from Yokohama, and Sensei had gone to see him off at Shimbashi. In those days, the boat train to Yokohama customarily left Shimbashi at eight-thirty in the morning. Sensei had left a message for me, however, saying that he would be back soon and that I should wait. While waiting for Sensei, therefore, I talked to his wife.

*

By then, I was already a university student.[2] I felt that I had become more mature since my first visit to Sensei's house. I had also become quite familiar with Sensei's wife. Therefore, when I found myself alone with her, I did not feel at all ill at ease. We talked of this and that. I should not have remembered the conversation at all, had it not been for the fact that, in the course of it, we talked of one matter which was of particular interest to me. Before I go on to say what this was, I should perhaps explain a few things about Sensei.

Sensei was a graduate of the university. I knew this from the first. But it was only after my return to Tokyo from Kamakura that I discovered he had no particular employment. I wondered at the time how he managed to support himself.

Sensei lived in complete obscurity. Apart from myself, there was no one who knew of Sensei's scholarship or his ideas. I often remarked to him that this was a great pity. But he would pay no attention to me. "There is no sense," he once said to me, "in such a person as myself expressing his thoughts in public." This remark struck me as being too modest, and I wondered whether it did not spring from a contempt of the outside world. Indeed, he was sometimes not above saying rather unkind things about those of his classmates who had since their graduation made names for themselves. This apparent inconsistency in his attitude, which was at once modest and contemptuous, I quite frankly pointed out to him once. I did not do this in a rebellious spirit. I simply regretted the fact that the world was indifferent to Sensei, whom I admired so much. In a very quiet voice, Sensei answered me: "You see, there is nothing we can do about it. I do not have the

2. He had been a "college" student before.

right to expect anything from the world." There was, as he said this, an expression on his face which affected me profoundly. I did not know whether what I saw was despair, regret, or grief. I had not the courage to say any more.

As Sensei's wife and I sat and talked, our conversation drifted naturally to the subject of Sensei.

"Why does Sensei," I asked, "not go out into the world and find himself some position that is worthy of his talents, instead of spending all his time studying and thinking at home?"

"There is no hope of that, I am afraid. He would hate it."

"I suppose he sees that it would be a vain thing to do?"

"Being a woman, I wouldn't know. But I doubt that that is the reason. I am sure he would like to do something, really. But somehow, he can't. I am very sorry for him."

"But he is in good health, is he not?"

"Certainly. He is perfectly well."

"Well then, why doesn't he do something?"

"I wish I knew. Do you think that I would be worrying so much if I did? I feel so sorry for him."

Her tone of voice held a great deal of sympathy. Her lips, however, were smiling slightly. As far as our outward manner was concerned, I must have seemed the more anxious of the two. I sat there, silent and serious. She looked up, as though she suddenly remembered something, and said:

"You know, when he was young, he wasn't at all the sort of person he is now. He was quite different. He has changed so much."

"When was he different?" I asked.

"Oh, in his student days."

"Then you knew him when he was a student?"

Sensei's wife blushed a little.

*

She was a Tokyo woman. Both Sensei and she herself had told me this before. Her father had actually come from some such place as Tottori, while her mother had been born in Ichigaya, when Tokyo was still known as Edo. For this reason, she once said, half-jokingly, "I am, as a matter of fact, of mixed blood." Sensei, on the other hand, was from the province of Niigata. It was clear to me, therefore, that her place of origin could not explain how she had come to know Sensei when he was a student. But seeing the blush on her face when I touched on the subject of their youthful acquaintance, I asked no more about it.

In the years between my first meeting with Sensei and his death, I came to know much of what he thought and felt, but, concerning the circumstances of his marriage, he told me almost nothing. I was inclined, sometimes, to regard this reserve on Sensei's part in a favorable light. After all, I would tell myself, he quite naturally would consider it indiscreet and in bad taste to speak of his early courtship to a youth such as myself. But sometimes I was inclined to regard his reserve unfavorably. I liked then to think that his reluctance to discuss such a matter was due to timidity born of the conventions of a generation ago. I thought myself more free, in this respect, and more open-minded, than either Sensei or his wife. Whatever my thoughts regarding Sensei's reserve might have been, they were, of course, only speculations. And there was always, at the back of my speculations, the assumption that their marriage had been the flowering of a beautiful romance.

My assumption was not proved entirely wrong. But I was imagining only a small part of the truth that lay behind their love story. I could not know that there had been in Sensei's life a frightening tragedy, inseparable from his love for his wife. Nor did his own wife know how wretched this tragedy had made him. To this day she does not know. Sensei died keeping his secret from her. Before he could destroy his wife's happiness, he destroyed himself.

I shall not speak here of the tragedy in Sensei's life. And, as I have said before, Sensei and his wife told me almost nothing of their courtship, which had come into being as though for the sake of the tragedy. Sensei's wife said little about it for modesty's sake, but there was a far profounder reason for Sensei's silence.

One day, during the flower-viewing season, Sensei and I went to Ueno. I remember that day well. While we were strolling there, we happened to see a good-looking couple walking, close together, beneath the flowering trees. They seemed unusually fond of each other. The place being rather public, they, rather than the flowers, seemed to be the object of interest for many people.

"They look like a newly married couple," said Sensei.

"They seem to be pretty fond of each other, don't they?" I said, in an amused tone of voice.

There was not even a trace of a smile on Sensei's face. He began deliberately to walk away from the couple. He then said to me:

"Have you ever been in love?"

I said no.

"Don't you want to be in love?"

I said nothing in reply.

"It isn't that you don't want to fall in love, is it?"

"No."

"You made fun of that couple, didn't you? But actually, you sounded to me like a person who is dissatisfied because he has not yet been able to fall in love, though he wants to."

"Did I sound like that?"

"Yes, you did. A person who has been in love himself would have been more tolerant and would have felt warmer towards the couple. But—but do you know that there is guilt also in loving? I wonder if you understand me."

I was surprised, and said nothing.

*

There was a large crowd around us, and every face in it looked happy. We had little opportunity to talk until we reached the woods, where there were no flowers and no people.

"Is there really guilt in loving?" I asked suddenly.

"Yes, surely," Sensei said. He seemed as certain as he did before.

"Why?"

"You will soon find out. In fact, you ought to know already. Your heart has been made restless by love for quite some time now."

Vainly, I searched my heart for an answer.

"But there is no one whom you might call the object of my love," I said. "I have not hidden anything from you, Sensei."

"You are restless because your love has no object. If you could fall in love with some particular person, you wouldn't be so restless."

"But I am not so restless now."

"Did you not come to me because you felt there was something lacking?"

"Yes. But my going to you was not the same thing as wanting to fall in love."

"But it was a step in your life towards love. The friendship that you sought in me is in reality a preparation for the love that you will seek in a woman."

"I think that the two things are totally different."

"No, they are not. But being the kind of man that I am, I cannot help you to rid your heart of that feeling of want. Moreover, peculiar circumstances have made me even more useless than I might have been as a friend. I am truly very sorry. That you will eventually go elsewhere for consolation is a fact I must accept. Indeed, I even hope that you will. But . . ."

I began to feel a strange kind of sorrow.

"Sensei, if you really think that I shall drift away from you, there is nothing I can do about it. But such a thought has so far never crossed my mind."

Sensei did not listen to me.

"But you must be careful," he continued. "You must remember that there is guilt in loving. You may not derive much satisfaction from our friendship, but at least, there is no danger in it. Do you know what it feels like to be tied down by long, black hair?"

I could imagine what Sensei meant, but inexperienced as I was, his words held no reality for me. Also, I had no notion of what Sensei meant by "guilt." I felt a little discontented.

"Sensei, please explain more clearly what you mean by 'guilt'. Otherwise, please let us not discuss this matter again, until I have myself found out what this 'guilt' is."

"It was wrong of me. I had intended to make you aware of certain truths. Instead, I have only succeeded in irritating you. It was wrong of me."

Sensei and I walked slowly in the direction of Uguisu-dani, past the back of the museum. Through the gaps in the fencing, we could see dwarf bamboos growing thickly in one part of the garden. There was about the scene an air of deep, secluded peace.

"Do you know why I go every month to my friend's grave in Zōshigaya?"

Sensei's question was totally unexpected. He should, of course, have known that I did not know. I remained silent. Then, as though realizing what he had just said, Sensei went on:

"I have said the wrong thing again. I was trying to explain my earlier remarks because I thought they had irritated you. But in trying to explain, I find that I have upset you once more. Let us forget the whole matter. But remember, there is guilt in loving. And remember too that, in loving, there is something sacred."

I was more mystified than ever by Sensei's talk. But I never heard him mention the word "love" again.

*

Being young, I was rather inclined to become blindly devoted to a single cause. At least, so I must have appeared to Sensei. I considered conversation with Sensei more profitable than lectures at the university. I valued Sensei's opinions more than I did those of my professors. Sensei, who went his solitary way without saying very much, seemed to me to be a greater man than those famous professors who lectured to me from their platforms.

"You must try to be more sober in your opinions about me," Sensei once said to me.

"But I am being sober," I cried, confidently. Sensei, however, refused to take me seriously.

"You are like a man in a fever. When that fever passes, your enthusiasm will turn to disgust. Your present opinion of me makes me unhappy enough. But when I think of the disillusionment that is to come, I feel even greater sorrow."

"Do you think me so fickle? Do you find me so untrustworthy?"

"I am simply sorry for you."

"I deserve your sympathy but not your trust. Is that what you mean, Sensei?"

He seemed vexed as he turned his face towards the garden. Not long before, the garden had been full of camellias. But now, the flowers, which had brightened the scenery with their rich, red color, were all gone. It had been Sensei's custom to look out from his room and gaze at them.

"It is not you in particular that I distrust, but the whole of humanity."

I could hear the cry of a goldfish vendor from the lane on the other side of the hedge. There was no other sound. The house was some distance from the main road, and we seemed to be surrounded by a complete calm. All was quiet, as usual, inside the house itself. I knew that Sensei's wife was in the next room, busy at her sewing or some such work. And I knew also that she could hear what we were saying. But I momentarily forgot this, as I said:

"Then you have no trust in your wife either?"

Sensei looked a little uneasy. He avoided giving a direct answer to my question.

"I don't even trust myself.- And not trusting myself, I can hardly trust others. There is nothing that I can do, except curse my own soul."

"Surely, Sensei, you think too seriously about these things."

"It is not a matter of what I think. It is what I have done that has led me to feel the way I do. At first, my own act shocked me. Then, I was terribly afraid."

I wanted to pursue the conversation, but we were interrupted by the voice of Sensei's wife, calling him from behind the door. "What is it?" Sensei said. "Can you come here a minute?" his wife said. I had hardly begun to wonder why Sensei had been called to the next room when he returned.

"At any rate," he continued, "don't put too much trust in me. You will learn to regret it if you do. And if you ever allow yourself to feel betrayed, you will then find yourself being cruelly vindictive."

"What do you mean?"

"The memory that you once sat at my feet will begin to haunt you and, in bitterness and shame, you will want to degrade me. I do not want your admiration now, because I do not want your insults in the future. I bear with my loneliness now, in order to avoid greater loneliness in the years ahead. You see, loneliness is the price we have to pay for being born in this modern age, so full of freedom, independence, and our own egotistical selves."

I could not think of anything to say.

*

After that day, I used to wonder each time I saw Sensei's wife whether Sensei's attitude towards her reflected his inner thoughts and, if so, whether she could be satisfied with her condition.

But I could discern neither satisfaction nor dissatisfaction in her manner. Of course, I was not close enough to her to know what her real feelings were. I rarely saw her away from Sensei: besides, in my presence, her behavior was always that of the conventional hostess.

I wondered also why Sensei felt the way he did towards mankind. Was it, I would ask myself, the result of a coldly impartial scrutiny of his own inner self and the contemporary world around him? And if one were as naturally reflective, intelligent, and as removed from the world as Sensei, would one inevitably reach the same conclusions? Such tentative explanations, however, which suggested themselves to my mind, did not completely satisfy me. Sensei's opinions, it seemed to me, were not merely the result of cloistered reflection. They were not, as it were, like the skeleton of a stone house which has been gutted by fire. They were more alive than that. True, Sensei, as I saw him, was primarily a thinker. But his thoughts, I felt, were based firmly on a strong sense of reality. And this sense of reality did not come so much from observation of the experience of others removed from himself, as from his own experience.

Such speculations, however, added little to my understanding of Sensei. Sensei, as a matter of fact, had already given me reason to believe that his thoughts were indeed forced upon him by the nature of his experience. But he had hinted only, and his hints were to me like a vast threatening cloud hanging over my head, vague in outline and yet frightening. The fear within me, nevertheless, was very real.

I tried to explain to myself Sensei's view of life by imagining a love affair in his youth—between Sensei and his wife, of course—involving violent passion at first, and perhaps regret later. Such an explanation, I liked to think, would more or less take into account the association in Sensei's mind of guilt with love. Sensei, however, had admitted to me that he was still in love with his wife. The cause of Sensei's pessimism, then, could not reasonably be traced to their relationship with each other. It seemed that Sensei's misanthropic views which he had expressed to me applied to the modern world in general, but not to his wife.

The memory of the grave in the cemetery at Zōshigaya would come back to me from time to time. That this grave was of some profound significance to Sensei, I knew well. I, who had come so close to Sensei and yet understood him so little, regarded the grave as something that held, in a sense, a fragment of his life. But whatever was buried in it was dead for me, and I knew that I would not find in it the key to Sensei's heart. Indeed, the grave stood like some monstrous thing, forever separating us.

Meanwhile, it so happened that I had another occasion to have a conversation with Sensei's wife. It was at the time of the year when the days grow shorter and there is everywhere a feeling of restless activity. There was already a chill in the air. During the previous week, there had been a series of burglaries in Sensei's neighborhood. They had all taken place in the early hours of the evening. Nothing of great value had been stolen. The houses had been broken into nevertheless, and Sensei's wife was uneasy. Unfortunately, Sensei was obliged to be away from the house one evening. A friend of his from the same part of the country as himself, and who was a doctor in some provincial hospital, had come up to Tokyo. Sensei and two or three others were taking him out to dinner that evening. Explaining the situation, Sensei asked me to stay with his wife until he returned. I agreed to do so willingly.

✳

It was dusk when I reached the house. Sensei, who was a punctilious man, had already left. "My husband did not want to be late. He left only a minute ago," said Sensei's wife, as she led me to her husband's study. The study was furnished partly in the Western style, with a desk and some chairs. A great number of books, bound beautifully in leather, gleamed through the glass panes of the book cases.

Sensei's wife bade me sit down on a cushion by the brazier. "There are plenty of books here for you to read, if you so wish," she said, and left the room. I could not help feeling ill at ease, rather like a chance visitor waiting for the master of the house to return. Sitting stiffly, I began to smoke. I could hear Sensei's wife talking to the maid in the morning room, which was along the same corridor as the study. The study, however, was at the end, and was therefore in a very quiet part of the house. When Sensei's wife stopped talking, I was surrounded by complete silence. Expecting the burglar to appear any minute, I sat very still and listened for any suspicious sound that might break the silence.

About half an hour later, Sensei's wife appeared at the door, "Well!" she said. She seemed both surprised and amused when she saw me sitting there, stiff and serious like a strange guest.

"You seem very uncomfortable," she said.

"Oh, no, I am not at all uncomfortable."

"Then you must be bored."

"Oh, no. I am all tense, waiting for the burglar, and so I am not at all bored."

She remained standing, with a European teacup in her hand, and laughed.

"This room, being in a rather remote corner of the house, is not an ideal place for a watchman," I said.

"Well, in that case, come along to the morning room, if you wish. I brought you some tea, thinking you must be bored. You can have it there."

I followed Sensei's wife out of the study. An iron kettle was singing on a handsome, long brazier in the morning room. There, I was given black tea and cakes. Sensei's wife refused to drink tea herself, saying that she would not be able to go to sleep if she did.

"Does Sensei often go out to dinner parties?" I asked.

"No, hardly ever. It seems that, of late, he has become less inclined than ever to see people."

Sensei's wife seemed to betray no anxiety as she said this, so I became more bold.

"You must then be the only person Sensei likes to be with," I said.

"Certainly not. I am like all the rest in his eyes."

"That is not true," I said. "And you know very well that that is not true."

"What do you mean?"

"Well, I think that he has tired of the company of others because of his fondness for you."

"I see that higher education has made you adept at empty rationalization. You might as well have reasoned that he cannot be fond of me, since I am a part of the world that he dislikes."

"True. But in this case, I am right."

"Let us not argue. You men certainly will argue about anything, and with such obvious pleasure too. I have often wondered how it is that you men can, without becoming bored, forever exchange empty saké cups with one another."

Her words, I thought, were a little harsh. But they did not seem offensive to me. Sensei's wife was not so modern a woman as to take pride and pleasure in being able to display her mental prowess. She valued far more that thing which lies buried in the bottom of one's heart.

∗

I wanted to say more. But I was afraid of being taken for one of these argumentative men, and so I became silent. "Would you like more tea?" Sensei's wife said to me, tactfully, when she saw that I was staring foolishly into the empty teacup. I quickly handed the cup over to her.

"How many? One lump? Two lumps?"

She had picked up a lump of sugar with a strange instrument, and was looking at me when she said this. She was not exactly trying to be ingratiating, but she was undoubtedly trying to eradicate the effect on me of her harsh words by her charming manner.

I drank tea silently. I remained silent even when I had finished the cup.

"You seem to have become very quiet," she said.

"Well, I don't want to be scolded for being argumentative," I answered.

"Come, come," she said.

We began to talk again. The conversation naturally wandered back to the subject of Sensei.

"Won't you allow me to go on with what I was saying?" I said. "It might have seemed to you that I was indulging in meaningless rationalization, but, truly, I was being sincere."

"Well, all right."

"You don't think that Sensei's life would be the same without you, do you now?"

"I certainly wouldn't know. Why don't you ask Sensei? It would be more sensible to ask him."

"Please, I am being serious. You mustn't try to evade my question so frivolously. I wish you would be more honest with me."

"But I am being honest. I honestly don't know."

"Then let me ask you a question that you, rather than Sensei, will be in a position to answer. You are very fond of Sensei, aren't you?"

"Surely, there's no need to ask a question like that. And with such a grave face, too!"

"You mean that the answer is obvious? That it's a silly question to ask?"

"More or less."

"Then what would happen to Sensei if such a loyal companion as yourself were suddenly to leave him? He seems to take little enough pleasure in this world as it is. What would he do without you? I don't want to know how he would answer this question. I want to know what you honestly think. Would he be happy, do you think, or unhappy?"

"Actually, I know the answer. (Though Sensei might not think that I do.) Sensei would be far more unhappy without me. Why, he might not even want to go on living, without me. It may seem very conceited of me, but I do really believe that I am able to make him as happy as is humanly possible. I believe that no one else would be able to make him as happy as I can. Without this belief, I would not be as contented as I am."

"Such a conviction must surely be known to Sensei."

"That is another matter entirely."

"You still wish to maintain that Sensei dislikes you?"

"Oh, no, I don't think for a moment that I am disliked. There is no reason why I should be. But you see, he seems to be rather weary of the world. Indeed, it would be more correct to say of Sensei these days that he is weary of people. And seeing that I am one of those creatures that inhabit this world, I can hardly hope to be regarded as an exception."

I began to understand Sensei's wife better.

*

I was deeply impressed by her capacity for sympathy and understanding. What also impressed me was the fact that, though her ways were not those of an old-fashioned

Japanese woman, she had not succumbed to the then prevailing fashion of using "modern" words.

I was a rather simple-minded young man; women, for example, were total strangers to the kind of world I knew or had experienced. True, being a man, I felt an instinctive yearning for women. But the yearning in me was little more than a vague dream, hardly different from the yearning in one's heart when one sees a lovely cloud in the spring sky. Often, when I found myself face to face with a woman, my longing would suddenly disappear. Instead of being drawn to the woman, I would feel a kind of repulsion. Such, however, was not my reaction to Sensei's wife. I did not even feel, when I was with her, that intellectual gulf which so often separates men from women. Indeed, I soon forgot that she was a woman, and came to regard her as the one person with whom I could share my sincere and sympathetic interest in Sensei.

"Do you remember," I said, "that time when I asked you why Sensei did not go out into the world more, and you replied that he was not always so much of a recluse?"

"Yes, I remember. And really, he was not."

"Then what was he like?"

"The kind of person you wish him to be, the kind of person I wish him to be . . . There was hope and strength in him then."

"What caused him to change so suddenly?"

"The change was not sudden. It came gradually."

"And you were with him all the time that this change was taking place?"

"Of course. I was his wife."

"Surely, then, you must know the cause of the change."

"Unfortunately, no. I am embarrassed to admit this, but no matter how much I think about it I don't seem to be able to find the answer. You have no idea how often I have begged him to tell me the reason for the change."

"What does he say when you ask him?"

"That there is nothing for him to tell, and that there is nothing for me to worry about. He says that it was simply in his nature to change so."

I said nothing. Sensei's wife also became silent. Not a sound came from the maid's room. I forgot all about the burglar.

"You don't think that I am to blame, do you?" she asked me suddenly.

"No," I said.

"Please tell me what you really think. The thought that you might secretly think me responsible is unbearable," she said. "You see, I like to tell myself that I do whatever I can to help Sensei."

"I am sure that Sensei knows that," I said. "Please don't worry. Believe you me, Sensei knows."

She leveled off the cinders in the brazier and poured more water from a jug into the iron kettle. The kettle stopped singing.

"Finally, I could not stand it any longer, and so I asked him to tell me frankly whether he found fault with anything I did. If he would only tell me what my faults were, I said, I would try if possible to correct them. His reply was that I had no faults and that it was himself that was to blame. His answer made me very sad. It made me cry and made me want to be told more than ever what my faults were."

As Sensei's wife said this, I noticed that there were tears in her eyes.

*

At first, I thought of Sensei's wife as a woman of understanding. But in the course of our conversation her manner began gradually to change, and I found that she had ceased to appeal to my mind and that she had begun to move my heart.

There was no ill-feeling between her and Sensei. Indeed, there was no reason why there should be. Yet, there was something that separated her from Sensei. But no matter how hard she tried, she could not find what this thing was that separated them. This, in short, was her predicament.

She claimed that since Sinsei disliked the world so much, it was inevitable that she should become a part of the object of Sensei's dislike. But she could not convince herself that this was the correct explanation. The poor lady could not avoid thinking that perhaps the very opposite of this was true: namely, that Sensei had become weary of the world because of her. But again, she could find no way of confirming her suspicion. Sensei's manner towards her was that of a loving husband. He was kind and thoughtful. Such, then, was her secret which she had kept in her heart all these years in gentle sorrow, and which she revealed to me that night.

"What do you think?" she said. "Is it because of me that he has become like that, or is it because of his view of life or whatever you men call it? Please don't hide anything from me."

I had no intention of hiding anything from her. But since I knew that there were things in Sensei's life that I did not understand, I could not, in my ignorance, hope to comfort Sensei's wife.

"I really don't know," I said.

A look of disappointment appeared on her face, and I felt pity for her. I said quickly:

"But I can assure you that Sensei does not dislike you. I am only repeating what he himself has told me. And you know that Sensei never lies."

Sensei's wife said nothing. After a while, she began to speak again.

"I remember something . . ."

"You mean something that might explain why Sensei changed?"

"Yes. If it was indeed the cause, then I was not responsible. There would be at least a little consolation in knowing that much, if I could be sure . . ."

"Won't you tell me?"

She hesitated, and gazed at her hands which lay folded on her lap.

"I will tell you," she said, "and you must tell me what you think."

"I will do my best."

"I can't tell you all. If I do, Sensei will be very angry. I will tell you only those parts of the story which he would not mind telling you."

I felt a growing tension inside me.

"When Sensei was still at the university, he had a very good friend. Just before this friend was due to graduate, he died. He died suddenly."

Then almost in a whisper, she added, "Actually, his death was not natural." She said this in such a way that I could not help asking immediately, "How?"

"I can't tell you any more about it. At any rate, it was after this friend's death that Sensei began to change gradually. I don't know why he died. I doubt that Sensei does either. On the other hand, when one remembers that the change came after the death, one wonders if Sensei really doesn't know."

"Is it this friend that is buried at Zōshigaya?"

"That again I'm not allowed to say. But can a man change so because of the death of one friend? I should very much like to know. That is what I want you to tell me."

I was forced to admit that I did not think so.

*

I tried, as far as I was able, to comfort Sensei's wife. And it seemed that she was trying to find some comfort in my company. We continued to discuss the death of Sensei's friend and the change in Sensei that followed it. However, I knew too little about the matter to be of much help. Sensei's wife did not seem to know very much about it either, and her uneasiness concerning it amounted to little more than a few grave doubts. Moreover, she was not free to tell me all that she knew. In a sea of uncertainty, then, the comforter and the comforted floated about hopelessly.

At about ten o'clock we heard Sensei's footsteps approaching the front gate. Seeming to forget all that we had been talking about, Sensei's wife quickly stood up and rushed out to meet him. I was left behind, as though my presence had been completely forgotten. I followed Sensei's wife. The maid, who was probably dozing in her room, failed to appear in the front hall to greet her master.

Sensei seemed to be in a rather good mood. But his wife was in even better spirits. I remembered the tears in her eyes and the anxiety in her face, and I could not but notice the quick change in her mood. I did not really doubt her sincerity. But had I been so inclined, I might with some justification have thought that she had been playing on my sympathy during our conversation, as is the way with some women. I was not in a critical frame of mind, however, and I was, if anything, rather relieved to see her so cheerful. There had been no need, I thought to myself, for such concern on my part.

Sensei grinned at me and said, "Thank you for your

trouble. So the burglar didn't come after all?" Then he added, "Are you disappointed?"

"Sorry to have caused you so much inconvenience," said Sensei's wife, as I was about to leave. She seemed not to be apologizing for having taken up so much of a busy student's time, but rather to be apologizing in a joking fashion, for the fact that the burglar did not appear. She then gave me the rest of the cakes, wrapped in a piece of paper, to take home. I put them in my pocket and went out into the cold night. I hurried along the winding and almost deserted alleys towards the busier streets.

I have written in great detail of the happenings of that evening because now, I see their significance. But that evening, by the time I had left Sensei's house with the cakes in my pocket, I attached little importance to the conversation I had with Sensei's wife. After lectures the following day, I went back to my lodgings, as usual, for lunch. On my desk was the package that Sensei's wife had given me. I opened it and, choosing a cake covered with chocolate, I began to eat it. I thought of the couple that had given it to me and decided that they must surely be happy with each other.

Autumn passed uneventfully. I began to take my clothes to Sensei's wife to be mended, and it was then too that I began to be more careful in my dress. She was even kind enough to say that being childless, she welcomed such work as a means of occupying her time.

"This is hand-woven," she once said, pointing to a kimono of mine. "I have never worked on such beautiful material. But it's awfully difficult to sew. I have already broken two needles on it."

But even when she complained thus, there seemed to be no real resentment in her voice.

*

That winter, I was obliged to go home. A letter had come from my mother, saying that my father's illness had taken a turn for the worse, and that though there was no immediate danger, I should come home if possible. As the letter reminded me, my father was, after all, an old man.

My father had been suffering from kidney trouble for some time. As is often the case with people who are past middle age, my father's disease was chronic. But he and the rest of the family had believed that with good care, the disease could be held in check, and my father had often boasted to his visitors that only through careful living had he managed to survive so far.

His condition, however, was worse than we had imagined. According to my mother's letter, he had fainted while pottering about in the garden. At first, it was believed that he had suffered a mild stroke, but the doctor, who later examined him, decided that the fainting fit had been brought on by his kidney disease.

The winter vacation was not far off and, thinking that there was no need for me to return immediately, I decided to stay on till the end of term. A day or two after the arrival of my mother's letter, however, I began to worry. I thought of my father lying in bed, and of my mother worrying, and I decided that I should return at once. I did not have enough money with me for the train fare and, in order to avoid the inconvenience of having to write home for it and wait for its arrival, I decided to go to Sensei for a loan. I wanted, in any case, to pay him a farewell visit.

Sensei was suffering from a cold. As he did not wish to come out into the sitting room, I was asked to see him in his study. Soft sunlight, such as we had rarely seen that winter, filled the study. Into this sunny room, Sensei had brought a large brazier. A metal basin, filled with water, had been placed on it so that the steam rising from it might ease Sensei's breathing.

"I would rather be truly ill than suffer from a trifling cold like this," Sensei said, and smiled unhappily at me.

Remembering that Sensei had never in his life been seriously ill, I was amused.

"I can bear a common cold," I said, "but I certainly don't want anything more serious than that. I am sure you will feel the same way about it as I do, Sensei, when you yourself have been really ill."

"I suppose so. As a matter of fact, my feeling is that if I must be ill, then I should like to be mortally ill."

I did not pay much attention to Sensei's words. I brought out my mother's letter, and I asked him for a loan.

"Certainly," he said. "If that is all you want, I am sure we can give it to you right away."

Sensei called his wife and asked her to bring the money. She returned and, politely placing the money on a sheet of white paper, said, "You must be worried."

"How often has he fainted?" Sensei asked.

"My mother didn't say. But is it usual in such cases to faint often?"

"Yes."

I was then told that Sensei's mother-in-law had died from a similar kidney ailment.

"At any rate," I said, "my father cannot be very well."

"I think not," Sensei said. "I would take his place if I could. . . . Does he suffer from nausea?"

"I don't know. Probably not. At least, there is no mention of it in the letter."

"He is all right," said Sensei's wife, "so long as there is no nausea."

I left Tokyo by train that night.

*

My father was not as ill as I had expected. When I returned, I found him sitting up in bed. "I've been in bed like this," he said, "to keep the others from worrying. I'm really well enough to get up." The next day, he left his bed, much against my mother's wishes. "Because you are here, your father has convinced himself that he is better," my mother said. But it did not seem to me that he was putting up a brave front for my sake.

My elder brother worked in distant Kyūshū, and therefore could not visit my parents, unless he felt that there was a pressing need for him to do so. My elder sister was married, and lived in another province. She also could not easily come home. I, being a student, was therefore the only one of the three children that my parents could call home freely. My father was nevertheless very pleased that I should have returned so soon after receiving my mother's letter, without waiting for the end of term.

"I am sorry that your studies had to be interrupted," said my father. "There has been altogether too much fuss about my slight illness. Your mother writes too many letters." He seemed to have recovered his normal health.

"You will be ill again," I said, "unless you take better care of yourself."

He brushed aside my admonition and said cheerfully:

"Don't you worry. I shall be all right so long as I look after myself as I always have done."

Indeed, my father seemed well enough. He wandered about the house with no sign of strain whatsoever. He looked very pale, it is true, but since this was not a new symptom, we paid little attention to it.

I wrote to Sensei, thanking him for the loan. I said that I would be returning to Tokyo in January and that, if he did not mind, I would wait till then to repay him. I told him that my father was better than I had expected, that there seemed little cause for immediate anxiety, and that he had suffered neither fainting fits nor nausea. I concluded the letter with a polite inquiry about his cold, which I was inclined to regard as a matter of little concern.

I wrote the letter with no expectation of receiving a reply from Sensei. After I had posted it, I told my parents about him. And as I did so, I found myself thinking of Sensei in his study.

"When you go back to Tokyo, why don't you take him some dried mushrooms?"

"Thank you. But I wonder if Sensei eats such things as dried mushrooms?"

"They may not be a delicacy, but surely, no one dislikes them."

Somehow, I could not bring myself to associate dried mushrooms with Sensei.

I was rather surprised when a letter from Sensei arrived. I was even more surprised when I read it, for it seemed to have been written for no particular purpose. Sensei had kindly written, I decided, in reply to my letter. That he should have troubled to do so made me very happy.

In case I have unwittingly given the impression that there was much correspondence between Sensei and myself, I should like to say here that in all the time I knew Sensei, I received from him only two pieces of correspondence that might strictly be called "letters." One of them was the simple letter that I have just mentioned, and the other was a very long letter which he wrote me shortly before his death.

My father, not being allowed to be very active, hardly ever left the house after he got up. Once, on a rather sunny day, he stepped out into the garden. I was worried, and kept close to his side. And when I tried to persuade him to lean on my shoulder, he laughed, and would not listen to me.

*

To help my father forget his boredom, I often played chess with him. We were both by nature very lazy. We would sit on the floor with a footwarmer between us, and a large quilt covering the footwarmer and our bodies from the waist down. We would then place the chessboard between us on the frame of the footwarmer. After every move, we would put our hands back under the quilt, determined not to sacrifice comfort for the sake of the game. Sometimes, we would lose a pawn or two and not discover the loss until we were ready to start another game. It amused us all when once my mother found the lost pieces among the cinders in the footwarmer, and had to retrieve them with a pair of tongs.

"One good thing about chess is that we can play it in this comfortable position," my father once said. "It's an ideal game for lazy people like us. The trouble with *go* is that the board is too high—and it has legs too—and we couldn't very well put it between us on the foot warmer and play on it . . . How about another game of chess?"

Whether he won or lost, my father always wanted to play another game. It seemed that he would never tire of playing chess. At first, I was willing enough to play with him. It was a novel experience for me to while away the time thus, as if I were an old man in retirement. But as the days went by, I began to weary of this inactive life. I was too full of youthful vigor to be contented with the role of playmate for my father. At times, in the middle of a game, I would find myself yawning heavily.

I thought of Tokyo. And it seemed that with each

46

heartbeat, the yearning within me for action increased. In a strange way, I felt as if Sensei was by my side, encouraging me to get up and go.

I compared my father with Sensei. Both were self-effacing men. Indeed, they were both so self-effacing that as far as the rest of the world was concerned, they might as well have been dead. They were, from the point of view of the public, complete nonentities. But while my chess-loving father failed even to entertain me, Sensei, whose acquaintance I had never sought for amusement's sake, gave me far greater intellectual satisfaction as a companion. Perhaps I should not have used the word "intellectual," for it has a cold and impersonal sound. I should perhaps have said "spiritual" instead. Indeed, it would not have seemed to me then an exaggeration to say that Sensei's strength had entered my body, and that his very life was flowing in my veins. And when I discovered that such were my true feelings towards these two men, I was shocked. For was I not of my father's flesh?

At about the time that I began to feel restless at home, my father and mother also began to tire of me. The novelty of having me was wearing off. This kind of situation is probably experienced by most people who return home after a long absence. For the first week or so there is a great deal of fuss, but, when the initial excitement is over, one begins to lose one's popularity. My stay at home had passed the initial stage. Moreover, each time I returned, I brought back with me a little more of Tokyo. This, my father and mother neither liked nor understood. As someone in days gone by might have put it, it was like introducing the smell of a Christian into the home of a Confucianist. I tried, of course, to hide whatever changes Tokyo might have wrought in me. But Tokyo had become a part of me, and my parents could not but notice that I

47

had changed. I ceased to enjoy being at home. I wanted to hurry back to Tokyo.

Fortunately, my father's condition did not seem to grow worse. To reassure ourselves, we had an eminent doctor, who lived some distance from us, come and examine my father carefully. The doctor was as well satisfied as we were. I decided to leave a few days before the end of the winter vacation. Human nature being the perverse thing that it is, my parents opposed my decision.

"Leaving so soon? But you haven't been home very long!" said my mother.

"Surely, you can stay four or five days longer!" said my father.

But I did not change my mind.

✳

When I returned to Tokyo, I discovered that all the New Year decorations had already been taken down. I detected little of the New Year spirit as I walked about the cold, windy streets.

Soon after my arrival, I visited Sensei to return the money I had borrowed. I also took with me the dried mushrooms. I thought it might seem odd to produce the mushrooms without some explanation, so, as I put them down in front of Sensei's wife, I carefully explained that my mother had wished me to present them to her and Sensei. The mushrooms had been put in a new cake-box. Sensei's wife thanked me politely, and picked up the box as she rose to go to the next room. She was probably surprised by its lightness, for she said to me: "What kind of cake is this?" The more familiar one became with Sensei's wife, the more often she seemed to show the innocent and childish side to her character.

They were both kind enough to ask after my father.

"It would seem," Sensei said, "that your father is well enough at the moment. But he must be careful and not forget that he is a sick man."

Sensei seemed to know all sorts of things about kidney diseases that I did not know.

"The trouble with your father's disease," Sensei continued, "is that the person who has it is often not aware of it. An officer I used to know died of it quite suddenly in his sleep. His wife, who was sleeping next to him, had not time to do anything for him. He woke her up once during the night, saying that he was not feeling well. The next morning, he was dead. The unfortunate thing was that his wife had been under the impression that he had gone back to sleep."

I, who had been inclined to be optimistic until then, suddenly became anxious.

"Do you think the same thing will happen to my father? One can't say that it won't happen, can one?"

"What does the doctor say?"

"He says that my father will never be cured. But he says also that there is no need to worry for a while."

"Well, if the doctor says so, then it's all right. The man I was telling you about was after all a careless sort of man. Besides, he was a soldier, and lived rather immoderately."

I was somewhat comforted by Sensei's last remarks. Sensei watched me for a while, observing my relief, and then said:

"But men are pretty helpless creatures, whether they are healthy or not. Who can say how they will die, or when?"

"You, of all people, think this?"

"Of course. I may be healthy, but that does not prevent me from thinking about death."

Sensei smiled faintly.

"Surely, there are many men who die suddenly, yet

49

quietly, from natural causes. And then there are those whose sudden, shocking deaths are brought about by unnatural violence."

"What do you mean by unnatural violence?"

"I am not quite sure; but wouldn't you say that people who commit suicide are resorting to unnatural violence?"

"Then I suppose you would say that people who are murdered die also through unnatural violence?"

"I had never thought of that. But you are right, of course."

Shortly afterwards, I left Sensei and went home. I did not worry very much about my father's illness that night, nor did I spend much time thinking back over what Sensei had said about death. I was more concerned with the problem of my graduation thesis, which I had tried to begin many times before but unsuccessfully. I should, I told myself, really get down to work on it very soon.

*

I was due to graduate in June that year and, according to the rules, my thesis had to be finished by the end of April. I counted the number of days that were left to me, and I began to lose confidence. While the others, it seemed, had been busy for some time collecting their material and accumulating notes, I alone had done nothing except promise myself that I would start work on my thesis in the New Year. I did indeed begin in the early part of the year, but it was not long before I found myself in a state of mental paralysis. I had fondly imagined that, by merely thinking vaguely about a few large problems, I was building up a solid and almost complete framework for my thesis. I discovered my folly as soon as I began to work seriously. I was in despair. I began to narrow down my thesis topic. And in order to avoid the trouble of having to present in a systematic manner my own ideas, I decided to compile relevant material from various books, and then add a suitable conclusion.

The topic that I had chosen was closely related to Sensei's field of specialization. When I asked Sensei whether he thought such a topic was suitable, he said that it would probably be all right. I was in a state of panic, and I soon rushed back to Sensei to ask what books I should read. He willingly gave me all the information he could, and then offered to lend me two or three books that were necessary for my work. But he steadfastly refused to give me any further guidance. "I have not been reading very much lately. I am not acquainted with up-to-date scholarship. You should ask the professors at the university."

When Sensei said this, I remembered the remark his wife once made to me that though Sensei was once an avid reader, he had since lost his old interest in books. Forgetting my thesis for the moment, I said to Sensei:

"Why is it, Sensei, that you are not as interested in books as you once were?"

"There is no particular reason . . . Well, perhaps it is because I have decided that no matter how many books I may read, I shall never be a very much better man than I am now. And . . ."

"And?"

"This is not very important, but to tell you the truth, I used to consider it a disgrace to be found ignorant by other people. But now, I find that I am not ashamed of knowing less than others, and I am less inclined to force myself to read books. In short, I have grown old and decrepit."

Sensei's manner was calm, as he said this. I was not much affected by what he said, perhaps because his tone held none of the bitterness of one who had turned his back on the rest of the world. I left the house thinking him neither decrepit nor particularly impressive.

From then on, my thesis hung over me like a curse, and with bloodshot eyes, I worked like a madman. I rushed to friends who had graduated the year before for advice on all matters. One of them told me that only by catching a rickshaw to the university offices did he succeed in handing in his thesis before the deadline. Another told me that he handed in his thesis fifteen minutes late, and it would not have been accepted but for the intervention of his principal professor. Such stories made me uneasy, but at the same time they gave me confidence. Every day, I worked as hard and as long as I could. If I was not at my desk, I was in the gloomy library, hurriedly scanning the titles on the high shelves, as though I were some kind of curio-hunter.

First, the plum trees bloomed, and then the cold wind veered towards the south. After a while, I heard that the cherry trees were beginning to flower. But I thought of nothing but my thesis. I did not visit Sensei once before the latter part of April, by which time I had finally completed my thesis.

*

I was free at last, when the double cherry blossoms had all fallen and in their place misty green leaves had begun to grow. It was the beginning of summer. I enjoyed my freedom like a little bird that has flown out of its cage into the open air. I soon paid Sensei a visit. On my way to his house, I noticed the young buds on the twigs of the quince hedges bursting into leaf, and I saw too the shiny brown leaves of the pomegranate trees softly reflecting the sunlight. I relished these sights as though I were seeing them for the first time in my life.

Seeing my happy face, Sensei said, "So you have finally finished your thesis. I'm glad."

"Yes, thanks to you, I have finished it at last," I said. "I have nothing more to do now."

I felt very happy and I did think then that, since I had done what was expected of me, there was indeed nothing left for me to do but relax and enjoy myself. I viewed my thesis with a great deal of confidence and satisfaction. I chattered endlessly to Sensei about what I had said in it. Sensei listened to me in his usual way, and except for an occasional "I see" or "Is that so?" he refused to make any comment. I felt not so much dissatisfied as deflated. However, I was so full of spirit that day that I wanted to shake Sensei out of his apathy. I tried to lure him out into the fresh green world outside.

"Sensei, let us go for a walk. It's such a nice day."

"Walk? Where?"

I did not care where we went. I simply wanted to go outside with Sensei.

An hour later, we had left the center of the city and were walking in a quiet neighborhood that seemed almost rural. I picked a young, tender leaf from a hawthorne hedge and began to whistle on it. I was a rather accomplished leaf-whistler, having once been taught the trick by a friend from Kagoshima. I proudly persevered with my whistling for a while, but Sensei kept on walking without paying the slightest attention to me.

After a while, we came to a little path which seemed to lead up to a house on a small hill. The hill was covered with a mass of green foliage. At the foot of the path was a gate, and on one of the columns was a sign telling us that we were at the entrance to a tree nursery. We knew then that the path did not lead to a private estate. Looking up at the gate, Sensei said, "Shall we go in?"

I answered quickly, "Yes. They sell trees here, don't they?"

We followed the winding path through the grove until we reached the house, which was on our left. The sliding doors had been left open, and we could see right into the house. There seemed to be no one about. In a large bowl in front of the house we could see some goldfish.

"It certainly is quiet around here," said Sensei. "I wonder if we should have come in without permission?"

"I am sure it's all right."

We walked on, and still we came across no one. All about us, azaleas flamed in all their splendor. Sensei pointed to an azalea which grew taller than the others and was reddish-yellow in color. "That is what we call '*Kirishima,*'[3] I think," he said.

There were also peonies covering an area of about ten *tsubo.*[4] It was too early in the summer for them to be in bloom. At the edge of this field of peonies was an old bench. Sensei stretched himself out on it. I sat down on the end and began to smoke. Sensei gazed at the sky, which was so blue that it seemed transparent. I was fascinated by the young leaves that surrounded me. When I looked at them carefully, I found that no two trees had leaves of exactly the same color. The leaves of each maple tree, for instance, had their own distinctive coloring. Sensei's hat, which he had hung on top of a slender cedar sapling, was blown off by the breeze.

I picked up the hat immediately. Flicking off the bits of red soil from it, I said:

3. Literally, this means "mist island."
4. Ten *tsubo* is about forty square yards.

54

"Sensei, your hat fell down."

"Thank you."

Sensei half rose to take his hat. Then remaining in that position—neither sitting nor lying down—he asked me a strange question.

"This may seem rather abrupt, but tell me, is your family very wealthy?"

"Well, I don't suppose what we have could be described as a fortune."

"About how much do you have? I don't mean to be rude."

"I really don't know. We own some woods and a few fields, but I suspect that we have hardly any money at all."

This was the first time that Sensei questioned me directly about my family's finances. And I had never asked Sensei about his source of income. Of course, I did wonder how Sensei managed to live in idleness. But I had thus far restrained myself from asking Sensei about his means of support, thinking that it would be crude to do so. Sensei's questions made me forget the trees that I had been peacefully contemplating, and I suddenly found myself asking:

"And you, Sensei? What kind of wealth do you possess?"

"Do I look like a rich man to you?"

Sensei was never expensively dressed. He had only one maid, and his house was by no means a large one. But even I, who was not of the family, could see clearly that he lived comfortably. One could hardly say that he lived in luxury, it is true, but on the other hand there was obviously no necessity for him to stint himself.

"You are rich, aren't you?" I said.

"I have some money, of course. But I am by no means rich. If I were, I would build myself a larger house for one thing."

Sensei was by this time sitting up on the bench and, as he finished talking, he began to trace a circle on the ground with his bamboo cane. When he had completed the circle, he drove his cane straight into the ground.

"I *was* a rich man, once."

Sensei seemed to be talking as much to himself as to me. I was at a loss as to what I should say. I kept quiet.

"I *was* once a rich man, you know," he said again. This time, he looked at me and smiled. Still, I remained silent. I felt awkward and I could not think of anything to say. Sensei then changed the subject.

"How is your father these days?"

I had received no news of my father's illness since January. My father had continued to write me a short letter every month when he sent me my money order, but he had said very little about his illness. Also, his handwriting had remained firm, and showed none of the hesitancy which one might have expected.

"He never tells me how he is. But I think he is quite well now."

"I hope you are right. But with his disease, you can never tell."

"I don't suppose there is much hope for him, is there? I do believe, however, that he will stay as well as he is for a while yet. At any rate, I have so far received no bad news."

"Is that so?"

I assumed then that Sensei's questions about my family's wealth and my father's illness expressed no more than a normal interest in my affairs and, not knowing much about Sensei's life history, I could not guess that they implied much more than appeared on the surface.

*

"If there is any property in your family, then I do think you should see to it that your inheritance is properly settled now. I know that all this is none of my business. But don't you think that, while your father is alive, you should make sure that you will receive your proper share? When a man dies suddenly, his estate causes more trouble than anything else."

"Yes, sir."

I did not pay much attention to Sensei's words. It was my conviction that, in all my family, there was no one that bothered about such matters. I was a little shocked, too, to see Sensei being so intensely practical. I said nothing, however, as I did not wish to seem impertinent.

"If I have annoyed you by seeming to anticipate your father's death, please forgive me. But we all have to die some time, you know. Even the healthy ones—how do we know when they will die?"

Sensei's tone seemed unusually bitter.

"I don't mind at all," I said, almost in apology.

"How many brothers and sisters did you say you had?" asked Sensei.

He went on to ask me about my other relatives, such as my uncles and aunts.

"Are they all good people?"

"Well, they aren't exactly bad. They are, after all, country people mostly."

"Why shouldn't country people be bad?"

I began to feel very uncomfortable. Sensei gave me no time to answer his last question.

"As a matter of fact, country people tend to be worse than city people. You said just now that there was no one amongst your relatives that you would consider particularly bad. You seem to be under the impression that there is a special breed of bad humans. There is no such thing as a stereotype bad man in this world. Under normal conditions, everybody is more or less good, or, at least, ordinary. But tempt them, and they may suddenly change. That is what is so frightening about men. One must always be on one's guard."

Sensei looked as if he wanted to continue. And I wanted to say something at this point. But suddenly a dog began to bark behind us. Surprised, we turned around.

Behind the bench, and next to the cedar saplings, dwarf bamboos grew thickly over a small patch of ground. The dog was looking at us over the bamboos, barking furiously. Then a boy of about ten appeared on the scene. He ran to the dog and scolded it. He then turned around towards Sensei and, without taking off his black schoolboy's cap, bowed.

"Sir," he said, "was there no one in the house when you came by?"

"No, there was no one."

"My elder sister and my mother were in the kitchen, you know."

"Is that so?"

"Yes, sir. You should have called out 'Good-afternoon' and then come in."

Sensei smiled faintly. He pulled out his purse and, finding a five-sen piece, gave it to the boy.

"Go to your mother and say that we would like her permission to rest here for a while."

With laughter in his intelligent eyes, he nodded.

"At the moment, I am chief of the army scouts," he said, and then rushed down the hill through the azaleas. The dog, with his tail held up, rushed after him. A moment or two later, two or three children of about the same age as the chief of scouts ran past us and disappeared down the hill.

*

Sensei would have made the purpose of his remarks clearer to me, had it not been for the sudden appearance of the dog and the boy. And I was left, for the moment, somewhat uncertain as to why Sensei should have spoken to me thus. Indeed, I did not share Sensei's interest in such matters as money, inheritance, and so on, partly because of my relatively easy circumstances, and partly because of my nature. Now, when I think of myself at that time, I see how unworldly I was. If I had known the meaning of material hardship then, I would have listened to Sensei more carefully. At any rate, money seemed to me a very distant problem.

Among the things that Sensei said, what interested me most was his remark that no man was immune to temptation. I knew, more or less, what Sensei meant, of course. But I wanted Sensei to talk more about the matter.

After the departure of the dog and the children, the large garden became quiet once more. We sat still for a moment or two, as though made immovable by the silence around us. The beautiful sky began slowly to lose its brightness. And before us, the delicate, green maple leaves, which looked like drops of water just about to fall from the branches, seemed to grow darker in color. From the road below, the sound of cart wheels reached our ears. I imagined that a man from the village had loaded his cart with plants or vegetables and was on his way to some fair to sell them. Sensei stood up, as though the sound had aroused him from his meditation.

"Let us go home," he said. "The days are becoming longer, but dusk seems to fall quickly when we are sitting about lazily like this."

The back of Sensei's coat was dirty, and I brushed it clean with my hand.

"Thank you. You don't see any resin marks, do you?"

"No. It's prefectly clean now."

"I had this coat made only recently. If I get it too dirty, my wife will scold me. Thank you."

On our way down the gently sloping path, we passed the house once more. This time, we saw the lady of the house on the front porch, winding thread onto a spool with the help of a young girl of about fifteen or sixteen. Stopping by the large goldfish bowl, we said: "Thank you for your hospitality."

"Not at all," said the woman, and then thanked us for the coin that her boy had received.

After we had walked a few hundred yards beyond the gate, I suddenly said to Sensei:

"What did you mean, Sensei, when you remarked that if tempted, any man may suddenly become evil?"

"What did I mean? There was no profound meaning in my remark. I was not theorizing, you understand. I was merely stating an obvious fact."

"I do not wish to deny that it is a fact. What I want to know is exactly what kind of temptation you were referring to."

Sensei began to laugh, as if he no longer wished to discuss the matter seriously.

"Money, of course. Give a gentleman money, and he will soon turn into a rogue."

Sensei's trite answer disappointed me. Sensei refused to be serious, and my pride was hurt. With a nonchalant air, I began to walk more quickly, leaving Sensei behind. "Hey!" he called to me.

"You see?" he said.

"What, sir?"

"One simple remark, and your whole attitude towards me, you see, has changed." I had turned around to wait for Sensei and, as he spoke, he looked straight into my eyes.

*

At that moment I hated Sensei. And after we had resumed our walk, side by side, I refrained from asking the questions I wanted to ask. I could not tell whether or not Sensei knew how I felt; at any rate, he seemed not to pay much attention to my behavior. He was his usual relaxed self as he walked silently by my side. I became spiteful. I wanted to say something that would humiliate him.

"Sensei," I said.

"Yes, what is it?"

"You became a little excited, didn't you, Sensei, when we were resting in the tree nursery? You are very rarely excited, and I feel that today, I was permitted to observe a rather unusual occurrence."

Sensei did not reply immediately. I thought that perhaps my remarks had had their effect on him, but at the same time I could not help being slightly disappointed. I decided to say no more. Then suddenly, Sensei left my side and, walking up to a neatly trimmed hedge, began to urinate. I stood by foolishly and waited for him.

"Pardon me," he said, as we set off again. I gave up all thought of trying to humiliate him. Gradually, the road became busier. The open fields that had been visible to us before were now almost completely hidden by rows of houses. Even then, there were sights that reminded us of the quiet countryside, such as peas growing around bamboo stakes in private gardens, and hens being kept in enclosures of wire netting. We passed an endless procession of cart horses, returning from the city. I, who was inclined to become absorbed in all such details of the scene around me, soon ceased to worry about what Sensei had said. Indeed, I had totally forgotten my last words to him, when he suddenly said to me:

"Did I seem so excited to you back there in the nursery?"

"Not very; perhaps a little . . ."

"I don't mind at all your saying that I was very excited. You see, I really do become excited when I start speaking of inheritances, and so on. It may not seem so to you, but I have a very vindictive nature. The indignities and injuries I suffered ten years ago—even twenty years ago—I have not yet forgotten." There was even less restraint in Sensei's words than there had been previously that day. What shocked me was not the tone of his voice so much as what he had actually said. I had never thought, of course, that I would ever hear such an admission from Sensei, nor imagined that there was such a tenacious streak in his character. I had believed him to be rather a weak person. And I had loved Sensei for this weakness, whether real or imagined, no less than for his virtues. I, who a short while ago had tried to pick a quarrel with him, began to feel small.

"I was once deceived," Sensei said. "Moreover, I was deceived by my own blood relations. I shall never forget this. When my father was alive, they behaved like decent people. But as soon as he died they turned into scoundrels. The effect of the injury that they did me in my youth is with me still. It will be with me, I suppose, until I die. What they did to me I shall remember so long as I live. But I have never taken my revenge on them. When I think about it, I have done something much worse than that. I have come to hate not only them, but the human race in general. That is quite enough, I think."

Not even words of consolation came to my lips.

*

We talked no more about the subject that day. I was somewhat awed by his manner, and I did not want to ask him any more questions.

When we reached the outskirts of the city proper, we boarded a tram. We hardly spoke to each other during the ride back. We parted shortly after we got off the tram. By that time, Sensei's mood had changed. Before leaving me, he said in a tone more cheerful than usual, "You will be really carefree from now till June, won't you? Perhaps you will never again in your life be so free from responsibility. Enjoy yourself as much as you can." I grinned as I took off my cap. And looking at his face, I wondered how such a man could carry so much hatred in his heart. His smiling eyes and lips showed nothing of the misanthrope.

I should like to say here that I profited considerably from my conversations with Sensei. Many times, however, I found Sensei very unsatisfactory as a mentor. I felt often that he was being purposely evasive: such was my feeling concerning our conversation that day.

Being a blunt and discourteous young man, I told Sensei one day that I had often found our conversation rather inconclusive. Sensei laughed, and I said:

"I would not mind so much, if I thought that you were too dull a person to realize that your remarks are often not very clear to me. But I do mind, because I know that you could tell me much more if you so wished."

"I hide nothing from you."

"Yes, sir, you do."

"It would appear that you are unable to distinguish between my ideas at present and the events of my past. I am not much of a thinker, but the few ideas that I do have, I have no wish to hide from others. I have no reason to. But if you are suggesting that I should tell you all about my past—well, that's another matter entirely."

"I do not agree with you. I value your opinions because they are the results of your experience. Your opinions would be worthless otherwise. They would be like soulless dolls."

Sensei stared at me in astonishment. I saw that his hand, which held a cigarette, was shaking a little.

"You are certainly an audacious young man," he said.

"No, sir, I am simply being sincere. And in all sincerity, I wish to learn about life."

"Even to the extent of digging up my past?"

Suddenly, I was afraid. I felt as though the man sitting opposite me were some kind of criminal, instead of the Sensei that I had come to respect. Sensei's face was pale.

"I wonder if you are being really sincere," he said. "Because of what happened to me, I have come to doubt everybody. In truth, I doubt you too. But for some reason I do not want to doubt you. It may be because you seem so simple. Before I die, I should like to have one friend that I can trust. I wonder if you can be that friend. Are you really sincere?"

"I have been true to you, Sensei," I said, "unless my whole life has been a lie." My voice shook as I spoke.

"Very well, then," said Sensei. "I will tell you. I will tell you all about my past. But remember—no, never mind about that. Let me simply warn you that to know my past may do you no good. It may be better for you not to know. And I cannot tell you just yet. Don't expect me to tell you until the proper time to do so has come."

I returned to my lodgings with an oppressive feeling— like a sense of doom—inside me.

*

My professors apparently did not have as high an opinion of my thesis as I did. I was, however, allowed to

graduate that year. On the day of the graduation ceremony, I brought out my old and musty winter uniform
from my suitcase and put it on. Everyone around me in
the graduation hall looked hot. My body felt as if it had
been sealed in an airtight envelope of thick wool. Very
quickly, the handkerchief that I was holding in my hand
became soaking wet.

I went back to my lodgings as soon as the ceremony
was over, and stripped to the skin. I opened the window
of my room, which was on the second floor and, pretend-
ing that my diploma was a telescope, I surveyed as much
of the world as I could see. Then I threw the diploma
down on the desk and lay on the floor in the middle of the
room. In that position, I thought back over my past and
tried to imagine what my future would be. I thought
about my diploma lying on the desk and, though it seemed
to have some significance as a kind of symbol of the
beginning of a new life, I could not help feeling that it was
a meaningless scrap of paper too.

That evening I went to Sensei's house for dinner. I had
promised him earlier that, if I graduated, I would dine
with him, and not with anyone else.

For this occasion, the table had been put in the drawing
room, near the verandah. On the table was an embroidered
cloth, heavily starched. It reflected the electric light beautifully. As always when I dined at Sensei's, I found the
bowls and chopsticks neatly laid out on white linen such
as one sees in the European-style restaurants. And the
linen was always spotless, having obviously been freshly
laundered.

"It is the same with shirt collars and cuffs," Sensei once
said. "If one is going to use soiled linen, one might as well
start with colored linen. But white linen must always be
spotless."

Indeed, Sensei was a very tidy person. His study, for instance, was always in perfect order. Being rather careless myself, Sensei's tidiness often attracted my attention.

"Sensei is rather fastidious, isn't he?" I once said to his wife. "Perhaps so," she said. "But when it comes to clothes, he certainly is not overcareful." Sensei, who was listening to us, said with a laugh, "To tell the truth, I have a fastidious mind. That is why I am always worrying. When you think about it, it's a terrible nuisance to have a nature like mine."

What he meant by "a fastidious mind," I did not know. Neither, it seemed, did his wife. Perhaps he meant to say that he was too intensely conscious of right and wrong, or perhaps he meant that his fastidiousness amounted to something like a morbid love of cleanliness.

That evening, I sat opposite Sensei at the table. Sensei's wife sat between us, facing the garden.

"Congratulations," Sensei said, and raised his saké cup to me. The gesture did not make me particularly happy, partly because, by then, I was not in such high spirits about having graduated, and partly because Sensei's tone of voice did not seem to invite a merry response from me. True, he grinned at me when he raised his cup, and I did not detect any irony in his grin. But neither did it convey happiness for my success. His grin seemed rather to say, "It is, for some strange reason, considered proper to congratulate people on such occasions as this."

Sensei's wife was good enough to say, "Well done. Your father and mother must be pleased." I was suddenly reminded of my sick father by this remark, and thought, "I must hurry home and show my diploma to him."

"What has become of your diploma, Sensei?"

"I wonder . . . You put it away somewhere, didn't you?" Sensei asked his wife.

"Yes, I think so. It should be somewhere in the house."

Neither of them seemed to know exactly where the diploma was.

*

When it was time for the main course to be served, Sensei's wife sent away the maid, who was sitting by her side and waited on us herself. This was their customary procedure, I believe, when they had friends, rather than formal guests, to dinner. The first two or three times I had dinner there, I felt somewhat ill at ease, but eventually I learned to ask Sensei's wife to refill my bowl without the slightest hesitation or embarrassment.

"Tea? Rice? You certainly eat a lot," she would say sometimes, in a pleasantly informal manner. That evening, however, I gave her no opportunity to tease me. It being summer, I did not have much of an appetite.

"Finished already? You certainly have become a small eater these days."

"I would eat as much as ever, if it weren't for the heat."

After the maid had cleared the table, Sensei's wife served fruit and ice cream.

"I made this myself, you know."

Sensei's wife, it seemed, had so little to do in the house that she could, if she wished, serve her guests homemade ice cream. I had three helpings of it.

"Now that you have finally graduated, what do you intend to do?" Sensei asked. He had moved his cushion towards the verandah, and was leaning against the sliding door.

My mind was preoccupied with the fact that I had graduated, and I had not begun to think seriously about my future. Seeing me hesitate, Sensei's wife said: "Do you intend to teach?" Again, I did not reply immediately, and she added: "Or work for the government, perhaps?" Sensei and I both began to laugh.

"To be honest, I have no idea. I have really not thought much about my career. I find it difficult to decide what profession would suit me best, since I have had no experience."

"That may be," she said. "But it is because your people have money that you can afford to be so unconcerned about your future. You would not be so easygoing, if you were in less fortunate circumstances."

I knew of course that she was right. Some of my friends at the university had started looking for posts in secondary schools long before their graduation. But I said:

"Perhaps I have been influenced by Sensei."

"Really!" she said. "You shouldn't allow yourself to be influenced in such a way."

Sensei smiled wryly, and said:

"I don't care if it's my influence or not. But as I have already said, make sure that your father will leave you a reasonable amount of money. Otherwise, you cannot afford to be so easygoing."

Then I remembered our conversation in the tree nursery, that day in early May when the azaleas were in bloom. And I remembered his words spoken in agitation on our way back from there. They had momentarily frightened me, but I, being ignorant of Sensei's past, had not given them much thought since.

"Madam," I said, "are you and Sensei very rich?"

"Why do you ask such a question?"

"I asked Sensei, and he wouldn't tell me."

She laughed and looked at Sensei.

"Perhaps he is reluctant to tell you because he hasn't very much."

"But I want to know what sum will be sufficient to

enable me to live as Sensei does, so that when I speak to my father about my inheritance, I shall have some idea of what I want."

Sensei was looking at the garden, calmly smoking a cigarette. His wife again had to do the answering:

"We don't have very much. We manage to make ends meet, that's all. Besides, what money we have has nothing to do with your future. You really must think seriously about your career. You must not live your life in complete idleness, like Sensei."

"I do not live in complete idleness," said Sensei, turning his head slightly in our direction.

*

I left Sensei's house a little after ten o'clock. As I was due to go home in two or three days' time, I said a few words of farewell before rising from my seat.

"I shall not be seeing you for some time."

"I suppose you will be back in Tokyo in September?" said Sensei's wife.

I had no intention of coming back to Tokyo in August in the full heat of the summer. I did not think that I would be seeking a post that soon. And in truth, there was no need to return in September either, since I had finished with the university. But I said:

"Yes, I shall probably be back in September."

"Take good care of yourelf," she said. "We are going to have a bad summer, apparently. We shall probably go away somewhere too. If we do, we'll send you a postcard."

"Where do you think you might go?"

Sensei, who had been listening to us with an odd grin on his face, said:

"We really don't know that we are going anywhere."

As I was about to rise, Sensei suddenly said, "By the

way, how is your father?" I said that I did not know, but that I assumed that he was no worse, since the letters from home had said nothing about his health.

"You must not regard your father's illness so lightly. Once there is uraemia poisoning, he will be finished."

I had no idea what uraemia poisoning was. The doctor, whom I saw during the winter vacation, had certainly said nothing about it.

"You really must take good care of him," said Sensei's wife. "When the poison reaches the brain, there's no hope, you know. It is no laughing matter, either."

I had been smiling uneasily, not knowing what to say.

"His disease is incurable, anyway," I said. "There is nothing to be gained by worrying."

"If you can truly be so resigned about it," she said quietly, "then there's nothing more to be said."

She lowered her eyes, as though she was thinking of her mother, who had died of the same illness. I too began to feel sad about my father's fate.

Then Sensei suddenly turned to his wife.

"Shizu, I wonder if you will die before me?"

"Why?"

"Why? I was just wondering. Or will I die first? It appears that women usually outlive their husbands."

"Perhaps, but how can one be sure? Of course, husbands are usually older than their wives."

"And so, you think, husbands will die sooner than their wives. In that case, I am certain to leave this world before you. Isn't that so?"

"No, not at all. You are different."

"Really?"

"You are so healthy. You have hardly ever been ill. No doubt, I shall be the first to go."

"Are you sure?"

"Yes, of course."

Sensei looked at me. I smiled.

"But if I die first," he continued, "what will you do?"

"What will I do . . . ?" Sensei's wife hesitated. For a moment, she seemed afraid, as though she had caught a brief glimpse of the life of sorrow she would lead when Sensei was gone. But when she looked up again, her mood had changed.

"What will I do? Why, what do you expect me to do?" she said lightheartedly. "I shall simply tell myself that 'death comes to old and young alike,' as the saying goes." She deliberately looked at me, when she said this.

*

I had been on the point of leaving when the conversation started, but I decided to stay a little while longer and keep the two company.

"What do you think?" Sensei asked me.

Which of the two would die first was obviously not a question that I could answer intelligently, so I smiled and said:

"I also do not know what your predestined span of life is."

"It certainly is a matter of predestination, if nothing else is," Sensei's wife said. "We are all given a certain number of years to live when we are born. Did you know that Sensei's father and mother died almost simultaneously?"

"On the same day?"

"Well, perhaps not on the same day. But one died very shortly after the other."

This, I had not known. I thought it rather curious.

"How was it that they died at the same time?"

Sensei's wife was about to answer me, when she was interrupted by her husband.

"Don't say any more about it. It is of no interest."

Sensei made as much noise as he could with his fan. He then turned to his wife again.

"Shizu, this house will be yours when I die."

Sensei's wife laughed.

"You might as well will me the land too."

"I can't give you the land, since it doesn't belong to me. But everything I own is yours."

"Thank you very much. But of what use would all those foreign books of yours be to me?"

"You can sell them to some secondhand bookshop."

"And what will I get for them, if I do?"

Sensei did not answer. He continued to talk, however, on the subject of his own death. And all the while, he seemed to have taken it for granted that he was going to die before his wife. At first, she seemed determined to treat the subject in a frivolous spirit. But eventually, the conversation began to oppress her sensitive woman's heart.

"How many more times are you going to say, 'When I die, when I die'? For heaven's sake, please don't say 'when I die' again! It's unlucky to talk like that. When you die, I shall do as you wish. There, let that be the end of it."

Sensei turned towards the garden and laughed. But to please her, he dropped the subject. It was getting late, and so I stood up to go. Sensei and his wife came to the front hall with me.

"Take good care of your father," she said.

"Till September, then," he said.

I said goodbye and stepped out of the house. Between the house and the outer gate there was a bushy osmanthus tree. It spread its branches into the night, as if to block my way. I looked at the dark outline of the leaves and thought of the fragrant flowers that would be out in the autumn. I said to myself, I have come to know this tree well, and it has become, in my mind, an inseparable part of Sensei's house. As I stood in front of the tree, thinking of the coming autumn when I would be walking up the path once more, the porch light suddenly went out. Sensei and his wife had apparently gone into their bedroom. I stepped out alone into the dark street.

I did not return to my lodgings immediately. There were a few things I wanted to buy before going home, and I felt also that I needed a walk after the big dinner I had eaten. I walked towards the busy part of the town. There, the night had only just begun. The streets were crowded with men and women who seemed to have come out for no particular purpose. I ran into a university acquaintance who had also graduated that day. He forced me to go into a bar with him. There, I had to sit and listen to my fellow graduate, whose talk was as frothy as the beer. It was past midnight when I returned to my room.

*

I had been asked by the family to buy a few things before leaving Tokyo, so I spent the next day shopping despite the heat. That morning as I set out on my errands, I found myself being very annoyed at the prospect of having to walk about the busy streets on such a hot day. And as I sat in the tram, wiping the perspiration from my face, I began to hate country people who were always ready to bother others busier than themselves with annoying requests.

I did not intend to spend the whole summer in idleness. I had already prepared a kind of daily schedule which I intended to follow when I got home, and so there were books that I had to buy. I went to the Maruzen Bookshop, and, prepared to spend half the day there if need be, I examined carefully all the books that dealt with my subject of study.

Of the items that I was asked to buy, the one that gave me most trouble was a chemisette. The apprentice at the shop was willing enough to bring out as many as I wished to see, but I found it very difficult to decide which I should buy. Also, prices varied greatly. Those that I thought would be cheap turned out to be very dear, and those that looked expensive to me turned out to be very cheap. Precisely what it was that made one chemisette better than another, I could not understand. I regretted not having asked Sensei's wife to buy one for me.

I bought a suitcase also. Of course, it was a cheap one, made in Japan. But it had metal fittings that shone brilliantly, and it was impressive enough to stun country people. My mother had asked me in one of her letters to buy such a bag for myself if I graduated, so that I could come home with all the presents packed in it. I laughed when I read the request. I understood my mother's motives, and I was not being unkind when I found it comical.

I left Tokyo three days later, as had been my intention when I took leave of Sensei and his wife. I was not overly worried about my father, in spite of the warnings that Sensei had given me since winter concerning his illness. Rather, I felt sorry for my mother, whose life after my father's death would, I knew, be very lonely. No doubt, I had come to regard it as inevitable that my father should die soon. In a letter to my elder brother in Kyūshū, I had said that there was no hope of my father's regaining his former health. In another letter, I had advised him to return home that summer if possible, to see my father before he died. I had even gone so far as to add, in a somewhat emotional strain, that we, their children, should feel pity for the old couple that led such lonely lives in the country. When writing such letters, I was quite sincere. But after writing them, my mood would change.

On the train, I thought about my own inconsistency. The more I thought about it, the more fickle I seemed, and I became dissatisfied with myself. I then thought of Sensei and his wife, and the evening of my last dinner with them. I remembered Sensei saying, "Which of us will die first?" And I thought: "How can anyone answer such a question? And if Sensei knew the answer, what would he do? What would his wife do, if she knew? Probably, they would behave exactly as if they did not know. As I am sitting here now, helpless, though I know my father is waiting to die . . ." I felt then the helplessness of man, and the vanity of his life.

MY PARENTS AND I

What surprised me when I got home was that my father's health seemed not to have changed much during the months I had been away.

"So you are back," he said. "I'm glad that you were able to graduate. Wait a minute, I'll go and wash my face."

I had found him in the garden. He was wearing an old straw hat, with a slightly soiled handkerchief attached to the back to shield his neck from the sun. The handkerchief swayed in the breeze as he walked towards the well behind the house.

I had come to regard a university education as commonplace, and I was touched by my father's unexpected pleasure at my graduation.

"I am glad that you were able to graduate," he said repeatedly. Inwardly, I compared my father's unaffected pleasure with the way Sensei had congratulated me that night at the dinner table. And I had greater admiration for Sensei with his secret contempt for such things as university degrees than I had for my father, who seemed to me to value them more than they were worth. I began at last to dislike my father's naïve provincialism.

"You shouldn't get so excited over such a trifling thing as a university degree," I blurted out. "After all, several hundred students graduate every year." My father looked at me strangely.

"It isn't simply your graduation that I am happy about, you know. Of course, I am glad that you graduated. But you don't know all the reasons why I say I am glad. If you could only understand . . ."

I asked him what he meant. He seemed reluctant to tell me, but finally said:

"You see, I am glad for my own sake. As you know, I am a sick man. When you were home last winter, I was convinced that I had no more than three or four months left to live. Providentially, I am still alive, and am able to potter about comfortably. And now, you have graduated. I am happy because you, who have worked so hard at your studies, managed to graduate before I died, and while I was in good health. Surely, I, as your father, have reason to be happy. Of course, you have bigger ideas than I, and it must annoy you to see me fuss over such an insignificant thing as your graduation. But try to look at it from my point of view. I am glad, not so much for your sake, as for my own. Do you understand?"

I said nothing. No word of apology would have expressed how I felt. I hung my head in deep shame. Calmly, he had been waiting for his death, believing that he would die before my graduation. And I had been too stupid to realize how much it meant to my father to be alive when I graduated. I brought out my diploma from my bag, and carefully showed it to my father and mother. I had not packed it well, and it was badly creased.

"You should have rolled it, and carried it in your hand," said my father.

"You should have protected it with something stiff," added my mother from his side.

My father looked at it for a while, then got up and went

to the ornamental alcove of the room, and placed it where everyone could see it. Ordinarily, I would have said something, but at that moment I was not my usual self. I had no desire to argue with my parents. I kept quiet and let my father do as he wished. The diploma was made of stiff paper, and, having become misshapen in the packing, it refused to stay still and collapsed each time my father tried to stand it up.

*

I drew my mother aside and asked her about my father's illness.

"Is it all right for my father to be so active? Going out into the garden, for instance . . ."

"There seems to be nothing the matter with him now. He has probably recovered."

My mother was surprisingly optimistic and unconcerned. As is commonly the case with women who live among woods and fields far from cities, my mother was quite ignorant about such matters. I remembered, a little uneasily, how surprised and frightened she had been when my father had fainted.

"But the doctor warned us then that father's illness was serious."

"That's why I think there is nothing stranger than the human body. Look at him now—so healthy, in spite of the doctor's anxiety. At first, I was worried, and tried to keep him still. But you know how he is. He does try to be careful, of course. But he is so stubborn. He has decided he is well, and won't listen to whatever I may have to say."

I remembered how, the last time I had come home, my father had insisted on leaving his bed. "I am all right now," he had said, after a shave. "Your mother fusses too much." And remembering that occasion, I thought that my mother was not entirely to blame. I had been on the verge of saying, "But you should take his illness more seriously, even if he doesn't," but decided to say nothing after all. It would be unjust, I thought, to chide her. Instead, I told her all I knew about my father's disease. Of course, I knew little more than what Sensei and his wife had told me. My mother seemed not particularly impressed or interested. She made only such remarks as: "Is that so? The lady died of the same disease? That's too bad. And how old was she, when she died?"

I gave up trying to convince my mother of the seriousness of my father's illness, and decided to speak to my father. He listened to me more attentively than my mother had done.

"Of course, you are right," he said. "But after all, my body is my own, and I know what's good for it and what is not. From experience alone, I should know how to look after it better than anyone else." My mother, when I told her what he had said, smiled wryly and said: "See? What did I tell you?"

"But," I said to her, "in spite of what he says, he is preparing to die, you know. That is why he was so glad when I came back with the diploma from the university. He himself was saying to me how fortunate he was that I should have graduated while he was still healthy, and not after his death as he had feared."

"What he says and what he thinks are quite different things," my mother said. "Secretly, he thinks that he has recovered."

"I wonder if you are right," I said.

"Why, he intends to live another ten or twenty years. True, he sometimes says depressing things to me too. Only the other day, he said to me: 'It doesn't look as if I'm

80

going to live much longer. What will you do when I'm dead? Do you intend to live all alone in this house?' "

I pictured to myself the large, old country house without my father, and with only my mother living in it. Could the house be kept up without him? What would my mother do? What would my mother say? Would I be able to leave home, and live without worry in Tokyo? And as I sat there, facing my mother, I began to think of Sensei's advice that I should try to get my share of the family fortune while my father was still alive.

Then my mother said: "There's no need to worry. When did anyone die who kept on saying that he was going to die? Despite the fact that your father says he expects to die soon, he will probably be living many years from now. Rather, it is we, who are so certain of our good health, that are in real danger."

Wondering whether she thought her ideas to be logically irrefutable or statistically demonstrable, I listened to my mother's platitudes in silence.

*

My parents began to discuss plans for a dinner party in my honor. Ever since my return, I had been secretly fearing that such a notion might enter their heads. I immediately objected.

"Don't do anything so elaborate for my sake, please," I said.

I hated the kind of guests that came to a country dinner party. They came with one end in view, which was to eat and drink, and they were the sort of people that waited eagerly for any event which might provide a break in the monotony of their lives. Since childhood, I had hated to see them at our house and to have to behave respectfully towards them. That they were now to be invited to dinner for my sake made me feel even less friendly towards them. But I could hardly say to my parents, "Don't invite those rowdy boors here." I pretended, then, that it was the elaborateness of such a party that I disliked. "Elaborate? Certainly not!" said my mother. "Such an occasion as this comes but once in a lifetime. It is only natural that we should have guests to celebrate. Don't be so retiring."

My mother seemed to attach about as much importance to my graduation as she would have done to my marriage.

"We don't have to invite them, of course," said my father, "but if we don't, there will be talk."

He was afraid of gossip. I was certain that our neighbors were hoping to be asked, and that if they were disappointed, they would indeed start gossiping.

"We are not in Tokyo, you know," said my father. "Country people are rather fussy and resentful."

"You must consider your father's reputation too," said my mother.

I could not go on being stubborn. I began to think that it would be better to let my parents do as they pleased.

"I was merely saying that you need not do it for my sake. But if you are afraid of gossip, then of course it's a different matter. Who am I to insist on something that may do you harm?"

"You embarrass me with your argumentative talk," said my father sourly.

"It isn't that your father is saying that we are not having a party for your sake," said my mother. "But even you must be aware of one's duty to one's neighbors."

My mother, like all women, was inclined, at times, to make incoherent remarks. In loquacity, however, she was more than a match for my father and me even when we sided together against her.

"The trouble with education," said my father, "is that it makes a man argumentative."

He said no more then. But in that simple remark, I saw clearly the character of his resentment towards me, which I had sensed before. Not realizing that I myself was being rather difficult, I felt strongly the injustice of my father's reproach.

That evening there was a change in my father's mood. He asked me when it would be convenient to hold the dinner party. He knew perfectly well that I was then spending my time in complete idleness. His asking the question was therefore his way of trying to bring about a reconciliation. I could not but be touched by my father's gentleness, and I became more obedient. After a short discussion, we agreed upon the date.

Before the day of the dinner party arrived, however, an important event took place. Emperor Meiji was taken ill. This news, which was spread throughout the nation by the newspapers, reached us like a gust of wind, blowing away the plans for a graduation party which had been tentatively made, not without difficulty, in an insignificant country house.

"I think that we had better cancel the dinner," said my father when he read the news, looking at me over the top of his spectacles. He then became silent, and it seemed to me that he was thinking of his own illness. I sat quietly too, thinking of the Emperor who had so recently attended the graduation ceremony at the university, as he was wont to do every year.

*

I brought out the books from my suitcase, and in the silent, old house, too large for the three of us, I began to read them. For some reason, I could not settle down. It had been easier to study in the middle of bustling Tokyo. In the small room on the second floor of the boarding house, where I could hear the distant sound of running trams, I had found no difficulty in concentrating on whatever I was reading.

Often, I found myself dozing over my books, and sometimes I went as far as to bring out my pillow and take a nap in earnest. I would wake to the cry of the cicadas, which at first would seem to have been a part of my dreams, and then, suddenly, I would be fully awake and find the harsh cry almost unbearable. Sometimes, I would lie still and listen to it for a moment or two, and my heart would fill with sadness.

I wrote to various friends. Sometimes, I sent short notes written on postcards, and sometimes, long letters. Some of my friends were still in Tokyo, and some had gone home to distant provinces. Some wrote back, and some did not. I did not, of course, forget Sensei. I wrote him a long letter, covering three double pages of foolscap paper with small handwriting, and told him all that had happened to me since my return. As I sealed the envelope, I wondered if Sensei would still be in Tokyo. It was the custom, whenever Sensei and his wife went away, for a lady of about fifty, with her hair cut and let down in the style affected by gentlewomen of her age, to come and look after the house. Once, when I asked Sensei who the lady was, he asked me in turn, "Who do you think she is?" When I said that I took her for some relation of his, he replied, "But I have no relations." Indeed, Sensei had come to ignore completely the existence of his family in his home province. The lady, it turned out, was related to Sensei's wife.

I thought of this lady, then, as I went out to post my letter, and I wondered whether she would have the sense and the kindness to forward it, should Sensei and his wife have left by the time it reached Tokyo. I knew, of course, that I had said nothing of importance in the letter. It was simply that I was lonely. I hoped for a reply from him, but it never came.

My father did not show as much interest in chess as he had done the previous winter. The chessboard lay in the corner of the ornamental alcove, covered with dust. He seemed more quiet than ever since the Emperor's illness. Every day, he would wait for the newspaper to arrive, and when it came, he would read it first. Then he would bring it to me, and say:

"Look, there's more news of His Majesty today."

He always referred to the Emperor as "His Majesty."

"I don't wish to seem irreverent," he once said, "but it does look as if His Majesty's illness is not unlike mine."

I could see deep anxiety on his face as he said this, and I thought to myself, "How long will it be before he faints again?"

"But I am sure His Majesty will be all right," my father said. "Why, if a worthless fellow like me can be up and about like this . . ."

Despite his attempts at being optimistic, however, I suspected that he feared the worst for himself.

"Father is really worried about his illness, you know," I said to my mother. "It doesn't look as if he expects to live another ten or twenty years, as you seem to think he did."

My mother appeared to be perplexed by my words.

"Why don't you persuade him to play chess with you," she said.

I brought out the chessboard and dusted it.

*

My father's health grew steadily worse. The old straw hat with the handkerchief attached to it, which had so amazed me when I first saw it on my father, now was laid aside. And every time I saw it lying on the smoke-blackened shelf, I felt pity for him. Before, when he had been active, I had wished that he would not move about so much. But I hated to see him lose his old vigor and to find him sitting about the house so quietly. My mother and I talked often of my father's health.

"It's just his mood," she once said. "He is depressed." She seemed to think that my father was depressed because of the Emperor's illness. I could not agree with her.

"I don't think that it is simply his mood," I said. "I think that he is feeling really ill."

I began then to consider seriously calling in a good specialist once more and have him examine my father.

"You can't be enjoying yourself very much this summer," my mother said. "We haven't even celebrated your graduation. Your father hasn't been well, and now, His Majesty . . . We should have had a dinner party immediately after your return."

I had come home on the fifth or sixth of July, and it was about a week after that that my parents had started discussing plans for the dinner. They had then decided to hold it the following week. One might say that due to the easygoing ways of my parents who, like all country people, could do nothing in a hurry, I had been spared an unpleasant social obligation. But my mother, who did not understand me, could not see this.

When the newspaper announcing the Emperor's death arrived, my father said: "Oh! Oh!" And then "Oh, His Majesty is gone at last. I too . . ." My father then fell silent.

I went to town to buy some black crepe. We wrapped a piece of it around the golden ball at the end of the flag pole. From another piece of crepe, we made a ribbon about three inches wide, and hung it from the pole near the top. The pole was then attached slantwise to one of the gate posts. The air was very still, and both the flag and the black ribbon hung limply. The old gate of our house had a thatched roof over it. The thatch had acquired a grey ashlike hue from years of exposure to wind and rain. One could see that, in places, it had become very uneven. I went out alone into the road and looked at the white muslin flag with the red rising sun in the center. The flag and the black ribbon dangling by its side stood out in relief against the dirty grey of the thatch. A question that Sensei had once asked me suddenly came to my mind. "What is your house like?" he had asked. "I wonder if the style of architecture in your part of the country is different from that in mine?" I wanted Sensei to see the old house where I was born. But, at the same time, I felt a little ashamed of it.

I went back to the house. I sat at my desk and, as I read the newspaper, I thought of far-off Tokyo. I imagined this city, the greatest in all Japan, immersed in gloom, yet bustling with activity despite the darkness. There was but one light shining, and that came from Sensei's house. I could not know then that this light too would be swallowed up by the silent whirlpool. I could not know that very soon, this light would be snuffed out, and that I would be left in a world of total darkness.

Thinking that I would write to Sensei about the death of the Emperor, I picked up my pen. After I had written ten lines or so, I decided not to write the letter after all. I tore up the paper and threw the bits into the wastepaper basket. (I thought that it would be senseless to write to him about such a matter. Besides, I had little hope of getting a reply from him.) If only he would write to me, I thought, knowing that I had begun the letter simply out of loneliness.

*

Some time towards the middle of August, I received a letter from a friend of mine, asking me if I would be interested in a post in a certain provincial secondary school. This friend, through economic necessity, had been spending a great deal of his time looking for such posts for himself. The post had been offered to him, but, since he had already accepted an offer from a school in a better district, he had been considerate enough to inform me of the opening. I wrote back immediately, saying that I was not interested, and suggesting that he write to a mutual friend of ours who, I knew, was desperately wanting a teaching post.

After I had posted the letter, I told my parents of the opening. They showed no displeasure when they heard that I had decided not to consider it.

"Surely, there is no need for you to go to such a place," they said. "You will get a better offer."

I began to suspect then that my parents had rather high hopes for my future. And it soon became clear that, in their ignorance, they were expecting their university-educated son to find an important position with a huge salary.

"You must realize," I said, "that good jobs are extremely hard to come by these days. Please remember that my field of specialization is quite different from my elder brother's. Things have changed too since his day. You mustn't think that I am in the same happy situation as he was when he graduated."

"But you are a university graduate all the same," said my father a little sullenly. "You mustn't blame us if we now expect you to be financially independent. It's rather embarrassing, you know, not to have an answer when I am asked, 'Now that your younger son has graduated, what is he going to do?' ''

The little community, of which my father had been a part for so many years, was his world, and he could not think beyond it. What he wanted me to do was find a position worthy of my qualifications, so that his reputation in the community would not be harmed. He did not wish to be embarrassed when his neighbors asked him: "I suppose your son will be earning a lot of money now that he has graduated from the university?" or "He will be earning about a hundred yen a month, perhaps?" To my parents, I, who was inclined to regard the great metropolis as my base of operations, must have seemed as weird as a creature that walked with its feet up in the air. Indeed, I myself sometimes felt as alien to my surroundings as such a being would have done. I decided to say nothing, rather than try to explain to them clearly what my feelings were. The gulf between us was too great.

"This is the sort of occasion when one tries to make use of one's contacts," said my mother. "Now, what about this man Sensei that you are constantly talking about?"

That was the extent of her understanding of my friendship with Sensei. She could not be expected to see that though Sensei might advise me to make sure of my inheritance before my father died, he was not the sort of person that would go out of his way to help me find a position.

"And what does this Sensei do?" asked my father.

"He does nothing," I replied.

It was my impression that I had already told both my father and my mother that Sensei did nothing; and if I was not mistaken in thinking so, then my father should have remembered this.

"Tell me," said my father, not without sarcasm, "why is it that he does nothing? One would think that such a man as he, whom you seem to respect so highly, would find some kind of employment."

What he really meant to say, it seemed to me, was that any man worth his salt would find some useful occupation, and that only a ne'er-do-well would be content to live in idleness.

"True, I don't earn a regular salary," my father continued. "But you must admit that even a simple fellow like me finds something to do. No one can say that I do nothing."

I still remained silent.

"If this man is as clever as you say he is," said my mother, "then I'm sure he will find you a job. Have you asked him?"

"No," I said.

"Well now, that won't do, will it?" said my mother. "Why don't you ask him? Write him a letter."

"Yes," I said half-heartedly, and left the room.

*

It was obvious that my father was afraid of his illness. But he tried to keep his fears to himself, and whenever the doctor came, he did not bother him with senseless questions. The doctor, in his turn, remained discreetly silent.

My father seemed to be thinking about what would happen after his death. It was apparent at least that he often tried to picture to himself life in the house with him gone.

"You know," he once said to me, "there are advantages and disadvantages in having one's children educated. You take the trouble to give them an education and, when they are through with their studies, they go away and never come home. Why, you can almost say that education is a means of separating children from their parents."

Indeed, it was because my elder brother had received a university education that he had gone away to a distant province. I too, because of my education, had resolved to live in Tokyo. It was not unreasonable, then, that my father should complain about his children. No doubt, it was very sad for him to imagine my mother left all alone in the country house where he had lived for so many years.

For him, the house was the family home, and he would never have contemplated living anywhere else. He took it for granted, too, that my mother would remain there until she died. The thought, therefore, of my mother living in solitude in the big house gave him considerable anxiety. That he should, at the same time, insist on my going to Tokyo to find a decent position struck me as being inconsistent. This inconsistency on his part amused me. Also, I welcomed it, since I could go to Tokyo with his full approval.

I dared not allow my father and mother to think that I was not trying hard to find a post. I wrote to Sensei and explained the situation at home. I said that I was willing to do any kind of work so long as I was qualified for it, and asked him to help me find an opening somewhere. I wrote the letter believing that Sensei would take no notice of my request. Besides, I thought to myself, even if he wished to help me, he could do very little, since he led such a secluded life. I was certain, however, that he would answer my letter.

Before I sealed the letter, I went up to my mother and said:

"See, I've written a letter to Sensei as you suggested. Won't you read it?"

As I had expected, my mother did not read the letter.

"Is that so?" she said. "In that case, you had better post it at once. You should have written it much sooner. One shouldn't have to be prodded to do these things."

My mother still treated me like a child. To be truthful, I did feel rather childish then.

"I should warn you, however," I said, "that merely writing a letter won't be enough. I must go up to Tokyo— perhaps in September."

"That may be so, but it never does any harm to write to one's friends first. How do you know that they won't suddenly find something for you?"

"Yes, of course. Well, let us talk about it again when I get a letter from Sensei. He is sure to write to me."

I believed that, in such a matter, Sensei would be quite conscientious. I waited confidently, therefore, to hear from him. But I was disappointed. A whole week passed, and there was no letter.

"He has probably gone away on holiday," I said to my mother, feeling that I should offer some sort of excuse for Sensei's silence. It was not only my mother, but myself also, that I was trying to convince. For my own peace of mind, I had to explain to myself that Sensei would not have ignored my request without good reason.

Sometimes I would forget my father's illness and toy with the idea of leaving immediately for Tokyo. My father too seemed occasionally to forget that he was ill and, though he was not unaware of the need to set his affairs in order before his death, he did nothing about it. No opportunity ever arose for me to approach him about my share of the estate as Sensei had advised.

*

Finally, at the beginning of September, I decided to go to Tokyo. I asked my father if he would continue sending me the allowance that I had received when I was at the university.

"I must go," I said, "if I am to find the kind of job that you have in mind for me."

I made it seem as though I wished to go to Tokyo merely to realize my father's hopes for me.

"Of course, I want the allowance only until I find a job."

Secretly, I felt that there was little chance of my finding a decent position. But my father, who was somewhat removed from the realities of the world outside, firmly believed otherwise.

"All right," he said. "Since it will only be for a short time, I'll see to it that you get your allowance. But only for a short time, mind. You must become independent as soon as you find employment. It really isn't right that one should, immediately after graduating, live on others. It would seem that the younger generation today knows only how to spend money. It doesn't seem to occur to them that money has to be made too."

He said other things in his lecture to me, among them being: "In my day, parents were supported by their children. Today, the children are supported forever by their parents." I listened quietly.

At last, the lecture seemed to be over, and I was about to get up when my father asked me when I intended to leave. I said that I should go as soon as possible.

"Ask your mother to choose a propitious day for your departure, then," said my father.

"Yes, I'll do that," I said.

I was being unusually obedient. I did not want to anger my father before leaving home. His last words to me, before I left the room, were: "With you gone, this house will seem lonely again. There will be no one but your mother and myself. I wish my health were better. As it is, one can't tell what will happen."

I comforted my father as well as I could and then went back to my desk. I sat down amongst my books, which were scattered all over the floor, and for a long time I thought about my father's plaintive words and the sadness in his eyes as he said them. I could hear the cicadas singing outside. These were different from those that I had heard in the early part of the summer. These were the little ones, the *tsuku-tsuku-bōshi*.[5] Every summer, when I was home for the holidays, I would often sit and listen to the piercing song of the cicadas and find myself falling into a strangely sorrowful mood. It was as if sorrow crept into my heart with the cry of these insects. And I would stay absolutely still, thinking of my own loneliness.

But that summer, the nature of my melancholy seemed gradually to change. I thought often of the fate of those that I knew, and sometimes I wondered whether it was not like that of the large cicadas of early summer, which had so soon been replaced by the *tsuku-tsuku-bōshi*. I thought of my sorrowing father, and then of Sensei, who had not yet answered my letter. It was natural that I should associate the two in my thoughts. The contrast between them was so sharp that I could not think of one without thinking of the other.

There was little that I did not know about my father. The regret I would feel if we were parted would be no more than that of any son who was fond of his father. On the other hand, there was much that I did not know about Sensei. He had not yet told me about his past, as he had promised. In short, Sensei still remained for me a figure half-hidden in the shadows. I could not be content until he

5. This name is supposed to resemble their song.

was fully revealed to me. I could not bear the thought of being parted from him before then.

My mother consulted the calendar, and we decided on a propitious day for my departure.

*

It was, I think, two days before I was due to leave that my father fainted once more. It was evening, and I had just finished roping up my trunk which was filled with books and clothing. My father had gone to take his bath. My mother, who had followed him to scrub his back, suddenly called to me in a loud voice. I found my father lying in my mother's arms. But as soon as he was back in his room he said, "I'm all right now." I sat down by his bed, however, and cooled his forehead with a wet cloth. It was nine o'clock before I was able to have a light snack, in lieu of the dinner I had missed.

The next day he seemed better than we had expected. Taking no notice of our remonstrances, he walked to the bathroom alone.

"I'm all right now," he would repeatedly say to me, as he had done the previous winter. Then, he had been more or less all right as he had claimed. I thought hopefully that he might be proved right once more. Despite persistent questioning, however, the doctor would tell me nothing, except that constant care was necessary. The day which had been fixed for my departure arrived, but through anxiety for my father, I decided to postpone my trip to Tokyo.

"I think I'll stay until things are more certain," I said to my mother.

"Yes, please do," she said imploringly.

When my father had shown himself well enough to wander about the garden or the backyard, my mother had been unduly optimistic. But now, she was more worried and nervous than I thought necessary.

"Were you not going to Tokyo today?" asked my father later that day.

"Yes, but I've decided to stay a little longer."

"Because of me?" he asked.

I hesitated for a moment. If I said yes, I would be admitting that I thought his condition serious. I wanted to spare his feelings if I could. But he seemed to read my thoughts.

"I am sorry," he said, and turned towards the garden.

I went back to my room and stared at the trunk lying on the floor. It was tightly bound, all ready for my journey. I stood before it for a while, wondering vaguely if I should start unpacking.

Three or four days went by. I was in such an unsettled frame of mind that I felt rather like a man who was neither sitting down nor standing up. My father then fainted again. This time the doctor ordered absolute quiet.

"What are we going to do?" said my mother in almost a whisper, so that my father would not hear. She looked rather frightened and helpless. I was prepared to send telegrams to my elder brother and younger sister. But my father, who was now confined to his bed, seemed hardly to be suffering at all. To look at him and to hear him chatting, one would have said that he had nothing more serious than a cold. Moreover, his appetite was even better than usual. He would not listen to us whenever we warned him against overeating.

"I am going to die anyway," he once said. "I may as well eat all the delicacies while I can."

My father's idea of a "delicacy" struck me as being at once comic and pathetic. He was not a townsman, and so did not know what real delicacies were. Often, late at night, he would ask my mother for grilled rice cake, and eat it with gusto.

"I wonder why he is always so parched?" my mother said. "It may very well be that there is still some strength left in him."

My poor mother had chosen the gravest of symptoms on which to pin her hopes. She had however said "parched,"[6] a word which in the old days meant hungry as well as thirsty, but only when applied to sick people.

When my uncle called, my father would not let him go. He wished him to stay mostly because he was lonely, of course, but I suspected also that he wanted someone to complain to about our reluctance to give him the kind of food he craved.

My father's condition remained the same for a week or so. During that time, I wrote a long letter to my brother in Kyūshū. I had my mother write to my sister. I thought that this would probably be the last time we would be writing them about my father's health. For this reason, I saw to it that they were warned that the next time they received any communication from us, it would be in the form of a telegram asking them to come home.

My brother was a busy man. My sister was with child. We could therefore not expect them to come home unless my father's condition became really serious. On the other hand, we did not want them to go to all the trouble of coming to see him only to find that they were too late. No one knew how much I worried over the problem of when to send the telegrams.

6. The Japanese word here is *kawaku*, which today means "to be thirsty," and not "to be hungry."

"I can't tell you precisely when the crisis will come," said the doctor whom we had brought in from the nearest big town. "All I can say is that it may come any time."

After talking it over with my mother, I decided to ask the doctor to send us a reliable nurse from the town hospital. The nurse arrived, dressed in her white uniform and, when she presented herself to my father, he looked at her rather strangely.

My father had known for some time that his disease was fatal. But when at last death was very close, he seemed unable to recognize it.

"When I am better," he said, "I must go to Tokyo once more, and enjoy myself. Who knows when any of us will die? We should do all the things we want to do while we can."

There was nothing that my mother could say, except: "When you go, please take me with you."

But sometimes, my father would become very sad, and say: "When I die, please look after your mother."

I was then reminded of that evening at Sensei's house, just after I had graduated, when Sensei had repeatedly used the phrase "when I die" in his wife's presence. And I remembered the smile on Sensei's face as he said it, and how his wife had refused to listen any more, saying, "Please don't say it again. It's so unlucky." Then, death had been simply a matter for speculation. But now, it was something that might soon become a reality. I could not very well imitate Sensei's wife. But I had to say something to divert my father's mind from the thought of death.

"Please don't talk like that. Remember, you are coming to Tokyo to enjoy yourself when you are better. And mother is coming with you. You will really be amazed to see how much Tokyo has changed since your last visit. For example, the tram lines have become numerous, and you know how they affect the appearance of streets. There's been a rearrangement of the boroughs too. Why, one can say that in Tokyo today, there's not a moment of quiet, day or night."

Perhaps, in my anxiety to please my father, I chattered more than I should. He seemed to enjoy listening to me, however.

Owing to his illness, the number of visitors to our house increased. Our relations living nearby came to see him frequently, perhaps at the rate of one every two days. Even those relations who lived far away, and who had become estranged from us, were among the visitors.

"Why," said one of them, after he had seen my father, "he is much better than I thought. I am sure he will be all right. He has no trouble talking, and his face isn't any thinner." Besides him, there were others who felt the same way about my father's condition.

Our household, which on my return had struck me as being almost too quiet, now became disturbingly busy. And my father, the only immobile figure in the growing commotion, became steadily worse. After consulting my mother and my uncle, I decided to send the telegrams. A reply came from my brother, saying that he would leave for home at once. There was a telegram from my brother-in-law, saying that he would be coming. My sister had had a miscarriage in her previous pregnancy, and he had sworn that, the next time, he would do everything possible to help prevent another such occurrence. We had thought it probable, therefore, that he would come alone.

*

Despite the unsettling circumstances, however. I was able to enjoy moments of privacy. Sometimes, I had even time enough to read ten pages of a book without interruption. The trunk, once so carefully packed, was now lying open on the floor. Every so often, I would go to it and pull out a book that I happened to want. Looking back on the daily schedule for the summer that I had set myself before leaving Tokyo, I decided that I had been able to complete only about one-third of the work that I should have done by then. The unpleasant feeling that I had not worked hard enough was one that I had often experienced before, though only very rarely had I ever accomplished so little as I had that summer. I was weighed down by the depressing thought that such perhaps was the normal state of things in every man's life.

Sitting thus unhappily, I thought again about my father's illness. I wondered how things would be after he was dead. And once more, side by side with the image of my father, there appeared in my thoughts the image of Sensei. With my mind's eye I gazed upon these two figures, so different from each other in position, in education, and in character.

My mother looked in around the door of my room and found me sitting amongst my scattered books with my arms folded. I had not long before left my father's bedside.

"Why don't you take a nap?" she said. "You must be tired."

She could not see that I was not suffering from physical fatigue. But I was not such a child as to expect my mother to guess my mood. I thanked her simply. My mother still stood in the doorway.

"How is father?" I asked.

"He is sleeping quite soundly at the moment," she said.

Suddenly, she walked into the room and sat down by me.

"Haven't you heard from Sensei yet?" she asked.

Before sending my letter to Sensei, I had assured her

that he would definitely write back, and she had believed me. But even then, I did not think that Sensei would write the kind of reply that my father and mother were expecting. In effect, I had knowingly lied to them.

"Why don't you write to him again?" she said.

I was not the sort to begrudge my mother the little comfort that the writing of useless letters, no matter how many, might give her. It was nevertheless painful for me to write to Sensei about such a matter. I feared Sensei's contempt far more than my father's anger or my mother's displeasure. I was indeed inclined to suspect that Sensei's silence was due to his contempt for my request.

"It's easy enough to write letters," I said, "but really, one can't arrange such things by mail. I must go to Tokyo and look around for myself."

"But with your father the way he is, there's no knowing when you will be able to go to Tokyo."

"I do not intend to go to Tokyo. I intend to stay here, until we know what will become of him."

"I should say so! Who would ever think of going to Tokyo at a time like this, when he is so critically ill!"

At first, I felt sorry for my mother who understood so little. And then, I began to wonder why it was that she had chosen such a time to reopen the question of my future. I had myself been able to forget my father's illness for a moment or two, and read and think in the privacy of my room. But did my mother, I wondered, have the same capacity to detach her thoughts from the invalid for a brief while and worry about other things? My mother began to speak again: "As a matter of fact . . . "

"As a matter of fact, I can't help thinking how much of a comfort it would be to your father if you could find a job. Of course, it may be too late now. But as you can see, he can still talk without any trouble, and his mind is perfectly clear. Won't you be a good son, and try to make him happy before he gets any worse?"

But the pity of it was that I could not be the good son my mother wished me to be. I did not write so much as a line to Sensei.

*

My father was reading the newspaper in bed when my elder brother arrrived. It had always been my father's custom never to let anything prevent him from at least glancing through the newspaper. But boredom, resulting from his confinement to bed, had made him more attached to it than ever. Neither my mother nor I had objected too strongly; thinking it best to leave him with his favorite pastime.

"I am glad to see you looking so well," said my brother to my father. "I came here thinking that you must be really ill, but you look very well indeed."

My brother seemed to me too cheerful, and his bright tone a little out of place. But later, when he had left my father and was alone with me, he seemed more depressed.

"He shouldn't be reading the paper like that, should he?" he said.

"No, I don't think he should either, but what can I do? He insists on being allowed to see it."

My brother listened to my excuses in silence. Then he said: "I wonder if he understands what he is reading?" He seemed to have decided that my father's mind had been considerably dulled by his illness.

"Certainly," I said. "He understands perfectly well. Why, only a short time ago, I talked to him about all sorts of things for about twenty minutes, and it was obvious then that he was in full possession of his faculties. At this rate, it is possible that he will be with us for quite a while yet."

My brother-in-law, who had arrived at about the same time as my brother, was more optimistic than any of us. My father asked him many questions about my sister, and then said: "In her condition, it is wise to avoid such discomforts as a train journey. I would have been worried, rather than pleased, had she gone to the trouble of coming to see me." He then added: "After all, I can always visit her myself, when I am better, and have a good look at the baby."

My father was the first to see the news of General Nogi's death in the paper.

"What a terrible thing!" he said. "What a terrible thing!"

We, who had not yet read the news, were startled by these exclamations.

"I really did think he had finally gone mad," said my brother later.

"I must say I was surprised too," agreed my brother-in-law.

About that time, the papers were so full of unusual news that we in the country waited impatiently for their arrival. I would read the news by my father's bedside, taking care not to disturb him, or, if I could not do this, I would quietly retire into my own room, and there read the paper from beginning to end. For a long time, the image of General Nogi in his uniform, and that of his wife dressed like a court lady, stayed with me.

The tragic news touched us like the bitter wind which awakens the trees and the grass sleeping in the remotest corners of the countryside. The incident was still fresh in our minds when, to my surprise, a telegram arrived frrom Sensei. In a place where dogs barked at the sight of a

Western-style suit, the arrival of a telegram was a great event. My mother, to whom the telegram had been given, seemed to think it necessary to call me to a deserted part of the house before handing it to me. Needless to say, she looked quite startled.

"What is it?" she said, standing by while I opened it.

It was a simple message, saying that he would like to see me if possible, and would I come up? I cocked my head in puzzlement. My mother offered an explanation. "I am sure he wants to see you about a job," she said.

I thought that perhaps my mother was right. On the other hand, I could not quite believe that Sensei wanted to see me for that reason. At any rate, I, who had sent for my brother and brother-in-law, could hardly abandon my sick father and go to Tokyo. My mother and I decided that I should send Sensei a telegram saying that I could not come. I explained as briefly as possible that my father's condition was becoming more and more critical. I felt, however, that I owed him a fuller explanation. That same day, I wrote him a letter giving him the details. My mother, who was firmly convinced that Sensei had some post in mind for me, said in a tone filled with regret, "What a pity that this should have happened at such a time."

*

The letter that I wrote was quite a long one. Both my mother and I thought that, this time, Sensei would write in reply. Then two days after I had posted my letter, another telegram arrived for me. It said that I need not come, and no more. I showed it to my mother.

"I think that he will soon be writing to you about it," she said. It never occurred to her that Sensei might have had something other than my future livelihood in mind when he sent me his first telegram. And though I thought that my mother might possibly be right, I could not but feel that it was not like Sensei to go to the trouble of finding me a job.

"Of course," I said, pointing to the second telegram, "Sensei cannot have received my letter yet. So he sent this without having read the letter."

My mother listened in all seriousness as I stated this obvious fact. "Yes, that is so," she said, after some careful thought. Needless to say, the fact that Sensei had not yet received my letter when he sent his second telegram was no indication as to why he had sent the telgrams at all.

We spoke no more about Sensei and his telegrams that day, since we were expecting our regular doctor to come with the chief physician of the town hospital. I remember that the two doctors, after examining my father, decided that he should be given an enema.

For the first few days after the doctor had ordered him to stay in bed, my father had found it particularly galling not to be able to go to the bathroom. But, gradually, he seemed to lose his habitual sense of propriety. As his condition grew worse, he became more uninhibited. At times, it seemed that he had lost all sense of shame in the matter of bodily functions.

His appetite slowly decreased. Even when he desired food, he found that he could only swallow a small amount. His strength went too, and he could no longer hold the newspaper that he loved so much. His spectacles, which still lay beside his pillow, now remained always in their black case. When a childhood friend of his whom we all called Saku-san, and who lived about three miles away from us, came to see him, he truned his lackluster eyes towards his friend and said, "Oh, it is you, Saku-san."

"It was good of you to come, Saku-san. I envy you your good health. I am finished."

"Come now, you must not say such things. You may be suffering from a slight illness, it is true, but what have you really to complain about? You have two sons with university degrees, haven't you? Look at me. My wife is dead, and I have no children. I am leading a meaningless existence. I may be healthy, but what have I to look forward to?"

It was two or three days after Saku-san's visit that my father was given the enema. He was very pleased, saying that, thanks to the doctors, he felt comfortable once more. He became more cheerful, as though he had regained confidence in his power to recover. Whether my mother was deceived into thinking that he was indeed getting better, or whether she was merely trying to encourage him, I do not know; but at any rate she told him about the telegrams from Sensei and talked as though a post had been found for me in Tokyo as he had hoped. I was sitting beside my mother then, and though I felt uneasy I could not very well interrupt her, and so I listened to her in silence. My father looked pleased.

"That's very good," said my brother-in-law.

"But don't you know yet what sort of a job it is?" asked my brother.

It was too late to tell the truth. I lacked the courage. I made a vague remark, so vague that I myself did not know its meaning, and abruptly left the room.

*

My father's illness advanced to the point where death was but another step away, and there it seemed to linger awhile. Every night, we went to bed thinking, "Will death wait another day, or is it to be tonight?"

He was not in great pain, and we were thus spared the strain of having to watch him suffer. From this point of view, nursing him was a relatively easy task. True, each one of us in turn stayed up at night to keep watch over him, but the rest of us were free to go to bed at a reasonable hour. One night, it so happened that I found difficulty in going to sleep. As I lay in my bed, I thought that I heard the faint sound of my father groaning. To make sure that there was nothing amiss, I got up and went to his room. It was my mother's turn to stay up that night. I found her asleep on the floor by his bedside, with her head resting on her bent arm. My father was absolutely still, as though someone had gently lowered him into a world of deep sleep. Softly, I went back to my bed.

My brother and I slept under the same mosquito net. But my brother-in-law, perhaps because he was regarded as a guest, slept alone in a separate room.

"It's rather hard on poor Seki-san," said my brother. "He has been kept away from home for days now." "Seki" was the surname of our brother-in-law.

"But he isn't a very busy man," I said. "That's probably why he's been good enough to remain here. Surely it must be far more inconvenient for you than it is for him. You can't have expected to stay so long."

"True, but there's nothing one can do about it. At a time like this, one can't start worrying about one's own affairs."

Lying in bed, we would talk thus before going to sleep. We both thought that there was no hope for our father. And sometimes the thought would enter our minds that since he was doomed, it would be better if the end came quickly. In a manner of speaking, the two sons were waiting for their parent to die. But we, as sons, could not in all decency openly express our thoughts, though each of us knew fully well what the other was thinking.

"It would seem that father intends to get better," said my brother to me.

My brother's opinion was not entirely unfounded. Whenever a neighbor came to our house, my father would invariably insist on seeing him. And then he would be sure to express his regret to the visitor that he had been unable to hold the graduation party in my honor as planned. Sometimes, he would add that when he got better, the visitor would certainly receive another invitation from him.

"It's just as well that the party was cancelled," said my brother, reminding me of his own unfortunate experience. "You're a very lucky fellow. As for me, I had a terrible time of it." I smiled sourly to myself as I remembered how disorderly and drunken the evening had been. And I remembered, with bitterness, how my father had gone around forcing food and drink on his guests.

There had never been much brotherly love between us. We had fought a great deal when we were children, and I, being the younger, had invariably left the fight in tears. Again, the fact that we had studied different subjects at the university was an indication of the difference in our characters. When I was at the university, and especially after my meeting with Sensei, I used to regard my brother from afar and pronounce him a kind of animal. He was then living far away from me, and we had not seen each other for some years. We had become alienated by both distance and time. Nevertheless, when we met again after so long a separation, we found ourselves being drawn together by a gentle, brotherly feeling which seemed to come naturally from I know not where. No doubt, the circumstances of our reunion had much to do with it. We had, so to speak, clasped each other by the hand over the dying body of one who was father to us both.

"What are your plans for the future?" asked my brother. I answered him with a question of my own:

"I wonder what has been decided about the family property?"

"I have no idea. Father has so far said nothing about it. In terms of cash, I don't suppose our property is worth very much."

As for my mother, she waited anxiously for the arrival of Sensei's reply.

"Haven't you heard from him yet?" she would say reproachfully.

"Who is this 'Sensei,' that I keep hearing about?" asked my brother.

"Why, I told you about him only the other day," I said. I was annoyed at him for so quickly forgetting what he had been told in answer to his own questions.

"You did tell me, it's true, but . . ."

What he meant to say of course was that Sensei was still a mystery to him. It should have mattered very little to me whether he understood Sensei or not. I was nevertheless angry, and began to think that my brother, after all, had not changed very much.

To his way of thinking, this man that I so admiringly referred to as "Sensei" must necessarily be a man of some importance and reputation. He was inclined to imagine that Sensei was at the very least a university lecturer. In this, he was no different from my father. He found it impossible to believe, and so did my father, that a man who was not known and did nothing could amount to very much. But while my father was quick to assume that only those with no ability at all would live in idleness, my brother seemed to think that men who refused to make use of their talents were worthless characters.

"That's the trouble with egoists,[7]" he said. "They are brazen enough to think they have the right to live idly. It's a crime not to make the best use of whatever ability one has."

I was tempted to ask my brother if he knew what he was talking about when he used the word "egoist."

"But one mustn't grumble," he went on to say. "Fortunately, it seems that he has found a job for you. Father is very pleased about that."

Without definite word from Sensei, I could hardly share my brother's optimism regarding my future. But I had not the courage to say what I really thought. My mother had indeed been very rash when she announced that Sensei was willing to help me, but it was now too late for me to say so. I was as eager as my mother was to hear from Sensei. And I prayed that the letter, when it came, would live up to my family's expectations. I thought of my father, who was so close to dying; of my mother, who so desperately wanted to give him as much comfort as she could; of my brother, who seemed to think that not to work for one's living was hardly human; and of my brother-in-law, my uncle, my aunt—and I asked myself, "What will they all think of me if Sensei has done nothing?" What was of itself quite unimportant to me began to worry me terribly.

When my father vomited some strange, yellow matter, I remembered Sensei's and his wife's warnings. "He has been lying in his bed for so long, no wonder his stomach is upset," said my mother. I could not help the tears in my eyes as I looked at her. She understood so little.

---

7. He uses the English word, and pronounces it *igoisto*.

My brother and I met in the morning room. "Did you hear?" he said. He was asking whether I had heard what the doctor said to him before leaving. There was no need for my brother to say more, for I knew.

"Do you think you can settle down here, and take over the house?" he said. I said nothing. My brother continued:

"Mother can hardly manage things by herself, can she?" The prospect of my slowly crumbling away with the odor of earth clinging to me bothered him very little. "If all you want to do is read books, then you can do that well enough here. Besides, you won't have to do any work. I should think the life would suit you very well."

"It would be more proper if you, being the elder brother, came home," I said.

"How can I do a thing like that?" he said crossly. My ambitious brother, I knew, was quite convinced that his promising career had just begun.

"Well, if you don't want to, I suppose we can always ask our uncle to manage our affairs for us. But even so, someone will have to look after mother. She will have to live with either you or me."

"That's the problem," I said. "Will she ever agree to leave this house?"

And so, while their father was still alive, the two brothers talked of what they would do after his death.

*

My father began to talk deliriously.

"Will General Nogi ever forgive me?" he would say. "How can I ever face him without shame? Yes, General, I will be with you very soon."

When he said such things, my mother would become a little frightened, and would ask us to gather around the bed. My father too, when he came out of his delirium, seemed to want everybody by his side so as not to feel lonely. He would want my mother most of all. He would look around the room and, if she was not there, he would be sure to ask. "Where is Omitsu?" Even when he did not say so, his eyes would ask the question. Often, I had to get up and find her. She would then leave her work, and enter the sickroom saying, "Is there anything you wish?" There were times when he would say nothing, and simply look at her. There were also times when he would say something quite unexpectedly gentle, such as: "I've given you a lot of trouble, haven't I, Omitsu?" And my mother's eyes would suddenly fill with tears. Afterwards, she would remember how different he used to be in the old days, and say, "Of course, he sounds rather helpless now, but he used to be quite frightening, I can tell you."

Among the tales she was fond of telling was the one about the time he had beaten her back with a broomstick. We had often heard the tale before, but now we listened more carefully, as though the tale was a keepsake to be treasured.

Even when death was casting its dark-grey shadow over my father's eyes, he said nothing about a will.

"Don't you think we should speak to him about it before it's too late?" said my brother.

"Well, I don't know," I said. I was not so sure that to force my father to consider such a matter at this stage would be right. Finally, we went to our uncle for advice. He was also hesitant.

"Of course, if he did have anything on his mind, it would be a pity to let him die without telling us about it. On the other hand, perhaps it would be wrong of us to bring up the subject."

Before we could reach a decision, my father fell into a coma. My mother, in her usual way, failed to see what had really happened. She was indeed very pleased, thinking that my father was sleeping peacefully. "Thank goodness he is still able to sleep like that," she said. "We can now relax."

My father would open his eyes from time to time, and would suddenly ask what had happened to so-and-so, referring always to someone who had been by his bedside in his last lucid period. It seemed that my father's understanding, like a white thread running through black material, was continuous though broken at intervals by patches of total darkness. It was not surprising that my mother should mistake his coma for natural sleep.

My father began to lose his power of speech. Often, his sentences would trail off into incoherent mumbling and we would fail completely to understand what he was trying to say. However, he would start each sentence in a voice stronger than one would have believed possible in one so ill. Also, he could no longer hear very well, and we were obliged to speak loudly into his ear.

"Would you like me to cool your head?"

"Yes."

With the help of the nurse, I renewed the water in the rubber pillow, and placed a bag of newly crushed ice on his forehead. I placed it gently, so that the sharp points of the ice would not hurt him. At that moment, my brother came into the room from the corridor and, without saying a word, handed me a letter. Much intrigued, I took the letter with my free hand.

It was very heavy, and too bulky to fit into an ordinary envelope. It was wrapped in a sheet of strong writing-paper, which had been carefully folded and sealed. I noticed at once that it was a registered letter. When I turned it over, I saw Sensei's name written in a restrained hand. I was too busy to open the letter just then, and so I put it into my pocket.

*

That day, my father's condition seemed to be very much worse. I left his bedside to go to the bathroom, and on my way there I met my brother in the corridor. "Where are you going?" he said, sounding rather like a sentry on duty. "He looks very bad, you know. You must try to stay with him as much as possible."

My brother was quite right. Leaving the letter unopened in my pocket, I went back to the sickroom. My father opened his eyes and asked my mother for the names of all those sitting around him. At the mention of each name, my father nodded, and when he seemed not to hear, my mother repeated the name loudly, saying, "Did you hear?"

My father said, "You have all been very kind. Thank you very much." Then again he fell into a coma. In silence, the people sitting around the dying man watched him for a while. Then one of the group got up and went into the adjoining room. Shortly after, another got up and left. The third to go was myself. I went back to my room with the intention of opening the letter there. No doubt, I could quite easily have done so while sitting with my father. But the letter, judging by its weight, was obviously very long, and I could not have read it through in the sickroom without interruption. I had been waiting for such an opportunity as this to read it undisturbed in my own room.

Almost violently, I tore open the tough paper which contained the letter. The letter had the appearance of a manuscript, with the characters neatly written between vertically ruled lines. I smoothed out the sheets which had been folded over twice for easier handling in the post.

I could not but wonder what it was that Sensei had written at such great length. I was, however, too much on edge to read the whole letter properly. My mind kept wandering back to the sickroom. I had the feeling that something would happen to my father before I could finish reading the letter. At least, I was sure that I would soon be called away by my brother, or my mother, or my uncle. In this unsettled state, I read the first page.

"You asked me once to tell you of my past. I did not have the courage then to do so. But now, I believe I am free of the bonds that prevented me from telling you the truth about myself. The freedom that I now have, however, is no more than an earthly, physical kind of freedom, which will not last forever. Unless I take advantage of it while I can, I shall never again have the opportunity of passing on to you what I have learned from my own experience, and my promise to you will have been broken. Circumstances having prevented me from telling you my story in person, I have decided to write it out for you."

I read thus far, and realized why it was that the letter was so long. That Sensei would not bother to write me about my future career, I had more or less known from the very beginning. What really worried me was that Sensei, who hated to write at all, had taken the trouble to write such a long epistle. Why had he not waited, I asked myself, until I was once more in Tokyo?

I said to myself repeatedly, "He is free now, but he will never be free again," and tried desperately to understand what the words meant; then all of a sudden I became uneasy. I tried to read on further but, before I could do so, I heard my brother's voice calling me from the sickroom. Frightened, I stood up, and hurried along the corridor to where the others were gathered. I was prepared to learn that the end had come for my father.

*

During my absence from the room, the doctor had arrived. In an attempt to make my father more comfortable, he was about to give him an enema. The nurse, tired from the previous night's vigil, had gone to the next room to sleep. My brother, who was not used to helping on such occasions, seemed at a loss. When he saw me enter, he said, "Here, give us a hand," and promptly sat down. I took his place and helped the doctor.

My father's condition seemed to improve a little. The doctor remained for another half-hour or so, then, satisfied as to the results of the enema, he stood up to go. He was careful to tell us before leaving that, if anything did happen, we should not hesitate to call him.

Once more I left the room with its atmosphere of approaching death, and returned to my own. There I tried again to read the letter. But I was too nervous. No sooner had I sat down at my desk than I was overcome by fear lest I should hear my brother's loud voice summoning me to the sickroom, perhaps for the last time. I turned the pages over mechanically, not taking in the meaning of the characters so neatly written along the ruled lines. I could not even grasp the gist of the letter. Finally I reached the last page, and was about to fold up the letter again and put it on the desk when suddenly a sentence near the end caught my eye.

"By the time this letter reaches you, I shall probably have left this world—I shall in all likelihood be dead."

I was stunned. My heart, which had till then been so restless, seemed suddenly to freeze. Hurriedly, I began to turn the pages over backwards, reading a sentence here and there. I tried desperately to pin down the words which seemed to dance before my eyes. All I wanted to know at that moment was that Sensei was still alive. Sensei's past, his dark past that he had promised to tell me about, held no interest for me then. But I could not find what I was seeking, and I refolded the letter in exasperation.

I returned to the doorway of my father's room to see how he was doing. The room was surprisingly quiet. There was only my mother sitting by the bedside, looking tired and forlorn. I beckoned her and, when she came to me, I asked, "How is he?" She said, "He seems to be holding out." I went up to my father, and putting my face close to his, I said, "How do you feel? Has the enema made you more comfortable?" He nodded, and then said quite distinctly, "Thank you." His mind seemed unexpectedly clear.

Once more, I returned to my room. I looked at my watch, and began to examine the railway timetable. I then stood up, rearranged my dress, and putting Sensei's letter in my pocket, went out through the back door. As though in a nightmare, I ran to the doctor's house. I wanted to ask the doctor whether my father would last another two or three days. I wanted to beg him to keep my father alive for a few days more, by injection or any other means in his power. The doctor was unfortunately out. I had not the time to wait for him. In any case, I was too agitated to stay still. I jumped into a rickshaw and urged the man to hurry to the station.

At the station, I scribbled a hurried note to my mother and brother and asked the rickshaw man to take it quickly to the house. I thought that it would be better to write even such a note than to leave without any word at all. Thus, in a desperate desire to act, I boarded the Tokyo-bound train. The noise of the engine filled my ears as I sat down in a third-class carriage. At last, I was able to read Sensei's letter from beginning to end.

SENSEI AND HIS TESTAMENT

I received two or three letters from you this summer. If I remember rightly, it was in your second letter that you asked me to help you find a suitable post. When I read it, I felt that the least I could do was to answer your letter. But I must confess that in the end, I did nothing. As you know, my circle of acquaintances is very small. Indeed, it would be more correct to say that I live alone in this world. How could I, then, have been of any help to you? However, that is of little importance. You see, when your letter came, I was trying desperately to decide what I should do with myself. I was thinking, "Should I go on living as I do now, like a mummy left in the midst of living beings, or should I . . .?" In those days, every time I thought of the latter alternative, I was seized with a terrible fear. I was like a man who runs to the edge of a cliff, and looking down, sees that the abyss is bottomless. I was a coward. And like most cowards I suffered because I could not decide. Unfortunately, it would not be an exaggeration to say that at the time I was hardly aware of your existence. To go further, such a matter as your future livelihood was to me almost totally without significance. I did not care what you did. It was not, to my way of thinking, worth all the fuss. I put your letter in the letter rack and continued to worry about my own problem. One brief and contemptuous glance in your direction, that is about all I thought you deserved. Why should a fellow, I asked myself, as comfortably placed as you, start whining for a job so soon after graduating? It is because I feel that I owe you some sort of explanation for my conduct that I tell you all this. I am not being purposely rude in order to anger you. I believe that you will understand when you have read my letter. At any rate, I should have at least acknowledged your letter. Please forgive me for my negligence.

Some time later, I sent you a telegram. To tell you the truth, I simply wanted to see you again. Also, I wanted to tell you the story of my past as you had once asked me to. When your telegram came, saying that you could not come to Tokyo, I was deeply disappointed. I remember I sat still for a while, staring at it. You too must have felt that a telegram was not enough, for you kindly wrote me a letter soon afterwards. The letter made it quite clear why you could not come to Tokyo. I had no reason to resent your not complying with my request. How could you have left home with your own father so ill? It was I who was at fault. I should have remembered your father's condition. As a matter of fact, when I sent you that telegram, I had forgotten all about him. I, who had previously warned you of the seriousness of his illness, could not remember . . . You see, I am an inconsistent person. This inconsistency may not be so much a natural part of my character as the effect that the remembrance of my own past has had on me. At any rate, I am well aware of my failing. You must forgive me.

When I read your letter—your last letter to me—I realized I had done wrong. I thought I would write to you and say so. I went so far as to pick up my pen but, in the end, put it back on the desk without writing a single line.

The truth is, the only things I would have thought worth saying at the time are those things which I shall say here, and it was then too soon for me to write such a letter. That is why I sent you that simple telegram, telling you that there was no need to come.

*

I began then to write this letter. I am not accustomed to writing, and it pained me much to find that many of the incidents and my own thoughts I could not describe as freely as I wished. Often, I was tempted to abandon the task, and so break my promise to you. But every time I dropped my pen thinking I could not go on, I found that, before a full hour had passed, I was writing once more. You may take this as a manifestation of my naturally strong sense of obligation. I will not contradict you if you do. As you know, I have led a very secluded life and have had little contact with the outside world. As I look about me, I find that I really have no obligations. Either through force of circumstances or through my own designing, I have lived in such a way as to free my life of obligation. But this is not because I have not it in me to feel a sense of obligation towards others. Rather, it is because I feel it so sharply that I have led such a negative kind of life. I am not strong enough to bear the pains that it inflicts on one. You will understand, then, that if I had not kept my promise to you I should have felt very uneasy. The desire to avoid such uneasiness was in itself enough to make me pick up my pen again.

But that is not the only reason why I wanted to write this. You see, apart from any sense of obligation, there is the simple reason that I want to write about my past. Since my past was experienced only by me, I might be excused if I regarded it as my property, and mine alone.

121

And is it not natural that I should want to give this thing, which is mine, to someone before I die? At least, that is how I feel. On the other hand, I would rather see it destroyed, with my life, than offer it to someone who does not want it. In truth, if there had not been such a person as you, my past would never have become known, even indirectly, to anyone. To you alone, then, among the millions of Japanese, I wish to tell my past. For you are sincere; and because once you said in all sincerity that you wished to learn from life itself.

Without hesitation, I am about to force you into the shadows of this dark world of ours. But you must not fear. Gaze steadily into the shadows and then take whatever will be of use to you in your own life. When I speak of darkness, I mean moral darkness. For I was born an ethical creature, and I was brought up to be an ethical man. True, my ethics may be different from those of the young men of today. But they are at least my own. I did not borrow them for the sake of convenience as a man might a dress suit. It is for this reason that I think you, who wish to grow, may learn something from my experience.

You will remember how you used to try to argue with me about contemporary ideas. You will remember too what my attitude was. Though I did not exactly disdain your opinions, I must admit I could not bring myself to respect them either. Your thoughts were without solid foundation, and you were too young to have had much experience. Sometimes, I laughed. Sometimes, you used to look at me discontentedly. In the end, you asked me to spread out my past like a picture scroll before your eyes. Then, for the first time, I respected you. I was moved by your decision, albeit discourteous in expression, to grasp something that was alive within my soul. You wished to cut open my heart and see the blood flow. I was then still alive. I did not want to die. That is why I refused you and postponed the granting of your wish to another day. Now, I myself am about to cut open my own heart, and drench your face with my blood. And I shall be satisfied if, when my heart stops beating, a new life lodges itself in your breast.

*

I was not yet twenty when I lost both my parents. I think that my wife once mentioned to you that they died of the same disease. Also, if I remember correctly, she told you, much to your surprise, that they died almost at the same time. My father, to tell the truth, was killed by that dreadful disease, typhoid; and my mother, who was nursing him, caught it from him.

I was their only son. Our family was well off, and so I was brought up in an atmosphere of generosity and ease. As I look back on my past, I cannot but feel that had my parents—or at least one of them—survived, I might have been allowed to keep my generous nature.

I was left behind alone, helpless as a lost child. I was inexperienced and knew nothing of the ways of the world. My mother could not be with my father when he died. And when my mother was dying she was not told that my father was already dead. I do not know whether she knew, or whether she actually believed us when we told her that he was recovering. All I know is that she asked my uncle to take care of everything. I was there at the time: she nodded towards me, and said to my uncle, "Please look after my child." It would seem that she wanted to say much more, but she succeeded only in saying, ". . . to Tokyo . . ." My uncle quickly said, "All right. You mustn't worry." It may be that my mother's constitution did not succumb too easily to fever, but at any rate my uncle later said to me praisingly, "She's a brave woman." I do not know whether those few words of my mother's were her last or not. She of course knew the terrible nature of her own disease, and that she had caught it from my father. But I am by no means certain that she truly believed that she would die from it. And no matter how clear those words which she spoke in high fever might have been, they often left no trace in her memory when the fever subsided. That is why I . . . but never mind. What I am trying to say is that even then I was beginning to show signs of a deeply suspicious nature which could not accept anything without closely analyzing it. Irrelevant as the above account may be to the main part of my narrative, I feel that it will help you to understand one side of my character. Please read all such passages, then, in this light. This nature of mine led me not only to suspect the motives of individual persons but to doubt even the integrity of all mankind, and to what extent it increased my capacity for suffering you will see for yourself.

I have digressed enough. Considering my situation, I am really quite calm. Even the sound of trams, which seems to become audible only when the rest of the world has gone to sleep, I can hear no more. The forlorn singing of the insects reaches me through the closed shutters, and one feels that their song is of the dews of coming autumn. My wife sleeps innocently in the next room. The pen in my hand makes a faint scratching sound as it traces one character after another down the page. My heart is tranquil as I sit before my desk. If the strokes of my characters seem sometimes ill-arranged, you must not think this due to my mental state. Attribute it, rather, to my inexperience with the pen.

✳

At any rate, I, who was left alone, had no choice but to rely on my uncle in accordance with my mother's wishes. My uncle, on his part, accepted full responsibility and looked after my affairs. And he arranged, as I had hoped, for me to go to Tokyo.

I came to Tokyo and entered the college. College students in those days were considerably more violent and barbaric than they are now. One student I knew, for example, got into a fight with a tradesman one night and hurt him rather badly on the head with his wooden clogs. He had been drinking, and so did not see the other fellow taking his college cap from him in the midst of the violent fight. His name, of course, was carefully written on a label inside the cap. The police were ready to report him to the college, but thanks to the intercession of his friends the matter was prevented from becoming public. You went to college in more gentle days, and so you must feel contempt for such rough doings. I also, when I look back on those days, feel that we were all pretty silly. There was, however, a certain kind of admirable simplicity in the life of the student then which one does not find today. My monthly allowance, which my uncle sent me, was considerably less than what your father used to send you. (Of course, the cost of living has gone up since my student days.) But I do not remember wanting any more money than I received. Besides, my financial position was such that there was no reason for me to envy my classmates. When I think of it, it is likely that many of them envied me. In addition to my regular allowance, I used to receive allowances for books—I was already fond of buying books—and for incidental expenses which I spent freely.

Being innocent, I not only trusted my uncle completely,

but admired him and even considered myself indebted to him. He was a businessman. He was also, at one time, a member of the prefectural assembly. I seem to remember that, through his membership in the assembly, he had connections with some political party. Though he and my father were brothers, it would seem that their characters developed in quite different directions. My father was a simple, upright man, whose main purpose in life was to keep intact the property left him by his ancestors. He took pleasure in the tea ceremony and in the arrangement of flowers, and he loved to read poetry. Paintings and antiques seemed to interest him too. Our house was in the country, and I remember that a dealer from the town used to visit my father, bringing with him paintings, incense burners, and so on. (The town was about six miles away, and it was there that my uncle lived.) My father was, I suppose, what one might call a "man of means,"[8] a country gentleman of taste. There was, therefore, quite a contrast between him and his active, worldly brother. Oddly enough, they seemed quite fond of each other. My father would often speak of my uncle in glowing terms, saying what a sound fellow he was, and how superior his brother's qualities were to his own. "The trouble with inheriting money from one's parents," he once said to my mother and to me, "is that it dulls one's wits. It's a bad thing not to have to struggle for one's living." I believe that he said this for my benefit. At least, he gave me a meaningful look at the time. That is why I remember his words so well. How could I doubt this uncle of mine, whom my father trusted and admired so much? It was natural that I should be proud of him. And when my father and mother died, he became more than someone to be proud of: he became a necessity.

8. The English term is used.

*

When I went home the following summer, my uncle had already moved into our house with his family, and was now its new master. This had been arranged between us before I left for Tokyo. So long as I was not going to be in the house all the time, some such arrangement was necessary.

My uncle was at that time connected with many business enterprises in the town. I remember that when we agreed that he should move into the house and manage the property during my absence, he said to me with a smile: "Of course, from the point of view of my own business, it would be much more convenient to live in my own house than to live six miles from town." My house had a long history, and was not unknown in the district. In the country, as you are probably well aware, it is a very serious thing to tear down or sell a house with a long tradition when there is an heir. Such things do not worry me now, but I was young then, and I was torn between the desire to go to Tokyo and the fear of shirking the responsibility of my inheritance.

Unwillingly, my uncle consented to move into my house. He insisted, however, that he be allowed to keep his old residence in town so that he might stay there whenever it was necessary. Naturally, I had no objections; I was willing to agree to any arrangement which would enable me to go to Tokyo.

As a child will, I loved my home; and when parted from it, there was a yearning for it in my heart. I was like a traveler who, no matter where he goes, never doubts that he will some day return to his place of birth. I came to Tokyo of my own free will, but I had little doubt that I should return when the holidays came. And so I studied and played in the great city, dreaming often of my home.

I have no idea how my uncle divided his time between the two residences during my absence. At any rate, when I arrived, he and his whole family were living in my house. I suppose that those of his children who were still at school lived normally in the town house, but had been brought to our house in the country for the holidays.

They were all pleased to see me. I was pleased too, for the house had become a gay place; much gayer certainly than when my parents were alive. My uncle chased out his eldest son who had taken over my own room, and put me in it. I objected, saying that since the house was so crowded, I did not mind staying in some other room. But my uncle would not listen: "This is your house, after all," he said.

There were unhappy moments when I thought of my father and mother, but on the whole I had an enjoyable summer with my uncle's family. There was one thing, however, which cast a slight shadow on my memory of the summer: my uncle and aunt had more than once tried to persuade me, who had only just entered college, to marry. The first time they mentioned marriage to me, I was somewhat shocked, for the subject had been introduced suddenly: the second time, I positively refused to consider it; and the third time, I was forced to ask them why they wanted to discuss such a thing. The reason they gave was quite simple: I should, they said, get married as soon as possible and succeed my father. I myself had been under the happy impression that, so long as I came home for the holidays, all would be well. Of course, I was too well acquainted with the ways of the country not to see the reasonableness of my uncle's wish that I should get married and settle down properly as my father's heir. Moreover, I do not think that I really disliked the prospect; but I had only recently begun my studies at college, and it was no more real to me than a distant scene observed from the wrong end of a telescope.

*

I forgot all about the subject of marriage. None of the young men in my group seemed to me to have that domesticated look. They all seemed to do as they liked, and, as far as I could tell, were all bachelors. It is possible that, if one had examined their personal histories carefully, one might have discovered that, despite their easygoing ways, some of them had already been forced into marriage; but I was too young to even suspect such a thing. Besides, even if there had been such men in our midst, it is doubtful that they would have wanted to talk about marriage, a subject far removed from the thoughts of young students. To think of it, I was myself in this position; but I was not worried, and managed to spend another year happily at the college.

At the end of that academic year, I packed my bag once more and returned to my parents' resting place. In my house, where once my father and mother had lived, I saw the cheerful faces of my uncle and his family. Again I was able to breathe the air of my native place, which was as dear to me then as it ever was before. It was good to be back after a year of student life.

But I was not allowed to enjoy for long the familiar surroundings which had become almost a part of me. Once more, my uncle brought up the subject of marriage. His reasons for wanting to see me get married were the same as those he gave the previous year. But this time, he had someone in mind for me, which made the matter all the more embarrassing. The person that he suggested as a suitable bride was his own daughter, my cousin. "It will be a convenient arrangement for both parties," he said.

129

"Your father, before he died, seemed to be of the same opinion." I could myself see the convenience of such a union; and I could quite easily believe that my father had been in agreement with my uncle. But the idea of marrying my cousin had never crossed my mind before, and had my uncle not pointed out the advantages of the marriage they would certainly have never occurred to me. I was therefore surprised; yet I had to admit to myself the reasonableness of my uncle's wishes. Perhaps I am a thoughtless sort of person. At any rate, I believe that the main source of my reluctance to marry my cousin lay in my complete indifference to her. As a child I had frequently gone to play at my uncle's home in town. I remember that I often spent the night there. My cousin and I were therefore childhood friends. You know of course that a brother does not fall in love with his sister. I may be simply repeating what has always been known, but I do believe that for love to grow there must first be the impact of novelty. Between two people who have always known each other, that necessary stimulus can never be felt. Like the first whiff of burning incense, or like the taste of one's first cup of saké, there is in love that moment when all its power is felt. There may be fondness, but not love, between two people who have come to know each other well without ever having grasped that moment. No matter how hard I tried, I could not bring myself to want my cousin for a wife.

My uncle said that if I should insist, he would be willing to postpone my wedding until I had graduated. "But," he added, "as the saying goes, 'don't put off the good things.' I should like, if possible, to announce the engagement now." As far as I was concerned, a fiancée was no more desirable than a wife; and so I refused. My uncle pulled a sour face. My cousin cried; not because she was saddened by the prospect of a life without me, but because her woman's pride had been hurt by my refusal to marry her. I knew very well that she was no more in love with me than I was with her. I returned once more to Tokyo.

*

The following summer, I went home for the third time. I had as usual awaited the end of the examinations impatiently, and then had hurried away from Tokyo as quickly as I could. Home was indeed very dear to me. You know of course that the very air of one's native place seems different from that of anywhere else. The smell of the earth, even, seems to have a special quality of its own. Besides, I found there to comfort me the tender memory of my father and mother. I looked forward to the months of July and August, when I could live like a snake hibernating in its hole, secure and comfortable in familiar surroundings.

I was so simple as to think that the question of marriage between my cousin and myself had been settled, and that there was no more need for me to worry about it. I believed that in life, so long as one rejected openly what one did not want, one would be left alone. And so the fact that I had not yielded to my uncle's persuasion worried me very little. After having spent a year without giving it much thought, I went home in my usual cheerful mood.

My uncle's attitude towards me, however, had changed. He did not receive me with open arms as he had done before. But being a rather easygoing sort of fellow, I did not notice this until I had been home for four or five days. Some incident or other brought it to my notice; and when I looked about me I saw that not only had my uncle become strange, but my aunt and my cousin also. Even my uncle's eldest son, who had not long before written to me for advice, saying that he was intending to go to a commercial college in Tokyo after his graduation from high school, seemed to behave strangely.

It was in my nature to begin wondering. "Why is it that my feelings have changed?" I asked myself. But quickly the question became: "Why is it that *their* feelings have changed?" And suddenly, I began to think that my dead father and mother had lifted the veil from my eyes so that I could see the world clearly for what it really was. You see, somewhere in my heart I believed that my parents, though they had departed from this world, still loved me as they had done when alive. I do not think that, even at that time, the rational part of me was undeveloped. But there was deeply rooted in my system a core of superstition bequeathed to me by my ancestors. I think that it is there still.

I went alone to the hill where my parents were buried and knelt down before their grave. I knelt partly in sorrow, and partly in gratitude. And as though my future happiness were held in the hands of these two buried under the cold stone, I prayed to them to watch over my destiny. You may laugh; and I will not blame you if you do. But I was that sort of person.

All of a sudden, my world had changed. I had had this experience before. It was, I think, in my sixteenth or seventeenth year that with a shock, I discovered that there was beauty in this world. I rubbed my eyes many times, not believing what they saw. And then my heart cried out: "How beautiful!" It is at the age of sixteen or seventeen that both boys and girls become—to use a popular expression—"love-conscious." I was no different from the others, and for the first time in my life I was able to see women as the personification of beauty in this world. My eyes, which had been blind to the existence of the opposite sex, were suddenly opened; and before them a whole new universe unravelled itself.

My awareness—my sudden awareness—of my uncle's attitude was, I suppose, a similar experience. It rushed at me without warning. My uncle and his family appeared before my eyes as totally different beings. I was shocked. And I began to feel that, unless I did something, I might be lost.

I thought that I owed it to my dead parents to find out from my uncle the details of the family fortune which I had left to his management. It seemed that he was as busy as he professed to be, for he never slept under the same roof for more than a few nights at a time. For every two days in our house, he would spend three in town. Whenever I saw him, I found him in a fidgety mood. "I am so busy, so busy . . ." he would automatically say, and then hurry away. Before I began to doubt him, I was inclined to believe that he was really busy, or, when in a cynical mood, I would tell myself that it was probably the latest fashion to appear busy. But after I had decided to have a long talk with him about my inheritance, I began to suspect that he was trying to avoid such a talk. At any rate, I did not find it easy to get hold of him.

Then I heard that my uncle was keeping a mistress in town. The rumor reached me through an old friend of mine, who had been a classmate at high school. Considering my uncle's character, his having a mistress was nothing to be surprised about, but I, who had never heard such rumors about him during my father's lifetime, was shocked. My friend told me of other things that were being said about my uncle: one of them was that though at one time his business enterprises were thought to be failing, his situation seemed to have improved considerably in the last two or three years. I was given another reason for suspecting my uncle.

At last, I had a conference with him. To say that "I had a conference" may sound odd, but that is about the only way I can describe our talk. My uncle persisted in treating me like a child, while I regarded him with suspicion from the beginning. There was certainly no chance of our talk ending amicably.

Unfortunately, I am in too much of a hurry to describe the results of the "conference" in detail. To tell the truth, there is something much more important that I want to write about. I am hardly able to restrain my pen, which seems anxious to reach the main part of the narrative. Having lost forever the opportunity of talking to you at my leisure, I cannot say all the things that I wish to say. I am a slow and inexperienced writer, and I have little time.

You remember of course that day when I said that there was no such thing in this world as a species of men whose unique quality is badness; and that one should always be careful not to forget that a gentleman, when tempted, may easily become a rogue. You were then good enough to point out to me that I was excited. You also asked what it was that caused good men to become bad; and when I answered simply, "Money," you looked dissatisfied. I remember well that look of dissatisfaction on your face. I now confess to you that I was then thinking of my uncle. With hatred in my heart, I was thinking of my uncle, who seemed to typify all those ordinary men who become evil for the sake of money, and who seemed to me the person-ification of all those things in this world which make it unworthy of trust. To you who wished to probe deeply into the realm of ideas, my answer must have been quite unsatisfactory: it must have seemed trite. But for me, the answer that I gave was a living truth. Was I not excited? I believe that words uttered in passion contain a greater living truth than do those words which express thoughts rationally conceived. It is blood that moves the body. Words are not meant to stir the air only: they are capable of moving greater things.

*

In short, my uncle cheated me of my inheritance. He managed to do so without much difficulty during the three years that I was away in Tokyo. I was incredibly naïve to have trustingly left everything under my uncle's management. It depends of course on the point of view: some, who do not consider worldliness a great virtue, may admire such a display of innocence. At any rate, I can never think of those days without cursing myself for being so trusting and honest. I find myself asking, "Why was I born so good-natured?" But, I must admit, I sometimes wish that I had never lost my old innocence, and that once more I could be the person that I was. Please remember that you met me after I had become soiled. If one respects one's elders because they have lived longer and have become more soiled than oneself, then certainly I deserve your respect.

There is little doubt that if I had married my cousin as my uncle wished, I would have profited materially. His real reasons for wanting me to marry his daughter were of course selfish. It was not simply the interest of the two houses that he had at heart: our marriage was to further his own base designs. I did not love my cousin, but I did not dislike her either. I find that now I take a certain amount of pleasure in the fact that I refused to make her my wife. It is true that I would have been cheated even if I had married her, but I have at least the consolation that in one matter at least, I had my way. This is, however, an unimportant detail. To you, it must seem that I am being rather silly and petty.

Other relatives of mine stepped in to settle the quarrel between me and my uncle. I had no trust in any of them. In fact, I regarded them as my enemies. I took it for granted that since my uncle had cheated me, they also would do the same. "If my uncle," I said to myself, "whom my father praised so much, could cheat me, then what reason have I to trust them?"

It was through their mediation, however, that I managed to receive all that remained to me. It amounted to far less than I had expected. There were two courses open to me: one was to accept quietly what was offered to me; and the other was to sue him. I was angry, but I hesitated. I feared that, if I took the latter course, I would have to wait a long time before the court reached a decision. I was a student, and time was very precious to me. I did not want my studies interrupted. I went to an old high school friend of mine who lived in town, and asked him to help me convert all my assets into cash. He advised me against doing so, but I would not listen. I had decided to leave, and stay away from home for a long time to come. I had made a vow never to see my uncle's face again.

Before leaving, I paid another visit to my parents' grave. I have not seen it since. I don't suppose I shall ever see it again.

My friend settled my affairs for me as I had asked, though he was not able to do so before a long time had passed after my return to Tokyo. It is not an easy thing to sell one's lands in the country. Besides, prospective buyers are always quick to take advantage of one's difficulties. The amount I finally received was much less than what my lands were worth. To tell the truth, my entire capital consisted of a few bonds that I had brought with me when I left home, and the money that I subsequently received through my friend. No doubt, my original inheritance was worth far more. What I found particularly galling was the fact that I myself had not been responsible for the dwindling of the family fortune. What I had, however, was certainly more than adequate for a student. As a matter of fact, I could not spend more than half the interest that accrued from my capital. Had I been in less easy circumstances as a student, I might not have been forced into such undreamt-of situations as later came my way.

As there was no more need for me to live as economically as I had done before, I began to toy with the idea of leaving the noisy boarding house and settling in a house of my own. I was, however, somewhat hesitant at first to put the idea into practice. I did not relish the thought of having to buy the necessary household goods, and of having to find an old housekeeper who was honest and whom I could depend upon to look after the house properly while I was away. At any rate, I decided one day to go for a walk and at the same time see if there were any vacant houses that I might find particularly attractive. I walked down the west side of Hongōdai Hill and then up the slope of Koishikawa towards Denzūin Temple. The whole area has changed in appearance since the trams started going through there but, in those days, there was merely the mud wall of the Arsenal on the left as one walked up the slope, and on the right there were only open fields. I stopped for a moment, and thinking of nothing in particular, looked towards the hill on the other side of the valley. The view is not bad even now, but it was much more pleasant then. All was green as far as I could see: it was a soothing sight. I then began to wonder whether a suitable house could not be found in the neighborhood. I walked across the fields until I came to a narrow lane, and then followed it northward. Even today, that neighborhood has a higgledy-piggledy look. You can imagine what it was like in those days. I walked around in circles through innumerable little alleys until I came upon a small confectioner's. I went in and asked the woman who kept the shop whether she knew of a small but neat house that I could rent. "Well, let me see now . . ." she said, and for a while appeared to be in deep thought. She then said, "I am afraid I can't think of one at the moment." I decided there was no hope, and was about to leave the shop when she said: "Would you mind living with a family?" I became interested. After all, I thought to myself, living as the only paying guest in a quiet household would probably be more convenient than having a house of one's own. I sat down, and the woman began to tell me about a family she knew of that might take me in.

It was an army family; or, to be more accurate, a family that had once been connected with the army. The head of it had been killed, the woman believed, in the Sino-Japanese War. The bereaved family had lived in their old house near the Officers' School at Ichigaya until the previous year, but had found it too large—it was the sort of house with stables attached to it—and so had sold it and moved into a smaller one. There were only three people living in the house, the woman told me: the widow, her daughter, and one maid. The widow had apparently said to the woman that it was rather lonely in the new house, and that she would like a boarder, if someone suitable could be found. I thought that the house would be very quiet and that it would suit me very well. But I was afraid that such a family would not wish to take in a student

about whom they knew nothing. I was tempted to give up
the idea of going to the house. I reminded myself, however, that for a student I looked quite respectable. Besides,
I was wearing my university cap. Of course, you will
laugh and say, "What is so impressive about a university
cap?" But in those days, university students were regarded
with more respect than they are now. My square cap,
then, gave me the confidence I needed. Following the
directions given me by the woman in the confectioner's,
and without proper introduction of any kind, I made my
way to the house.

I introduced myself to the widow and told her the
purpose of my visit. She questioned me closely concerning
my background, my university, my field of study, and so
on. My answers must have satisfied her, for she did not
hesitate to say that I could move in as soon as I wished.
The lady had an honest and direct manner. I was quite
impressed, and thought to myself: "Are all soldiers' wives
like her?" At the same time, I was surprised that a lady of
such obvious strength of character could ever feel lonely.

I moved immediately. I was given the room in which
our interview had taken place. It was the finest room in
the house. I had by no means been living in squalor before:
by my time, there were already a few high-class boarding
houses in existence in the Hongō area. I had become
accustomed to living in rooms which, by student standards, were more than adequate. But my new room was
far more impressive than any I had had before in Tokyo.
When I first moved into it, I felt that it was perhaps a little
too grand for a student.

It was an eight-mat room. There was an alcove, and
beside it, some ornamental shelves. On the side opposite

the verandah, there was a closet six feet wide. There were no windows, but the room opened onto a sunny verandah facing the south.

As soon as I moved into the room, I noticed a vase of flowers in the alcove. A *koto* stood against the wall of the alcove, next to the flowers. Neither the flowers nor the *koto* pleased me. Having been brought up by a father who was fond of such things as Chinese poetry, calligraphy, and the tea ceremony, I was from childhood inclined to severity in my taste. I had learned to be contemptuous of such obvious attempts at charm as I found in the alcove.

Thanks to my uncle, the greater part of my father's art collection had disappeared, but there still remained to me a few items of value, most of which I had left with my friend at home for safekeeping. There were, however, four or five hanging scrolls that had struck my fancy, and these I took out of their wooden cases and put at the bottom of my trunk before leaving for Tokyo. I had been looking forward to hanging one of them in the alcove of my new room, but when I saw the flowers and the *koto,* I lost heart. When I learned later that the flowers had been put there to please me, I was secretly amused and exasperated. The *koto* apparently had always been there, and I suppose they could not find another place for it.

I think it likely that the shadow of a young woman has already begun to pass before your mind's eye. I must admit that I began to be curious about the young lady even before I moved in. Perhaps this vulgar curiosity on my part made me self-conscious, or perhaps I had not yet overcome my youthful shyness; but whatever the reason may have been, I behaved very awkwardly when I was introduced to Ojōsan.[9] She, on her part, blushed.

9. Close equivalent in meaning and usage would be *mademoiselle.*

I had already formed a picture in my mind of what she would be like from my observation of her mother's appearance and manner. The picture was not altogether flattering. Deciding that her mother was the soldier's wife *par excellence,* I had gone on to imagine what a typical soldier's daughter would be like. But all my preconceptions about Ojōsan vanished as soon as I saw her face. And I was filled with a new awareness, far greater than any that I had ever experienced before, of the power of the opposite sex. After that, the flowers in the alcove ceased to displease me. The presence of the *koto* did not annoy me any more.

Whenever the flowers in the vase showed signs of wilting, she would come to replace them. Sometimes, she came in to take the *koto* away to her room, which was diagonally opposite mine. I would then sit quietly at my desk, my chin resting on my hands, and listen to the sound of the *koto*. I could not be sure whether her playing was good or bad. But as she never played a piece that sounded complicated, I was inclined to suspect that she was not quite an expert. In fact, I thought it likely that her *koto*-playing was no better than her flower arrangement. I know something about the latter art, and I can safely say that Ojōsan was by no means a master of it.

Unblushingly, however, she persisted in decorating my alcove with flowers of all kinds. They were arranged always in the same way and always in the same vase. Stranger still was the music. All that one heard was a series of hesitant, disconnected plucking sounds, and one could hardly hear the singing that these sounds were meant to accompany. I do not say that she did not sing. But her singing was rather timid, and had what one might call a confidential tone. When scolded by the teacher, she became even less audible.

Happily, however, I gazed at the badly arranged flowers and listened to the strange music.

*

I was already a misanthrope when I left home for the last time. That people could not be trusted must already have become a conviction deeply rooted in my system. It was then that I began to think of my uncle, my aunt, and all the other relatives whom I had come to hate as typical of the entire human race. On the Tokyo-bound train, I found myself watching suspiciously my fellow passengers. And when anyone spoke to me, I became even more suspicious. My heart was heavy. I felt as though I had swallowed lead. But my nerves were on edge.

I am quite sure that my state of mind was largely responsible for my wanting to leave the boarding house. It would of course be simpler to attribute my desire to have a house of my own to my sudden affluence; but I am convinced that I would not have gone to the trouble of moving if the change had been merely economic.

For quite a while after I had moved to Koishikawa, I could not relax. I looked at everything around me with such obvious shiftiness that I became ashamed of myself. Strangely enough, I became less and less inclined to talk, while my mind and eyes increased their activity enormously. I sat silently at my desk and, like a cat, watched the movements of others in the house. I was so much on my guard that sometimes I had the grace enough to feel guilty towards them. "I am behaving like a pickpocket who doesn't steal," I would tell myself disgustedly.

You are probably asking yourself: "If he was indeed in such a state, how is it that he was able to feel affection for Ojōsan? How could he have enjoyed her bad flower arrangement and her *koto*-playing?" I can only answer that I truly did experience these conflicting emotions at the time, and that I can do no more than describe them to you as faithfully as I can. I am sure that you are quite capable of finding a satisfactory explanation yourself. But let me say this: I had come to distrust people in money matters, but I had not yet learned to doubt love. And so, strange as it may seem to another person and inconsistent as it may seem even to me when I think about it, I was quite unaware of any conflict between the two states of mind.

It was my custom to call the widow "Okusan,"[10] so I shall refer to her as such from now on. Okusan was wont to comment on my calm disposition—as she would call it—and my quietness, and on one occasion praised me for being so studious. She said nothing about insecurity or shiftiness. I don't know whether she failed to notice my odd behavior or whether she was too polite to mention it, but she certainly seemed inclined to view me in a favorable light. She once went so far as to say to me in an admiring tone that I had a generous heart. I was honest enough to blush and to say that she was mistaken. She said quite seriously, "You say that because you are unaware of your own virtues." It seems that she had not expected to have a student in her house. When she let it be known in the neighborhood that she was willing to take in a boarder, she was apparently hoping for some kind of civil servant to apply. I suspect that she was quite resigned to the fact that only an underpaid petty official would want a room in someone else's house. When she called me a generous-hearted person, she must have been comparing me with this shabby civil servant of her imagination. True, I had some money, and, I suppose, lived in a way which is impossible for those who are financially embarrassed. In

10. Close equivalent in meaning and usage would be *madame*.

money matters, then, I could afford to be liberal. But this kind of liberality has nothing to do with one's nature. It seems that Okusan, in the way that women have, was apt to assume that my attitude towards money was an indication of the generosity of my heart.

*

Okusan's manner towards me gradually changed my own state of mind. I became less shifty, and began to feel more relaxed. I suppose the fact that Okusan and the rest of the household took no notice of my suspicious and withdrawn manner gave me great comfort. Since there was nothing in my surroundings that seemed to justify watchfulness, I began to calm down.

Okusan was a woman of some understanding, and it is possible that she behaved as she did because she knew my mood. It is also possible that she really did think me a peaceful, generous, and easygoing person. The latter is more likely, for I do not suppose that my outward behavior betrayed the confusion within very often.

Gradually, as I grew more calm, I came to know the family better. I began to exchange witticisms with Okusan and Ojōsan. There were days when I was invited to drink tea with them. There were evenings when I would go out and buy sweets and then invite them to my room. I felt that suddenly, my circle of acquaintances had been considerably enlarged. True, many hours were wasted in conversation which should have been spent in study. But I was surprised to find that I did not mind this at all. Okusan, of course, had little to do all day. But to my surprise, Ojōsan, who not only attended school but was studying flower arrangement and the *koto* as well, never seemed busy either. And so the three of us were willing enough,

144

whenever the opportunity presented itself, to get together and entertain one another with small talk.

It was usually Ojōsan that came to call me. She would sometimes appear on the verandah, and sometimes she would come through the morning room and appear at my door. She would stand still for a moment, and then call my name and say, "Are you studying?" I was usually staring hard at some heavy tome lying open on my desk, and so I must have seemed a rather scholarly fellow. But to tell the truth, I was not much of a student in those days. I might have looked at a lot of books, but I was usually waiting for Ojōsan to appear. If by chance she failed to do so, then I would get up and go to her room and say, "Are you studying?"

Ojōsan's was a six-mat room next to the morning room. Okusan would sometimes be sitting in the morning room and sometimes in her daughter's room. The two rooms were really used like one large room by the two ladies, neither of whom seemed to regard either room as exclusively hers. Whenever I called to them from outside the door, it was invariably Okusan who said, "Come in." Ojōsan, even when she was there, hardly ever joined her mother in the invitation.

Occasionally, when Ojōsan came to my room on some errand, she would sit down for a chat. At such times, I felt strangely uneasy. Afterwards, I would try, with little success, to convince myself that my uneasiness was no more than the natural embarrassment of a young man finding himself alone with a young woman. It was not so much embarrassment as a feeling of restlessness; and the cause of this restlessness was the unnatural feeling that I was somehow being a traitor to my true self. She, on her part, seemed perfectly at ease. She was, in fact, so self-possessed that I would ask myself, "Is this the same girl that is so self-conscious about her voice during her *koto* lessons?" Sometimes, when she stayed too long, her mother would call her. I remember that on more than one occasion she merely answered, "I'm coming," and remained where she was. Ojōsan was by no means a child, however. This was quite clear to me. What was also clear to me was that she wanted me to know she was no longer a child.

*

After her departure I would sigh with relief. At the same time, the room would seem empty, and I would apologize to her inwardly for the releif I had felt. Perhaps I was behaving like a woman. It must certainly seem so to a modern young man like yourself. But most of us were like that in those days.

Okusan hardly ever went out of the house. Whenever she did so, she was sure to take Ojōsan with her. I could not tell whether she did this for a particular reason or not. Perhaps it is not quite proper for me to say this, but it did seem to me, after I had carefully watched Okusan for a while, that she was encouraging me and her daughter to become better acquainted with each other. On the other hand, there were times when she appeared to be on her guard against me. The first time she gave me this impression, I was a little annoyed.

You see, I wanted to know precisely what her attitude was. From my point of view at least, her conduct was quite illogical. And having only recently been cheated by my uncle, I could not stop myself from suspecting Okusan of duplicity, and from assuming that one of her two attitudes was a deliberate deception. I could not understand the reason for her seemingly inconsistent behavior. "Why should she behave so strangely?" I would ask myself. And finding no answer to the question, I would angrily mutter to myself, "Women!" Then I would try to find comfort in the thought that Okusan behaved as she did because she was a woman, and women, after all, were idiots.

In spite of my contempt for women, however, I found it impossible to be contemptuous of Ojōsan. It seemed that reason was powerless in her presence. My love for her was close to piety. You may think it strange that I should use this word, with its religious connotation, to describe my feeling towards a woman. But even now I believe—and I believe it very strongly—that true love is not so far removed from religious faith. Whenever I saw Ojōsan's face, I felt that I had myself become beautiful. Whenever I thought of her, I felt a new sense of dignity welling up inside me. If this incomprehensible thing that we call love can either bring out the sacred in man or, in its lowest form, merely excite one's bodily passions, then surely my love was of the highest kind. I am not saying that I was not like other men. I am made of flesh too. But my eyes which gazed at her, and my mind which held thoughts of her, were innocent of bodily desire.

As you can well imagine, relations between the three of us became rather complicated. I was growing more and more fond of the daughter while my antagonism towards the mother increased. Our feelings, however, were hardly ever allowed to appear on the surface, and the change of atmosphere in the house was not openly recognized. And then suddenly, for some reason or other, I began to wonder if I had not been mistaken about Okusan. I began to think that perhaps her apparent inconsistency was not a sign of dishonesty, and that, contrary to my previous suspicion, perhaps neither of her two attitudes was a conscious attempt to deceive me. I came to acknowledge the possibility that the two seemingly conflicting attitudes existed side by side, and that the existence of one need not necessarily preclude the other. I decided finally that even when she seemed suddenly to become watchful after having encouraged her daughter to be friendly with me, she was not truly changing her mind: she was merely preventing us from becoming closer to each other than her sense of propriety allowed. I, who had no dishonorable intentions, did feel that Okusan was worrying unnecessarily, but I ceased to bear her a grudge.

Shortly thereafter, when I had observed Okusan's behavior towards me in a different light, I came to the conclusion that she put considerable trust in me. Moreover, I was given reason to believe that she had begun to trust me from the time of our first meeting. This discovery was a great shock to me, who had learned to be distrustful of everybody. "Are women endowed with intuitive powers so great," I asked myself, "that they know at a glance whom to trust and whom not to trust?" But later, I said to myself: "Is it not because women are so trusting that they are constantly being deceived by men?" It is amusing to think that it never occurred to me then to examine my own confidence in Ojōsan, which was based on nothing more than intuition. Though I had vowed never to trust people, I trusted Ojōsan absolutely. Yet I found Okusan's trust in me quite incredible.

I told them very little about my home. Concerning the incident that caused me to leave, I said nothing. It was unpleasant for me to think about it, let alone talk about it. I tried always, therefore, to steer the conversation to Okusan's past life. But she would not co-operate. She insisted many times on hearing about my home. Finally, I

148

told them everything. When I said that I would never go home again since there was nothing left for me there except my parents' grave, Okusan seemed very moved. Ojōsan cried. I felt that I had done the right thing in telling them my story. I was glad.

After our conversation, Okusan began to act as though her intuitions about me had been confirmed and to treat me as she would a young relation of hers. This did not annoy me. I was even pleased. Before long, however, I began once more to suspect her motives.

It was only something very petty that put me in a suspicious frame of mind. But this did not prevent me from becoming more and more suspicious as time went by. Some small incident—I forget what—put the idea into my head that Okusan was forcing her daughter onto me from the same motives as those which prompted my uncle when he wished me to marry his daughter. Okusan, whom I had taken for a kindly person, quickly became a cunning schemer in my eyes. I was filled with disgust.

When Okusan first told me that loneliness was the reason why she had wanted a boarder, I believed her; and after I had come to know her well, I found no cause to change my mind. On the other hand, she was by no means a wealthy woman and, from the financial point of view, I was certainly not unattractive as a prospective son-in-law.

Once more, I found myself on the defensive. Of course, I stood to gain nothing from such an attitude, since I remained very much in love with Ojōsan. I laughed at myself in scorn. I told myself that I was an idiot. If my suspicions had gone no further, I should not have suffered very much, and I should simply have laughed at myself for being such an inconsistent fool. But I began to be really miserable when the thought occurred to me that perhaps Ojōsan was no less of a schemer than her mother. It was unbearably painful to imagine the two of them plotting behind my back. I was not merely unhappy: I was desperate. But there was another part of me that trusted Ojōsan absolutely. I stood still, unable to move away from the half-way point between conviction and doubt. To me, both seemed like figments of my imagination, and yet both seemed real.

*

I continued to attend lectures at the university. But the professors who stood on the platforms seemed very far away, and their voices faint. I could not study either. The printed characters that my eyes saw disappeared like rising smoke before they reached my mind. Also, I became silent. Two or three of my friends misconstrued my silence, and reported to the others that I seemed to be deep in some kind of philosophic meditation. I did not try to undeceive them. Indeed, I was happy to hide behind the mask that they had unwittingly put on me. I cannot have been entirely satisfied with the role, however. I would sometimes throw fits of riotous merrymaking that would shock them considerably.

There were not many visitors to the house. Okusan seemed to have few relatives. Ojōsan's school friends visited her occasionally, but they were so quiet that one could hardly tell that they were in the house. They were being quiet for my sake; but I did not know this. My own friends who came to the house were none of them rowdy fellows, but they were not so demure as to start whispering for the sake of other people's comfort. At such times, I seemed to enjoy all the rights due to the owner of the house, while Ojōsan's position was hardly better than that of an unwanted guest.

This is not of great importance, however. I wrote it

down simply because it came to my mind: besides, it leads me to something less insignificant. One day, I heard a man's voice coming from Ojōsan's room. Being Ojōsan's guest, he spoke far more quietly than any of my friends would have done. I found it impossible, therefore, to hear what he was saying. I remained seated at my desk in helpless indignation. Was he a relative, I asked myself, or was he merely an acquaintance? Was he young, or was he old? It was of course impossible to find answers to these questions in my room. But I could hardly barge into Ojōsan's room to inspect the visitor. I was more than irritated: I was truly in agony. As soon as the man went away, I left my room to ask who he was. They gave me a simple answer. It was too simple to satisfy me. I looked at them discontentedly, lacking the courage to question them further. I had no right, of course, to be so curious. I had to maintain my dignity and my self-respect which I had been taught to value. But the fact that this self-respect was not succeeding too well in overcoming my vulgar curiosity showed in my discontented face. They laughed. Whether they did so in derision, or out of friendliness, I was too flustered at that moment to find out. Afterwards, I repeatedly asked myself: "Did they make a fool of me, or didn't they?"

I was free to do anything I liked. Without consulting anyone, I could leave the university at any time, I could go anywhere, live in any way that suited me, and get married if I wished. Often, I was on the verge of asking Okusan for permission to marry her daughter. But each time I decided to do so, I quickly changed my mind. The prospect of being refused did not frighten me. True, life would be different without Ojōsan, but I thought that there would at least be the compensation of being able to look at a new world from another vantage point. Besides, I thought that I had the necessary courage to accept such a change. But I hated the idea of being enticed by Okusan to swallow her bait. No matter what happened, I vowed to myself, no one would ever dupe me as my uncle had done.

Seeing me buy nothing but books, Okusan said that I should buy myself some new clothes. Indeed, all the clothes that I possessed had been made at home, of cotton woven locally. It was not the custom for students to wear silk in those days. I remember that a friend of mine once received a heavy silk garment from home. His father, incidentally, was a Yokohama merchant whose tastes were rather ostentatious. When the garment arrived, we all laughed at the fellow. He was quite embarrassed, and made all sorts of excuses. He tossed it into his trunk, and would not put it on. We finally bullied him into wearing it. Unfortunately, it caught fleas from somewhere. My friend must have been pleased, for he wasted no time in getting rid of the famous garment. He rolled it up into a bundle, and taking it with him on one of his walks, threw it into the large ditch in Nezu. I was with him at the time. I remember standing on the bridge and watching my friend with amusement. It never occurred to me then to think that he was being wasteful.

All this happened when I was still living in a boarding house. I had matured somewhat since then, but I was not yet so clothes-conscious as to start worrying about being well-dressed. I still had the odd notion that good clothes, like a mustache, came after graduation. This is why I remarked to Okusan that though books were necessary, clothes were not. She knew that I bought a great number of books, and she asked me: "Tell me, do you read them all?" Amongst them were, of course, such necessary books

of reference as dictionaries, but there were also many that
I had not yet even opened. I was at a loss for an answer.
And I thought that, as long as I was going to buy unnecessary things, I might just as well spend money on clothes
as on books. Besides, I had been wanting to buy Ojōsan a
present, such as a sash or a length of material, under the
pretext of showing my appreciation for their many kindnesses. I asked Okusan, therefore, if she would be good
enough to buy something suitable for her daughter, and
for myself.

Okusan refused to go by herself. She commanded me
to accompany her. She insisted also that her daughter
come too. Brought up as we were in an atmosphere quite
different from that of today, we students were not accustomed to being seen in the streets in the company of
young women. Then, I was even more of a slave to
convention than I am now. I hesitated at first, but I finally
overcame my scruples and set out with the two ladies.

Ojōsan had taken great care over her appearance.
Though she was naturally very light-complexioned, she
had covered her face liberally with white powder, which
made her conspicuous. Passers-by stared at her. What gave
me a strange feeling was the fact that after they had had a
good look at her, they would begin to stare at me.

The three of us went to a shop in Nihonbashi and
bought what we wanted. It was difficult to decide what to
buy, and we spent more time there than I had expected.
Okusan insisted on my giving an opinion on everything
that was shown to us. She would drape a piece of cloth on
Ojōsan's shoulder, then ask me to step back a few paces,
and say: "Well, how do you like it?" I tried to play my part
properly, and never failed to give some kind of opinion.
"I don't think that looks very good," I would say; or "Yes,
that would suit her very well."

When we finally left the shop, it was time for dinner. Okusan said that to thank me for being so kind, she would like to take me out to dinner. She led us into a narrow side street called Kiharadana where there was, I noticed, a small old-fashioned theater. The restaurant we went into was as poky as the street. I was not at all familiar with the neighborhood, and I was amazed that Okusan should know it so well.

It was quite late in the evening when we returned home. The next day was Sunday, and I spent it in my room. As soon as I appeared at the university on Monday morning, a classmate of mine came up to me and began to tease me. "When did you get married?" he said in mock seriousness. "Your wife is quite a beauty, I must say!" He must have seen the three of us in Nihonbashi.

*

When I got home, I told Okusan and Ojōsan what my friend had said. Okusan laughed. She then gave me an odd look, and said: "It must have been rather annoying for you." I immediately thought that this was probably a woman's way of sounding out a man's inner thoughts. Perhaps I should then have told her frankly how I felt towards her daughter. But I was too suspicious to be honest. I restrained my impulse to tell her the truth, and deliberately steered the conversation away from myself to the subject of Ojōsan's marriage.

I tried to find out what Okusan's plans were for her daughter. She clearly implied that Ojōsan had already received some offers of marriage. She explained that since her daughter was still at school, she felt that there was no need to hurry. Though she did not say so outright, it was obvious that she set great store by her daughter's good looks, and hinted that she could marry her off any time she wished. Ojōsan was her only child, and of course she was reluctant to part from her. I suspected that she was in a quandary as to whether she ought to allow her daughter to marry into another family, or whether she should arrange to adopt a son-in-law who would become a member of her own household.

As the conversation progressed, I felt that I was learning much that was of interest to me from Okusan. But I had lost the opportunity of talking about myself. Thinking that I could not, at this late stage in the conversation, put in a word on my own behalf, I decided to leave as soon as I could do so without seeming rude.

Ojōsan was sitting near me when I told them what my friend had said that morning: she even said merrily, "That's going too far!"; but she had quietly withdrawn to the corner of the room in the course of the conversation, and was now sitting with her back turned towards me. I was not aware that she had moved until I was about to get up and go. I saw her back when I turned around to look at her. It was of course impossible to read her thoughts without seeing her face. I could not even begin to guess how she felt about marriage. She sat near the closet. The door was open, and I decided that she had taken something out of it, placed it on her lap, and was looking at it. Through the open door of the closet, I caught a glimpse of the pieces of cloth that I had bought two days before. The cloth that I had bought for her, and the cloth that I had bought for myself, were lying one on top of the other.

I said no more, and I was about to stand up when Okusan suddenly said to me in a serious tone, "What do you think?" Her question was so sudden that for a moment I wondered what she was talking about. Then I realized that she was asking me whether or not her daughter should get married soon. "Oh, I think that she should wait a while, don't you?" I said. Okusan said that she thought so too.

The relationship between the three of us had developed thus far when another man appeared on the scene. He became a member of the household and, by doing so, changed the course of my destiny. If this man had never crossed my path, I don't suppose there would ever have arisen the necessity for me to write this long letter to you. The devil had passed before me, so to speak, casting his shadow over me for a moment. And I did not know that his passing had darkened my life for ever. I must tell you that it was I who dragged this man into the house to live with us. Needless to say, I had first to get Okusan's permission to do so. I told her everything about the man, and asked her if he might come and stay with me. At first she said no. But while I felt myself absolutely obliged to invite him, she seemed to have no reasonable basis for her objection. Finally, I had my way. I was able to do what I thought was right.

I shall here call my friend "K." K and I were friends from the time we were children. Needless to say, then, we were from the same part of the country. K was the son of a priest of the Shinshū sect. He was the second son, and was sent as an adopted son to the house of a certain doctor. The Hongan church was very powerful in my native district, and so Shinshū priests were more affluent than the priests of other sects. For example, if a Shinshū priest happened to have a daughter of marrying age, he would have little trouble marrying her into a suitable family through the kind offices of a parishioner. Of course, wedding expenses would not come out of the priest's pocket. For reasons such as this, Shinshū priests were generally quite prosperous.

K's family lived comfortably. But whether they possessed enough means to send their younger son to Tokyo to complete his studies, I do not know. Nor do I know that arrangements for his adoption were made in order that his chances of further education might be improved. Whatever the reason, then, K went as an adopted son to the house of the doctor. This happened when we were still in the secondary school. I remember even now my surprise when, during roll call in class one day, I found that my friend's name had suddenly been changed.

K's new family was a wealthy one, and his education was to be financed by them; so he came to Tokyo. Though K and I did not travel up together, we moved into the same boarding house. In those days, it was common practice for two or three students to live and sleep in one room, and work at desks placed next to each other, as did K and myself. We were like wild beasts captured in the mountains, that hug each other and stare angrily from their cage at the world outside. We feared Tokyo and the people in it. Nevertheless, when we were in our little six-mat room, we would talk contemptuously of the whole world.

But we were in earnest, and seriously intended to become great men one day. Indeed, K was very earnest. Having been born in a temple, he often spoke of "concentration of mind." And to me, it seemed that this phrase described completely his daily life. My heart was filled with reverence for K.

From the time we were at school, K was in the habit of embarrassing me by bringing up such difficult matters as religion and philosophy. I do not know whether this was the result of his father's influence, or the result of having been born in a house possessing an atmosphere peculiar to temples. At any rate, it seems to me that he had more of the priest in him than the average priest. K's foster parents had originally sent him to Tokyo with the intention of making him a doctor. But K, who was very stubborn, had come to Tokyo resolved never to become a doctor. I reproached him, pointing out that he was deceiving his foster parents. Undaunted, he agreed with me, and then answered that he did not mind doing such a thing, so long as it led him to "the true way." In all likelihood, even he did not know what he meant by "the true way." I certainly did not know. But to us who were young, these vague words seemed quite sacred. Ignorant though I was, I was certain that there was no meanness in his enthusiastic decision to follow the dictates of what seemed to me to be noble sentiments. I fully agreed, therefore, with K's views. To what extent K was encouraged by my agreement, I do not know. Undoubtedly, K, single-minded as he was, would not have altered his opinion, no matter how much I might have disagreed with him. And though only a child, I was, I think, more or less aware of my future responsibility through having encouraged K, should anything happen to him as a result of his decision. My enthusiastic approval implied that in the future, if such an occasion should arise when we would cast our more mature eyes back on what he had done, I would be fully prepared to bear my proper share of responsibility, even though at this moment I might not have felt fully prepared for such a necessity.

*

K and I entered the same faculty. Without any show of bad conscience, he began to follow his beloved "true way" with the money that his foster parents sent him, and I can only say that he was less troubled than I by his deception; he seemed quite certain that he would never be caught, and he seemed assured enough that, even if he were caught, he would not mind at all.

When the time came for our first summer vacation, K did not go home. He said that he was going to rent a room in some temple in Komagome. And true enough, when I returned to Tokyo in early September, I found him holed up in a dirty temple by the Great Kannon. His room was a small one very close to the main temple building; he was very happy that there he had been able to study to his heart's content. It was then, I think, that I saw that his life was becoming more and more like that of a priest. He was wearing a rosary around his wrist, and when I asked him what it was for, he showed me how he counted the beads with his thumb, saying one, two, and so on. Apparently, he counted them many times a day. But the meaning behind all this counting I did not understand. Surely, I thought, there is no end to counting beads strung together in a circle. With what thoughts in his mind did K count those beads? This worthless question often comes to my mind now.

I also noticed a Bible in his room. I was a little surprised. Though I could recall that on occasion he had spoken of the sutras, I could not remember his ever having mentioned Christianity. I could not therefore resist asking him why the Bible was there. K said that the Bible was there for no particular reason, except that he thought it only natural that one should read a book so highly valued by others. He added that he intended to read the Koran when he had the opportunity. He seemed particularly interested in the phrase "Mohammed and the sword."

Finally, after being urged to do so by his people, he went home for the following summer vacation. It seems that, when at home, he said nothing about his field of study. His family seemed not at all suspicious. You, being a well-educated person, are obviously well-informed about such matters, but the world in general is surprisingly ignorant about student life, academic rules, and so on. These things, which are common knowledge to us, are not known at all in the outside world. Also, we who live in a comparatively isolated atmosphere are not entirely blameless, in that we tend to assume that academic matters, whether important or not, are well-known throughout all walks of life. In this particular matter, however, it seems that K was more worldly than I. Looking quite unperturbed, he left home. We were traveling to Tokyo together, and as soon as we boarded the train I asked K how things stood between him and his family. He answered that all was well.

At the beginning of the third summer vacation—it was at the end of this that I decided to leave forever the birthplace of my parents—I urged K to go home; but he would not listen. Indeed, he asked me why it was that I went home every year. Evidently he wished to remain in Tokyo and study. With reluctance I left him in Tokyo and went home alone. Concerning the two months that I spent at home, which so affected my future life, I shall not write again, since I have already done so. With my heart filled with dissatisfaction, melancholy, and loneliness, I saw K again in September. And I found that circumstances had changed for the worse for him too. Without my knowing, he had written to his foster parents, confessing that he had been deceiving them. Apparently, he had from the start intended to write such a confession eventually. Perhaps he hoped they would say that it was too late to change his plans, and permit him, no matter how grudgingly, to pursue his studies as he wished. At any rate, it seems K had no desire to deceive his foster parents once he was ready to enter the university. He may have perceived that he could not possibly go on with the deception indefinitely, even if he wanted to do so.

*

K's foster father was furious when he read K's letter. He sent back a severe reply, in which he said that he could not possibly finance the education of one so unprincipled as to cheat his parents. K showed the letter to me. He also showed me another letter that arrived about the same time as the first. It was from his original family. It was a letter of reprimand as severe in tone as the other. Perhaps the severity was due to his family's sense of obligation to those that had adopted K. At any rate, K was told that for anyone to worry about him would be a waste of time. Whether he should return to his original family because of the unhappy incident, or whether he should consider some way of compromise and remain with his adopted family, was a problem for the future, but what required his immediate attention was the question of how he was to pay for his education.

I asked K whether he had any definite ideas about the matter. K said that he thought he might teach in some night school. Compared with now, conditions were surprisingly easy in those days, and it was not as difficult as you might think to find some way of supplementing one's income. I therefore thought that K would manage well enough. At the same time, I felt my own responsibility in the matter. When K decided to go against his foster father's wishes and to follow his own inclinations, it was I that encouraged him. At this stage, then, I could not very well stand aside and idly watch my friend in his predicament. I immediately offered K material assistance. K refused without hesitation. It was in his character to feel greater pleasure in being able to fend for himself than in receiving assistance from his friend. His view, in short, was that once having entered the university, it would be a disgrace to him as a grown man not to be able to solve his own problems by himself. I could not hurt K's feelings merely to satisfy my own sense of responsibility. I therefore withdrew, leaving K to do as he saw fit.

Shortly after, K found the kind of work he wanted. You can well imagine how painful it was for K, who valued his time so much, to have to do such work. And with this new burden on his shoulders, he drove himself harder than ever, so that he might study as he had done before. I began to worry about his health. But he was a stouthearted fellow, and took no notice of my anxious warnings.

About this time, relations between him and his adopted family grew steadily worse and more complicated. As K had now no time to spare, we had little opportunity to talk as we had done before, and I did not hear all the particulars; but I knew how much more difficult of solution the whole problem had become. I knew also that one person had tried to act as mediator between the two parties. This person had actually tried by letter to persuade K to come home. But K refused, saying that it was absolutely impossible. This stubbornness on his part—or so it seemed to the people at home, though K had pointed out to them that he could not leave Tokyo during term-time—made the situation worse; not only did he hurt his foster parents' feelings, but he angered his original family as well. In my anxiety, I wrote a conciliatory letter to soothe their feelings, but it seemed to have no effect whatsoever. My letter, it seems, did not merit even a word in reply. I also became angry. Circumstances had so far made me sympathize with K; but now I was determined to stand by K, whether he was right or wrong.

In the end K decided to become officially a member of his original family once more. They arranged to pay back to K's former foster parents the money spent on his education so far. However, beyond this, his family would do no more. They had washed their hands of him, they said. He was, I suppose, "expelled from his father's house," to use an old-fashioned phrase. On the other hand, perhaps his family did not intend to be so final in their treatment of K; but K, at least, felt that he had been disinherited. K was motherless, and it is more than likely that a part of his character was the result of his having been brought up by a stepmother. I cannot but feel that had his real mother been alive, such a wide gulf might not have come to exist between him and his family. I have already said that K's father was a priest. But I believe that in his unbending regard for honor, he was perhaps more like a samurai than a priest.

*

The excitement over K had abated somewhat when I received a long letter from his elder sister's husband. K told me that this man was related to his foster parents, and had therefore played an important part in the proceedings when he was adopted and when his adoption was revoked.

In the letter, the brother-in-law asked me to let him know if all was well with K. He said that K's sister was worried, and that she would like to have news of him as soon as possible. K was fonder of his sister than he was of his elder brother, who had succeeded to his father's rectory. They were born of the same mother, but there was a considerable difference in age between K and his sister. To

K, she must have seemed more of a mother than his stepmother ever did.

I showed the letter to K. He made no comment, except that he himself had received two or three letters similar in content from his sister, and that he had written back saying that there was no need to worry. Unfortunately, his sister had not married into a well-to-do family. Though she sympathized with K, she could give him no material assistance.

I wrote a reply to the brother-in-law, repeating more or less what K had already said in his letters. I did add, however, a strongly worded assurance that K could always count on my assistance whenever it was necessary. I was, of course, sincere in my assurance. I felt too that I should try to comfort K's sister as best I could. But there is no doubt that in insisting so strongly that I would and could assist K, I was also being indirectly spiteful to his father and to his foster parents, who had, it seemed, treated me with contempt.

K's adoption was revoked in his first year at the university. For a year and a half after that, he worked hard to support himself. Eventually, I began to think that this continual strain was affecting his physical and mental condition. Of course, the squabbling that preceded his decision to leave his adoptive family must have left its mark on him. He became more and more sentimental,[11] and occasionally he would talk as though he carried on his own back the misfortune of all mankind. When one pointed out the unreasonableness of such an attitude, he would become infuriated. Then he would begin to worry about his future, which seemed not as promising as it did before. It is true that everybody begins his university career cher-

11. The English word is used.

ishing great ambitions, like a man who sets out on a long journey; and that, after a year or two, most students suddenly realize the slowness of their progress and, seeing that graduation is not far off, find themselves in a state of disillusionment. K had, no doubt, reached this stage in his career. But his despondency was far greater than was normally found among his fellow students. I finally decided that the only thing to do was to try to calm him down a little.

I said to him that he should do no more work than was necessary. I told him that for the good of his own great future, he should rest and enjoy himself. Knowing K's stubbornness, I did not expect to find my task easy. But once begun, I found it far more difficult and exasperating than I had ever imagined. He held that scholarly knowledge was not his only objective. What was important, he said, was that he should become a strong person through the exercise of will-power. Apparently, this could be done only by living in straitened circumstances. Judged by the standards of a normal person, he was perhaps a little mad. Moreover, straitened circumstances seemed not at all to be strengthening his will-power. Indeed, they were making a neurotic out of him. In desperation, I pretended to be in wholehearted agreement with his views. It had always been my wish, I said, to lead a life such as his. (I was not being totally insincere. I had always found K persuasive in argument, and he could momentarily convince me of almost anything.) Finally, I suggested that he live with me, so that I might learn to lead his kind of life. Because of his stubbornness, I was forced to bow to him. At last, I succeeded in bringing him to the house.

*

There was attached to my room a small anteroom of four mats. One had to go through it to get to my room from the front hall. It was not therefore very conveniently situated. I put K in there. It had been my intention to share my own room with K, and to leave the other room free for both of us to use as the occasion demanded. But K would not listen to my suggestion, saying that he would rather have a room of his own, however small it might be.

As I said, Okusan was against this arrangement from the first. In a boarding house, she said, two lodgers would be more convenient than one, and three would be more profitable than two. But, she pointed out, she was not running a boarding house, and she had no wish to take in another lodger. I said that my friend would give her no trouble. Trouble or no trouble, she answered, she disliked having a stranger in the house. But I was a stranger too, I said. Her answer was that she had from the first known that she could trust me. I smiled. She then changed her tactics. She said that I would later regret having brought such a person into the house. I asked her why she thought so. It was her turn to smile.

Indeed, there really was no reason why I should insist on sharing my apartment with K. But I felt that he would hesitate to accept my assistance if I were to offer it to him every month, in the form of money. He was a very independent-minded person. For this reason, I thought it advisable to have him live with me, and to give Okusan, without his knowledge, enough money to pay for our food. But I had no wish to tell Okusan about K's financial difficulties.

I did, however, say that I was worried about K's health. I said that, if allowed to keep on living in solitude, he was sure to become more eccentric than ever. I told her also of the troubles he had had with his foster parents, and of his later expulsion from his original family. It was, I said, in the hope of lending warmth to his cold and lonely life that

I wanted him to come and stay with me. Would not Okusan and Ojōsan, I asked, look after him with the warm kindness that he so much needed? Okusan raised no more objections. I said nothing about this conversation to K. I was glad that he had no inkling of what had been said with regard to his entering our household. He arrived with a dignified and absent-minded air. In my normal manner, I received him.

Okusan and Ojōsan helped him unpack his bags, and were otherwise very kind to him. I was very happy—despite the fact that K remained his usual moody self—for I felt that their kindness to him arose out of their regard for me.

When I asked K what he thought of his new home, all he said was: "'Not bad." His answer struck me as being somewhat incongruous, considering that he had been living, until then, in a squalid, damp room which faced the north. His food had been in keeping with his room. As far as I was concerned, he had been raised from the bottom of a dark valley to the top of a sunlit mountain. No doubt his stubbornness was partly responsible for his apparent indifference towards the change; but I am sure also that he was being indifferent on principle. Having grown up under the influence of Buddhist doctrines, he seemed to regard respect for material comfort as some kind of immorality. Also, having read stories of great priests and Christian saints who were long since dead, he was wont to regard the body and the soul as entities which had to be forced asunder. Indeed, he seemed at times to think that mistreatment of the body was necessary for the glorification of the soul.

I decided that the best thing for me to do was to avoid arguing with him at all costs. I decided to leave the piece of ice out in the sun, and wait until it had melted and turned into warm water. Then, I thought, he would begin to see the error of his ways.

*

Okusan was giving me a similar treatment, and I was gradually becoming more cheerful. Knowing the efficacy of this treatment when applied to myself, I decided to try it on K. I had known him too long not to know that there was a considerable difference in our characters, but I thought nevertheless that just as my nervousness had become less acute since I entered the household, so also would K be soothed by its atmosphere.

K had more will-power than I. He must have studied twice as much as I did. Moreover, he had greater natural intelligence. I cannot say much concerning his academic standing at the university, since we were in different fields; but at both secondary school and college, where we were in the same class, he was always ahead of me. I had indeed come to regard myself as inferior to K in every way. But when I talked K into moving in with me, I believed that I was for once displaying greater common sense than he. It seemed to me that he did not see the difference between stubbornness and patience. I want you to pay attention to what I am now going to say; it is intended for your benefit. The development—or the destruction—of man's body and mind depends upon external stimuli. Unless one is very careful, and unless one sees to it that the intensity of the stimuli is gradually increased, one will find too late that the body, or the mind, has atrophied. According to doctors, there is nothing that requires more attention than the human stomach. Give it nothing but gruel, and you will apparently find one day that it has lost the power to digest anything else. That is why the doctors tell us to accustom our stomachs to all kinds of food. But I do not think that it is simply a matter of habituation. It is, I think, more a question of increasing the efficiency of the stomach through the gradual adding of stimuli. You can imagine what will be the effect if the process were reversed. K was a much abler fellow than I, but he seemed not to see the simple truth of this principle. He seemed to be under the impression that once one had become accustomed to hardship, one would quickly cease to notice it. The mere repetition of the same stimulus was to him a virtue. He believed, I think, that there would come a time when he would become insensitive to hardship. That it might eventually destroy him never entered his head.

I wanted to say all this to K. But I knew that he would violently disagree with me. And no doubt, I thought to myself, he would in the course of his argument refer to those men of the past. Meek as I was in his presence, I would then be obliged to point out the difference between him and them. He would take this as a rebuke, and would advance to a position more extreme than ever before in order to prove his consistency. And having done this, he would later feel compelled to put into practice what he had maintained in his argument with me. In this respect, he was really quite frightening—and very impressive. He would wilfully proceed to his own destruction. But, however one looked at him, he was certainly no ordinary fellow. At any rate I knew his character too well to think that I could tell him what I honestly thought. Moreover, I was afraid that he had become a little neurotic of late; and supposing that I could have worsted him in an argument, he would still have become terriby agitated. I was not afraid of quarreling with him, but remembering what pain my own loneliness had given me, I did not have the heart to place K, who was my friend, in a state of lonely isolation such as mine had been—or, worse still, push him into far greater loneliness than I myself had ever experienced. And so I tried not to be openly critical of his ways even after he had moved in with me. I decided to wait quietly and see what the change of surroundings would do for him.

*

Secretly, I went to Okusan and Ojōsan and asked them to talk to K as much as possible. It was my opinion that the silent life K had so far been living had had bad effects on him. I could not help thinking that his heart, like a piece of iron, had gone rusty from disuse.

Okusan laughingly said that K was an unapproachable sort of person. Ojōsan, by way of illustration, told me of an encounter she had had with K. She had apparently gone to K and asked him if there was any fire in his brazier.

"No," he had said.

"Well, would you like a fire?"

"No, thank you."

"Aren't you cold?"

"Yes, I am. But I don't need a fire." And he had refused to discuss the matter any further.

I could hardly laugh such an incident off with some such comment as, "Eccentric, isn't he?" I felt that I owed them some kind of explanation. True, it was spring, and a fire was not absolutely necessary. But I could not blame the two ladies for thinking that K was a difficult man to handle.

I tried very hard, in the role of perpetual go-between, to establish a harmonious relationship between K and the two ladies. If I happened to be conversing with K, I would ask the ladies to join us. If I happened to be with the ladies, then I would try to get K to come out of his room and be with us. Suiting my tactics to the occasion, I did everything I could to bring them together. K did not like this, of course. Sometimes, he would suddenly get up and leave our company, without a word. Sometimes, he would refuse to come out of his room when I called him. "Why is it," he once asked me, "that you take so much pleasure in useless small talk?" I merely laughed—though I knew in my heart that I was being despised.

It is possible that, in a sense, I deserved his contempt. His point of view of everything was much loftier than mine. I do not deny this. But when the loftiness is merely in one's point of view, then one is hopelessly handicapped as a human being. I decided that what he needed, above all else, was humanizing. No matter how full one's head might be with the image of greatness, one was useless, I found out, unless one was a worthy man first. In an attempt to make him more human, then, I tried to encourage him to spend as much time as possible with the two ladies. And, I thought, when he had once become accustomed to that atmosphere which the presence of women seems to bring about, he would become less of a recluse and more lively.

My experiment seemed gradually to succeed. What had at first seemed difficult of accomplishment became more and more easy. K, I thought, was learning to acknowledge the existence of a world other than his own. He said to me one day that women were, after all, not as contemptible as one might think. K had always expected the same kind of knowledge and education from women as he did from men. And in his disappointment, he had come to regard them with contempt. He had not known that there was a way to judge women and a way to judge men. "If you and I," I said to him, "were to spend the rest of our lives as bachelors, forever talking to each other, we would advance merely in straight parallel lines." "Of course," he said.

My mind was full of Ojōsan at the time, and my opinions were naturally influenced by this fact. But I said not a word to K about the underlying cause of my remark.

It was very pleasing to me to see him gradually emerge from his fortress of books, and to see his heart beginning to thaw. Such had been my hope when I first brought him to the house, and it was natural that I should be happy to see my plan succeeding so well. I told Okusan and Ojōsan—though not K himself—how happy I was to see the change in him. They seemed pleased too.

*

Although K and I were students in the same faculty, we studied different subjects. We would therefore leave the house and return to it at different times. If I was the first to get back, I would simply walk through his room to get to my own; but if I happened to return after him, then I would say a word or two to him in passing. K would look up from whatever he was reading when he heard me opening the door, and say, in answer to my greeting: "Did you just get back?" I would nod silently, or say "Yes," as I walked past his desk.

One day, it so happened that I had to go to Kanda on my way home, and I returned much later than usual. With hurried steps I walked up to the front door and slid it open, not without some noise. Just as I did so, I heard Ojōsan's voice. I was certain that it came from K's room. Facing the front hall was the morning room, and behind it, Ojōsan's room. To the left of the front hall was K's room, and then mine. I had lived in the house too long not to be able to tell where the voice was coming from. Quickly, I closed the door behind me. Then Ojōsan stopped talking. While I was taking off my boots—I had just begun wearing those cumbersome lace-up boots

which were then fashionable—there was not a sound in
K's room. I thought this strange. I began to think that
perhaps I had been mistaken. But when I opened the door
to K's room as usual, I found the two of them seated
comfortably, facing each other. "Did you just get back?"
said K. Ojōsan remained seated, and said: "Welcome
home." It may have been my imagination, but I thought I
detected a little stiffness in her simple greeting. Her tone
struck me as being somehow unnatural. I said to Ojōsan,
"Where's Okusan?" My question contained no subtle
meaning. I asked it simply because the house seemed
unusually quiet.

Okusan, it turned out, was not at home. She had gone
out with the maid. K and Ojōsan, then, were alone in the
house. I could not but wonder at this. Okusan had never
left *me* alone in the house with Ojōsan; and I had lived
with them considerably longer than K. I asked Ojōsan if
Okusan had left on some urgent business. She merely
laughed. I disliked women who laughed at such times. I
suppose one can dismiss this weakness as something that
is common to all young women. At any rate, Ojōsan was
wont to find cause for laughter in the most trivial things.
When Ojōsan saw the expression on my face, however,
she became serious again. No, it was nothing urgent, she
said. As a boarder, I had no right to question her further.
I said no more.

I had hardly changed my clothes and settled down in
my room when Okusan and the maid returned. Shortly
thereafter, we sat down to dinner. Before I came to know
the family well, it used to be the custom for the maid to
bring all my meals to my room on a tray. But they soon
ceased to treat me like a boarder, and I began to eat
regularly with them. When K moved in, therefore, I asked
them to invite him to join us at mealtimes. And to show

my appreciation for doing as I asked, I bought them a light dining table made of thin wood, with folding legs. It would seem that such tables are to be found in all houses now, but in those days, there were very few families that owned them. I took the trouble of having one specially made by a furniture maker in Ochanomizu.

It was while we were seated around this table, then, that Okusan told me the fish vendor had failed to come that day at the usual hour, and that she had consequently gone out to buy some fish for us. Why, of course, I said to myself, one had to do such things when one had boarders. Ojōsan looked at me, and began to laugh. She stopped quickly enough when her mother scolded her.

*

Again, about a week later, I returned home to find K and Ojōsan talking to each other in his room. On that occasion, Ojōsan began to laugh as soon as she saw me. I suppose I should have asked her then what it was that she found so amusing. Instead, I went straight to my room without saying a word. I gave K no time to greet me with his usual "Did you just get back?" Very soon afterwards, I thought I heard Ojōsan going back to the morning room.

At dinner, Ojōsan said that I was a strange person. I did not ask her why she thought so. I did notice, however, that Okusan was glaring at her.

After dinner, I persuaded K to go for a walk with me. From the back of Denzūin Temple, we went around the botanical garden and returned to the bottom of the slope at Tomizaka. It was a fairly long walk, but we said very little during it. K was by nature less talkative than I. I was not a very talkative person myself. But on this occasion, I tried to carry on a conversation with him. I wanted mostly to discuss the family with whom we were staying. I wanted to know how K regarded Okusan and Ojōsan. But to my questions he gave replies so vague that one could not tell whether they came from the mountains or the sea. Despite their vagueness, however, they were rather simple answers. The subject of his special study seemed to interest him more than the two ladies. True, our second-year examinations were drawing near, and I suppose that from the point of view of a normal person, K was behaving more like a student than I was. I remember that he amazed me—I was not very scholarly—with references to Swedenborg and so on.

When we had successfully completed our examinations, Okusan was very pleased for our sake, and said: "Well, you now have only one year to go." Ojōsan too, who was Okusan's one real pride, was due to graduate soon. K remarked to me that women seemed to graduate without having learned a thing. He attached no importance whatsoever to those things which Ojōsan was studying outside of school, such as the *koto,* flower arrangement, and sewing. I laughed at his stupidity. Once more, I told him that his was not the proper way to judge the worth of a woman. He did not argue with me. On the other hand, he did not appear to be convinced. This pleased me. His attitude, which seemed to suggest that the subject did not merit serious discussion, I took to be an indication of the contempt with which he still regarded women. I decided that Ojōsan, whom I looked upon as the embodiment of womanly qualities, was of little significance to K. It is obvious to me now that I was already more than a little jealous of him.

I suggested to K that we should go somewhere during the summer holidays. He said that he was not very anxious to leave Tokyo. He was certainly in no position to go anywhere he liked, but there was nothing to prevent him from joining me if I invited him. I asked him why he did not wish to go away. There was no particular reason, he said; he simply wanted to stay and read books. I pointed out that it would be far better for our health if we went to some cool resort and read our books there. Well, he said, if that was why I wanted to go away, then I should go alone. But I did not want to leave him in the house. I had already come to regard his growing familiarity with the two ladies with some discomfort. "But wasn't that what you wanted?" you might ask. "Didn't you force K on them?" Certainly, I was a fool. Okusan, seeing that we would never reach an agreement if left alone, stepped in and helped us make up our minds. At last it was decided that the two of us should go to the coast of Bōshū.

*

K had not traveled very much, and it was my first trip to Bōshū. Knowing nothing about that part of the country, therefore, we got off the boat as soon as we could. We found ourselves—I remember quite clearly—in a place called Hota. It may be quite different now, but in those days it was a very unpleasant fishing village. There was the smell of fish everywhere and, whenever we tried to bathe, we were beaten down by the waves and knocked about among huge pebbles, until we emerged with our hands and feet quite raw.

I soon tired of the place. But K showed neither approval nor disapproval. Despite the fact that he never came out of the sea unwounded, he seemed, at least outwardly, quite indifferent to his surroundings. Finally, I managed to convince him of the unpleasantness of Hota, and we left for Tomiura. From there, we went to Nako. That part of the coast was by then very popular with students, and we found no difficulty in finding suitable places for bathing.

K and I often sat on the rocks near the shore, and watched the sea stretching far beyond towards the horizon, or the sandy bottom visible through the water nearby. The scene below the rocks was especially beautiful. We could see brightly colored fish, some of them red and some of them deep blue, which one would never find in the fish markets, swimming about in the clear water.

Often, I took books with me to the rocks, and read them there. K, on the other hand, usually did nothing, and sat near me in silence. I could not decide whether he was meditating, or drinking in the beauty around him, or simply daydreaming. I would occasionally look up and ask him what he was doing. "Nothing," he would say. Often, I found myself thinking how nice it would be if the person sitting so quietly by my side was not K, but Ojōsan. Unfortunately, this pleasant thought invariably led me further to the point where I would begin to wonder whether K was not sitting there indulging in exactly the same reverie. Then I would become restless and cease to enjoy the book I happened to be reading; and I would begin to shout in a loud voice. I could find no satisfaction in such mild forms of emotional release as reciting a poem or singing a song. Instead, I shouted as an uncontrolled savage might have done. Once, I grabbed K's neck from behind. "What would you do," I said, "if I pushed you into the sea?" K did not move. Without looking back, he said: "That would be pleasant. Please do." Quickly, I withdrew the hand that had been holding his neck.

It would seem that by then, K's nervous condition had improved considerably. My nerves, on the other hand, had become increasingly high-strung. I envied K who was so much calmer than I. I hated him. What annoyed me was that he took no notice of me, no matter what I did. I took this as a sign of K's self-confidence. But that K had grown more confident of late gave me little satisfaction. I wanted to discover the real cause of the change in him. Had he simply become optimistic about his studies and his future career once more? If so, there was no reason why there should be any rivalry between us. Indeed, I would find satisfaction in the fact that my efforts to help him had not been in vain. But if his new serenity had come as a result of his contact with Ojōsan, then I would find it impossible to forgive him. K seemed totally unaware of my love for Ojōsan. Of course, I had been careful not to be too obvious about it. But there is no denying that, in such matters, K was quite insensitive. And I must confess that it was because I was aware of this insensitivity in him that I was less reluctant than I might have been to invite him to live with us.

I decided to confide my secret to K. Actually, I had been wanting to do so for some time. But I had found myself incapable, when talking to K, of seizing, or creating, the right moment to introduce the subject casually. When I think about it, my acquaintances in those days were all rather odd. There was not one among them that showed any inclination to discuss his own romantic problems without restraint. I suppose many of them really had nothing to talk about. At any rate, it would seem that it was the custom not to exchange confidences concerning women. You, who are used to a more liberal atmosphere, must think this strange. Whether we were still under the influence of Confucian teachings, or whether we were only being shy, I shall leave you to decide for yourself.

K and I were close friends, and there was little that we did not feel free to discuss with each other. On rare occasions, we would talk about love, but never was the subject allowed to go beyond abstract theorizing. And as I said, it was very seldom discussed. We hardly ever talked of matters other than our future careers, our ambitions, means of disciplining our minds, our scholarly interests, books, and so on. Though we were good friends, there was a stiff formality about our friendship, and it was difficult for me to break through this wall of formality. The character of our friendship had already been formed, and we could come closer only in a very limited way. Many times, I was on the verge of telling him about Ojōsan, but always I was checked by the insurmountable wall that stood between us. Often, in exasperation, I would feel like hammering a hole somewhere in his head, so that a gentle, warm breeze might blow into it.

All this must seem quite absurd to you. I was nevertheless in great torment at the time. I was no less timid than I had been in Tokyo. I watched K closely, hoping that he would give me a chance to confide in him. But not once did he emerge from his forbidding aloofness. It was as though his heart was encrusted with a layer of black lacquer, so thick that no warm blood could ever penetrate through it.

There were times, however, when I found some consolation in his apparent high-mindedness. And I would regret having suspected such a person, and inwardly apologize to him. I would then begin to hate myself for my baseness. I was never contrite for long, however. For very soon I would be assailed by the same old doubts. At such times, I would compare myself with K—always unfavorably, of course, since the desire to compare originated in doubt. Surely, I would tell myself, he is better-looking than I; and his nature too, which seemed so much less fussy than my own, must be more appealing to the opposite sex. As for his absent-minded air, would not women say that that was a sign of manly strength? True, we were studying different subjects, but I knew only too well that, in intellectual ability, I was not his equal either. All in all, I would decide, I was a rather unappealing fellow in comparison. And so my momentary relief would soon be replaced by my old fears.

K noticed my unsettled state, and said that it would be all right with him if we went back to Tokyo. When he said this, the idea of returning to Tokyo suddenly became distasteful to me. It is possible that I did not want to let him go back. At any rate, we decided to continue our trip. We went around the headland of Bōshū. Groaning in the heat of the midsummer sun, we walked on. The walk began to seem quite senseless to me, and I said so, in a half-joking manner, to K. "We are walking because we have legs," he answered. When it got too hot for us, we would take our clothes off, and jump into the sea. What with the swimming and the broiling heat, we were completely exhausted by the end of the day.

Such strenuous walking in the heat cannot but affect one's body. It is not like being ill. Rather, one feels as though one's soul has found for itself a strange home. I talked to K as usual, but my feelings had somehow changed. My affection and my hatred for K acquired a character peculiar to that journey on foot. What I mean is that perhaps because of the heat, the swimming, and the walking, our relationship shifted temporarily to a different plane. We were like two far-traveling peddlers who had met by chance on the road. We talked to each other, but we said nothing that was of serious concern to us.

In this way, we finally reached Chōshi. There was, however, one exceptional incident which I still remember.

Before leaving Bōshū, we stopped at a place called Kominato, and went to see the Bay of *Tai*[12]. Many years have passed since then, and I have never been interested in such things, so I cannot remember very clearly; but it seems that it was at Kominato that Nichiren[13] was born. According to the local legend, two *tai* were thrown up on the beach at the time of his birth. In deference to this legend, the men of the village have always abstained from fishing in the bay. Hearing that the bay was full of *tai* for this reason, we hired a small boat and went out to look at them. I was enthralled by the scene under the water, and I felt that I would never tire of watching the violet-tinged fish twisting and turning beneath the waves. K, however, seemed not as interested as I was in the fish. He seemed rather to be thinking about Nichiren. We had found a temple in the village by the name of Tanjō-ji[14]. I presume it was called this because Nichiren had been born there, in Kominato. It was certainly an impressive temple. K said that he wanted to meet the chief priest. To tell the truth, we were at the time a shabby-looking pair. K looked especially disreputable. His cap had been blown away during the hike along the coast, and he was now wearing a sedge hat. Our clothes were soiled, and smelled of sweat. I did not think that the priests would welcome our company, and I said so to K. But he was stubborn, and would not listen to me. "If you don't want to come in, you can wait out here," he said, when we had reached the gate of the temple. I was obliged to accompany him into the front hall. I was quite certain that we would be refused admit-

12. *Tai* is a red fish, a kind of bream, and is in Japan a symbol of good fortune.
13. Nichiren (1222–1282) is one of the greatest figures in the history of Japanese Buddhism.
14. It means "Temple of the Birth."

tance. But I was mistaken. Priests, I discovered, are on the whole more gracious than one might expect. We were shown into a large and fine room, and there received by the chief priest. In those days, my interests were very different from K's, and so I did not listen very carefully to what K and the priest were saying; but I do remember that K asked him many questions about Nichiren. When the priest remarked that Nichiren was such a master of the grass script that he was called "Grass" Nichiren, I remember that K, who was a poor calligrapher himself, looked impatient. I suppose he regarded such facts as irrelevant and trivial. Obviously, he wanted the priest to say something more profound about the great man. I do not know whether K was satisfied with the conversation or not: at any rate, when we came out of the temple, he began to give me a lecture on Nichiren. I was too tired and hot to be much interested, and my comments were half-hearted and bored. Eventually, I stopped saying anything at all.

It was, I think, the following evening that we had an argument. We had had our dinner at the inn, and were preparing to go to bed. I discovered that he had resented my lack of interest in his comments on Nichiren the day before. Saying that anyone who had no spiritual aspirations was an idiot, he began to attack me for my frivolity. My apprehensions concerning Ojōsan had made me more sensitive than I might have been to K's almost insulting remarks. I began to defend myself.

*

I remember that I used constantly the word "human" in defending my position and in attacking his. K insisted that I was trying to hide all my weaknesses behind this word. Now, I see that he was right. But in trying to point out his limitations I had become aggressive, and I was in no mood to be objective about myself. I became more dogmatic than ever. Finally, he asked me why it was that I considered him unhuman. I told him that he was indeed human—perhaps too much so; but that one would never guess this from his words. Moreover, I said, he was trying too hard to live and act in a way that was not natural to human beings.

When I said this, he did not argue with me. He merely said that it was his own lack of training that was responsible for the low opinion I seemed to have of what he was trying to accomplish. Not only did his remark take the wind out of my sails, but I began to be sorry for what I had said. I stopped arguing then. K's tone also became more quiet. "If you only knew those men of the past as I know them," he said sadly, "you would not be so critical of me." The men of the past that he was referring to were not, of course, heroic figures in the conventional sense, but ascetics who had tyrannized over their flesh for the freedom of their souls, who had lashed their bodies so that they might find the way. "How I wish," he said, "that you could understand my suffering."

K and I went to bed. The next day, we resumed our sweaty and tortuous walk. Once more, our relationship became like that of two peddlers on the road. During the walk, however, I thought now and then of the argument of the night before, and cursed myself for having missed such a good opportunity to confide in him. I should have been more honest, I said to myself, and instead of criticizing him for not being human and so on, I should have admitted to him openly the true cause of my grievance. After all, it was Ojōsan that was at the bottom of my troubles, and, for my own good, I should not have tried to hide this fact under half-true generalities. But, I must confess, the tone of our friendship had become intellectualized, and I did not have the courage to rebel openly against the established pattern of our relationship. You may attribute this weakness on my part to affectation or vanity. So long as you try to understand that it was not the ordinary kind of affectation or vanity, I shall not mind.

Burnt almost black by the sun, we returned to Tokyo. My state of mind had changed greatly by then, and such petty considerations as K's human qualities or his lack of them had ceased to worry me very much. K, too, had lost most of his piousness. I doubt that the problem of body and soul was worrying him at all then. Like two barbarians, we stared at the busy scene around us. We stopped at Ryōgoku and, despite the heat, treated ourselves to a meal of game hen. This seemed to fortify K, and he suggested that we walk all the way to Koishikawa. I had a more robust constitution than K, and I assented readily enough.

Okusan, when she saw us, was shocked by our appearance. Not only were we black, but the walking had made us terribly thin. She soon recovered from her shock, however, and was good enough to say that we looked very healthy. "But you are so inconsistent," said Ojōsan, and laughed at her mother. I felt cheerful, forgetting that I had left Tokyo not without resentful feelings towards her. After all, I had not seen her for some time, and the occasion was, I suppose, a happy one.

*

Moreover, I soon noticed that Ojōsan's manner towards me had changed. After such a long absence, there was much that had to be done before we could settle down once more to our normal routine. The two ladies came to our aid. Okusan, of course, was very helpful. But what pleased me particularly was that Ojōsan seemed to pay greater attention to my needs than she did to K's. Now, if she had done so at all crudely, I should have been embarrassed. Indeed, I might even have been annoyed. But she showed great sense here, and there was only a delicate suggestion of favoritism, which made me very happy. She was kind to us both, but she simply gave me the greater share of her natural kindness, in such a way that only I noticed it. K had no reason to be annoyed therefore, and as far as he was concerned, nothing out of the ordinary had happened. I had scored a victory over K, and my heart was filled with a sense of triumph.

Summer finally came to an end. About the middle of September, we began once more to attend lectures at the university. Our schedules were again different, and we came and went at different times during the day. Approximately three days a week, I remember, K got home before me, but not once during the first few weeks of term did I find Ojōsan in his room when I returned. K would greet me with his customary "Did you just get back?" My reply too would be mechanical, simple, and almost meaningless.

It so happened that one morning—it was about the middle of October, I think—I overslept, and having no time to put on my uniform I rushed off in Japanese dress. And instead of the usual lace-up boots, I wore my sandals. Normally, on that day of the week, my lectures ended earlier than K's, and so I went home assuming that K would not yet be back. When I opened the front door, however, I heard K's voice. And then the sound of Ojōsan's laughter reached my ears. Since I was wearing sandals that day, and not those boots which took so long to unlace, I was very soon in K's room. I found K sitting at his desk as usual. But Ojōsan was no longer there. I had opened the door just in time to catch a glimpse of her fleeing figure. I asked K why he was back so early. He had not been feeling very well, he said, and so had decided to stay at home. I went to my room and sat down. A few minutes later, Ojōsan came in with a cup of tea. "Welcome home," she said. I was too awkward a fellow to smile at her and make some such comment as, "Well, why did you run away from me just now?" And of course I was not the sort to make light of such an incident. She stayed with me for only a moment or two. She then got up and left my room by the verandah. She stopped outside K's room and exchanged a few words with him. They were, I gathered, continuing the conversation that my return had interrupted. Not having heard the earlier part of it, I could not guess what it was all about.

As time passed, Ojōsan's manner became more nonchalant, and I noted that she was becoming more openly friendly with K. Even when I was at home, she would call K's name from the verandah, and then go into his room for a long chat. But, you would say, how else could two people living under the same roof behave? And I will admit that she could hardly avoid going into his room; there were, after all, such things as his letters and his laundry that she had to take to him. But to me, who was so intent on monopolizing her company, it seemed that she was seeing him far more than was necessary. Sometimes, indeed, I could not help the impression that she was purposely avoiding my company in order to be with K. You may ask, "Why then did you not ask him to leave the house?" But it was I that had forced K to come and live with me for his own good. To ask him to leave would have been an unprincipled thing to do, and humiliating.

*

On a cold, rainy day in November, I walked home as usual through the grounds of the temple of Konnyaku-Emma and up the narrow lane that led to the house. My

overcoat was wet, and I was chilled. K was not in his
room, but there was a good fire going in his brazier.
Looking forward to seeing as good a fire in my own
brazier, I hurried to my room. But there were only cold,
white ashes where I had expected to find red-hot charcoal.
I was overcome with annoyance.

I then heard footsteps approaching my door. It was
Okusan. She saw me standing silently in the middle of the
room. She must have felt sorry for me, for she came in
and helped me change into my Japanese dress. When I
complained of the cold, she went into the next room and
returned with K's brazier. I asked Okusan if K had already
been back. Yes, he had, she replied, but had gone out
again. K's lectures were held later than mine that day, and
so I wondered why it was that he had come back before
me. Okusan said that he probably had some business to
attend to.

I sat down and tried to read. There was not a sound to
be heard in the house. The cold of early winter and my
own loneliness seemed to grip my whole body. I soon put
my book down and stood up. You see, I had the sudden
desire to go somewhere that was gay. It seemed to have
stopped raining, but the sky still looked cold and heavy,
like a sheet of lead. I decided to take my umbrella out with
me. I went down the hill towards the east, alongside the
back wall of the Arsenal. The city authorities had not yet
undertaken the improvement of roads in that area, and so
the slope was then very much steeper than it is now. The
road was also narrower, and not as straight as it is today.
What with bad drainage and big buildings on the south
side which blocked the sun, the road became terribly
muddy when you reached the valley. It was particularly
bad between the narrow stone bridge and Yanagichō. You
had to watch your step even if you were wearing high rain

clogs or Wellingtons. There was a narrow strip of well-trodden ground in the middle of the road which was comparatively dry, and you had to walk carefully so as not to step beyond it. It was not more than a foot or two wide, so it was like walking on a woman's sash which had been stretched along the road. Slowly and in single file, the pedestrians made their way through the mud. It was on this narrow sash that I met K. I had not noticed him walking towards me, since keeping to the path had required all my attention. Seeing that someone was in front of me, I looked up and found myself standing face to face with K. "Where have you been?" I asked. "Just down the road," he answered, in his usual curt tone. We squeezed past each other. And then I discovered that a young woman had been standing a pace or two behind K. Being shortsighted, I had to peer at her before I realized, to my amazement, that I was looking at Ojōsan. She blushed slightly, and greeted me. Women in those days did not wear their hair over their foreheads, but twisted it in snake-like coils on top of their heads. I stood still and stared vacantly at her head. Then I remembered that one of us had to step aside to let the other pass. I moved quickly and stepped into the mud, thus allowing Ojōsan to get by.

I finally reached the main street of Yanagichō but, once there, I could not decide where to go. It did not seem to matter where I went. I walked about angrily and aimlessly in the mud, not caring whether I got splashed or not. I then went home.

*

I asked K if he had gone out with Ojōsan. No, he said. He went on to explain that he had met her by chance in Masagochō, and so had walked home with her. I had to restrain myself from asking him more questions. At dinner, however, I could not resist asking Ojōsan where she had been that afternoon. She answered with a laugh—that laugh of hers which I hated so much. Then she said, "I'll let you guess." I was a touchy fellow in those days, and I was considerably irritated at being treated in such an offhand manner by a young woman. The only person around the table who seemed to notice this was Okusan. K appeared as usual indifferent to his surroundings. As for Ojōsan, I could not be sure whether she was annoying me on purpose or whether she was being innocently playful. For a young woman, she was on the whole a considerate sort of person, but there is no denying that she had some traits which were common to all young women and which I disliked. Moreover, I began to notice these traits only after K had moved into the house. Perhaps, I told myself, they were no more than figments of my imagination, caused by my jealousy of K; or perhaps they were quite real, and sprang from the coquetry of a young woman in the presence of two men. Mind you, I have no intention of denying that I *was* jealous. And as I have often said to you, I was quite aware then of the presence of great jealousy in my love for Ojōsan. Moreover, I became jealous for reasons which must have seemed quite trivial to others. I am digressing here, but don't you think that this kind of jealousy is a necessary concomitant of love? I have noticed that since my marriage, I have become less and less subject to fits of jealousy. I have noticed also that my love is by no means as passionate as it once was.

Once more, I was tempted to tear the secret out of my heart and hurl it at her breast. By "her," I do not mean Ojōsan, but Okusan. I began again to think of asking Okusan for her daughter's hand. But I could not bring myself to speak to her about marriage. You must think me a very irresolute person. That you may do so does not worry me very much. All I want to point out here is that my irresolution was not due to lack of will-power on my part. Before K moved in with us, it was my fear of being duped that had stopped me from approaching Okusan about her daughter. After K's entrance on the scene, however, it was the suspicion that Ojōsan might prefer him to me that was responsible for my inaction. I decided, you understand, that if K did indeed mean more to her than I did, then my love would not be worth declaring.

You must not think that I was frightened of being humiliated. I simply abhorred the idea of living with a woman who had secretly preferred someone else to me. There are many men, I grant, who seem happy enough to marry women who strike their fancy, not caring whether or not they themselves are found satisfactory by the other party. I was firmly convinced that such men were either far more worldly and cynical than I, or were contemptible dullards who had no understanding of the true nature of love. Also, I was too ardently in love to tell myself, for instance, that once we were married, all problems would somehow disappear. In other words, I was far from lacking high-minded convictions about love; but when I discovered that it necessarily involved some decisive action on my part, I became hesitant, timid, and rather devious.

During the long period of time that we lived in the same house, there were of course many opportunities for me to tell Ojōsan directly how I felt towards her, but I purposely ignored them. I was then very conscious of the fact— perhaps too much so—that to speak to Ojōsan about marriage before I had spoken to Okusan would be a flagrant breach of Japanese custom. On the other hand, it was not this alone that prevented me from confessing my love to Ojōsan. I was also afraid that if she did not by any chance want me for a husband, she would not say so outright. I thought that Japanese people, especially Japanese women, lacked the courage to be bluntly truthful on such occasions.

✳

And so I stood still, not daring to take a step in any direction. I was like a sick person in bed, who falls into an uneasy sleep during the day. He opens his eyes as he comes out of his sleep, and sees clearly what is going on around him. Then for a moment or two he is overcome by the feeling that, in the midst of a world that moves, he alone is still. I was beset by the same kind of fear, though the others did not know it.

The old year came to an end. One day, during the New Year season, Okusan said that we all ought to play a game of cards, and asked K if he would like to invite a friend to join us. "But I have no friends," he answered. Okusan was shocked. K indeed had no friends. There were, of course, a few students with whom he had a nodding acquaintance, but he knew none of them well enough to ask them to join him and the family in a game of cards. Okusan then turned to me and said, "Well, in that case, why don't *you* bring someone along?" I gave a noncommittal reply, since I was in no mood for merry games. That evening, however, Ojōsan dragged K and me out of our rooms and forced us to play cards with them. Since there were no guests, the gathering was small, and we had a very quiet game.[15] K, who was unused to such lighthearted pastimes, sat like a block of wood. I said to him, "Don't you know the

15. In this game, which is played in the New Year, picture cards are laid out on the floor. Each of them corresponds to a poem belonging to a collection called *Hyakunin Isshu*. As a poem is read out, one tries to be the first to pick up the appropriate card. It is an innocent game involving little skill, and is meant to be played with much gaiety.

Hyakunin Isshu poems?" "Not very well," he answered. Ojōsan must have thought that I was being unkind to K. She began conspicuously to help him whenever she could, and very soon the game developed into a contest between me and these two. I might have picked a quarrel with them but for K's manner, which showed no elation when Ojōsan started taking his side. We were able to finish the game peacefully.

It was, I think, two or three days later that Okusan and Ojōsan left the house early in the morning, saying that they were going to visit a relative of theirs in Ichigaya. K and I remained in the house, since we were still on holiday. I had no inclination to go outside. I sat down by the brazier, and resting my elbows on it, began to think in a vague and disconnected way. K, who was in his room, was also very quiet. Neither of us gave the other any indication that he was still in the house. The silence did not worry me, however: both K and I were accustomed to it.

At about ten o'clock, the door between our rooms was suddenly opened, and I saw K looking at me from the doorway. "What are you thinking about?" he said. I could not in all honesty say that I was *thinking* about anything at all. If the confusion in my mind then could have been called "thought," then I suppose I might have answered: "Ojōsan." And I might have added: "I have been thinking about Okusan too; and, as a matter of fact, about *you,* who seem recently to have made matters far more complicated than ever for me. Yes, you are a haunting, albeit vague, figure that refuses to leave me alone. I have been thinking of you as a confounded nuisance." But I could hardly say all this to his face. I continued to look at him in silence. K then strode into the room and sat down opposite

192

me. I moved my elbows away from the edge of the brazier, and pushed it just a little nearer to him.

K began to talk to me about Okusan and Ojōsan. I was surprised, since he had never shown any inclination before to talk about them. "Whom are they visiting in Ichigaya?" I said that in all likelihood they had gone to see Ojōsan's aunt. "What does this aunt do?" he asked. I explained that she also was a soldier's wife. "But is it not the custom," he said, "for women to pay New Year visits after the middle of January? I wonder why they went so early?" "I have no idea," I was forced to reply.

*

K continued to question me about Okusan and Ojōsan. Eventually, I found myself unable to answer his questions, which became increasingly complicated and personal. I thought his behavior not so much irritating as odd. Previously, it had always been I that had tried to introduce the subject of the two ladies into our conversation. I could not but take notice, therefore, of the sudden interest that K was showing in them. I asked him finally, "Why is it that today, in particular, you are asking me all these questions?" He became suddenly very quiet. I saw that his mouth was trembling. K was normally a man of few words. He also had the habit of opening and shutting his lips like a stutterer before he said anything, as though they were not altogether under the control of his will. Perhaps this difficulty was partly responsible for the impression of weightiness that his words conveyed to the listener. His voice, when it broke through the barrier, was twice as strong as that of the average man.

Seeing the trembling of his lips, I knew that he was about to say something. But, of course, I had no inkling of what he was going to say. And so I was shocked.

Imagine my reaction when K, in his heavy way, confessed to me his agonized love for Ojōsan. I felt as if I had been turned into stone by a magician's wand. I could not even move my lips as K had done.

Exactly what the emotion was that I felt then, I am not sure. Perhaps it was fear; or perhaps it was terrible pain. Whatever it was, its physical effect was to make me feel rigid from head to toe, as though I were a piece of stone or iron. I do not think that I even breathed then. Fortunately, this condition did not last long. A moment or two later, I began to feel alive again. And my first thought was: "He's beaten me to it!" Beyond this, however, I could not think of anything to do or say. I suppose I was not yet composed enough to think coherently.

I sat still, feeling the cold sweat seeping through my clothes. In his usual ponderous manner, K continued with his confession. The pain within me was almost unbearable. I thought, "Surely, it must show on my face?" Indeed, the way I felt then could not have been any less obvious than a large advertisement stuck on my head, and I am sure that even K, had the conditions been normal, would have observed it. But I suppose he was so busy talking about his own troubles that he had no time to watch my reaction to his words. His confession was uttered in the same monotonous tone from beginning to end, and its very ponderousness imparted to the speaker an air of immovable strength. I did not listen too closely to what he was saying. For my heart seemed all the while to be crying out, "What shall I do? What shall I do?" I was nevertheless fully aware of the tone of his voice, which seemed to drone on and on interminably and to beat against my consciousness like the waves of the sea. That is why I felt then not only torment but a kind of fear. It was the fear of a man who sees before him an opponent stronger than himself.

When finally K stopped talking, I found myself unable to say anything. I want you to understand that I was not silent because I was debating with myself whether I should make a similar confession to K or whether it would be wiser policy to say nothing about my love for Ojōsan. I was simply unable to speak. Besides, I had no desire to break the silence.

At lunch we faced each other across the table. The maid waited on us. It seemed to me that the food was unusually tasteless. K and I hardly spoke to each other all through the meal. We had no idea when Okusan and Ojōsan would return.

*

We went back to our rooms. K was as quiet as he had been that morning. I also sat still, deep in thought.

I told myself that I should be honest with K, and tell him that I too had fallen in love with Ojōsan. I could not help feeling, however, that it was now too late to do so. I began to curse myself for not having interrupted K's confession with one of my own. If I had done that, I thought, I might have outmaneuvered him. The fact that I had not even tried to tell him the truth about myself after he had stopped talking now seemed a terrible mistake. Moreover, I felt that to begin confiding in him at this late stage would somehow be inappropriate: it would seem unnatural, perhaps contrived. I saw no way out of the dilemma. My head seemed to throb with despair and regret.

I wished that K would once more open the door and stride into my room. That morning, K had taken me by surprise, and I had been totally unprepared. I wanted the same scene repeated, so that this time, I might receive K with the initiative on my side. Time and again I glanced at

195

the door, but it did not open. The silence in K's room seemed eternal.

Eventually, I was driven almost to distraction by the quiet. I could not prevent myself from wondering nervously what K was thinking in the next room. Before that day, we had spent many hours not making a sound, and I had found that the longer the silence lasted the easier it became to forget K's existence. That it should have had the opposite effect on me that afternoon shows how frayed my nerves were. I might have stood up and opened the door to K's room myself, it is true; but this I could not do. Having lost the opportunity that morning to unburden myself to K, I was forced to wait passively for another opportunity to present itself.

I began to feel that if I stayed in the room any longer, I might suddenly lose control and rush into K's room. And so I got up and went out to the verandah. From there I went into the morning room, where, for lack of anything better to do, I poured some hot water from the kettle on the brazier into a cup, and drank it. Then I went to the front hall. And thus managing to avoid K's room, I made my way into the street. Needless to say, I did not care where I went so long as I was not in my room. Aimlessly, I walked about the streets that were bright with New Year decorations. And no matter how much I walked, K remained the sole object of my thoughts. I want you to understand that I was not walking in order to forget K. Indeed, one might say that I was wandering about the streets in pursuit of K's image.

I must confess that K was a puzzle to me. I asked myself: "Why did K confide in me at all? Why did he allow his love for the girl to become so intense that he could no longer keep it a secret? What has happened to the K that I once knew?" I could not find an easy answer to any of these questions. I knew that he was strong-minded, serious, and sincere. But there was much that I did not know about him; and I realized then that before I could decide what I should do, I had to know much more than I did about K. At the same time, I felt inside me a strange fear—amounting almost to a superstitious dread—of the person that had become my rival. With the image of K sitting still in his room constantly before my mind's eye, I walked about the streets in confusion. And I thought I could hear a voice whispering into my ear: "You'll never get rid of him . . ." Perhaps I was beginning to think of him as a kind of devil. Once, I even had the feeling that he would haunt me for the rest of my life.

When I reached home, exhausted, I noticed that his room was as quiet as ever. One would have thought that there was no one in it.

*

Soon afterwards, I heard the wheels of rickshaws approaching the house. In those days, rickshaw wheels did not have rubber tires as they do now. They were therefore unpleasantly noisy, and one could hear them from quite a distance. A moment or two later, the rickshaws stopped in front of the house.

It was only about half an hour after this that we were called to dinner. As I passed Ojōsan's door on my way to the dining room, I saw the ladies' going-out dresses lying in colorful disarray on the floor. They had apparently hurried home so that they might prepare our dinner. Okusan's kindness, however, was wasted on us. During the meal, I behaved as though words were too precious a commodity to squander, and I was very brusque with the ladies. K was even more taciturn than I was. The ladies on the other hand, having returned from a rare outing, were unusually gay, which made our gloomy behavior all the more noticeable in contrast. Okusan asked me if anything was wrong. I told her that I was not feeling well. And I was being quite truthful, I assure you. Then Ojōsan asked K the same question. K gave a different answer: he was simply not in a talkative mood, he said. "Why not?" she asked. I lifted my eyes, which felt dull and heavy, and looked at K. I was very curious as to what he would say. Once more, his lips were trembling slightly. To innocent eyes, it must have seemed that he was only having his usual difficulty with words. Ojōsan laughed and said that he must have been thinking about something very profound. K blushed slightly.

I went to bed earlier than usual that night. At about ten o'clock, Okusan, remembering that I had said I was not feeling well, kindly brought me some buckwheat gruel. She found my room in darkness when she opened the door. "Well!" she said, looking in. Through the other door, which was closed, a shaft of light from the lamp on K's desk sneaked in. He was apparently still up. Okusan sat down by my bed, and holding out the cup of gruel, said: "Here, drink this. It will warm you up. You have probably caught a cold." I dared not refuse, and drank the thick liquid while she watched.

I lay in the dark thinking until the early hours of the morning. All I could think about, of course, was the problem of K and Ojōsan. Then suddenly I wanted to know what K was doing in his room. Almost involuntarily, I called out, "Hey!" "Yes?" he answered. So K had not yet gone to sleep either, I thought. "Haven't you gone to bed yet?" I said. He answered simply, "I will soon." Then I said, "What are you doing?" This time, there was no reply. Five or six minutes later, I heard him open the closet door, then spread out the bedding on the floor. "What time is it?" I asked. "Twenty past one," replied K. I heard him blow out the lamp. The house was now completely dark. I felt suddenly the silence around me.

But I could not go to sleep. My eyes would not close, and they stared into the darkness. Once more, I heard my own voice cry out, "Hey!" Again, K answered, "Yes?" Not being able to restrain myself any longer, I said: "Look here, I want to have a good talk with you . . . you know, about what you said this morning. How about it?" I had no wish, of course, to carry on a complicated conversation through the closed door: all I wanted was a simple answer from K. But he became noncommittal all of a sudden. "Well, perhaps . . ." he said, quietly and unwillingly. Once more, I was stricken with fear.

∗

K's attitude remained noncommittal all through the following day, and the day after that. He showed absolutely no sign of wanting to talk to me again about Ojōsan. True, we were given no opportunity to have such a talk. So long as Okusan and Ojōsan were in the house, we could not very well have a long conversation of so involved and private a nature without interruption. I was quite aware of this. Nevertheless, I was irritated. Having prepared myself for another talk with K, I was in no mood for protracted silence. I decided finally to bring up the subject myself, rather than wait for him to do so, at the earliest opportunity.

Quietly, I watched the conduct of the two ladies. It showed no change, and I was satisfied that K had confided in me only: I was certain that neither Ojōsan herself nor her strict and observant mother knew K's secret. I was relieved. With the relief came the conviction that it would be better to wait for an opportunity to present itself naturally and be sure not to miss it, than to approach K impatiently and force him to discuss the affair with me.

I may have given you the impression that my reaching the decision to be patient was a simple process. It was nothing of the sort. For a long time, I could not make up my mind: my mental state then could be likened to a tide, which ebbs and flows continually. I was not certain as to how I should interpret K's calm and noncommittal manner. I even wondered if what the two ladies said and did truly expressed their thoughts. I asked myself: "Can one expect the complicated mechanism of the human mind to betray its purposes so obviously, as though it were some kind of clock?" In short, please understand that it was after a great deal of vacillation that I finally decided to wait for the right moment to talk to K. Mind you, my decision by no means eased my troubled mind.

Our holidays were at last over. On days that our lectures coincided, we walked to the university together. We often walked home together too. Outwardly, we were as friendly as ever; but I am sure each of us was very much immersed in his own problems. One day, as we were walking home, I suddenly asked him: "Am I the only one that knows your secret? Or have you told Okusan and Ojōsan too?" What tactics I would adopt in the future depended, I thought, on his answer. He answered that he had told no one but me. So I was right after all, I said to myself, feeling rather pleased. I knew very well that he was more brazen than I. He was also more bold. On the other hand, I did trust him in a strange way. Even the fact of his having deceived his foster parents for three years had by no means impaired my confidence in him. Indeed, I had come to trust him more because of it. Despite my suspicious nature, then, I felt no inclination to doubt his word.

"What do you intend to do?" I asked. "Are you going to keep your love for Ojōsan a secret, or are you going to do something about it?'" This time, he gave no reply. He lowered his eyes and went on walking. "Please don't hide anything from me," I begged him. "Please tell me what you intend to do." He said, "There is no need to hide anything from you." But he refused to tell me what I wanted to know. I could hardly stop him in the middle of the street and force him to be more explicit. We walked on in silence.

*

Not many days later, I paid one of my rare visits to the university library. I had been told by my supervisor to acquaint myself, before the following week, with certain facts concerning my field of specialization. I had to get up from my seat in the reading room and return to the stacks two or three times before I could locate what I wanted. I sat down at the end of the large desk and began to read carefully the article in the newly arrived foreign journal. The sun shone through the window, warming the upper part of my body. Then suddenly, I heard someone whispering my name from the other side of the desk. I looked up and saw K standing there. He leaned over the desk so that he could get closer to me. As you know, we were not permitted to disturb others in the library by talking too loudly. K was therefore doing what any other student would have done in a similar situation. Nevertheless, K's behavior gave me an odd sensation.

"Studying?' he asked, still whispering. "There was something I had to look up," I said. K would not move. His face was only a few inches away from mine. "Come out for a walk," he said. "I will," I said, "but you will have to wait." "All right," he said, and sat down in the

201

empty chair opposite me. I found that I could not concentrate on the article any more. I was disturbed by the idea that K had come to discuss something serious with me. I gave up trying to read, and closing the magazine, I made as if to get up. Calmly, K asked, "Finished?" "No," I answered, "but it doesn't matter." I returned the magazine and left the library with K.

We had no particular destination in mind. We walked through Tatsuokachō towards Ikenohata, and then went into Ueno Park. He suddenly began to talk about the affair. Judging by the way he introduced the subject, it would seem that he had asked me out specifically for the purpose of talking to me about it. I learned that the situation had remained unchanged for all practical purposes since the time of his confession to me. "What do you think?" he asked vaguely. What he wished to know was how I regarded him, who had fallen so deeply in love. He wanted my opinion of him as he was then. I felt that this desire of his to find out what I thought of him was a sure indication that he was not altogether his usual self. I want to emphasize here—though you may think me rather repetitious—that K was normally an independent-minded fellow, and what others thought of him worried him very little. He had the courage and strength to do anything if he thought he was right. I saw this trait in him only too clearly in his dealings with his foster parents. No wonder, then, that I thought his question in the park rather out of character.

I asked him why he thought it necessary to seek my opinion. In an unusually dejected tone, he said, "I have found I am a weak man, and I am ashamed." Then he added, "You see, I am lost. I have become a puzzle even to myself. What else can I do, but ask you for your honest opinion?" "What do you mean," I asked quickly, "by 'lost'?" He said, "I mean that I can't decide whether to take a step forward or to turn back." Once more, I prodded him: "Tell me, can you really turn back if you want to?" Suddenly, he seemed lost for an answer. All he said was: "I cannot bear this pain." His expression, as he said this, was indeed tormented. If Ojōsan had not been involved, I would surely have spoken to him kindly and have tried to ease his suffering. He needed kind words, as dry land needs rain. I believe I was born with a compassionate heart. But I was not my usual self then.

I watched him carefully, as though he were my fencing opponent. There was not one part of me that was not on guard. I did not relax for one single moment my eyes, or my heart, or my body. To say that K did not guard himself well would be an understatement. In his innocence, he put himself completely at my mercy. I was allowed to observe him at leisure, and to note carefully his most vulnerable points.

I could think of only one thing, and that was K's defenselessness. He was hovering uncertainly between the world of reality and the world of his ideals. Now is the time, I thought, to destroy my opponent. I waited no longer to make my thrust. I turned to him with a solemn air. True, the solemnity was a part of my tactics, but it was certainly in keeping with the way I felt. And I was too tense to see anything comical or shameful in what I was doing. I said cruelly, "Anyone who has no spiritual aspirations is an idiot." This was what K had said to me when we were traveling in Bōshū. I threw back at him the very words that he had once used to humiliate me. Even my tone of voice was the same as his had been when he made the remark. But I insist that I was not being vindictive. I confess to you that what I was trying to do was far more cruel than mere revenge. I wanted to destroy whatever hope there might have been in his love for Ojōsan.

K was born in a Shinshū temple. But I remember that at secondary school, he was already showing signs of moving away from the doctrines of his family's sect. I am quite aware of my ignorance concerning the various Buddhist doctrines. But it was clear to me that at least in the matter of men's relationship with women, K was in disagreement with Shinshū teachings.[16] K had always been fond of the phrase, "concentration of mind." When I first heard K mention it, I thought it likely that "concentration of mind" implied, among other things, "control of passions." When I learned later that much more than this was implied, I was surprised. It was K's belief that everything had to be sacrificed for the sake of "'the true way.'" Even love without bodily desire was to be avoided. Pursuit of "the true way" necessitated not merely restraint of appetite, but total abstinence. K made all this clear to me when he was living alone and trying to support himself. I was already in love with Ojōsan by that time, and I used to argue with him whenever he brought up the subject of "the true way." K would listen to me with a look of pity on his face. Always, it was contempt that lay behind his pity: I found hardly any trace of friendly tolerance in it. In view of all that we had said to each other in the past, I knew that K would be much hurt by my remark. I had no intention of destroying his old beliefs. I said what I did say in order to make him even more righteous than he had been before. Of course, it mattered little to me whether he really followed "the true way" or not; or whether he would ever reach heaven. What I feared was the harm he

16. Shinshū, a protestant sect, discourages celibacy.

might cause me if he decided to change his ways. It was simply self-interest that prompted my remark.

I said again: "Anyone who has no spiritual aspirations is an idiot." I watched K closely. I wanted to see how my words were affecting him.

"An idiot . . ." he said at last. "Yes, I'm an idiot."

He stood still as he spoke, and stared at his feet. I was suddenly frightened that, in desperation, K had decided to accept the fact that he was an idiot. I was as demoralized as a man who finds that his opponent, whom he has just knocked down, is about to spring up with a new weapon in his hand. A moment later, however, I realized that K had indeed spoken in a hopeless tone of voice. I wanted to see his eyes, but he would not look my way. Slowly, we began to walk again.

∗

I walked by K's side, waiting for him to speak again. I was waiting for another chance to hurt him. I lurked in the shadows, so that I might take him by surprise. I was not an ignorant man, and I was not without conscience. Had a voice whispered into my ear, "You are a coward," I might at that moment have returned to my normal self. And had the voice been that of K, I would surely have blushed with shame. But K was not the one to admonish me. He was too honest, too simple, and altogether too righteous to see through me. I was in no mood to admire his virtues, however. Instead, I saw them only as weaknesses.

After a while, K turned towards me, and addressed me. This time, it was I that stopped walking. Then K also stopped. At last, I was able to look into his eyes. He was taller than I, and so I had to look up at him. I was like a wolf crouching before a lamb.

"Let us not talk about it any more," he said. I was strangely affected by the pain in his eyes and in his words. For a moment, I did not know what to say. Then, in a more pleading tone, he said again: "Please, don't talk about it." My answer was cruel. The wolf jumped at the lamb's throat.

"Well, so you don't want me to talk about it! Tell me, who brought up the subject anyway? If I remember rightly, it was you. Of course, if you really want me to stop, I will. But not talking about it isn't going to solve the problem, is it? Can you will yourself to stop thinking about it? Are you prepared to do that? What's become of all those principles of yours that you were always talking about?"

K seemed to shrivel before my eyes. He seemed not half as tall as he once was. As I have said before, he was a very stubborn fellow; but he was also too honest to ignore his own inconsistency when it was bluntly pointed out to him by another. I saw the effect my words had had on him, and I was satisfied. Then he said suddenly: "Am I prepared . . .?" Before I could say anything, he added: "Why not? I can will myself . . ." He seemed to be talking to himself. And the words sounded as though they were spoken in a dream.

In silence, we started to walk towards the house in Koishikawa. It was not very cold that day, for there was little wind. It was winter nevertheless, and the park looked bleak. I turned my head once and looked back at the row of cedars. They were brown, and looked as if the frost had eaten all the greenness out of them. Over them stretched the grey sky. The coldness of the scene seemed to bite into my spine. Hurriedly, in the twilight, we walked over Hongō Hill. It was only after we had reached the bottom of the valley and started walking up the hill in Koishikawa that I began to feel warm under my overcoat.

We hardly spoke to each other on our way home. Perhaps this was because we were in such a hurry to get back. At dinner, Okusan asked us, "Why were you so late?" I said that K had asked me to walk with him to Ueno. Okusan seemed surprised, and said, "But it's so cold!" Ojōsan asked, "Why Ueno? Was there something in Ueno you wanted to see?" "No," I said, "we were simply taking a walk." K said even less that night than usual. Okusan spoke to him; Ojōsan laughed at him; but he would not respond. He gulped his food down and went back to his room, leaving us at the table.

In those days, such phrases as "the age of awakening" and "the new life" had not yet come into fashion. But you must not think that K's inability to discard his old ways and begin his life anew was due to his lack of modern concepts. You must understand that to K, his own past seemed too sacred a thing to be thrown away like an old suit of clothes. One might say that his past was his life, and to deny it would have meant that his life thus far had been without purpose. That K was hesitant in love does not mean that his love was in any sense lukewarm. He was unable to move, despite the violence of his emotion. And since the impact of his new emotion was not so great as to allow him to forget himself, he was forced to look back and remind himself of what his past had meant. And in doing so he could not but continue along the path that he had so far followed. Moreover, he had the kind of stubbornness and forbearance that is unknown these days. I think that thus far, I understood K's reaction to his own predicament well enough.

That evening, after our walk to Ueno, I felt unusually relieved. I quickly got up from the table and followed K into his room. I sat down by his desk and began to chatter about some trivial matter. He looked pained. It is possible that my eyes betrayed the triumph that I was then feeling. I know that there was a note of self-congratulation in my voice. A few minutes later, I withdrew my hands from the brazier and returned to my room. For the first time in my life, I felt that, in one matter at least, I was more than a match for K.

I was soon fast asleep. Then suddenly I was awakened by someone calling my name. The door was open, and I saw K's shadowy figure standing in the door-way. The lamp was still burning in his room. The change from sleep to wakefulness had been too abrupt, and I lay for a moment or two in a daze, unable to speak.

"Were you asleep?" K asked. K himself always went to bed late. I addressed myself to the shadow: "Did you want something?" "No, not really," he said. "I went to the bathroom a minute ago, and on my way back I wondered whether you were still up or not." The light was behind him, and so I could not see his face clearly. But I could tell by the tone of his voice that he was unusually calm.

K stepped back into his room and closed the door. The room became dark once more. I closed my eyes in the darkness, to return to my peaceful dreaming. I fell asleep immediately. The next morning, I thought about the incident, and began to wonder why K had behaved so strangely. I was half-inclined to believe that it was all a dream. At breakfast, I asked K if he had indeed opened the door in the middle of the night and called me. "Yes, I did," he replied. "Why?" I asked. He would not answer my question. Then after a brief silence he asked unexpectedly: "Have you been sleeping well lately?" His question gave me an odd sensation.

We left the house together, as our lectures were to begin at the same hour that day. The previous night's incident was still bothering me. I began questioning him again during our walk to the university. But K would not answer me satisfactorily. Finally I said, "Are you sure you weren't intending to continue yesterday's conversation?" He said, "Certainly not!" His short answer, I felt, was his way of reminding me that, in the park the previous afternoon, he had said: "Let us not talk about it any more." I then remembered how fiercely proud K was; and the words he had muttered began strangely to oppress me: "Am I prepared? . . . Why not? . . ."

I was well aware that K possessed a resolute nature. I understood also why it was that, in this affair only, K was unable to act decisively. But I soon realized that I did not know K as well as I had thought. K's conduct under stress was not as predictable, I learned, as it was under normal circumstances. The more I thought over K's last words in the park, the less clear their meaning seemed to become. Perhaps, I thought uneasily, he is as confident as ever; perhaps he is "prepared" not to forswear his love for Ojōsan, but to reject his past once and for all so as to be free from all doubt and suffering. The realization that K's words could be thus interpreted came as a shock to me. The shock itself should have revealed to me my own foolishness in jumping to conclusions about K; and I should perhaps have asked myself, "But is it not possible that there is yet another meaning hidden behind his words?" Unfortunately, I was unable to see things clearly then: it is sad to think how blind I was. At any rate, I persuaded myself that it was K's intention to submit to his love for Ojōsan. I became convinced that K, in his usual determined manner, would now do all he could to win her.

A voice whispered into my ear, "It is up to you to make the final move." The voice gave me new courage. I must act before K does, I thought, and without his knowledge. I decided to talk to Okusan about her daughter when both K and Ojōsan were out of the house. Quietly, I waited for the right moment: two days passed, then three, but it did not come. Always, when I was in the house, one of the two was there also. I became very impatient.

A week went by, and I decided I could not wait any longer. I could think of no better plan than to feign illness and stay at home all day. Okusan, then Ojōsan, and finally K himself came into my room to get me out of bed; I gave noncommittal answers to their questions and allowed them to go away with the impression that I was not feeling very well. It was about ten o'clock when I finally crawled out of bed. Both K and Ojōsan had gone out. There was not a sound in the house. Okusan, when she saw me, said: "You can't be feeling well. Why don't you stay in bed? I'll bring you something to eat." I was feeling perfectly healthy of course, and I had no desire to go back to bed. I washed my face and had my breakfast in the morning room as usual. Okusan sat on the other side of the long brazier and waited on me. It was a strange meal, being neither breakfast nor lunch; and during it, I remained silent, wondering uneasily how I should word my proposition. I have no doubt that Okusan misconstrued my preoccupation as a sign of illness.

When the meal was over, I lit a cigarette. Okusan was obliged to remain seated by the brazier: she could hardly leave the room before I did. She called the maid and had her take the tray. For lack of anything better to do, Okusan poured water into the iron kettle and then began polishing the brazier. I said: "Okusan, are you busy?" "No," she said; then, "Why do you ask?" "Well," I said, "there's something I should like to talk to you about." "Yes?" she said, watching me. Okusan's manner was so casual that I began to lose courage.

Finally, after a minute or two of beating about the bush, I said: "Has K said anything to you lately?" Okusan seemed taken aback by my question. "What do you mean?" she asked. Before I could answer her she said, "Did he say something to you?"

*

I had no inclination to tell her what K had told me that day in my room, so I said, "No." I was immediately ashamed of the lie. To ease my conscience, I added: "What I want to say has nothing to do with K. He has not asked me to say anything to you on his behalf." "Is that so?" she said, and waited. There was nothing left for me to do but come to the point. "Okusan," I blurted out, "I want to marry Ojōsan." She was not half as surprised as I had expected. She seemed at a loss for an answer, nevertheless, and gazed at me in silence. I had gone too far now to be intimidated by mere silence. "Please," I said, "let me marry her. I want Ojōsan very much." Okusan, being older, was much calmer than I. "Mind you," she said, "I am not saying no. But this is all so sudden . . ." "I want to marry her soon,'" I said quickly, and she began to laugh. Then she said seriously, "Have you thought about it carefully? Are you sure?" I assured her in no uncertain terms that though my manner of proposing might have seemed hasty, I had had Ojōsan in mind for a very long time.

211

There were a few more questions and answers, but I forget what they were. Okusan was an easy person to talk to on such an occasion as this: there was nothing elusive about her. In this respect, she was more like a man than a woman. "All right," she said finally. "You may have her." Then she said in a more formal tone, "Of course, it is I who should be doing the asking. Who am I to say, 'you may have her'? She is, as you know, a wretched, fatherless child."

I do not think that the entire conversation lasted more than fifteen minutes. It remained simple and direct throughout. Okusan made no stipulations. She said that there was no need to consult her relatives, though of course she would have to inform them of the decision. She seemed also to take it for granted that her daughter would raise no objections. I had some misgivings here. Despite my education, I must have been the more conventional of the two: I said, "I don't care about the relatives, but don't you think you should ask Ojōsan first?" She assured me that there was no need for me to worry. She had no intention, she said, of forcing her daughter to marry anyone she did not like.

I returned to my room. Surely, I thought a little uncomfortably, it can't be as easy as all this! I found new relief, however, in the thought that my future had at last been settled. On the whole, I was satisfied.

I went back to the morning room about noon and asked Okusan when she intended to inform Ojōsan of my proposal. "Does it really matter when I tell her?" she said. "The important thing is that I know about it, don't you think?" I was somehow made to feel that I was being more of a woman than she was. I was about to withdraw in embarrassment when she stopped me and said, "All right. Since you seem to be in a hurry, I will tell her today if you like. I'll talk to her when she gets back from her lessons. Will that do?" "Yes, thank you," I said, and went back to my room. The thought of having to sit quietly at my desk while the two ladies whispered to each other in their room was unnerving. I put on my cap and went out. I met Ojōsan at the bottom of the hill. She seemed surprised to see me. I took off my cap, and said: "So you're back." She said in a puzzled tone, "You have recovered?" "Oh yes," I said, "I am quite well now—quite well." I walked away hurriedly towards Suidōbashi.

From Sarugakuchō I entred the main street of Jimbochō and turned in the direction of Ogawamachi. It was my custom to browse through the secondhand bookshops whenever I found myself in that area, but I was in no mood that day for musty books. I thought ceaselessly of what was happening at the house. I thought of Okusan and what she had said to me that morning, then tried to imagine the scene in the house after Ojōsan's return. I walked on, not caring where my feet led me. My mind was filled with thoughts of the two ladies. I would suddenly stop in the middle of the street and think, "They must be talking about it at this moment"; or, "They will have finished their talk by now."

I crossed Mansei Bridge and walked up the slope past the Temple of Myōjin. Then from Hongō Hill I went down to the valley of Koishikawa. During this long walk— my route had formed a rough circle cutting through three separate boroughs—I gave K very little thought. Why, I do not know. Is it not strange that I did not think about him? I felt very tense that afternoon, it is true; but where was my conscience?

I returned to the house. As usual, I went into K's room

in order to get to mine. It was then that I felt guilty for the first time. He was of course at his desk, reading. And as always, he looked up at me. But this time, he did not give me his customary greeting—"Did you just get back?" Instead, he said: "Are you feeling better now? Have you seen the doctor?" Suddenly, I wanted to kneel before him and beg his forgiveness. It was a violent emotion that I felt then. I think that had K and I been alone in some wilderness, I would have listened to the cry of my conscience. But there were others in the house. I soon overcame the impulse of my natural self to be true to K. I only wish I had been given another such opportunity to ask K's forgiveness.

I saw him again at dinner. He sat quietly, deep in some melancholy thought. There was not the slightest sign of suspicion in his eyes. How could there be, when he knew nothing of what had happened in his absence? Okusan, ignorant of the truth about us, seemed unusually happy. Only I knew everything. I found difficulty in swallowing my food. It was like lead. Ojōsan, whose custom it was to eat with us, did not appear at the table that evening. When Okusan called her, she answered from the next room: "Yes, I'm coming!" K became curious. Finally, he asked Okusan: "What's the matter with her?" Okusan threw a glance in my direction, and said: "She's probably embarrassed." This made K all the more curious. "Why is she embarrassed?" he wanted to know. Okusan merely smiled, and looked at me again.

I had guessed, immediately upon sitting down at the table, the reason for Okusan's pleased look. The last thing I wanted her to do was explain the whole situation to K in my presence. The thought that Okusan was wont to show little reserve in such matters gave me acute discomfort. Fortunately, K became silent again. And Okusan, despite her unusually cheerful mood, did not reveal the secret after all. Sighing with relief, I returned to my room. But I could not help worying about my future relations with K. "What am I going to say to him?" I asked myself. I thought of one excuse after another, but none satisfied me. Eventually, the mere thought of having to explain my conduct to K became distasteful to me. I was a cowardly soul.

*

Two or three days passed. Needless to say, I remained very apprehensive. What made matters worse was the changed attitude of Okusan and Ojōsan towards me. It acted as a constant and painful reminder of the fact that the least I could do was tell K the truth. It added to my feeling of guilt. Moreover, I was fearful lest Okusan, who had a directness of manner rarely found in women, should one evening decide to tell K the happy news when we were all gathered round the dinner table. And I could not be sure that K would not begin to brood on Ojōsan's manner, which seemed to me to have conspicuously altered. I was compelled to admit that K had to be informed of the new relationship between myself and the family. Knowing the weakness of my own position, I thought it a terrible hardship to have to face K and tell him myself.

In desperation, I began to toy with the idea of asking Okusan to tell K of our engagement. (She would speak to him when I was out of the house, of course.) However, if Okusan were to tell him everything truthfully, my action would seem no less shameful than it would if I were to break the news to him myself. It did not seem so much of a consolation, after all, that K should learn the truth about me indirectly. Moreover, Okusan was sure to demand an explanation from me, if I were to ask her to give K a conveniently false account of how her daughter and I had become engaged; and I would then have to expose my weakness not only to my future mother-in-law, but to the person that I loved. In my naïve and earnest way, I believed that such an exposé would seriously affect the ladies' future opinion of me. I could not bear the thought of losing even a fraction of my sweetheart's trust in me before we were married.

And so, despite my sincere desire to follow the path of honesty, I strayed away from it. I was a fool; or, if you like, a scheming rogue. Apart from myself, only heaven knew me for what I was. Having once done a dishonest thing, I found that I could not redeem myself without telling everyone of my dishonesty. I wanted desperately to keep my shame a secret. At the same time, I felt that I had to win back my self-respect. Finding myself in this dilemma, I stood still.

It was five or six days later that Okusan suddenly asked me: "Have you told K about the engagement?" "Not yet," I answered. "Why not?" she demanded. I felt my whole body stiffen. I said nothing.

"No wonder he looked so odd when I told him," she said. Her words shocked me. I remember them clearly still. She continued: "You ought to be ashamed of yourself. He is, after all, a very close friend, isn't he? You really mustn't treat him so callously."

"What did K say?" I asked. "Oh, nothing of great interest," she said. But I pressed her to tell me in detail what K had said. Okusan of course had no reason to hide anything from me. Saying that there was really nothing much to tell, she proceeded to describe K's reaction to the news.

It would seem that K received his final blow with great composure. He must have been surprised, of course. "Is that so?" he had said simply when told of the engagement of Ojōsan and myself. Okusan had then said: "Do say that you are pleased." This time, apparently, he had looked at her and smiled: "Congratulations." Just as he was leaving the morning room he had turned around and said: "When is the wedding? I would like to give a present, but since I have no money, I am afraid I can't."

As I sat before Okusan, listening to her words, I felt a stifling pain welling up in my heart.

*

K, then, had known about it for over two days, though one would never have guessed this from his manner. I could not but admire his calm, however superficial it may have been. It seemed to me that he was much the worthier of the two of us. I said to myself: "Through cunning, I have won. But as a man, I have lost." My sense of defeat then became so violent that it seemed to spin around in my head like a whirlpool. And when I imagined how contemptuous K must be of me, I blushed with shame. I wanted to go to K and apologize for what I had done, but my pride—my fear of humiliation—restrained me.

I finally tired of my own inability to decide whether I would speak to K or remain silent. It was, I remember, on a Saturday night that I told myself: "Tomorrow, I will make up my mind one way or the other." But that night, K killed himself. Even now, I cannot recall the scene without horror. I do not know what strange forces were at work that night; for I, who had always slept with my feet pointing towards the west, decided that evening to arrange my bedding so that my feet would point towards the east.[17] Some time in the night, I was awakened by a

---

17. To lie with one's feet towards the west—i.e., in the direction of the Pure Land where the dead abide—is unlucky.

cold draught on my head. As I opened my eyes, I saw that the door between K's room and mine was ajar. This time, however, I did not see K's shadowy figure standing in the doorway. Like a man who has been suddenly warned of some appoaching disaster, I sat up and peered into K's room. In the dim lamplight, I could see his bed. The counterpane had been flung back. K sat with his back turned towards me. The upper part of his body was bent forward.

"Hey!" I called. He did not answer. "Hey! What's the matter?" His body did not move. I stood up, and went as far as the doorway. From there, I took a quick glance around the room in the half-light.

I experienced almost the same sensation then as I did when K first told me of his love for Ojōsan. I stood still, transfixed by the scene I beheld. My eyes stared unbelievingly, as though they were made of glass. But the initial shock was like a sudden gust of wind, and was gone in a moment. My first thought was, "It's too late!" It was then that the great shadow that would for ever darken the course of my life spread before my mind's eye. And from somewhere in the shadow a voice seemed to be whispering: "It's too late . . . It's too late . . ." My whole body began to tremble.

But even at such a moment I could not forget my own welfare. I noticed a letter lying on K's desk. I saw that it was addressed to me, as I had hoped. Frantically, I tore open the envelope. The purport of the letter was not in the least what I had expected. I had been afraid that in it, I would find many things that would cause me great pain. I had feared that its contents would be of such a nature that, should Okusan and Ojōsan happen to see it, they would cease to regard me with respect. When I had quickly read it through, my first thought was: "I'm safe." (I was thinking only of my reputation: at the time, what others thought of me seemed of great importance.)

The letter was simply written. K explained his suicide only in a very general way. He had decided to die, he said, because there seemed no hope of his ever becoming the firm, resolute person that he had always wanted to be. He thanked me for my many kindnesses in the past: and as a last favor to him, would I, he asked, take care of everything after his death? He asked that I apologize to Okusan on his behalf for causing her so much trouble. And he wanted me to notify his relatives of his death. In this brief, businesslike letter, there was no mention of Ojōsan. I soon realized that K had purposely avoided any reference to her. But what affected me most was his last sentence, which had perhaps been written as an afterthought: "Why did I wait so long to die?"

With trembling hands I folded up the letter and returned it to the envelope. I deliberately put it back on the desk, where everybody could see it. Then I looked around, and for the first time, I saw the blood on the wall.

I held his head—almost in embrace—and lifted it a little. I wanted to take just one look at his face in death. I bent down towards the floor and peered at his face from beneath. I quickly withdrew my hands. Not only had the sight filled me with sudden horror, but the head had felt inordinately heavy. I sat still for a while, looking at the cold ears that I had just touched, and the thick, close-cropped hair, which seemed to belong to someone alive. I felt no desire to cry. I felt only frightened. The fear I experienced then was not caused merely by the proximity of a bloodstained body. What truly frightened me was my own destiny; it seemed to have been irrevocably shaped by this friend of mine, who now lay cold and lifeless before me.

I could think of nothing better to do than return to my room. There, I began to pace restlessly up and down. My mind commanded me to do this for a while, useless though it might be. "I must do something," I said to myself; then, "But what can I do? It's too late." It was impossible for me to sit still. Like a caged bear, I had to be constantly on the move.

I was tempted to go and wake Okusan. But, at the same time, I felt that it would be wrong to allow her to see the dreadful sight in the next room. I was particularly anxious that Ojōsan should not see it. I knew that she would be terribly shocked if she did.

I lit the lamp in my room. Time and again, I looked at my watch. How slowly its hands seemed to move that night! I could not be sure exactly when it was that I had been awakened by the draught, but I knew that it had been close to dawn. And so I paced up and down, waiting impatiently for the sun to rise. Sometimes, I almost believed that night had fallen for ever.

It had been our custom to get up at seven, for many of our morning lectures began at eight. The maid, therefore, had to get up at six. It was some time before that hour that I decided to wake her. On my way to her room, however, I was stopped by Okusan. "This is Sunday, you know," she said. She had heard me walking down the corridor. 'Since you are already awake," I said, "will you be good enough to come to my room?" She slipped on a coat over her nightgown and followed me. As soon as I entered my room, I shut the door to K's room. I then said to Okusan, almost in a whisper: "A terrible thing has happened." "What do you mean?" she asked. I nodded towards the closed door, and said: "You must be calm." She went pale.

"Okusan," I said, "K has killed himself." She stood absolutely still and stared at me in silence. All of a sudden I knelt down and, bowing my head low before her, I said: "Please forgive me. It was all my fault. Will you and Ojōsan ever forgive me?" Until that moment, I had felt no inclination to say such things to Okusan. It was only when I saw her staring at me that I had the sudden urge to kneel down and blurt out my apology. Please take it that I was compelled to apologize to Okusan and Ojōsan because I could no longer apologize to K himself. I was forced by my conscience to apologize against my will. Fortunately for me, Okusan did not know the real reason why I had asked her forgiveness. Her face still pale, she said gently: "You mustn't blame yourself. Who could have foreseen such a thing?" Despite her gentleness, however, I could see unmistakable signs of fear and shock in her eyes.

*

Though I felt sorry for Okusan, I opened the door that I had only recently closed. K's lamp had gone out, and the room was almost pitch dark. I returned to my room and picked up my lamp. When I reached the doorway once more, I turned around and looked at Okusan. She walked slowly towards me and peered fearfully over my shoulder into the small room. But she would not go in. "You must open the storm windows," she said, "and let the light in."

Okusan's conduct throughout that day was exemplary, as one would expect of a soldier's wife. It was in obedience to Okusan's orders that I went to the doctor and then to the police. And until they had come and gone she would not allow anyone to enter K's room. K had cut open a carotid artery with a small knife and died instantly. He had no other wound. I learned that the blood which I had seen on the wall in the semi-darkness—as though in a dream—had gushed out in one tremendous spurt. I looked at the stains again, this time in daylight; and I marveled at the power of human blood.

Okusan and I cleaned up the room as well as we could. Fortunately, most of the blood had been absorbed by the quilted bedding, and very little had touched the floor mats. We moved K's body to my room and laid it out in a sleeping position. I then went out to send a telegram to his family.

When I returned, I found incense sticks already burning by his pillow. Their scent, so reminiscent of death, filled the air. The two ladies were sitting in the haze. I had not seen Ojōsan since the previous evening. She was crying. Okusan must have been crying too, for her eyes were red-rimmed. I, who had not remembered to shed one tear since K's death, was able to feel sorrow then for the first time. You have no idea what comfort this gave me. My heart, which until then had felt tight with pain and fear, seemed to find relief in sorrow.

Silently, I sat down beside the two ladies. "Offer an incense stick," said Okusan. I obeyed her in silence. Ojōsan did not speak to me. She exchanged a few words with her mother, but only concerning pressing business. She could not bring herself to talk of K as she remembered him. I was glad that she had not witnessed the terrible scene immediately after his death. I was afraid that a beautiful person such as she could not behold anything ugly and frightful without somehow losing her beauty. Even when the fear within me became so strong that it seemed to touch the very roots of my hair, I refused to move, not daring to expose her beauty to ugliness. I thought that to help destroy such beauty would be no less cruel and meaningless than to beat down a pretty, innocent flower.

222

When K's father and elder brother arrived, I gave my opinion as to where he should be buried. K and I had often walked to Zōshigaya. K was very fond of the place. I remembered saying to him jokingly: "All right, I'll see to it that you're buried here." I thought to myself, "What good will it do now to remember my promise to K?" But I wanted K to be buried in Zōshigaya, so that I could visit his grave every month and ask his forgiveness. His father and brother raised no objections. I suppose they felt that I had the right to decide where his grave should be, since I, and not they, had looked after K before his death.

*

On our way back from the funeral, a friend of ours asked me: "Why did he commit suicide?" I had been asked the same painful question many times before—by Okusan and Ojōsan, by his father and brother, by acquaintances who had been notified of his death, and even by newspaper reporters, who had never known him. My conscience pricked me each time I was asked the question. It seemed that the question was in reality an accusation. It seemed that what the questioner meant to say was: "Why not be truthful, and admit that you killed him?"

My answer was always the same. I merely repeated what K had said in his last letter to me. My friend, who had asked me the question after the funeral, produced a newspaper from his pocket when I had given him the usual answer. He pointed to the report of K's death. It explained that he had been disowned by his family and, in a fit of depression, had killed himself. I folded the paper and handed it back to my friend. He then told me that in another newspaper, K's suicide had been attributed to insanity. All this I did not know, for I had been too busy to read the papers. I had nevertheless been wondering what

223

they were saying about K's death. I was afraid that they
might say something that would embarrass the two ladies.
The mere thought of Ojōsan's name being mentioned in
connection with the affair upset me. "What else did you
see in the papers?" I asked. "Oh, nothing else," he answered.

It was not long after the funeral that the three of us
moved into the house where I now live. Both Okusan and
Ojōsan disliked the idea of staying in the old house, and I
could not bear to be constantly reminded of that night.

About two months later, I was able to graduate from
the university. Half a year after that, Ojōsan and I were
married at last. On the surface at least, I suppose it was a
happy occasion. After all, my hopes had been realized.
Okusan and Ojōsan both appeared happy. I will admit
that I was too. But over my happiness, there loomed a
black shadow. It seemed that my momentary contentment
led nowhere, except to a sorrowful future.

Soon after the wedding, Ojōsan—"my wife," I shall call
her from now on—for some reason suggested that we visit
K's grave together. I should have known better, but I was
at once suspicious. "Why this sudden desire to go there?"
I asked. "I thought that K would be pleased," she said. I
gazed at her innocent face in silence. I pulled myself
together when she said, "Why do you look at me like
that?"

I complied with my wife's request, and we went to
Zōshigaya. I washed the dust off the tombstone with
water. My wife put some flowers and incense sticks before
it. We then bowed our heads in silent prayer. My wife was
probably telling K of her new happiness. All I could think
of to say was: "I was wrong . . . I was wrong . . ."

Touching the stone gently, my wife said: "This is a fine
grave." It was really not so impressive, but I suppose she

praised it because I myself had chosen it at the stonemason's. I thought of the new stone, of my new wife, and of the newly buried white bones beneath us, and I felt that fate had made sport of us all. "Never again," I promised myself, "will I come here with my wife."

*

I did not cease to blame myself for K's death. From the beginning, I was afraid of the suffering my own sense of guilt would bring me. One might say that I went through my marriage ceremony, which I had looked forward to for so long, in a state of nervous insecurity. But since I did not know my own self very well, I had a vague hope that perhaps marriage would enable me to begin a new life. That this hope was no more than a fleeting daydream, I realized soon enough. It was my wife who unwittingly reminded me of harsh reality every time we were together. How could I continue to have hope, no matter how forlorn, when the sight of her face seemed always to bring back haunting memories of K? Sometimes, the idea occurred to me that she was like a chain that linked me to K for the rest of my life. At such times, I would behave coldly to my wife, whom I found otherwise faultless. She would immediately sense my aloofness and ask: "What are you thinking about? Have I done something wrong?" There were times when I managed to ease her mind with a smile. But there were times when she would show signs of irritation and say: "Are you sure you don't dislike me?" or "You are hiding something from me." And I would look at her in misery, not knowing what to say.

Often, I was on the verge of telling her everything, but each time, at the crucial moment, I would be stopped by something that was beyond my conscious control. You know me well, and I suppose there is no need for me to explain what this was that prevented me from confessing to my wife. Nevertheless, I feel that I owe you an explanation. Please understand that I did not wish my wife to believe me better than I actually was. I am sure that if I had spoken to her with a truly repentant heart—as I did always to the spirit of my dead friend—she would have forgiven me. She would have cried, I know, from happiness. That I refused to tell her the truth was not due to selfish calculation on my part. I simply did not wish to taint her whole life with the memory of something that was ugly. I thought that it would be an unforgivable crime to let fall even the tiniest drop of ink on a pure, spotless thing.

A whole year passed, but my heart remained restless. I tried to bury this restlessness in books. I began to study furiously, and waited for the day when I would make public the result of my efforts. But I found little comfort in striving towards a goal which I had artificially set myself. Eventually, I found that I could not find peace in books. Once more I sat still and gazed at the world around me.

It would seem that my wife attributed my ennui to the fact that I had no material worries. This was understandable, since not only did my mother-in-law have enough money to support herself and her daughter, but there was enough on my side to enable me to live without working. Besides, there is no doubt that I had learned to take my easy circumstances for granted. But material comfort was by no means responsible for my inaction. When I was cheated by my uncle, I felt very strongly the unreliableness of men. I learned to judge others harshly, but not myself. I thought that, in the midst of a corrupt world, I had managed to remain virtuous. Because of K, however, my self-confidence was shattered. With a shock, I realized that

I was no better than my uncle. I became as disgusted with myself as I had been with the rest of the world. Action of any kind became impossible for me.

*

Having failed to bury myself alive among books, I tried for a while to forget myself by drowning my soul in saké. I do not say that I liked drinking. But I can drink if I want to, and I hoped that saké would bring at least momentary oblivion. I was being naïve, of course. All that drinking did for me in time was to make me more depressed than ever. Occasionally, in the midst of a drunken stupor, I would suddenly remember myself: I would realize how idiotic it was to try to deceive oneself. Then my eyes and my heart would be jerked back to sobriety. Sometimes, I would fail even to reach that stage of self-deception, and find myself becoming more keenly aware of my own sorrow. Moreover, when I did succeed in reaching a state of artificially induced gaiety, I would be sure to sink into deep gloom afterwards. It was always in the latter state that my mother-in-law and my wife, whom I loved so much, found me after I had been drinking. The way in which they interpreted my behavior was, under the circumstances, quite understandable.

It would seem that my mother-in-law sometimes complained about me to my wife. My wife never told me what her mother had said. But she reproached me on her own account. I suppose she could not bear to watch me live as I did without saying something. I say that she "reproached" me, but I assure you that she never used strong words. She hardly ever gave me cause to be angry with her. She asked me more than once if she was not in some way responsible for my behavior; she wanted to be told what her faults were. Sometimes, she begged me to stop drinking for the sake of my own future. Once, she cried and said: "You have changed." The words that followed hurt much more: "You would not have changed so, had K-san been alive." "Perhaps you are right," I answered. Secretly, I grieved for my wife, who did not know how right she had been.

Sometimes—usually the morning after I had come home late in a very drunken state—I would apologize to her. She would listen to my apology and then laugh; or she would remain silent; or she would begin to cry. Whatever she did, I was invariably disgusted with myself at such times. I suppose that, in a sense, I was apologizing as much to myself as to her. Finally, I gave up drinking: one might say that it was self-disgust, rather than my wife's reproaches, that made me stop.

I did not touch saké any more, it is true, but I was at a loss as to what I should do instead. In desperation, I began to read again. I read with no object in view, however. I would finish a book, then cast it aside and open another. My wife asked me, on more than one occasion, why it was that I studied so hard. I was saddened by the thought that she, whom I loved and trusted more than anyone else in the world, could not understand me. And the thought that I had not the courage to explain myself to her made me sadder still. I was very lonely. Indeed, there were times when I felt that I stood completely alone in this world, cut off from every other living person.

Time and again, I wondered what had caused K to commit suicide. At first, I was inclined to think that it was disappointment in love. I could think of nothing but love then, and quite naturally I accepted without question the first simple and straightforward explanation that came to my mind. Later, however, when I could think more objectively, I began to wonder whether my explanation had not been too simple. I asked myself, "Was it perhaps because his ideals clashed with reality that he killed himself?" But I could not convince myself that K had chosen death for such a reason. Finally, I became aware of the possibility that K had experienced loneliness as terrible as mine, and wishing to escape quickly from it, had killed himself. Once more, fear gripped my heart. From then on, like a gust of winter wind, the premonition that I was treading the same path as K had done would rush at me from time to time, and chill me to the bone.

*

Then my mother-in-law fell ill. The doctor told us she would not recover. I devoted all my energy to caring for her. I did so for the invalid's sake, and for my dear wife's too; but I felt also that I was in some way helping the whole of mankind. There is no doubt that, in a sense, I had been waiting for such a chance to prove to myself that I was not totally useless. For the first time since my retirement from the world, I was able to feel that I could still be of some use to others. There is no way to explain my state of mind, except to say that I was seeking a means of atoning for the wrong I had done.

My mother-in-law died. There remained only my wife and myself. My wife said to me: "In all the world, I now have only you to turn to." I looked at her, and my eyes suddenly filled with tears. How could I, who had no trust in myself, give her the comfort she needed? I thought her a very unfortunate woman. One day, I said so to her. "Why do you say that?" she asked. She could not understand what I meant. And I could not tell her. She began to cry. "It is because you have always looked at me in your twisted way," she said reproachfully, "that you can say such things."

After her mother's death, I tried to treat my wife as gently as I could. I loved her, of course. But again, I was not being gentle merely for her sake. I suppose that my heart was moved in the same way as when my mother-in-law had fallen ill. My wife appeared content. But in her contentment, there seemed to linger a vague uneasiness that sprang from her own inability to understand me. Mind you, I do not think for a moment that her uneasiness would have decreased had she been allowed to understand the nature of my gentleness towards her. Indeed, I think that she would have become even more uneasy. A woman is more happy when she is the sole object of affection— whether or not this kindness may involve injustice elsewhere does not seem to matter very much—than when she is loved for reasons which transcend particular individuals. At least, I have noticed this tendency more in women than in men.

My wife once asked me: "Can't a man's heart and a woman's heart ever become a part of each other, so that they are one?" I gave a noncommittal answer: "Perhaps, when the man and the woman are young." She sat quietly for a while. She was probably thinking of the time when she herself had been a young girl. Then she gave a little sigh.

From then on, a nameless fear would assail me from time to time. At first, it seemed to come over me without warning from the shadows around me, and I would gasp at its unexpectedness. Later, however, when the experience had become more familiar to me, my heart would readily succumb—or perhaps respond—to it; and I would begin to wonder if this fear had not always been in some hidden corner of my heart, ever since I was born. I would then ask myself whether I had not lost my sanity. But I had no desire to go to a doctor, or anyone else, for advice.

I felt very strongly the sinfulness of man. It was this feeling that sent me to K's grave every month, that made me take care of my mother-in-law in her illness and behave gently towards my wife. It was this sense of sin that led me to feel sometimes that I would welcome a flogging even at the hands of strangers. When this desire for punishment became particularly strong, I would begin to feel that it should come from myself, and not others. Then I would think of death. Killing myself seemed a just punishment for my sins. Finally, I decided to go on living as if I were dead.

I wonder how many years have passed since I made that decision. My wife and I continued to live in harmony. We were by no means unhappy. We were, I assure you, quite a happy couple. But there was always this shadow which separated us. I could never push it away, and it lay like a dark streak across my wife's happiness. She has always sensed its presence. As I think about it now, I cannot but feel terribly sorry for her.

Though I had resolved to live as if I were dead, my heart would at times respond to the activity of the outside world, and seem almost to dance with pent-up energy. But as soon as I tried to break my way through the cloud that surrounded me, a frighteningly powerful force would rush upon me from I know not where, and grip my heart tight, until I could not move. A voice would say to me: "You have no right to do anything. Stay where you are." Whatever desire I might have had for action would suddenly leave me. After a moment, the desire would come back, and I would once more try to break through. Again, I would be restrained. In fury and grief I would cry out: "Why do you stop me?" With a cruel laugh, the voice would answer: "You know very well why." Then I would bow in hopeless surrender.

Please understand that though I might have seemed to you to be leading an uncomplicated, humdrum life, there was a painful and unending struggle going on inside me. My wife must have felt very impatient with me sometimes; but you have no idea how much more impatient I was with myself. When at last it became clear to me that I could not remain still in the prison much longer, and that I could not escape from it, I was forced to the conclusion that the easiest thing I could do would be to commit suicide. You may wonder why I reached such a conclusion. But you see, that strange and terrible force which gripped my heart whenever I wished to make my escape in life, seemed at least to leave me free to find escape in death. If I wished to move at all, then I could move only towards my own end.

I tried two or three times to follow this only course which destiny had left open to me. But each time, I was restrained by my feelings for my wife. Needless to say, I lacked the courage to take her with me. As you know, I could not even bring myself to confess everything to her: how could I, then, rob her of her allotted life and force her to share my own destiny? The mere thought of doing such a cruel thing was terrible to me. Her fate had been pre-ordained no less than mine had been. To throw her into the fire that had been built for me would be an extremely unnatural and heartless thing to do.

At the same time, the thought of my wife living alone after I had gone aroused my compassion. How could I ever forget my wife's words after her mother had died?—"In all the world, I now have only you to turn to." And so I hesitated. Afterwards, I would look at my wife and say to myself: "It's a good thing that I hesitated." And I would once more begin to live in hopelessness and frustration, feeling my wife's disappointed eyes on me.

Look back on those days when you knew me: my life then was as I have just described it. My state of mind was always the same—at Kamakura where we met, or in the suburbs where we walked. A dark shadow seemed always to be following me. I was no more than bearing the weight of life for her sake. My mood was no different that night after your graduation. Believe me, I was not lying when I said that we would meet again in September. I really did mean to see you—even after the passing of autumn, even after winter had come and gone.

Then, at the height of the summer, Emperor Meiji passed away. I felt as though the spirit of the Meiji era had begun with the Emperor and had ended with him. I was overcome with the feeling that I and the others, who had been brought up in that era, were now left behind to live as anachronisms. I told my wife so. She laughed and refused to take me seriously. Then she said a curious thing, albeit in jest: "Well then, *junshi*[18] is the solution to your problem."

I had almost forgotten that there was such a word as *"junshi."* It is not a word that one uses normally, and I suppose it had been banished to some remote corner of my memory. I turned to my wife, who had reminded me of its existence, and said: "I will commit *junshi* if you like; but in my case, it will be through loyalty to the spirit of the Meiji era." My remark was meant as a joke; but I did feel that the antiquated word had come to hold a new meaning for me.

A month passed. On the night of the Imperial Funeral I

18. *Junshi* is an old-fashioned word, meaning "following one's lord to the grave."

sat in my study and listened to the booming of the cannon. To me, it sounded like the last lament for the passing of an age. Later, I realized that it might also have been a salute to General Nogi. Holding the extra edition in my hand, I blurted out to my wife: *"Junshi! Junshi!"*

I read in the paper the words Genral Nogi had written before killing himself. I learned that ever since the Seinan War,[19] when he lost his banner to the enemy, he had been wanting to redeem his honor through death. I found myself automatically counting the years that the general had lived, always with death at the back of his mind. The Seinan War, as you know, took place in the tenth year of Meiji. He must therefore have lived for thirty-five years, waiting for the proper time to die. I asked myself: "When did he suffer greater agony—during those thirty-five years, or the moment when the sword entered his bowels?"

It was two or three days later that I decided at last to commit suicide. Perhaps you will not understand clearly why I am about to die, no more than I can fully understand why General Nogi killed himself. You and I belong to different eras, and so we think differently. There is nothing we can do to bridge the gap between us. Of course, it may be more correct to say that we are different simply because we are two separate human beings. At any rate, I have done my best in the above narrative to make you understand this strange person that is myself.

I am leaving my wife behind me. It is fortunate that she will have enough to live on after I am gone. I have no wish to give her a greater shock than is necessary. I intend to die in such a way that she will be spared the sight of my blood. I shall leave this world quietly while she is out of

19. Sometimes known as the Satsuma Rebellion.

the house. I want her to think that I died suddenly, without reason. Perhaps she will think that I lost my mind: that will be all right.

More than ten days have gone by since I decided to die. I want you to know that I spent most of the time writing this epistle about myself to you. At first, I wanted to speak to you about my life; but now that I have almost finished writing this, I feel that I could not have given as clear an account orally, and I am happy. Please understand, I did not write this merely to pass the time away. My own past, which made me what I am, is a part of human experience. Only I can tell it. I do not think that my effort to do so honestly has been entirely purposeless. If my story helps you and others to understand even a part of what we are, I shall be satisfied. Only recently, I was told that Watanabe Kazan postponed his death for a week in order to complete his painting, *Kantan*.[20] Some may say that this was a vain sort of thing to do. But who are we to judge the needs of another man's heart? I did not write simply to keep my promise to you. More compelling than the promise was the necessity which I felt within me to write this story.

I have now satisfied that need. There is nothing left for me to do. By the time this letter reaches you, I shall probably have left this world—I shall in all likelihood be dead. About ten days ago, my wife went to stay with her aunt in Ichigaya. The aunt fell ill, and when I heard that she was short of help I sent my wife there. Most of this long document was written while she was away. Whenever she returned, I quickly hid it from her.

I want both the good and bad things in my past to serve as an example to others. But my wife is the one exception—I do not want her to know about any of this. My

20. "Illusion."

first wish is that her memory of me should be kept as unsullied as possible. So long as my wife is alive, I want you to keep everything I have told you a secret—even after I myself am dead.

Sōseki as Lecturer:
Autonomy and Coercion

The Lecture Tour of 1911

"The Civilization of Modern-day Japan" was the second of four lectures that Sōseki delivered in August 1911 on a tour organized by the *Asahi Shimbun,* the newspaper in which Sōseki published his fiction after he became staff novelist in 1907. "Pastime and Profession," "The Civilization of Modern-day Japan," "Content and Form," and "Literature and Morality" all dealt with the question of personal freedom, as did Sōseki's most famous lecture, "My Individualism" of 1914.[1]

There was perhaps a special urgency to the theme of freedom in the lectures of August 1911, however, coming as they did near the end of the second administration of Katsura Tarō, which had been one of the most reactionary and repressive regimes of the Meiji period since its rise to power in 1908.

In the "festive" atmosphere following the Russo-Japanese War (1904–1905), the country's leaders perceived the loss of a unified sense of national purpose, especially among the younger generation. Everywhere, it seemed, there were anguished young men seeking the meaning of life and spouting philosophies such as free love and women's liberation that clashed with the traditional Confucian family system. Naturalist fiction, with its emphasis on the liberation of the individual, was gaining in popularity and threatening to corrupt the morals of an entire nation. In conservative minds, these developments became confused with the upsurge of socialism and anarchism.[2] All came from the West and all were equally "dangerous thoughts." In response, Katsura's administration embarked on a campaign to resuscitate the good, old Confucian values of loyalty and filial piety through stepped-up programs of indoctrination and censorship.[3]

It was the Katsura Cabinet that staged a nationwide roundup of leftists beginning on June 1, 1910, later trying twenty-six of the suspects *in camera* on largely trumped-up charges of plotting to assassinate the emperor, and sentencing twenty-four of them to death. (Twelve of the sentences were commuted to life imprisonment in a show of imperial magnanimity, and the final twelve were promptly executed in January 1911.) During most of this rumor-filled, frightening period, Natsume Sōseki was in bed, recovering from nearly fatal hemorrhaging of stomach ulcers on August 24, 1910.

A year later, Katsura was still in charge and Sōseki was well enough to embark on a lecture tour at the request of the Osaka *Asahi Shimbun.* He was not eager to go, but he felt obligated to accept the assignment after having been out of commission for so long with his illness.[4] He left Tokyo on the morning of Friday, August 11, and was met in Osaka that night by a small contingent of *Asahi* colleagues. There followed a fairly grueling schedule of touring and lecturing for the next seven days. Despite sweltering, sometimes violently stormy weather, the lecturers played to capacity crowds wherever they went. They delivered three lectures in a three-hour program in nearby Akashi that Sunday afternoon, three more lectures to an audience of 1,700 in a four-hour program in rather more distant Wakayama on Tuesday afternoon, three again in Sakai on Thursday, and, finally, the next evening, a marathon five-lecture performance in Osaka that lasted from six o'clock until after eleven o'clock, drawing an audience of more than 4,700 men and as many as 50 women in their own special section.

Sōseki's was always the third lecture, following talks on such topics as "Conditions in French Annam," "The Manchurian Problem," "Interests of the World Powers in China," and "My Observations in Sakhalin." "Fundamental Problems of the Economy" and "Revision of the Anglo-Japanese Alliance" followed Sōseki's lecture in Osaka. Each session was publicized as an *Asahi* company event, bearing such titles as "*Asahi* Reporters' Lecture Meeting" or "Osaka *Asahi Shimbun* Reporters' Invitational Lecture Meeting." The company supplied stenographers and in November published a volume containing all the talks as revised by their authors.[5]

As it turned out, Sōseki's reluctance to join the tour proved all too well founded. After the second session, he and the other speakers were invited to a banquet, where he overindulged in octopus, one of the local specialties. A wild storm blew in that evening which made it necessary for the lecturers to change hotels, and Sōseki had a restless night. They transferred to Osaka the next day, and by the time he was due on the podium in Sakai on the seventeenth, his stomach was beginning to bother him. With only one lecture left in the series, he decided to press on to Osaka. He ate nothing after the marathon presentation there on the eighteenth, but a wave of nausea struck him as he lay in bed at the inn that night, and he was shocked to find himself vomiting blood. Admitted to a hospital, he was unable to return to Tokyo until mid-September.

Sōseki did not hesitate to tell his audiences that he was less than thrilled to be there. "I never imagined I would be coming to a place like this to deliver a lecture," he told the folks in Akashi, but he had done so because the company had insisted.[6] In Wakayama, he pointed out that the company had added that particular venue to his itinerary even though he had requested the Kyoto-Osaka area.[7] In Sakai he told his listeners with a touch of humor that he did not normally reside in their fair city but had received "an order—or was it a notice or a request? In any case, they made it clear I had to participate."[8] On the way from the station to the lecture hall, he had seen posters on every street corner with his name in bold characters advertising the meeting as if it were some kind of vaudeville show.[9] "The company may prefer this approach," he sniffed, "but Natsume Sōseki is not terribly pleased to be made such a spectacle of." To his Osaka audience he said, "I could tell you that I am standing up here on the podium like this entirely for your benefit, like the Salvation Army, but you wouldn't believe me. For whose benefit am I up here, then? I'm up here for the company. I'm up here as an advertisement for the *Asahi Shimbun*. Or maybe I'm up here to make Natsume Sōseki better known to the world. . . . I certainly wouldn't have been fired if I had refused to speak," he added, concluding that he had accepted the assignment out of mixed feelings of obligation and good will.[10]

Sōseki was not being entirely ungracious with these remarks. Taken out of context, they are missing the charm and humor with which he delivered them. Indeed, such comments were the device Sōseki typically used to put his audiences at ease.[11] The fact remains, however, that Sōseki had felt more or less coerced into participating in the *Asahi*'s sideshow, and his resentment not only surfaced at several points in the talks but provided additional illustrative material for the central theme of his lectures, which revolved around the question of individual autonomy versus external coercion. This remained his focus whether he was discussing the position of the novelist in modern society, or criticizing the government's folly in attempting to impose outmoded moral concepts on an increasingly individualistic populace, or analyzing the tragic relationship of Japan to the Western world.

Conscious of his anomalous position as company novelist—that is, as an independent artist on the payroll of a major newspaper—Sōseki exploited the opportunity of the lecture tour to warn the company that he meant to retain his independence as a novelist, whatever compromises he may have made in accepting this assignment to speak. "I am connected with a newspaper," he said, "but fortunately I have never to this day been subjected to external pressure. There have been no orders from the boss to write more marketable novels or to step up my production. The company generally lets me write as I see fit, in return for which they never raise my pay. But even if they were to raise my pay, I would find it intolerable if they suddenly changed their policy and began giving me orders concerning the nature and volume of my writings for commercial purposes."[12] The imposition of external forms without regard to internal need is what brings about student riots, national revolutions, and, he adds most pointedly, employee rebellions—"even in a newspaper such as that of our dear *Asahi* Company."[13]

Ever since he left Tokyo Imperial University to join the *Asahi* staff in 1907, Sōseki had been thinking about his social role as a novelist. In the lecture "Pastime and Profession," Sōseki saw the relentless advance of civilization turning modern men into specialists incapable of function-

ing outside their narrow fields. Isolated as we make ourselves, he said, it becomes increasingly difficult for us to
know or understand or sympathize with each other; our
inner lives have no connectedness.[14] It was here that Sōseki
perceived a useful function for the novelist. As he said to
his audience:

> Works of literature are, by their very nature, nonspecialist
> books. They were written to criticize or depict matters of com-
> mon concern to all men. They bring people together, stripped
> naked, regardless of profession or class, and break down all such
> walls that separate us. Thus I believe them to be the most worthy
> and least harmful means for binding us together as human be-
> ings.[15]

As respectable a profession as Sōseki saw novel writing
to be, however, he also suggested in the lecture that he
might have had some misgivings about having changed his
writing from a pastime to a profession when he joined the
Asahi staff because all professions, by definition, require
some loss of autonomy. Pastimes are done entirely for
oneself, but "the moment a pastime changes into a profession, the authority that lay entirely in one's own hand
suddenly moves into that of another, and pleasure turns
quickly and inevitably into pain."[16] Artists, however, belong to a special "class" of people whose professions
cannot survive if they cede their autonomy to others.[17]
They cannot produce art unless they are entirely true to
themselves, and they cannot produce income unless the
work they do for themselves happens—purely by chance—
to be pleasing to others. "Unless the works of the artist,
who deals directly with the public, succeed in arousing a
response from some part of society and that response takes
the form of material remuneration, then all the artist can
do is starve to death."[18]

Sōseki was not entirely comfortable identifying himself as an artist and to some extent continued to view himself as a scholar. In "Pastime and Profession," Sōseki holds scholars up as the extreme example of compartmentalization forced on people by the pace and intensity of modern civilization, and he includes himself among the ones so "crippled": "I don't know how to do the most ordinary things—how to fill out a change of domicile notice for the ward office, how to go about selling a piece of land, how to make cotton from what part of the plant, how to cook an egg."[19] A character in the novel *Until After the Spring Equinox* (*Higan-sugi made,* 1912) summarizes Sōseki's own "Modern-day Civilization of Japan" as a lecture he says he heard delivered by "a certain scholar."[20]

Just as inner direction and the freedom from external coercion were indispensable for the artist, they were also necessary for modern individuals. Under Katsura, however, intellectuals found themselves struggling against forces in politics and education that sought to turn the clock back. The men in high office simply could not fathom the new ways of thinking. Katsura had been in power for almost a year when Sōseki recorded his disgust for the leaders' blindness after attending a reception at which Katsura and other major political figures had delivered resounding toasts. His diary entry observes "Those who make their way through life spouting such nonsense are the same as hermits living in ignorance of the world. No, they are worse than hermits the way they fill their speech with lies."[21]

This was Sōseki's private view, but twice in 1911, the year of the lecture trip, Sōseki had also come into public conflict with the government. In February, he openly rejected the Ministry of Education's award of the Doctorate of Letters, largely out of resentment for the government's arrogance in failing to ask him whether he even wanted the degree. And, in May, he published a three-part critique of the Ministry's new Committee on Literature, which was a transparent attempt to promote the writing of "wholesome" literary works to counter the new naturalist writing with its modern values. In his August lectures, Sōseki never mentioned the Prime Minister by name nor did he refer to any specific government measures, but his audiences—whose support for him became obvious when they applauded at his mention of having rejected the doctorate—could not have missed his point.[22]

In the lecture "Content and Form," Sōseki called on the government and educators to adjust their policies to the inner needs of the individualistic new Meiji generation instead of attempting to impose outmoded forms on them without regard to the vast changes that had occurred in the inner lives of the Japanese since the fall of the Tokugawa regime.

> We hear a lot of fuss these days about individualism and naturalist fiction, but the appearance of such phenomena is proof that the content of our lives has naturally undergone a change since the old days. I suspect there will be more and more cases in which those who seek to preserve the old forms try to crush individualism and naturalism because they might conflict with those traditional forms, while those who seek to create their own forms in accordance with the content of their lives resist these attempts.[23]

Sōseki, a supposedly antinaturalist writer, came even more vigorously to the defense of naturalism in the lecture he called "Literature and Morality," praising the new literature for the wholesome moral effect of its honesty. In labeling naturalism as "wholesome" *(kenzen),* Sōseki was pointedly rejecting the Katsura regime's censorship and its attempts to counter naturalism by promoting the creation of what they called "wholesome" literature—specifically, literature based on Confucian moral values. These old concepts were nothing but "lies," Sōseki declared.[24] Having won the Russo-Japanese War, he said, the Japanese people could begin to worry less about the fate of the nation and live more for themselves as individuals; and the ethic of self-sacrifice had begun to ring hollow. "And when we look closely at the old Confucian moral slogans—loyalty, filial piety, chastity—we realize that they were nothing but duties imposed solely for the benefit of those who possessed absolute power under the social system of the time." If they were merely a cynical ploy even in their heyday, they could only cause even more hardship when artificially resuscitated in late Meiji.[25]

Although he was addressing large roomfuls of men and was himself a fairly typical Meiji male chauvinist, Sōseki was aware that the death of Confucian morality applied to women as well. "Look at how differently we relate to our wives and daughters now as compared with before the Restoration. . . . If, even in dealing with our housemaids the old rules no longer apply, then educators and governments will have to go out of their way to accommodate the general mass of students and citizens."[26]

"The Civilization of Modern-day Japan" is the best known of the four August lectures. It is cited at least as often in historical and literary studies as "My Individualism." Here is where Sōseki had the most to say about the relationship of Japan to the West. Modern readers might wish that he had said it more succinctly, but in the lecture's many rambling excursions, Sōseki is continually drawing parallels between personal experience and national tendencies. Again the theme is autonomy and coercion but on an international scale. He has little of an encouraging nature to say to civilized nations, either East or West, but for Japan he sees an additional source of suffering in the form of external coercion.

Whether Japanese or Western, "civilization," in general, is, for Sōseki, a dynamic, ever-changing process that results from the interplay of two inborn human impulses—the positive desire of the individual to do what pleases him, and the negative desire of the individual to avoid tasks imposed on him by others.[27] Over the centuries, the interplay of autonomy and coercion have led to progress in terms of an improved living standard, but not in terms of comfort for the human psyche. Progress brings with it heightened competition, which only tends to increase the "psychological pain" of existence for each individual.

For the individual Japanese, it is even worse than for the modern Westerner because the country as a whole has lost its autonomy. Japan's civilization is motivated by the external pressure of the West, and this has its effect on the minutest details in the lives of individuals—matters as seemingly inconsequential as how to hold a knife and fork. The Japanese must endure not only the stress of competition but the additional psychological pain of keeping current with the latest developments that have been imported only half understood from the West.

This is true in all fields, but it is especially evident in the case of the university professor, for whom "succumbing to a nervous breakdown is more or less to be expected." Scholars come in for a good deal of self-deprecating humor from Sōseki's pen (it is the job of the scholar "to make the comprehensible incomprehensible," he tells his audience here), but finally they symbolize the nervous strain that all Japanese must experience to some extent because their values are established for them elsewhere. In "My Individualism," Sōseki confesses the discomfort he felt as a young scholar spouting Westerners' opinions, "boasting of borrowed clothes, preening with glued-on peacock feathers." And where the later talk advocates "self-centeredness" *(jiko-hon'i)* as the single most indispensable value for individual development, it is precisely Japan's having "lost its ability to be self-centered" in the face of the onslaught of Western culture that has caused the nation and its inhabitants such stress.

The loss of his autonomy was the greatest threat that Sōseki envisioned for himself—as an artist, as a citizen, and as a Japanese. His most broadly applicable insights came from the pain he found inside himself. To validate his remarks, Sōseki tells his audience at one point that they need only "experiment" on themselves: stop a moment to observe how their minds work, then apply those observations to the larger issues at hand. This gives us a glimpse at the method that served Sōseki so well as a novelist. Sensei in *Kokoro*, Daisuke in *And Then* (*Sore kara,* 1909), Ichirō in *The Wayfarer* (*Kōjin,* 1912–13), and other Sōseki protagonists are not merely isolated individuals struggling with their limited personal problems but tortured minds that represent the most fundamental forces at work in their society and in the modern experience.

"My Individualism"

Sōseki delivered this now widely quoted lecture on November 25, 1914, at Gakushūin—literally, the Academy for Study and Training, best known in English as the Peers' School. Gakushūin was founded in 1877 for the education of Japan's new aristocracy—the former low-ranking samurai who had effected the "restoration" of the emperor and wanted fancy titles to go with their new

247

status. It was the only educational institution under the direct jurisdiction of the Imperial Household Agency, and, by Sōseki's time, it had courses from primary to university levels.[28]

Sōseki did not have to leave Tokyo to deliver this solo performance, but he did have to venture into an area of the city unknown to him, as he told his audience at the outset. If he did not exactly see himself as forging into enemy territory to engage in single-handed combat, he was at least hoping to influence members of the coming generation of Japan's elite. He wanted these rich young men to have some appreciation for the individual human beings who would feel the impact of the power and money that would be theirs someday to wield. In effect, he wanted them to behave differently from the arrogant officials who had tried to force on him the "honor" of the Doctorate of Letters. Nor was the problem of the doctorate far from his thoughts. In a letter to the Gakushūin professor who had arranged for his talk, Sōseki had insisted that announcements of the event not append the "mistaken" title to his name, especially since Gakushūin had such close ties with officialdom. (He also asked in the letter whether Gakushūin was, in fact, as he recalled, "just beyond the girls' school in Mejiro.")[29]

Katsura Tarō was no longer in power when Sōseki came to speak at Gakushūin, but his regime's substantial contributions to Japan's "modern myths" were still intact, and succeeding events—among them the spectacular funeral of the Meiji emperor in September 1912—had kept the "course of the ship of state" essentially unchanged.[30] Thus, when Sōseki arrived at the podium in November 1914, he was more than ever prepared to warn his listeners against an excessive devotion to the nation at the expense of its individual citizens.

Sōseki had been invited to speak by the Hojinkai, the "[Confucian] Virtue-Promotion Society," which had been founded in 1889 for students and faculty of Gakushūin and which continues functioning at the school to the present day. The Society's magazine, *Hojinkai zasshi,* would print "My Individualism" and, in later years, would carry the juvenilia of such Gakushūin Higher School literary types as the Shirakaba group and the novelist Mishima Yukio.[31]

An odd coincidence links Mishima with Sōseki's talk. On November 25, 1970, fifty-six years to the day after Sōseki spoke at Gakushūin, Mishima exhorted the members of Japan's Self-Defense Force to rally in support of the emperor and, when they failed to respond, Mishima committed ritual disembowelment. Sōseki would have been appalled at Mishima's actions, and would certainly have balked at the suggestion that individuals should willingly lay down their lives for the state, but he was undoubtedly moved when General Nogi Maresuke, one of the foremost military figures of his time and President of Gakushūin from 1907 until his death, committed the same traditional form of suicide following the death of the Meiji emperor in 1912. Nogi's suicide had been a "success," Sōseki concluded, despite the undesirable effect it had had of inspiring imitators, because the General's act had been performed in utter sincerity.[32]

Critics of *Kokoro* have had difficulty explaining exactly how the suicide of General Nogi is related to the suicide of Sōseki's protagonist, but it is clear that this traditional display of devotion is meant to open wellsprings of feeling in Sensei that he had assumed had long since dried up, thanks to his education in "this modern age, so full of freedom, independence, and our own egotistical selves."[33]

Equally difficult to explain may be the relationship between *Kokoro* and "My Individualism." With irrepressible passion, Sōseki the lecturer "confesses" to the key role played in his life by his discovery of self-centeredness, and he urges his young audience to develop their own individual natures. Three months earlier, *Kokoro* had brought Sōseki's continuing fictional study of the "egotistical self" to its logical conclusion in Sensei's death. As Edwin McClellan has written, "It is in *Mon* (The gate) (1910) and *Kōjin* (The wayfarer) that Sōseki asks: 'How is man to escape from his own sense of isolation and purposelessness?' And it is in *Kokoro* that he finally gives the only answer he knows."[34]

About ten days before the lecture on individualism, Sōseki wrote to a young friend that he believed "death to be man's last and greatest happiness," and it was also at this time that he wrote, with reference to an episode involving a suicidal woman, "Death is more precious than life."[35] In both instances, however, he rejected suicide as an answer to life's problems, and, like Sensei, whose escape from life came only after the writing of his testament to the sincere, young student/narrator, Sōseki began drawing closer to the young "disciples" who gathered at his home, opening up to them in order to pass on something of his past experience, as he does with his audience at Gakushūin.[36] The resulting examination of his formative years emerged in many of the sketches in the essay series "Within My Glass Doors" ("Garasudo no uchi") (January–February 1915) and in the novel *Grass on the Wayside* (*Michikusa*) (June–September 1915), whose protagonist, Kenzō, learns from the ghosts of his past that beneath the "veneer" of his modern education, he shares more with other people than he had supposed.[37]

Finally, however, Kenzō is not comforted by the realization of his collective identity, any more than Daisuke in the novel *And Then* can content himself with rusticating in the cool shadows of his father's feudal heritage, or the artist in *The Three-Cornered World* (*Kusamakura*) (1906) can linger in the passionless, dehumanized world of eastern aestheticism. Determined commentators have been able to discover Sōseki's ultimate answer to the problem of alienation in only one place: the unwritten chapters of *Light and Darkness* (*Meian*), the novel he left unfinished at the time of his death in 1916.

Among Sōseki's disciples, Komiya Toyotaka was foremost in popularizing the idea that, after his brush with death in 1910, Sōseki was turning away from individualism to a more characteristically Eastern stance which he epitomized as *sokuten kyoshi* ("Follow heaven, abandon the self"). This view was exposed as all but groundless by Etō Jun in his brilliantly iconoclastic *Natsume Sōseki*, but the Japanese urge to find a sage in every great artist has kept the myth alive.[38]

Nowhere in his works do we find Sōseki preaching a passive acceptance of the world or holding out the possibility of a saving union with nature. Even where he adopts Zenlike terminology in discussing the function of literature, Sōseki envisions a mystical union of individual minds—the writer's and the reader's—in a successful work of fiction, not—as was the tendency in some Zen-influenced naturalist theory—a union between the author and the natural object of his observation.[39] The best comfort men could hope for was a momentary union of separate minds, and if, as *The Wayfarer* concludes, perfect bridges can never be built from one mind to another, the only alternative—obliteration of mind (or the "succession of consciousness, which is life") was never a real alternative for Sōseki, either in his fiction or his life.[40]

Although his battle with the ego is presented on a heroic scale, comparable in gravity to the tumultuous events that brought the great Meiji period itself to a close, Sensei is not to be seen as a model, any more than Sōseki thought people should attempt to emulate General Nogi. Sensei was one of those who, "while they hold their own egos in the highest esteem, . . . make no allowance for other people's egos." He is so obsessed with his own loneliness and guilt that he makes no allowance for his wife's equivalent capacity for suffering. To him, she is not an individual on a par with himself but "a pure, spotless thing" to be protected from the ugly truth.[41] What is missing in Sensei is the one quality that Sōseki tried to impress on his young audience: that recognition of the individuality of others that distinguishes individualism from egoism and gives it an ethical foundation.

It is said that there was a military man at Gakushūin who had come prepared to be outraged by Sōseki's advocacy of individualism but who left the hall pleased and relieved after Sōseki explained what he had meant by "my individualism," in contrast to the term that had been receiving so much attention.[42] Individualism was not the antisocial stance that most Japanese assumed (and still assume) *kojinshugi* to be. And while Sōseki honestly warned his young listeners of the loneliness experienced by the individual who stands apart from the group, he did not hesitate to affirm the importance to them of taking that step.

Notes

1. The original titles, with abbreviations, dates, and places of the lectures are "Dōraku to shokugyō" (DS, Akashi, August 13), "Gendai Nihon no kaika" (GNK, Wakayama, August 15), "Nakami to keishiki" (NK, Sakai, August 17), "Bungei to dōtoku" (BD, Osaka, August 18), and "Watakushi no kojinshugi" (WK, Tokyo, November 25, 1914). All passages translated or referred to here

are based on texts contained in *Sōseki zenshū* (SZ), 17 vols (Iwanami shoten, 1974), 11: 295–388, 431–63. The two other lectures that Sōseki revised for publication, "Bungei no tetsugakuteki kiso" (The philosophical foundations of literature) (1907) and "Sōsakka no taido" (The attitude of the creative writer) (1908), are also in this volume, pp. 30–183. Unrevised stenographic notes of five other lectures can be found in SZ 16: 369–433.

2. Oka Yoshitake, "Nichiro sensō-go ni okeru atarashii sedai no seichō," Part I (*Shisō*, February 1967), pp. 137–40. The term "festive" comes from the opening line of Tanizaki Jun'ichirō's 1911 story, "Hōkan."

3. On the repressive Katsura years, see my *Injurious to Public Morals: Writers and the Meiji State* (Seattle: University of Washington Press, 1984).

4. He was also concerned both that he had refused a similar request three years earlier and that he had accepted a private invitation to lecture in Nagano that June. See Komiya Toyotaka, *Natsume Sōseki*, 3 vols. (Iwanami shoten, 1953), 3:115. Other biographical information has been derived from Ara Masahito, *Zōho kaitei: Sōseki kenkyū nenpyō*, ed. Odagiri Hideo (Shūeisha, 1984).

5. Ara, pp. 654–55. The four lectures plus "Bungei no tetsugakuteki kiso" and "Sōsakka no taido" comprised a volume of Sōseki's lectures that appeared in 1913 under the title of *Shakai to jibun* (Society and self). Ara, p. 740.

6. DS, SZ 11:296.

7. GNK, SZ 11:320.

8. NK, SZ 11:344.

9. Literally, as if the *naniwabushi* singer Kumoemon (1873–1916) had blown into town for a show. NK, SZ 11:346. On Kumoemon, see SZ 8:61.

10. BD, SZ 11:372.

11. See, for example, the laughter noted in SZ 16:400.

12. DS, SZ 11:317.

13. NK, SZ 11:359.

14. DS, SZ 11:310.

15. DS, SZ 11:312. Cited in my *Injurious to Public Morals: Writers and the Meiji State*, p. 73.

16. DS, SZ 11:313.

17. DS, SZ 11:314.

18. DS, SZ 11:316–17.

19. DS, SZ 11:307–10. Cooking *tamago-dōfu* is, in fact, a rather complicated procedure.

20. "Matsumoto no hanashi" SZ 5:308. Translated by Kingo Ochiai and Sanford Goldstein as *To the Spring Equinox and Beyond* (Rutland: Tuttle, 1985); see p. 291.

21. Diary, May 30, 1909, SZ 13:389. Sōseki also names Itō and Ōkuma among those attending this gathering at the International Press Association.

22. DS, SZ 11:308, 309. On Sōseki's refusal of the doctorate and his critique of the Committee on Literature, see my *Injurious to Public Morals*, pp. 195–98, 201–205.

23. NK, SZ 11:363–4.

24. BD, SZ 11:382–83.

25. BD, SZ 11:384, 387. Sakaguchi Ango would find it necessary to make essentially the same argument in 1946. See my "From Wholesomeness to Decadence: The Censorship of Literature under the Allied Occupation," *Journal of Japanese Studies* 11:1 (1985), pp. 76–80.

26. NK, SZ 11:363. Notice that the "general mass" *(ippan no)* of students and citizens *(jinmin)* is being contrasted to "women" almost as if they constituted separate ethnic groups.

27. I have chosen to translate Sōseki's *kaika* as "civilization" for several reasons, not the least of which is the rich ambiguity of the English term. Webster's Ninth Collegiate defines civilization both as "a relatively high level of cultural and technological development . . . the culture characteristic of a particular time or place" and as "the process of becoming civilized." Sōseki emphasizes frequently that he is talking about a dynamic process ("Civilization is the process of the manifestation of human vitality / Kaika wa ningen-katsuryoku no hatsugen no keiro de aru," 11:324), but he uses *kaika* in the more static sense as well.

For Sōseki and his audience, *kaika* had the additional association with early Meiji *bunmei-kaika*, that officially promoted process of Westernization intended to bring Japan on a par with the civilized imperialistic powers of the West. "Accepting the Western concept of progress as expounded by Buckle and Guizot, the more Western-oriented among Japan's leaders assumed that their people had reached a level of semi-civilization in their advance from savagery to civilization. Moreover, if Japan were to achieve the prosperity and strength necessary for the nation to compete on equal terms with the West, they believed it essential to raise the Japanese people to the level of civilization and enlightenment achieved by the West" (William Reynolds Braisted, tr., *Meiroku Zasshi: Journal of the Japanese Enlightenment* [Cambridge: Harvard University Press, 1976], pp. 18–19). *Bunmei-kaika* (sometimes *kaika-bunmei*) was originally a more-or-less arbitrary translation for the English phrase "civilization and enlightenment." Indeed, *bunmei*, with its bright *mei* character, might have been a more fitting term for "enlightenment" than for "civilization," while *kaika* ("opening-changing"), with its connotation of progress, seems closer to the dynamic sense of "civilization." Carmen Blacker translates *bunmei-kaika* as "civilization" and restricts "enlightenment" to *keimō*. See her *Japanese Enlightenment: A Study of the Writings of Fukuzawa Yukichi* (Cambridge University Press, 1964), esp. pp. 34–35, 146.

In any case, when Sōseki used the term *kaika* in his fiction forty years later, it was as an essentially interchangeable synonym for his more frequently invoked *bunmei*, with the added sense of "development" or "progress." (See Kindai sakka yōgo kenkyūkai and Kyōiku gijutsu kenkyūjo, eds., *Sakka yōgo sakuin: Natsume Sōseki*, 15 vols. [Kyōikusha, 1986], 7:679, 854, 5:582, 10:175, 11:342, 415, 15:259, 1196, etc.) Thanks to Al Craig for some timely help here.

28. Kuroda Shigejirō and Tsuchidate Naganori, *Meiji gakusei enkaku shi* (Kin-kōdō, 1907), p. 1189.

29. Letter of November 9. SZ 15:409, 413.

30. Carol Gluck, *Japan's Modern Myths: Ideology in the Late Meiji Period* (Princeton University Press, 1985), p. 227. On the Meiji funeral, see pp. 213–27 and *Injurious to Public Morals*, pp. 219–24.

31. Ara, p. 788. D.T. Suzuki, when a Gakushūin professor, also published in the magazine. For a stimulating discussion of the subsequent publication of "My Individualism" and the possible political implications thereof, see Takayoshi Matsuo, "A Note on the Political Thought of Natsume Sōseki in his Later Years," in Bernard Silberman and H.D. Harootunian, eds., *Japan in Crisis* (Princeton University Press, 1974), pp. 67–85.

32. "Mohō to dokuritsu" (Imitation and independence, 1913), SZ 16:423.

33. SZ 6:41.

34. "The Implications of Sōseki's *Kokoro*," in *Monumenta Nipponica* 14 (1959), p. 357. For a discussion of the timing of "My Individualism," see Tamai Takayuki, " 'Watakushi no kojinshugi' zengo," in Nihon bungaku kenkyū shiryō kankōkai, ed., *Nihon bungaku kenkyū shiryō sōsho: Natsume Sōseki* (Yūseidō, 1970), pp. 236–44.

35. For the letter, see SZ 15:414–15. The episode with the woman is described in *Garasudo no uchi* (1915), sections 6–8, in SZ 8:425–32; quotation from p. 430. Both are cited by Tamai, p. 240.

36. Tamai, pp. 240–41.

37. SZ 6:483. See Edwin McClellan's translation, *Grass on the Wayside* (University of Chicago Press, 1969), p. 109.

38. See Etō's discussion of the Sōseki myth and *sokuten kyoshi* in *Natsume Sōseki* (Keisō shobō, 1965), pp. 5–15, or in any of the earlier or later editions, beginning with 1956. The first book-length study, *Natsume Sōseki*, by the disciple Akagi Kōhei (Shinchōsha, 1917) places great emphasis on *sokuten kyoshi* (the phrase is emblazoned on the cover), but it never mentions the existence of "My Individualism," drawing from the lecture only to the extent of paraphrasing Sōseki's account of his early job difficulties (pp. 89–91).

39. Compare "Bungei no tetsugakuteki kiso," SZ 11:90–92, 94–96, with Shimamura Hōgetsu, "Ima no bundan to shizenshugi," in *Waseda Bungaku* (June 1907); or Sōma Gyofū, "Bungei-jō shukaku ryōtai no yūkai," in ibid., (October 1907).

40. "Bungei no tetsugakuteki kiso," SZ 11:39; "Danpen" (ca. 1907), SZ 13:257.

41. Indeed, if we take the last, resonant line of the book literally—"*So long as my wife is alive*, I want you to keep everything I have told you a secret"—the narrator has released Sensei's testament (i.e., the novel) to the public only because the wife has followed her husband in death, just as Madame Nogi followed her own husband. The parallel is almost certainly intentional. One of the few characters in the novel with a personal name, Sensei's wife is called "Shizu." General Nogi's wife was known as "Shizuko." But where Shizuko died in keeping with traditional norms, Shizu would have died in response to her

husband's blindness to her individuality. I see the parallels between Shizu and Shizuko and the heavy emphasis in the last line as more persuasive than the remark in the first part of the book concerning Sensei's suffering, "To this day she does not know" (SZ 6:34; McClellan, p. 25), which would seem to imply that in the mind of the narrator the wife is still alive. Serialization occasionally led to inconsistencies in Sōseki's novels. In fact, Sōseki originally intended *Kokoro* to be a series of interrelated short stories in the manner of *Until the Spring Equinox*. Instead, the entire novel grew uncontrollably out of an episode called "Sensei's Testament" (Sensei no isho) and only on book publication did Sōseki divide it into three sections, the last of which is called "Sensei and His Testament" (Sensei to isho). (See Etō, *Asahi shōjiten: Natsume Sōseki*, p. 72). Of course, it can be argued that the "suppression" of personal names in the book was a means of justifying its release during Shizu's lifetime, or that the narrative presented by the nameless student is merely a privileged look into his mind and experience, which is not identical with the text published by Natsume Sōseki in 1914.

42. Komiya 3:221.

The Civilization of
Modern-day Japan

With the weather as hot as it is, I imagine the last thing anyone would want to do is pack into a hall and listen to a bunch of lectures. Or should I say *another* bunch of lectures: I understand you had a meeting like this just yesterday. And even if these talks came with guarantees that they wouldn't make you sick, it is possible to have too much of a good thing. So I appreciate your discomfort. Not that it's easy for me to be up here, either. Especially after the introduction my friend Mr. Maki[1] has just bestowed on me—practically an advertisement claiming that Sōseki's lectures are filled with all sorts of fascinating twists and turns. If I'm going to live up to his praise, I'll never be able to leave this podium until I've accomplished all the twists and turns I supposedly am here to fascinate you with, which puts me in a pretty uncomfortable position.

To tell you the truth, I had a little talk with Mr. Maki before coming to the hall this afternoon. It was something just between the two of us, but now I think I'll let you in on it, too. Not that it's a major secret. I was simply concerned that I might not have enough material to speak about for an extended period of time, so I asked Mr. Maki if he could stretch his talk a little. He assured me that he could talk as long as I wanted him to, which came as a tremendous relief to me. In other words, that praise of my lecture style you heard at the beginning of his speech was, in fact, the result of my own request that he extend his talk, and while I am very grateful for his remarks, I must admit that his praise has made things difficult for me. Let's face it: Anyone who has to make such a pitiful request as I did is not likely to favor you with twists and turns—such a person's lecture is going to forge straight ahead from beginning to end.

The simple fact is that I don't happen to have the kind of material with me that provides for twists, turns, thrills, chills, toil, moil, shakes, quakes, or anything else you might be hoping for. Not that I have climbed to the lecture stand completely blank, either. I *have* done some preparation. Of course it's true that I wasn't planning to come here to Wakayama. I had asked for the Kyoto-Osaka area, and the company added Wakayama to my itinerary—which worked out fine for me. I've been able to visit several tourist spots I had never seen before. While touring I give my lectures—no, wait, it's the other way around. I've had the opportunity to visit famous spots like Tamatsushima or Kimiidera in the course of presenting my lectures, so I couldn't even go sightseeing empty-handed. I had decided on the titles of my lectures before I ever left Tokyo.

This lecture is entitled "The Civilization of Modern-day Japan." Of course, it could just as well be called "The Modern-day Civilization of Japan." As long as it contains the words "civilization," "modern-day," and "Japan," the "of" can go just about anywhere. That is a simple matter. But if you ask me what we're supposed to *do* about this present-day civilization of ours, I won't have an answer for you. I merely plan to explain what "civilization" means and leave the rest to you.

Well, then, what do we mean by "civilization"? My guess is that you do not understand the civilization of modern-day Japan. By this I mean no disrespect toward you. None of us really understands it, and that includes me. I just happen to be in a position that gives me more time than you have to think about such matters, and this lecture allows me to share my thoughts with you. All of you are Japanese, and so am I; we live in the modern age, not the past or the future, and our civilization influences us all; it is obvious that the three words "modern," "Japan," and "civilization" bind us together inseparably. If, however, we remain unconscious of the civilization of modern-day Japan, or if we do not have a clear understanding of what it means, this can adversely affect everything we do. We will all be better off, I believe, if, together, we study this concept and help each other understand it.

Now, this may sound somewhat academic, but I believe that the first thing we must do is define the nature of "civilization" in general, unrestricted by such modifiers as "modern" and "Japan." We use the term everyday, we hear it all the time, but if we closely examine what it actually means, I think we will find that, as so often occurs with words, our definitions clash with each other or turn out to be far more vague than we would have imagined. So let us begin by defining the word "civilization."

Of course, when defining words, we have to be very careful or the results might be disastrous. A definition can cause the object it is defining to harden up like a papier-mâché figure. As much as I admire the skill and intelligence of scholars who can summarize complex characteristics with the utmost simplicity, I also find that I often deplore their stupidity when I see the definitions they come up with. It's as if they've sucked the life out of a thing and set it in a coffin, stiff with rigor mortis. Of course there are some definitions, like those in geometry, say, that are perfectly all right; a circle is a figure in which the distance from the center to the perimeter is equal at all points. Nothing wrong with that definition. It's a great convenience. But it works at all times and in all situations for only one reason, and that is because rather than describing round objects that actually exist in the world, it is a convention that merely establishes the *idea* of a circle, as it exists in the mind. Once we have constructed a figure according to our definition—be it a square, a triangle, or what have you—we may never have to change it as long as that figure exists only in the realm of geometry. But, unfortunately, there are very few circles or squares or triangles in the real world that remain unchanged through the past, the present, and the future. This is especially true of objects that possess the ability to move, for these are always accompanied by change. Today's square could become tomorrow's triangle, and tomorrow's triangle could be worn down the next day to a circle. If we are attempting to fashion a definition to explain something that actually exists (and not, as in geometry, trying to describe something according to a pre-existing definition), then we must anticipate in our definition that the object is going to change. Otherwise, we end up with a useless hide-bound rule. It would be as if we insisted that a still photograph of a train, captured in an instant as the train roars by, is a complete representation of a train, when of course it lacks the one quality most indispensable to a train: motion. Or there are the flies we sometimes see caught in amber. A fly in amber is undeniably a fly, but it is a fly that has neither life nor motion. And so it is with the definitions we often get from scholars. They may be as clear as the train in the photograph or the fly in the amber, but they are also clearly dead. That is why you must approach these definitions with caution. The one element they eliminate is the potential for change. If heaven suddenly decreed that a policeman, for example, was a man in a white uniform with a saber at his side, then an actual policeman would have a terrible time. He wouldn't be able to change into comfortable clothing when he went home at night. The poor fellow would have to carry around a sword with him all day, even in this hot weather. Or say that "a cavalry officer is a man on a horse." True enough, but he can't stay on that horse from the beginning to the end of the year. He will want to get down *some* time. Well, enough of these examples: there's no end to them. I'm supposed to be providing you with a definition of "civilization," and before I know it I've forgotten all about civilization and have gotten lost in the theory of definitions. I must apologize. But if we approach our definition of civilization with this degree of caution, we might be able to avoid some of the pitfalls scholars are prone to while still benefiting from the convenience that a definition can provide.

Now, back to "civilization." Civilization, like a train or a fly or a policeman or a cavalry officer, is something that moves.[2] We may be able to capture a single instant of it with a camera, but what we will have will not be civilization. The same is true of Wakanoura, which I toured yesterday. Some who have been to Wakanoura say the sea is rough there; others insist it is very calm. I don't know which view is correct. The contradiction derives from the simple fact that one person visited Wakanoura on a stormy day, the other when the sea was calm. Both are reporting what they saw, but what they tell us is neither false nor true. Such a definition is not entirely useless, but it can obviously be harmful. If possible, I'd like to avoid such harmful elements in my definition of "civilization." Unfortunately, though, if I'm too careful my definition will be vague. Still, vague though it may be, it will serve the purpose as long as it establishes the necessary distinctions. I'm sorry to burden you with these thoughts, but I seem to be living up after all to Mr. Maki's introduction, when he said that my talks resemble my writing: sometimes you're fed up with them by the time you go from the gate to the front door. Well, at last we have reached the front door, so let me now launch into my definition.

Civilization is the process of the manifestation of man's vital energies. This is how I define it. And I'm not the only one: you would define it that way, too. Not that this is a definition you will find in books. It is simply how I wish to define the word. And though it is my own definition, it isn't the least bit unusual. It *is*, however, extremely vague. I know you must think I'm trying to fool you, coming up with such a puny definition after that long, long lead-in, but, really, I must approach it this way to avoid becoming too vague. Well, then, "man's vital energies," as I said, continue manifesting themselves through time, giving form to civilization, and, as this process goes on, I want to, indeed, I *do* take note that it consists of two fundamentally different types of motion.

The first type of motion is positive, the second negative. I'm sorry this sounds so trite, but let me continue. The word "positive," when applied to the manifestation of man's vital energies, implies the consumption of those energies. And because the second type is a motion or a measure designed, conversely, to prevent the consumption of energy insofar as that is possible, I have called this type of motion "negative." Civilization, then, is what emerges when these two contradictory, incompatible types of motion become entangled with one another.

262

I suppose this is too abstract and you are having trouble following me, but I believe that my meaning will become clear soon enough. Depending on the interpretation one adopts, human life can be seen to have various meanings or to be merely incomprehensible, but insofar as it is a phenomenon that we can only construe to be, as I have said, the manifestation or the progress or the continuation of a vital force, then we can achieve a reasonably full understanding of the condition of our life as human beings if we minutely observe the ways in which this vital force responds to the stimuli of the outside world, and we can see that "civilization" is no more nor less than that which the mass of humanity has experienced together from the past to the present day.

Because the stimuli of the outside world are complex, the ways in which our vital energies respond to these stimuli are, of course, many and varied, but, as I see it, they can be boiled down to two fundamental responses. One is to conserve our vitality and use as little of it as possible whenever a stimulus impinges on us; the other is to take it on ourselves to seek out desirable stimuli and to attain pleasure by consuming as much vitality on these stimuli as we can. For the sake of convenience, we can call the former "vitality conserving actions," and the latter "vitality consuming contrivances."

Now, vitality conserving actions occur in response to the type of stimuli that can be labeled "duties," as we modern people ordinarily use the word. In traditional moral training—and in present-day education as well—it seems the development of an uncompromising determination in people to carry out their duties is encouraged, but this is simply a matter of public morality, instructing us that "from a moral point of view, such-and-such is necessary" or "society will be better off if you do so-and-so." Once we have observed the manifestation of man's vital energies, however, the general principle governing any single act of duty within that system requires us to view it as I have suggested. We all have a strong and constant desire to do our duty, and after we have done our duty we always feel very good about it. But if we dig beneath the surface and examine ourselves honestly, we would find that what we really would like to do is to escape the shackles of duty and become free, to take it easy and reduce as much as possible the volume of work that is forced on us by others. That is the true desire that lurks in our hearts, and it is precisely that desire which takes the form of contrivances to conserve our vital energies and constitutes one of the great motive forces of what we call civilization.

In contrast to this negative struggle to conserve our vital energies is the positive desire to consume them in accordance with our own wishes, and this desire comprises the other half of civilization. As the world advances, of course, the ways in which this desire manifests itself increase in complexity, but, simply stated, it is something that arises in response to those stimuli commonly known as pastimes. Of course, everyone knows what these are. Fishing or billiards or *go* or hunting: many different pastimes give us pleasure. We gladly consume our energies on these activities without being forced to do so by others, entirely on our own initiative. Advancing a step, this mentality leads to literature and science and philosophy. Some rather weighty activities are obviously nothing more than manifestations of the pursuit of enjoyment.

In sum, then, I believe that this infinitely complex phenomenon we call civilization arises from the advancement, entanglement, and ongoing change of these two parallel mentalities: the conservation of our vital energies as a negative response to the stimulus of duty, and the consumption of our vital energies as a positive response to the stimulus of pleasurable pastimes. The results are immediately apparent if we witness the state of the society in which we ourselves live. The conservation of energy is obvious in the ways we contrive to labor as little as possible, to accomplish the maximum amount of work in the minimum amount of time. These contrivances take amazing shapes: not only trains and steamships, but the telegraph, the telephone, and the automobile—all of which are, finally, nothing more than conveniences developed from an unabashed desire to avoid effort. Suppose someone tells you to run an errand from here in Wakayama over to Wakanoura: you're going to try to get out of it if possible. If you can't get out of it, you're going to go there the easiest way you know how and come back as soon as you can. You want to avoid as much physical exertion as you possibly can. And so, inevitably, the rickshaw is born. You want something better, so you get a bicycle. You insist on more, and the bicycle becomes a streetcar, which then becomes an automobile or an airplane in conformance with the laws of nature.

Despite these laws, however, there may well come a day—perhaps two or even three days—in the year when the desire for enjoyment takes over and you decide that you feel like walking instead of taking the streetcar or making a phone call. You purposely seek out the physical exertion. The extravagance of those daily walks we take belongs among the positive uses we make of our lives and thus belongs to this category of the consumption of vital energy. If the order to walk happens to come during one of those times when our desire for enjoyment has taken over, that is a fortunate coincidence, but most of the time things don't work out so well and the order comes when we aren't in the mood for walking. So we must find a way to complete the task without walking. And thus the visit becomes a letter, or the letter becomes a telegram, and the telegram becomes a phone call. In other words, these marvelous devices are but the sudden transformation of some fairly low-level human instincts: Faced with the need to perform some task in the interest of survival, our first reaction is to try to get by without doing it as long as we can go on living to our own satisfaction. Or else we react in anger: "Get out of here! Life's too short, I'm not going to break my back!" The next thing we know, we have the telephone. Like magic.

Thanks to this kind of magic, distances are shortened, time is diminished, bother is eliminated, all compulsory effort is reduced to a minimum, then reduced again, and before we find out how far we can push this process, along comes the opposite, "energy-consuming" impulse, the desire for enjoyment, urging us to do exactly as we please, and this, too, goes on and on, developing naturally, advancing without a moment's intermission.

The moralists may grumble about the development of our desire for enjoyment, but that is strictly an ethical question, not a practical one. The simple fact is that the impulse to find ways to consume our energies by doing what pleases us keeps working around the clock, developing without a break. Only the existence of society causes a man to have compulsory actions thrust upon him, but give that man his freedom and he will inevitably try to consume his mental powers, his physical powers, on stimuli that please him because it is perfectly natural for him to operate from an egocentric standpoint.

Now, of course, to consume one's powers freely in response to preferred stimuli doesn't necessarily mean behaving badly. Women are not the only source of enjoyment in this world. Doing what you want to do takes in the whole range of civilization. If you like to draw, you'll spend as much time as you can drawing. If you like to read books, you'll spend all the time you can reading.

Let's say, for example, that there's a fellow who likes scholarly pursuits. He spends all of his time in the study, pasty-faced, completely unaware of how his parents feel about this. And they can't figure him out. The father has scrimped and saved all his life to pay the boy's tuition, and now that the son has graduated he wants him to start bringing home a salary so that he can retire soon. The boy, meanwhile, couldn't care less about such practical matters as making a living. He stays hunched over his desk all day, scowling at his books and spouting daydreams about discovering the great truths of the universe. What the father envisioned as training for a livelihood, the son sees as scholarship for enjoyment.

Thus we see that no moralist can obstruct the vital energies we devote to enjoyment. After a moment's reflection, even the most industrious soul—one who feels that enjoyment has no right to exist in these brutally competitive times—will be forced to recognize the various forms in which these vital energies become manifest in our world.

Last night I stayed in Wakanoura, where I saw many interesting sights: the drooping pine trees, the shrine of Ieyasu, the Kimiidera Temple, but I was especially impressed with the elevator that goes to the top of Ishiyama. That is a fairly high hill, and the sign claimed that the elevator is the highest in the Orient: 200 feet above sea level. It carried an endless stream of tourists up and down Ishiyama from the rear of the hotel. I must admit that I was one of those who rode to the top in the steel cage, like a bear at the zoo. But make no mistake: that elevator isn't there out of necessity, nor is it a particularly important machine. It's there for fun. It goes up and down, nothing more. Without a doubt, it is a manifestation of the desire for enjoyment, aided perhaps by a combination of curiosity and a desire for publicity, but, in any case, it has precious little to do with life's basic necessities. This is just one example, but I think everyone will agree that the number of such useless luxuries is going to increase as civilization advances. Not only will there be more of these idle luxuries, but they will become more precise and specialized with each passing day, like a series of concentric circles inside a big funnel, each smaller and deeper than the previous one. At the same time, they will develop in directions that no one ever imagined before, the breadth of their coverage becoming greater year by year.

In any case, we have these two intertwining processes: one involving inventions and mechanisms that spring from the desire to conserve our labor as much as possible, and the other involving amusements that spring from the wish to consume our energies as freely as possible. As these two intertwine like a textile's warp and woof, combining in infinitely varied ways, the result is this strange, chaotic phenomenon we know as our modern civilization.

If this is what we mean by "civilization," a strange paradox arises, a phenomenon that at first glance seems rather odd, but whose truth everyone must recognize. Why, we might ask, has man followed the stream of civilization from its beginnings to the present day, manifesting these two types of energy? The answer is simply that we are born that way. In other words, everything we have today is the result of these inborn tendencies of ours. We could not have survived if we had simply stood by with our arms folded. Pushed along from one thing to the next, we have toiled and toiled for thousands of years, finally developing to the point where we find ourselves today.

As a result of the contrivances wrought by these two kinds of vital energy from ancient times to the present, life should be far easier for us than it was for our ancestors. But is life, in fact, easier for us? I would have to say that it is not. For you and for me, life is enormously painful. You and I both know that we live with pain no less extreme than that which was felt by the men of old. Indeed, the more civilization progresses, the more intense the competition becomes, only adding to the difficulty of our lives. True enough, thanks to the violent struggle of the two energies, civilization has attained its present triumph, but "civilization" in this sense means only that our general standard of living has risen; it does not mean that the pain of existence has been softened for us to any extent. Just as academic competition is equally painful for both the grammar school child and the university student, though at different levels, there may be a huge difference between people in the old days and people now where energy-consuming and energy-conserving mechanisms are concerned, but when it comes to relative degrees of happiness (or unhappiness), the anxieties and exertions that arise from the struggle for existence are no less for us today than they were for our ancestors. If anything, they may even be more painful. Back then it was a matter of life and death: if you didn't make the necessary exertions, you died and that was that. You did it because you had no choice. You didn't think about enjoyment; the means for seeking pleasure had not been developed. People were satisfied just to stretch out their legs or let their arms hang down: It was probably all the enjoyment they could hope for.

Today, we have long since transcended the problem of

life and death. Now, it's more a matter of life and life. I know that sounds funny, but by this I mean that now our most taxing problem is whether to live in circumstances A or in circumstances B. To cite an example of the energy-conservation type, competition now raises the question of whether a man is going to make a living by dragging a rickshaw around the streets or by grasping the steering wheel of an automobile. Whichever he chooses, this will not determine whether he lives or dies. The amount of labor involved, however, will certainly not be the same. He will sweat a lot more pulling that rickshaw. If he drives passengers around in an automobile (of course if he can afford an automobile, he won't have any need to drive passengers around), he can cover longer distances in shorter times. He doesn't have to exert himself physically. As a result of the conservation of vital energy, he has an easier job. In contrast to the old days, now that the automobile has been invented, the rickshaw will inevitably fall behind. Having fallen behind, the rickshaw will have to struggle to keep up.

In this way, when something appears on the horizon that is superior by virtue of its ability, however small, to conserve energy, and this provokes a wave of disruption, a phenomenon resembling a kind of low-pressure zone occurs in the civilization, and until its components return to a state of balance and proportion, the people of that civilization have no choice but to continue in restless motion. Indeed, it is their very nature to do so.

This wave of disturbance is the same when viewed from the perspective of the manifestation of the positive consumption of energy. Say, for example, a man is satisfied smoking his Shikishimas until he sees the next fellow enjoying Turkish cigarettes. He decides he wants those. He tries them, and in fact they do taste better, so now he feels that anyone who smokes Shikishimas is beyond the pale of humanity, and soon there's competition to see who is going to switch to the Turkish brand.

Simply put, people have a taste for luxury. The moralists are always warning us against extravagance, and that's all very well, I suppose, but if you stop and think about what a taste for luxury mankind has developed over the centuries, you know that such warnings are bound to fail because they fly in the face of nature.

Assuming, then, that the momentum of civilization consists of increasingly ferocious competition in both the positive and negative areas, it would appear that we have done our utmost over the ages to wring out some bit of wisdom, developing at last to where we are today, and yet it seems to me that the psychological pain that life thrusts upon us may be no more nor less than it was fifty or even a hundred years ago. Even with all the machines we have today to reduce our labors, even with all the means of amusement we now have for the free enjoyment of our vital energies, the pain of existence is far more intense than one would have imagined. Perhaps I would not be overstating the case to call the pain extreme. What else can we call it when we fail to appreciate the sheer fact of our having been born in an age of such vastly reduced labor and when the magnified means and scope of our amusements fail to arouse in us the appropriate sense of gratitude? This is the great paradox to which civilization has given birth.

And now the time has come to discuss the civilization of Japan. If civilization in general is as I have described it, and Japan's civilization is simply another example, that would pretty well take care of what I wanted to say, and I could end this lecture. Unfortunately, however, Japan's case is special and cannot be dispensed with so easily. Why not, you might ask. Well, explaining "why not" is exactly the point of this lecture. You will probably be shocked to learn that, after all this, we have just entered the front door and gotten only as far as the living room. But don't worry, it won't take much longer. The distance from the front door to the back door of this lecture will be surprisingly short. Long talks are tiring for the speaker, too, so I intend to wind this up as quickly as possible, in keeping with the law of the conservation of energy. I ask only a little more of your patience.

So, then, the question facing us is this: How does the civilization of modern-day Japan differ from civilization in general as I have been discussing it? Simply stated, Western civilization (that is, civilization in general) is internally motivated, whereas Japan's civilization is externally motivated. Something that is "internally motivated" develops naturally from within, as a flower opens, the bursting of the bud followed by the turning outward of the petals. Something is "externally motivated" when it is forced to assume a certain form as the result of pressure applied from the outside.

Western civilization flows along as naturally as clouds or a river, which is not at all what we see in the case of Japan since the Restoration and the opening of relations with the West. Of course, all countries are influenced, to some degree, by their neighbors, and Japan is no exception: We have certainly not developed separately, relying exclusively on our own vital energies. There have been periods in our history when we were profoundly under the sway of foreign cultures—of Korea, for example, or China. But overall, viewed in the long course of events, we can say with some confidence that we have advanced to where we are today with a more or less internally motivated civilization. Certainly, Japan had never experienced any foreign influence as intense as that of the sudden influx of Western culture. There we were, slumbering for two hundred years in an atmosphere of sealed ports and foreign exclusion, when it jolted us awake.

From that time on, Japan's civilization began twisting and turning dramatically. The impact of the West was so great that we simply had no choice but to continue twisting and turning. To rephrase it in terms I used earlier, we were a country that had until then developed according to our own internal motivation. But then we suddenly lost our ability to be self-centered[3] and were confronted by a situation in which we could not survive unless we began taking orders from the external force that was pushing us around at will. Nor was this by any means a temporary situation. The year is Meiji 44, after all: We've been bracing ourselves for close to fifty years. And not only have we been pushed and shoved along from that day to this, but unless we continue to be pushed along for years to come—perhaps forever—Japan will not be able to survive as Japan. What else can we call ourselves but externally motivated?

The reason for this is obvious. If I may return to the definition of civilization that I formulated earlier at such length, Western civilization, this civilization we first collided with some fifty years ago and are incapable of avoiding contact with today, possesses labor-conserving means many times more powerful than our own, and it is equipped, too, with the ability to utilize its vital energies in the area of amusement and enjoyment many times more actively than we can. As a rough illustration, say Japan has gone along developing by internal motivation until, at long last, it brings its civilization to a complexity level of ten. We've just barely managed to reach that point when, all of a sudden, out of the clear blue sky, a civilization that has advanced to a complexity level of twenty or even thirty

273

comes along and crashes into us. Because of the pressure this new civilization exerts on us, we have no choice but to develop in unnatural ways. And so the civilization of Japan today does not plod along at its own steady pace, but instead it leaps ahead from one desperate round to the next. Lacking the freedom to climb the stairway of civilization one step at a time, we take a stitch here and a stitch there with the biggest needle we can find. For every ten feet of ground we cover, we touch down on only one, virtually missing the other nine. Now, perhaps, you see what I mean by the term "externally motivated."

What kind of psychological impact does such an externally motivated civilization have on us? Well, it's a rather strange one. I hesitate to introduce difficult material into this lecture, which is not supposed to be concerned with psychology, but please bear with me for a short while: I will just touch on the necessary points briefly and then return to the topic at hand.

Our minds are constantly on the move. Now you're listening to my lecture, and I'm up here talking to you, and we are both aware of this. Our minds are active, working. This is called "consciousness." Now, if we were to take one unit of consciousness—say one minute, as measured in terms of time—remove it from this constantly moving larger consciousness and examine it, we would find that this unit, too, is moving. This movement is not something that I have discovered; I am simply introducing to you some ideas written by Western scholars that I have found convincing. In any case, whether we examine one minute of consciousness or thirty seconds' worth in terms of the clarity with which the contents are reflected in the mind, we find that nothing remains fixed in the same spot, with the same level of intensity as everything else, unaffected by the passage of time. The contents of our minds are in motion. And with this motion bright areas and dark areas are formed. If we were to represent this ebb and flow on a graph, it would not require a straight line but rather an arc.

My explanations may be making this more complicated rather than simplifying things but, after all, scholars are supposed to make the comprehensible incomprehensible, while laymen are supposed to appear as though they have understood perfectly what they in fact find incomprehensible, so we are equally at fault.

Now, let me explain this business about the arc, or the curve, or whatever we wish to call it. Say that we catch sight of an object, a certain amount of time is required for us to grasp fully what this object is. Our consciousness starts at a low point, passes through a certain period of time, rises to a peak, comes into focus, and then the moment arrives when we think, "Aha, it's this!" As we continue to look at the object, our visual perception begins to blur, and our consciousness, which had for the moment been turning upward, heads down again and begins to darken.

You'll see what I mean if you experiment a bit. No, you won't need any apparatus for this "experiment." It's simply a matter of noticing what goes on in your head. Consider reading, for example. We have three words before us, call them Word A, Word B, and Word C, written in that order, so of course we comprehend them in that order. While our minds focus clearly on A, B has yet to enter our consciousness. When B begins to mount the stage of awareness, A has already begun to blur and to move gradually toward the threshold. The same thing happens when B gives way to C, and so on.

Scholars have used this model to dissect consciousness over an extremely short period of time, but I believe that this dissection works not only for a minute of an individual's consciousness but can be applied to the collective consciousness of society in general, as well as to shorter periods of a day or a month, or to longer periods of a year or even ten years. For example, you, the audience, are a group of individuals sitting here now, listening to my lecture. Alright, maybe some of you aren't listening, but let's just say that you are. The consciousness of each individual member of the group (which is itself not an individual) is now focused clearly on the contents of my lecture. As the lecture increasingly occupies each of your minds, the events you experienced before you came here—the rain on the way that drenched your clothes, or the hot muggy weather that made getting here an ordeal—this consciousness begins to become more and more blurred and uncertain. And when the lecture ends and the cool breeze hits you as you step outside, your awareness of how good the breeze feels will occupy your minds and you'll forget all about this lecture—which is not a very comforting thought for me, but it's a fact, so there's nothing I can do about it. I can order you to keep my lecture in mind at all hours of the day and night, but no one can act so contrary to the natural functioning of the mind.

Now, if we examine the group's consciousness as a whole, I would conclude that there exists a clear consciousness that can encompass a long unit of time, be it a month, a year, or whatever, and that this consciousness ebbs and flows, moving in turn from one event to another. We all do this individually when we look back on our lives and discover distinct units of consciousness—our middle school years, say, or our university years: periods that stand out distinctly enough to have special names attached to them. A few years ago, in 1904 to 1905, the collective consciousness of the Japanese as a whole was focused exclusively on the Russo-Japanese War. Then came the period when we were occupied with a consciousness of the Anglo-Japanese Alliance. When, through induction, we thus expand the psychologists' analyses and apply them to the collective or long-term consciousness, we must conclude that the process of the development of man's vital energies—that is, civilization—progresses in waves, stringing one arc after another in a constantly advancing line. Of course, the number of waves thus traced is infinite, the length and height of each potentially different from all the others, but finally they must move along in order, wave A calling forth wave B, B calling forth C, and so on. Simply stated, the progress of civilization should be internally motivated. I am lecturing to you now, for example. Listening to me, you probably couldn't tell what I was getting at for the first ten minutes. Finally, after some twenty minutes, a theme began to take shape. After half an hour, things were warming up and maybe even getting a little interesting, but by about the fortieth minute your mind began to wander. After fifty minutes, you were bored, and when the first hour came, you were yawning. Well, perhaps it didn't go exactly as I'm describing it, but suppose that it did and I continued to talk relentlessly for two hours, three hours, or more. I would be asserting myself in opposition to the natural functioning of your minds and my lecture couldn't possibly succeed. It would fail because it would be an external force that had nothing whatsoever to do with your internal needs. I could shout myself hoarse at this podium, but you would have long since passed beyond the bounds of my lecture's demands. You would be wanting something to eat or to drink, not thinking about my lecture. Your own internal motivations would have taken over as a natural matter of course.

Now, after this lengthy explanation, I suppose I can

return to the civilization of modern-day Japan. The question facing us is whether or not Japan's civilization is advancing by means of internal motivation, tracing a natural motion from wave A to B to C. The answer, unfortunately, is that it is not, and that is the trouble. Because of external pressure, Japan has had to leap all at once from a barely attained complexity level of twenty to a level of thirty in the two great areas of energy conservation and energy consumption. The country is like a man who has been snatched up by a flying monster. The man clings desperately to the monster, afraid of being dropped, hardly aware of the course he is following.

In the normal order of events, wave A of a civilization yields to wave B only when people have drunk their fill of A and have become satiated, at which time new desires arise from within and a new wave develops. A new stage of life opens before us after we have tasted the old one to the full, both the good and the bad, the bitter and the sweet. Then we leave the first wave behind without regret, as a snake sheds its skin. And then whatever difficulties we may experience with the new wave, at least we never feel that we are dressing up in borrowed clothing, putting on a false front. But the waves that govern Japan's present civilization roll in on us from the West. We who ride these waves are Japanese, not Westerners, and so we feel out of place with each new surge, like uninvited guests. There is no question of our understanding the new wave, for we have not had time to appreciate the features of the old one that we have cast off so reluctantly. It is like sitting at a dinner table and having one dish after another set before us and then taken away so quickly that, far from getting a good taste of each one, we can't even enjoy a clear look at what is being served.

A nation, a people that incurs a civilization like this can

278

only feel a sense of emptiness, of dissatisfaction and anxiety. There are those who gloat over this civilization of ours as if it were internally motivated, but they are wrong. They may think that they represent the height of fashion, but they are wrong. They are false and shallow, like boys who make a great show of enjoying cigarettes before they even know what tobacco tastes like. This is what the Japanese must do in order to survive, and this is what makes us so pitiful.

Here is an example that may not come under the heading of "civilization," but just look at how we socialize with Westerners—always according to *their* rules, never ours. Why, then, do we not just stop socializing with them? Sadly enough, we have no choice in the matter. And when two unequal parties socialize, they do so according to the customs of the stronger. One Japanese may make fun of another for not knowing the proper way to hold a knife or fork, but such smug behavior only proves that the Westerners are stronger than we are. If we were the stronger, it would be a simple matter for us to take the lead and make them imitate us. Instead, we must imitate them. And because age-old customs cannot be changed overnight, all we can do is mechanically memorize Western manners—manners which, on us, look ridiculous.

All of this talk about silverware and manners may seem very trivial and have nothing to do with civilization, but that is exactly my point: everything we do—every trivial little act—is not internally, but externally motivated. This tells us that the civilization of modern-day Japan is superficial: it just skims the surface. Of course, I am not saying that this is true of absolutely everything. Such radical pronouncements should be avoided in dealing with complex problems, but the fact remains that no matter how much we view our civilization in our own favor, we cannot escape the conclusion that a part—perhaps the greatest part—of our civilization is superficial. This is not to say that we must put a stop to it. There is really nothing we can do about it. We must go on skimming the surface, fighting back our tears.

You may wonder, then, whether it is finally impossible for us to cease being the child carried along on a grown-up's back, for us to forge ahead on our own through all the proper stages of development. I would answer no: it is not impossible. But if the Japanese were able to condense into ten years all the developments that it took the West a hundred years to accomplish—to do this in such a way as to avoid the accusation of hollowness and convince all onlookers that the progress was internally motivated—the results would be devastating. Even a beginner in mathematics could see that our vital energies would have to increase tenfold in order for us to accomplish a hundred years' worth of experience in a tenth of the time without skimming the surface.

I can illustrate this point most easily by referring to the academic world. Let us suppose that, through the forty-odd years of educational efforts that we have expended since the Restoration, we were able to arrive at the high degree of academic specialization that the Westerners reached after a hundred years, and that we were able to do this entirely through internal motivation and without re-lying on any half-digested theories imported from the West, passing through a natural series of stages from theory A to B to C, entirely as a result of our own original research. If the Westerners, whose mental and physical powers far surpass ours, took a hundred years to get where they are now, and we were able to reach that point in less than half that time (forgetting for the moment the difficul-ties they faced as pioneers), then we could certainly boast of an astounding intellectual accomplishment, but we would also succumb to an incurable nervous breakdown; we would fall by the wayside gasping for breath. And this is in no way farfetched. If you stop and think about it, a nervous breakdown is exactly what most university professors end up with after ten years of hard work. The healthy ones are merely phony scholars, or, if that's putting it too bluntly, let's just say that succumbing to a nervous breakdown is more or less to be expected in that profession. I use scholars here simply because their example is so easy to grasp, but I believe the logic can be applied to all areas of civilization.

I said earlier that, for all its progress, civilization favors us with so little peace of mind that, if we consider the added anxieties thrust on us by competition and the like, our happiness is probably not very different from what it was in the stone age. If we add to that what I just now said about the nervous breakdown we experience from trying not to skim the surface as our civilization is forced to change mechanically because of the unique situation Japan now finds itself in, we Japanese come out looking pretty miserable, or—shall I say?—pathetic: our situation is simply appalling. That is my only conclusion. I have no advice to give, no remedies to suggest, because I do not believe there is anything anyone can do about it. I am simply lamenting the sad fact of it all.

Perhaps it would have been better not to have arrived at any conclusion rather than to have reached one so utterly pessimistic. The truth is often something we long for until we get it, and then we wish we didn't have it.[4] Guy de Maupassant wrote a story that illustrates this point. A man grew tired of his common-law wife, so he left her a note and went into hiding at a friend's place. Furious, she hunted him down and burst in on him, shouting at the top of her lungs. He tried to offer her money in return, but she dashed it to the floor, and screamed, "I didn't come here for this. If you really mean to leave me, I'll kill myself. I'll jump from that window and die." They were on the third or fourth floor. The man smiled and gestured toward the window, all but inviting her to make good on her threat—which she did without a moment's hesitation. The fall didn't kill her, but it left her crippled for life. Confronted with such proof of the woman's true feelings, the man became filled with remorse for the way he had doubted her fidelity and for treating her as if she were a common prostitute. He took her back and devoted himself to caring for his ailing wife.

So much for the plot of de Maupassant's story.[5] Now, if the man hadn't let his doubts get out of hand, this disastrous turn of events might never have taken place, but his suspicions probably would have remained unresolved for the rest of his life. Although it's true that only by taking things to such extremes was he able to verify her sincerity, I'm sure that with the benefit of hindsight after such an irreversible tragedy he would have far preferred to keep the woman whole than to have gained absolute certainty at such a cost. And the same applies to the true nature of Japan's modern civilization. As long as it remains obscure, we feel we want to study it, but when the naked truth about it emerges, we feel we would have been better off with our former ignorance.

Assuming that my analysis is correct, we can only view Japan's future with pessimism. There seem to be fewer of us nowadays ridiculous enough to boast of Mt. Fuji to foreigners, but we do hear many people proclaiming that victory over Russia made Japan a first-class power.[6] I suppose one can make such claims if one is an incurable optimist. But what are we to do? How are we to cut our way through this desperate situation? As I said before, I have no clever solutions. The best answer I can come up with is that we probably should go on changing through internal motivation while trying our best to avoid a nervous breakdown.

I apologize for having exposed you so mercilessly to the bitter truth as I see it and for having given you something unpleasant to think about, if only for an hour or so, but I hope that you will appreciate the fact that I have shared with you today my own most deeply held opinions, based on substantial evidence and on my fullest intellectual efforts, and that this will allow you to forgive the weak points in my presentation.

Notes

1. Maki Kanjirō (Hōrō), editorialist and chief of the correspondence section, Osaka *Asahi Shimbun*. SZ 11:674.

2. For a discussion of images of movement and stillness in Sōseki's fiction, see my translation, *Sanshiro, A Novel by Natsume Soseki* (Seattle: University of Washington Press, 1977), p. 237.

3. Sōseki here uses one of his most deliberately controversial terms for personal independence in drawing the parallel between individual and national independence, *jiko-hon'i*, a word that today still retains its pejorative connotations as a critique of egoism (which is also true, though to a lesser extent, of *kojinshugi*, or "individualism").

4. To illustrate the ineradicable pain caused by knowledge of a secret better left hidden, Sōseki has a character in *Until After the Spring Equinox* give the gist of this lecture as delivered by "a certain scholar." "Matsumoto no hanashi": 5, SZ 5:308.

5. This is a reasonably accurate summary of "Le Modèle" (1883).

6. This echoes a conversation in the opening chapter of *Sanshirō* (1908). SZ 4:21; translation, p. 15.

My Individualism

This is my first visit to the famous Gakushūin. I had always imagined the campus to be out here somewhere, but I was never quite sure—until today.

As Mr. Okada mentioned in his introduction, he originally asked me to speak to you last spring. I was unable to oblige him at the time—exactly why this was so, Mr. Okada seems to remember better than I, and I trust that his explanation has been sufficient. In any case, I had to refuse. Rather than simply turn the invitation down, however, I volunteered to deliver the next lecture in the series and learned that it was scheduled for October. After some calculating, I concluded that I should be able to get something together, what with so many months left to go, and I accepted. Unfortunately, however—or perhaps fortunately—I became ill and spent the entire month of September in bed.[1] I was up by October, it is true, but I was still too unsteady for lecturing. On the other hand, I could hardly ignore my promise, and the thought that they were going to be after me any day now was a constant source of anxiety.

Soon the unsteadiness went away, but the end of October came with no communication from Gakushūin. I had not sent word of my illness, but a few of the newspapers had apparently carried the item, which led me to the comforting belief that the Gakushūin people had realized the problem and asked someone to give a lecture in my place. Then, all of a sudden, Mr. Okada showed up again—in boots, no less. Of course, the fact that it was raining that day may have had something to do with it. But there he was, having trekked in his rain boots all the way to my house in Waseda to announce that the lecture had been postponed to the end of November, at which time he hoped I would make good on my promise. Meanwhile, I had assumed that I had evaded my responsibility, and I was more than a little taken aback. But there was still over a month left and I thought I should be able to manage something. Again I agreed to give a talk.

One would think that from spring to October, or from the end of October to the twenty-fifth of November, I could have found plenty of time to organize a lecture of some kind. But I wasn't feeling well, and just thinking about a talk became burdensome. No, I simply wouldn't bother with the talk until the twenty-fifth of November, I decided, and then let it go day after day. At last, with barely three days left, I had a twinge of feeling that I had better think of something to talk about, but it was still such an unpleasant prospect that I spent the day painting.

Now, please don't think that I really know how to paint. I simply dashed off this little thing, stuck it to the wall, and then spent two or three days alone, staring vacantly at what I had done. Yesterday—I think it was—a friend came by and said he thought my picture was very good—no, not that the painting itself was good, but that it looked like something I must have done when I was in a very good mood. I told him he was all wrong: I had done the painting not because I was feeling good but because I was feeling bad. And I went on to explain my mood. Just as there are those who turn their overflowing happiness into paintings or calligraphy or books, there are others who take up the brush to create paintings or literature as a way to attain happiness. And when we see the results that spring from these two very different psychological states, oddly enough they are often identical. I won't go any deeper into this subject. It is just something I wanted to mention and has nothing to do with the main idea of my talk.

At any rate, there I was, passing the time looking at this funny painting and doing nothing to organize my lecture. And so the twenty-fifth arrived, today, the day I must appear to give my talk whether I liked it or not. I spent some time this morning trying to organize my thoughts, but it seems I am inadequately prepared. I must ask that you bear with me and not expect too much.

I do not know how long your club has been in existence, but I see nothing wrong with your practice of bringing in outsiders and having them lecture. On the other hand, it seems to me that you are not likely to hear the kind of entertaining lectures you would like, no matter whom you bring in. I suspect that what interests you is the novelty of someone from the outside.

Here is an ironic tale I heard from a *rakugo* storyteller. Once, two feudal lords were enjoying falconry near Meguro. After they had been galloping about for several hours, they became famished, but they had brought no food with them and had strayed away from their retainers. All they could do was demand something to eat at a nearby peasant's shack. Taking pity on them, the old farmer and his wife broiled some mackerel they happened to have on hand and served this with barley-rice—crude fare for such grand warriors. The lords enjoyed the meal enormously—so much so that the aroma of the fish lingered in their nostrils the next day, and they could hardly stop thinking about the wonderful flavor. One of the lords then invited the other for a mackerel dinner, much to the surprise of his retainers. There was no gainsaying the commands of the lord, however. The retainers ordered the cook to remove all of the mackerel's slender bones, marinate the fish in sweet *sake*, and roast it exactly so before serving it to the lord and his guest. This time, of course, the two men were not famished, and the ridiculous care with which the cook had prepared this odd dish had long since expunged any flavor of mackerel. After a few perfunctory pokes with their chopsticks, the two lords looked at each other and said, "If you want mackerel, you've got to go to Meguro."[2]

As I see it, your inviting me to speak to you, your willingness to listen after having been kept waiting from spring to late autumn—despite the fact that you are at the excellent Gakushūin and in constant contact with excellent teachers—exactly resembles the case of the two lords who, satiated with the finest delicacies, long to taste that mackerel from Meguro.

I see Professor Ōmori is here today.[3] Professor Ōmori and I graduated from the university at about the same time. Once, I remember, he complained to me that the students were not really listening to his lectures, that they were lacking in seriousness. He was not talking about Gakushūin students, I believe, but students at a private college. In any case, my reply to him then was rather impolite. I am embarrassed to repeat it here, but I said to him, "There's not a student anywhere in the world who would come running to hear *your* lectures." Professor Ōmori may well have misunderstood what I meant by that, so let me take this opportunity to correct any misunderstanding. When we were your age, or perhaps a little older, we were far less well behaved than you. It would not be too much of an exaggeration to say that we never listened to lectures. I speak from my own experience and observations, of course, and what I have to say may not apply to anyone outside my immediate acquaintance, but, looking back, I can't help thinking that my impression is quite accurate. Certainly in my own case, I looked docile enough, but I was not the type to pay attention to lectures. I did nothing but loaf.[4] With memories like these, I can't find it in me to criticize the earnest young men I see in school today, and it was merely this idea that I sought to convey to Professor Ōmori when I spoke to him so rashly. My purpose in coming here today was not to render an apology to Professor Ōmori, but now, in your presence, let me take the opportunity to do so.

Having strayed so far from the subject, I will now try to return to it.

You are all students at an excellent school under the constant guidance of excellent teachers, whose lectures—both specialized and general—you attend every day. And I would imagine, as I said before, that you have bothered to bring me here for a talk much as the two lords enjoyed the mackerel from Meguro: You want to take a bite of something new. But, in fact, I am sure the lectures of the professors you see every day, the men employed by Gakushūin, are of far greater value and interest than anything I might have to say. You know as well as I do that if I were a professor here, there would not be so many of you in the audience today, and the enthusiasm and curiosity with which you are listening to me now would not have been forthcoming.

The reason I have bothered to mention this at all is because, in fact, many years ago, I tried to become a Gakushūin instructor. No, I did not come looking for a job: A friend of mine here recommended me. Back then, I was the kind of dull-witted fellow who still didn't know what he wanted to do to make a living right up to the moment of graduation. Once you go out into the world, of course, the rent money does not come in while you wait with arms folded. I had to find a position for myself. And so, without considering whether I was in fact qualified to become an educator, I did as my friend advised and began to maneuver for an opening here. There was a rival applicant, but my friend assured me that I had nothing to worry about. Deciding that I was as good as hired, I went so far as to ask him how instructors were expected to dress. A morning coat would be essential, he told me. So before anything was decided, I had myself fitted for a morning coat—this, mind you, while I still had only the vaguest notion of where Gakushūin was located!

Well, the coat was finished soon enough, but the hoped-for position did not come to me. The other man was chosen to fill the post of instructor of English. I can't seem to recall his name—probably because I was not especially chagrined at the loss, but apparently he had just come back from studying in America. If, by some fluke, they had hired me instead of him, and if I had continued teaching here all these years, then I might never have received your courteous invitation or been given the opportunity to speak to you from on high like this. Indeed, look how long you have waited for me: this in itself is proof that you see me as a delicious Meguro mackerel only because I failed in my bid for a job here at Gakushūin![5]

I would now like to say a few words about what has happened to me since my failure to enter Gakushūin—not simply because it follows logically on what I have been saying, but because it is an essential part of my talk today.

I was turned down here, but I still had my morning coat. And I wore it—because I had nothing else to wear.

And where do you suppose I wore it? Finding a job was a very simple matter in those days, unlike the situation today. There was a shortage of people, and you could be sure of finding a fair number of openings no matter where you looked.[6] Even I had almost simultaneous offers from the First National Higher School and the Higher Normal School. To the faculty member who was negotiating for me with the Higher School, a former teacher of mine, I more or less said that I would accept their offer. Meanwhile, I was still giving noncommittal answers to the Normal School. As a result, I got myself into a very difficult situation. I suppose this was just what I deserved for such youthful irresponsibility, but the fact remains that I felt terrible. My former Higher School professor who was negotiating for me called me in and scolded me for putting him in such an awkward position. With a foolishly short temper to match my youth, I decided to turn down both offers, and I set about doing so.

But then a note arrived from President Kuhara of the Higher School, asking me to come and see him.[7] I hurried over to find there the President of the Normal School, Kanō Jigorō, and my former Higher School professor.[8] Everything had been decided, they said: I need feel no obligation toward the Higher School but should take the Normal School job. I had no choice but to accept the post. Secretly, however, I was greatly annoyed at the way things had turned out, for I did not think very highly of the Normal School, an opinion I know now to have been unjustified. I even attempted to convince President Kanō of my unworthiness. I insisted that I was unfit to teach at the Normal School if what he had said were true—that as a teacher I must be a model for the students.[9] But he went me one better: Hearing me decline with such simple honesty, he said, made him want me all the more. He refused to let me go. It had never crossed my mind to be so greedy as to hold both jobs at once, but in my immaturity I had managed nevertheless to cause everyone concerned a lot of needless difficulty. And so I ended up taking the job at the Normal School.

The fact was, however, that I had never been qualified to make anything of myself as an educator, and now I found myself in an exceedingly uncomfortable position. Perhaps I could have shirked my duties if I had been cleverer; Mr. Kanō had complained that I was *too* simple and honest. But I could not escape the feeling that I was in the wrong place. I felt like a fishmonger working in a pastry shop.

A year later I finally went to work in a provincial middle school. This was in Matsuyama.[10] I see this amuses you. No doubt, then, you have read my novel, *Botchan*. When I wrote *Botchan*, many people asked me who the model for the character nicknamed "Redshirt" could have been. It so happens that I was the only one in Matsuyama Middle School at the time to have a university degree, so if you're going to try to find living models for each of the characters, then Redshirt must be me—a cheering thought indeed![11]

I remained at Matsuyama for just one year. The prefectural governor asked me not to leave, but I had made an arrangement with another school, the Fifth National Higher School in Kumamoto. My teaching experience goes, thus, from Middle to Higher School, then on to the university. The only places in which I haven't taught are elementary school and girls' school.

My stay in Kumamoto was a long one. Then suddenly, after I had been there several years, a confidential inquiry came from the Ministry of Education inviting me to go to England to study. At first, I thought of declining.[12] After all, I reasoned, how would it serve the nation for someone like me to go abroad with no clear-cut objective? But my superior who had conveyed the Ministry's inquiry would have none of this. "The Ministry knows why it has chosen you," he said. "There is no need for self-appraisal on your part. Just go." Having no good reason to refuse, I followed the government's orders and went to England.[13] But sure enough, when I got there, I had nothing to do.

This requires some explanation, for which I will have to speak about my life and experiences up to the time I went abroad. You may assume that we have come to an important part of today's talk.

At the university, I majored in English literature. What exactly *is* English literature, you may well ask. I myself did not know the answer to that after three years of furious study. Our instructor in those days was Professor Dixon.[14] He would make us read poetry aloud, read prose passages to him, do composition; he would scold us for dropping articles, explode when we mispronounced words. His exam questions were always of one kind: give the dates of Wordsworth's birth and death, give the number of Shakespeare's folios, list the works of Scott in chronological order. Even as young as you are, surely you can see what I mean: can *this* be English literature? Is *this* any way to instill an understanding of what literature is, English or otherwise? Alright, you say, forge ahead on your own. But this is like the proverbial blind man peeking through the fence.[15] I would wander about in the library searching for something that would get me started. But there was nothing. This was not simply because I lacked motivation; the field was represented by the most meager collection of books. For three years I studied, and, at the end, I still did not know what literature was. This was the root source of my agony.

With this ambivalent attitude, I emerged from school to take my place in the world. I became—or rather, was made into—a teacher. Questionable as my language ability was, I knew enough to get along and managed to squeak by each day. Deep inside, however, I knew only emptiness. No, perhaps if it had been emptiness I could have resigned myself more completely, but there was something continually bothering me, some vague, disagreeable, half-formed thing that would not let me alone. To make matters worse, I felt not the slightest interest in my work as a teacher. I had known from the start that I was no educator, but I saw it was hopeless when just teaching English classes seemed like an enormous burden. I was always in a crouch, ready to spring into my true calling as soon as the slightest opening should present itself. But this "true calling" of mine was something that seemed to be there and, at the same time, was not. No matter where I turned, I could not bring myself to make the plunge.

Having been born into the world, I had to find something to do. But what that something was, I had no idea. I stood paralyzed, alone and shut in by a fog, hoping that a single ray of sunlight would shine through to me, hoping even more that I could turn a searchlight outward and find a lighted path ahead, however narrow. But wherever I looked, there was only obscurity, a formless blur. I felt as if I had been sealed in a sack, unable to escape. If only I had something sharp, I could tear a hole in the sack, I thought, struggling frantically, but no one handed me what I needed, nor could I find it for myself. There was nothing for me to do but spend day after day in a pall of gloom that I concealed from others even as I kept asking myself, "What will become of me?"

I graduated from the university clutching this anxiety to my breast. I took it with me to Matsuyama and from

Matsuyama to Kumamoto. And when, at last, I journeyed to England, the anxiety was still there, deep within me.

Given the opportunity to study abroad, anyone would feel some new sense of responsibility. I worked hard. I strove to accomplish something. But none of the books I read helped me tear my way through the sack. I could search from one end of London to the other, I felt, and never find what I needed. I stayed in my room, thinking how absurd this all was. No amount of reading was going to fill this emptiness in the pit of my stomach. And when I resigned myself to the hopelessness of my task, I could no longer see any point to my reading books.

It was then that I realized that my only hope for salvation lay in fashioning for myself a conception of what literature is, working from the ground up and relying on nothing but my own efforts. At long last I saw that I had been no better than a rootless, floating weed, drifting aimlessly and wholly centered on others—"other-centered"[16] in the sense of an imitator, a man who has someone else drink his liquor for him, who asks the other fellow's opinion of it and makes that opinion his own without question. Yes, it sounds foolish when I put it like this, and you may well doubt that there could be people who would imitate others in this manner. But, in fact, there are. Why do you think you hear so much about Bergson these days, or Eucken? Simply because Japanese see what is being talked about abroad and, in imitation, they begin shouting about it at home.

In my day, it was even worse. Attribute something—anything—to a Westerner, and people would follow it blindly, acting meanwhile as though it made them very important. Everywhere, there were men who thought themselves extremely clever because they could fill their speech with foreign names. Practically everyone was doing it. I say this not in condemnation of others, however: I myself was one of those men. I might read one European's critique of another European's book, for example. Then, never considering the merits of the critique, without in fact understanding it, I would spout it as my own. This piece of mechanically acquired information, this alien thing that I had swallowed whole, that was neither possession nor blood nor flesh of mine, I would regurgitate in the guise of personal opinion. And the times being what they were, everyone would applaud.

No amount of applause, however, could quiet my anxiety, for I myself knew that I was boasting of borrowed clothes, preening with glued-on peacock feathers. I began to see that I must abandon this empty display and move toward something more genuine, for until I did, the anxiety in the pit of my stomach would never go away.

A Westerner might say a poem was very fine, for example, or its tone extremely good, but this was his view, his Western view, and while certainly not irrelevant, it was nothing that I had to repeat if I could not agree with it. I was an independent Japanese, not a slave to England, and it was incumbent on me *as* a Japanese to possess at least this degree of self-respect. A respect for honesty, as well, the ethic shared by all nations, forbade me to alter my opinion.

The fact remained, however, that as a specialist in English literature, it made me terribly uneasy to find that my ideas clashed with those of native English critics. Whence, indeed, did this clash arise? From differences in habits? Mores? Customs? Surely, if you traced it back far enough, national character was a source. But the usual scholar, confounding literature with science, mistakenly concludes that what pleases country A must of necessity win the admiration of country B. This, I was forced to recognize, was where I had made my mistake. All right, then, perhaps it *was* impossible to reconcile the contradiction between the English critics' views and my own. But if it could not be reconciled, at least it could be explained, and that explanation could cast a ray of light on the world of letters here.

It embarrasses me to confess that I was realizing such obvious notions for the first time so late in life, but I have no intention of concealing the truth from you.

My next step was to strengthen—perhaps I should say to build anew—the foundations on which I stood in my study of literature. For this, I began to read books that had nothing whatever to do with literature. If, before, I had been other-centered, it occurred to me now that I must become self-centered.[17] I became absorbed in scientific studies, philosophical speculation, anything that would support this position. Now the times are different and the need for self-centeredness should be clear to anyone who has done some thinking, but I was immature then, and the world around me was still not very advanced. There was really no other way for me to proceed.

Once I had grasped this idea of self-centeredness, it became for me an enormous fund of strength, even defiance. Who did these Westerners think they were anyway? I had been feeling lost, in a daze, when the idea of ego-centeredness[18] told me where to stand, showed me the road I must take.

Self-centeredness became for me a new beginning, I confess, and it helped me to find what I thought would be my life's work. I resolved to write books, to tell people that they need not imitate Westerners, that running blindly after others as they were doing would only cause them great anxiety. If I could spell this out for them with unshakable proof, it would give me pleasure and make them happy as well. This was what I hoped to accomplish.

My anxiety disappeared without a trace. I looked out on London's gloom with a happy heart. I felt that after years of agony my pick had at least struck a vein of ore. A ray of light had broken through the fog and illuminated my way.

At the time that I experienced this enlightenment, I had been in England for more than a year. There was no hope of my accomplishing the task I had set for myself while I was in a foreign country. I decided to collect all the materials I could find and to complete my work after returning to Japan. As it happened, then, I would return to Japan with a strength I had not possessed when I left for England.

No sooner was I back in Japan, however, than I was obliged to chase about in order to make a living. I taught at the First National Higher School in Tokyo. I taught at the university.[19] Later (my income was still insufficient to make ends meet), I took another job with a private college. On top of all this, I came down with nervous exhaustion. Finally, I ended up having to write stories for magazines.[20] Circumstances compelled me to give up my contemplated task long before it was completed. My *Theory of Literature* is thus not so much a memorial to my projected "life's work" as its corpse—and a deformed corpse, at that.[21] It lies like the ruins of a city street that has been toppled by an earthquake in the midst of its construction.

The idea that came to me at the time, however, the idea of self-centeredness, has stayed with me. Indeed, it has grown stronger with the passing of each year. My projected work ended in failure, but I had found a belief that I could get my hands on, the conviction that I was the single most important person in my life while others were only secondary. This has given me enormous confidence and peace of mind, and I feel that it will continue to make it possible for me to live. Its strength may well be what enables me to be standing here like this lecturing to young men like yourselves.

In my talk so far I have tried to give you a rough idea of what my experience has been, my only motive being a sort of grandmotherly hope that it will be of some relevance to your own situations. All of you will leave school and go out into the world. For many of you, this will not happen for some time yet. Others will be active in the real world before long. But I suspect that all of you are likely to repeat the agony—perhaps a different kind of agony— that I once experienced. There must be those among you who, as I once did, want desperately to break through to something but cannot, who want to get a firm hold on something but meet with as maddeningly little success as you would in trying to grasp a slippery, hairless pate. Those of you who may have already carved out a way for yourselves are certainly the exception.

There may be some who are satisfied to travel the old, proven routes behind others, and I do not say you are wrong in doing so—*if* it gives you genuine, unshakable peace of mind and self-confidence. If it does not, however, you must continue to dig ahead with your very own pick until you strike that vein of ore. I repeat, you *must* do it, for anyone who is unable to strike home will be unhappy for life, straying through the world in an endless, uneasy crouch.[22] I urge you on so emphatically because I want to help you avoid such a predicament. I have absolutely no intention of suggesting that you take me as a model for emulation. I know that I have succeeded in making my own way, and however unimpressive it may appear to you, that is entirely a matter of your observation and critical judgment and does me no injury at all. I am satisfied with the route I have taken, but let there be no misunderstanding: It may have given *me* confidence and peace of mind, but I do not for a moment believe that it can, for that reason, serve as a model for you.

In any case, I would suspect that the same kind of anguish I experienced lies in store for many of you. And if indeed it does, then I hope you will see the necessity for men such as yourselves engaged in learning and education to forge ahead until you collide with something, whether you must work at it for ten years, twenty years—a lifetime. "I have found my way at last! I have struck home at last!" Only when this exclamation echoes from the bottom of your heart will your heart find peace. And with that shout will arise within you an indestructible self-confidence. Perhaps a goodly number of you have already reached that stage, but if there are any of you now suffering the anguish of being trapped somewhere in a fog, I believe that you should forge ahead until you know that you have struck home, whatever the sacrifice. I urge you to accomplish this, *not* for the nation's sake, nor even for the sake of your families, but because it is absolutely necessary for your own personal happiness.[23] If you have already taken a route similar to mine, then what I have to say here will be of little use to you, but if there is something holding you back, you must press on until you have trampled it to dust. Of course, simply pressing on will not in itself reveal to you the direction you must take: All that you can do is go forward until you collide with something.

I do not mean to stand up here and preach to you, but I cannot keep silent when I know that a part of your future happiness is at stake. I speak out because it seems to me that you would hate it if you were always in some amorphous state of mind, if deep down inside you there were nothing but some half-formed, inconclusive, jellyfish sort of thing. If you insist that it does not bother you to feel like that, there is nothing I can say; if you insist that you have gone beyond such unhappiness, that is splendid, too: It is everything I wish for you. But I myself was unable to go beyond that unhappiness even after I had left school—indeed, until I was over thirty. It was, to be sure, a dull ache that afflicted me, but one that persisted year after year. That is why I want so badly for you—any of you who have caught the disease that I once had—to forge bravely onward. I ask you to do this because I believe that you will be able to find the place where you belong and that you will attain peace of mind and self-confidence to last a lifetime.

This concludes the first part of my lecture, and I shall now move on to part 2.

Gakushūin is generally thought of as—and, in fact, it surely is—a school for young men of good social position. If, as I suspect, the sons of the upper classes gather here to the exclusion of the genuinely poor, then foremost among the many things that will accrue to you in the years to come must be mentioned power. In other words, when you go out into the world, you will have a good deal more power at your disposal than would a poor man.

I did say earlier that you must forge ahead in your work until you strike home in order to attain happiness and peace of mind, but what is it that brings that happiness and peace of mind? You make peace with yourself when the individuality with which you were born arrives where it belongs. And when you have settled on the track and move steadily forward, that individuality of yours proceeds to grow and develop. Only when your individuality and your work are in perfect harmony can you claim to have found the place where you belong.

With this understood, let us consider what is meant by the word "power." Power is a tool by means of which one forces his individuality on others. If this sounds too arbitrary, let us say that power *can be used* as such a tool.

After power comes money. This, too, is something that you will have more of at your disposal than would a poor man. Viewed in the context in which I have viewed power, money—financial power—can be an exceedingly useful tool for aggrandizing one's individuality through the temptation of others.

Thus, we would have to characterize power and money as enormously convenient implements, for with them one is able to impose one's individuality on other men or to entice them in any direction, as a poor man never could. A man with this kind of power seems very important; in fact, he is very dangerous.

Earlier, I spoke primarily with reference to education, literature, and culture when I said that individuality could develop only when one has reached the place where one belongs. But individuality functions in areas well beyond the confines of the liberal arts. I know two brothers, the younger of whom likes to stay at home reading, while the elder is fanatically devoted to fishing. The elder is disgusted with his brother's reclusive ways, his habit of staying bottled up in the house all day long. He's decided that his brother has turned into a world-weary misanthrope because he doesn't go fishing, and he does all he can to drag him along. The younger brother hates the idea, but the elder loads him down with fishing gear and demands that he accompany him to the pond. The younger brother grits his teeth and goes along, hoping he won't catch anything. But luck is against him: He spends the day pulling in sickening, fat carp. And what is the upshot of all this? Does the elder's plan work? Does his brother's personality change for the better? No, of course not. He ends up hating fishing all the more. We might say that fishing and the elder brother's personality are a perfect match; they fit together without the slightest gap in between. It is strictly a matter of *his* personality, however, and has nothing to do with his brother's nature.

What I have tried to do here is to explain how power is used to coerce others. The elder's individuality oppresses the younger and forces him to go fishing against his will. Granted, there are situations where such oppressive methods are unavoidable—in the classroom, say, or the army, or in the kind of dormitory that stresses military discipline. But all I have in mind in this instance is the situation that will prevail when you become independent and go out into the world.

So then let us suppose you are fortunate enough to collide with something you think is good, something you like, something that matches your personality. You go on to develop your individuality, meanwhile forgetting the distinction between yourself and others, and you decide that you are going to get this fellow or that fellow into your camp—even if it means dragging him into it. If you have power, then you end up with a strange relationship like that of the two brothers. If you have money, you spread it around, trying to make the other fellow over in your own image. You use the money as a tool of enticement, and with its seductive power you try to change the other fellow into something that pleases you more. Either way, you are very dangerous.

And so it is that my ideas on the subject have come down to this: first, that you will be unhappy for life unless you press on to the point where you discover work that suits you perfectly and enables you to develop your individuality; second, that if society is going to allow you such regard for your own individuality, it only makes sense for you to recognize the individuality of others and show a similar regard for their inclinations. To me, this seems not only necessary but proper. I think it is wrong for you to blame the other fellow for facing left simply because you, by nature, face right. Of course, when it comes to complex questions of good and evil, right and wrong, some fairly detailed examination of the facts may be called for. But where no such questions are involved, or where the questions are not particularly difficult, I can only believe that so long as others grant us liberty, we must grant equal liberty to them and treat them as equals.

There has been a good deal of talk about "the ego" and "self-awareness" these days as a justification for unrestrained self-assertion. You should be on your guard against those who spout such nonsense, for while they hold their own egos in the highest esteem, they make no allowance whatsoever for other people's egos. I firmly believe that if one has any sense of fairness, if one has any idea of justice, one must grant others the freedom to develop their individuality for the sake of their personal happiness, even as one secures it for oneself. Unless we have a very good reason, we must not be allowed to obstruct others from developing their individuality as they please for the sake of their own happiness. I speak of "obstruction" because many of you here will surely be in positions from which you will one day be able to obstruct others; many among you will be able one day to exploit your power and your money.

Properly speaking, there should be no such thing as power that is unaccompanied by obligation. As long as I reserve the right to stand up here looking down at you and to keep you listening quietly to what I have to say for an hour or more, I should be saying something worthy of keeping you quiet. Or at least if I am going to bore you with a mediocre talk like this one, I had better make certain that my manner and appearance have the dignity to command your respect. Oh, I suppose we could say that you have to behave yourselves because you are the hosts and I am the guest, but that is quite beside the point. It stops short at superficial etiquette—convention—and has nothing whatsoever to do with the spirit.

Let me give you another example. I am certain you all know what it is like to be scolded by your teachers. But if there is in this world a teacher who does nothing but scold, that teacher is simply unqualified to teach. A teacher who is going to scold must give himself entirely to his teaching, for a teacher who has a right to scold also has a duty to teach. Teachers, as you know, make full use of the right they are given to maintain order and discipline. But there is a duty inseparable from that right, and if they do not discharge it, they cannot live up to the functions implicit in their profession.

The same holds true of money. As I see it, there should be no financially powerful man in this world who does not understand responsibility. Let me explain what I mean. Money is exceptionally handy to have around. It can be used for anything with the utmost flexibility. Let's say I make a hundred thousand yen on the stock market. With that money, I can build a house, I can buy books, I can even have a good time in the pleasure quarters. Money can take any form at all. But I think you will agree when I say that the most frightening thing money can do is buy men's minds. This means throwing it down as bait and buying out a man's moral sense, making it a tool to corrupt his soul. Now, assuming that the money I've made on the stock market can have a great ethical and moral impact, we would have to conclude that this is an improper application of money—or so it would seem. And yet this is how money functions; this is a fact we must live with. The only way to prevent it from corrupting the human heart is for those who have money to have a sense of decency and to use their money wisely so that it will do no moral damage. This is why money must always be accompanied by responsibility. One must cultivate sufficient discrimination to appreciate the influence one's money will have in any given situation, and one must manage one's money as responsibly as one's discrimination demands. To do less is to wrong not only the world at large, but to wrong oneself.[24]

Everything I have said thus far comes down to these three points: First, if you want to carry out the development of your individuality, you must respect the individuality of others. Second, if you intend to utilize the power in your possession, you must be fully cognizant of the duty that accompanies it. Third, if you wish to demonstrate your financial power, you must respect its concomitant responsibilities.

To put this another way: Unless a man has attained some degree of ethical culture, there is no value in his developing his individuality, no value in his using his power or wealth. Or, yet again: In order for him to enjoy these three privileges, he must submit to the control imposed by the character that should accompany such privileges. When a man is devoid of character, everything he does presents a threat. When he seeks to develop his individuality without restraints, he obstructs others; when he attempts to use power, he merely abuses it; when he tries to use money, he corrupts society. Some day you will be in a position where you can do all of these things quite easily. That is why you must not fail to become upstanding men of character.

Let me change the subject for a moment. England, as you know, is a country that cherishes liberty. There is not another country in the world that so cherishes liberty while maintaining the degree of order that England does. I am not very fond of England, to tell you the truth. As much as I dislike the country, however, the fact is that no nation anywhere is so free and at the same time so very orderly. Japan cannot begin to compare with her. But the English are not merely free: They are taught from the time they are children to respect the freedom of others as they cherish their own. "Freedom" for them is never unaccompanied by the concept of duty. Nelson's famous declaration, "England expects every man to do his duty," was by no means limited to that particular wartime situation. It is a deep-rooted ideology that developed as an inseparable concomitant of liberty. They are like two sides of a single coin.

When the English have a complaint, they often stage protest demonstrations. The government, however, never interferes but takes an attitude of silent disinterest. The demonstrators, meanwhile, are fully appreciative of this and never engage in reckless activities that will embarrass the government. We see headlines nowadays about "suffragettes" committing violence, but these women are the exception. One might object that there are too many of them to be dismissed as an exception, but I think that is the only way we can view them. I don't know what it is with these "suffragettes"—perhaps they can't find husbands or they can't find jobs; maybe they are taking advantage of the long-ingrained ethos of respect for women. In any case, this is not the way the English have always behaved. Destroying famous paintings, going on hunger strikes in prison which makes life miserable for their jailers, tying themselves to benches in Parliament and shouting in order to drown out the proceedings: Perhaps these women go through these unimaginable contortions because they know the men will use restraint in dealing with them. Whatever their reasons, they are an exception to the rule. In general, the English temperament cherishes liberty that does not depart from the concept of duty.

I am not suggesting that we take England as a model. I simply believe that freedom without a sense of duty is not true freedom, for such self-indulgent freedom cannot exist in society. And if, for a moment, it did, it would quickly be expelled, stamped out by others. I sincerely wish for all of you to be free. At the same time I want to make very certain that you understand what we mean by "duty." I believe in and practice individualism in this sense, and I do not hesitate to declare this before you now.

There must be no misunderstanding in what I mean by "individualism." I ask your undivided attention on this point, for it would be particularly unforgivable of me to instill misunderstanding in young men such as yourselves. Time is running short, so let me explain individualism as simply as I can. Individual liberty is indispensable for the development of individuality that I spoke of earlier. And the development of your individuality will have a great bearing on your happiness. Thus it would seem to me that we must keep for ourselves and grant to others a degree of liberty such that I can turn left while you turn right, each of us equally unhindered so long as what we do has no effect on others. This is what I mean when I speak of individualism.

The same is true of power and money. What will happen if people abuse these things, if they exploit their wealth and power to attack men they happen not to like? This will surely destroy individuality and give rise to human misery. For example, what if the Police Commissioner had his men surround my house for no better reason than that the government did not take a fancy to me? The Commissioner may actually have that much power, but decency will not permit him to use it in this manner. Or, again, what if one of the great magnates—Mitsui, say, or Iwasaki—were to bribe our maid and have her oppose me in everything? If these individuals have the slightest bit of what we call character behind their money, it would never occur to them to commit such an injustice.

All such evils arise because people like that are incapable of understanding ethical individualism. They try, instead, to aggrandize themselves at the expense of the general public, to use their power—be it financial or otherwise—to further their own selfish ends. Thus it is that individualism—the individualism I am describing here—in no way resembles the danger to the nation that ignorant people imagine it to be. As I see it, individualism advocates respecting the existence of others at the same time that one respects one's own existence. I find that a most worthy philosophy.

More simply stated, individualism is a philosophy that replaces cliquism with values based on personal judgment of right and wrong. An individualist is not forever running with the group, forming cliques that thrash around blindly in the interests of power and money. That is why there lurks beneath the surface of his philosophy a loneliness unknown to others. As soon as we deny our little groups, then I simply go my way and I let the other man go his unhindered. Sometimes, in some instances, we cannot avoid becoming scattered. That is what is lonely.

Back when I was in charge of the literary column of the *Asahi Shimbun*, we ran an article with an unflattering

remark about Miyake Setsurei. It was a critical commentary, of course, not a personal attack, and it consisted of a
mere line or two. I don't remember exactly when it was
printed—perhaps while I was sick, or possibly I *was* the
one who gave the go-ahead—but, in any case, this bit of
criticism appeared in the *Asahi* literary column, which
made them very angry over at Setsurei's magazine, *Nihon
oyobi Nihonjin*. They didn't deal directly with me but
approached a subordinate of mine, demanding a retraction. Setsurei himself, of course, had nothing to do with
this. It was something that a few of his henchmen took it
upon themselves to do. (Perhaps I should call them his
"colleagues." "Henchmen" makes them sound like a
bunch of thugs.)[25] Well, these "colleagues" of his insisted
on a retraction. We would have been happy to oblige them,
of course, if it had been a question of factual error, but
this was a critique, after all, and there was nothing we
could do but insist on our right to publish what we
wanted. Their demand was surprising enough in itself, but
then some of these men at *Nihon oyobi Nihonjin* started
writing negative comments about me in every issue, which
truly came as a shock. I never dealt with them directly,
but when I heard what was going on, it made me feel very
odd, for while I was acting out of individualism, they
seemed to be functioning strictly as a clique.[26] At times, I
had gone so far as to publish negative reviews of my own
novels in the literary column that I myself controlled, so it
shocked me and made me feel very strange to see these
"colleagues" of Setsurei angered by a little criticism.[27] I
know this will sound disrespectful, but I could not help
feeling that they were living in the wrong century. They
were like something out of the feudal age.

But even as I concluded this of Setsurei's men, I myself
could not deny a sense of loneliness. Differences of opin-

ion, I know, are bound to arise between the closest of friends. That is why I may have given advice to the many young men who frequent my home but have never—unless for some other substantial reason—tried to keep any of them from expressing their views.[28] I acknowledge the existence of others; I grant them this degree of freedom. Thus I can never hope for another man to support me against his will, however wronged by someone I may feel. Herein lies the loneliness of individualism. Before the individualist will take a stand based on what others are doing, he chooses a course of action based on the merits of the case. Sometimes, as a result, he will find himself quite alone. He will miss the comfort of having allies. And that is as it should be: Even matchsticks feel secure in a bundle.

I would like to add just another word to prevent any misunderstanding. Many people seem to think of individualism as something opposed to—even destructive of—nationalism. But individualism in no way justifies such a misguided, illogical interpretation. (Actually, I don't like these labels I've been using. People are not to be neatly defined by any single "ism." For clarity's sake, however, I am forced to discuss a variety of subjects under one heading.) Some people nowadays are spreading the idea—and they believe it—that Japan cannot survive unless she is entirely nationalistic. Many go so far as to assert that our nation will perish unless this terrible "individualism" is stamped out. What utter nonsense! All of us, in fact, are nationalists *and* internationalists *and* individualists as well.

Freedom is the essential substance of individualism, which, in turn, forms the foundation of individual happiness. Each man's share of freedom, however, rises and falls like a thermometer in accordance with the relative security or insecurity of the nation. This is not so much an abstract theory as a generalization determined by the facts; it is the way things happen in the natural course of events. The individual's liberty contracts when the country is threatened and expands when the nation is at peace. This is all obvious.[29] No man of character is going to aim solely at the development of his individuality when the very survival of the nation is at stake. On the other hand, do be sure you see that the individualism I am talking about implies a warning against becoming the kind of fellow who insists on keeping his helmet on even after the fire is out, the man who wants to keep in lock-step when that is no longer necessary.

Here is another example. When I was in Higher School, some of the students organized a club. I've forgotten now what they called it and just what its aims were, but the club was a particularly severe advocate of nationalism.[30] There was nothing wrong with this club, of course; it had plenty of support, including that of the school president, Kinoshita Hirotsugu.[31] All of the members wore badges on their chests. I did not intend to wear any badges, but I was made a member nevertheless. Not being one of the club's originators, I knew that many of my opinions were at odds with theirs, but I joined because I had no good reason not to. When it came time for the inaugural meeting in the big lecture hall, one of the students apparently decided that the occasion deserved a speech. I was, to be sure, a member of the club, but there was much in it that conflicted with my opinions and I recall having strongly attacked its aims. But here, at the opening meeting, everything this fellow had to say was a rebuttal of what I had said! I had no idea if he was doing it on purpose or by coincidence, but, in any case, I was going to have to answer him, and when he was through I stepped to the podium. I suppose I handled myself very badly, but at least I said what was on my mind. My remarks were quite simple, and they went something like this:

The nation may well be important, but we cannot possibly concern ourselves with the nation from morning to night as though possessed by it.[32] There may be those who insist that we think of nothing but the nation twenty-four hours a day, but, in fact, no one can go on thinking only of one single thing so incessantly. The bean-curd seller does not go around selling bean curd for the nation's sake. He does it to earn a living. Whatever his immediate motives may be, he does contribute something necessary to society and, in that sense, perhaps, the nation benefits indirectly. The same might be said of the fact that I had three bowls of rice today for lunch and four for supper. I took a larger serving not for the nation's sake but, frankly, to suit my stomach. These things might be said to have some very indirect influence on the country, and, indeed, from certain points of view, they might bear some relation to the entire drift of world affairs. But what a horror if we had to take that into account and eat for the nation, wash our faces for the nation, go to the toilet for the nation! There is nothing wrong with encouraging nationalism, but to pretend that you are doing all of these impossible things for the nation is simply a lie. This was more or less what I said.

No one—and I do mean no one—is going to be unconcerned about the nation's safety when one's country is in danger. But when the country is strong and the risk of war small, when there is no threat of being attacked from without, then nationalism should diminish accordingly and individualism enter to fill the vacuum. This only stands to reason. We are all aware that Japan today is not entirely secure. Japan is a poor country, and small. Anything could happen at any time. In that sense all of us must maintain our concern for the nation. But this country of ours is in no danger of suddenly collapsing; we are not about to suffer annihilation; and as long as this is true, there should be no need for all the commotion on behalf of the country. It is like running through the streets dressed in firefighting clothes, filled with self-sacrifice, before any fire has even broken out.[33]

Finally, however, this is all a matter of degree. When war does break out, when a crisis involving the nation's survival does arise, anyone with a mind that can think—anyone who has cultivated sufficient character such that he cannot help but think—will naturally turn his attention to it. Nature itself will see to it that he gives his all for the nation, even if this means placing restrictions on his individual liberty and cutting back on personal activity. Thus, I do not for a moment believe that nationalism and individualism are irreconcilable opposites engaged in a constant state of internecine warfare.

I would like to say more on the subject but time does not permit, so I will limit myself to these remarks. There is just one other point that I would like to bring to your attention—namely, that a nationalistic morality comes out a very poor second when compared with an individualistic morality. Nations have always been most punctilious over the niceties of diplomatic language, but not so with the morality of their actions. They swindle and cheat and trick each other every chaotic step of the way. That is why you will have to content yourself with a pretty cheap grade of morality when you take the nation as your standard, when you conceive of the nation as an indivisible monolith. Approach life from a foundation of individualism, however, and you arrive at a far loftier morality; the difference between the two deserves a good deal of thought. To me, therefore, it seems obvious that in a time of tranquility for the nation, we should place the greater emphasis on individualism with its lofty moral sense. I am afraid I have no time to say anything further on this subject today.

I want to thank you for inviting me here. I have tried my best to explain to you how necessary individualism will be for young men such as yourselves who will have the opportunity to live lives of individual fulfillment, and I have done so in the hope that it might be of some use to you once you have gone out into the world. Whether or not I have, in fact, made myself understood, I of course cannot know, but if there should be points that are still unclear to you, it is because I have expressed myself insufficiently or poorly. If you do find that something I have said remains vague, please do not assign some random meaning to my words, but come to see me at my home whenever you wish and I will do my best to explain. Of course, nothing could give me greater satisfaction than to have gained your understanding of my true meaning without this extra effort.[34]

And now I shall step down, lest I overstay my welcome.

Appendix

Sōseki and *Nihon oyobi Nihonjin*

Sōseki had been hoping to institute a literary column in the *Asahi Shimbun* for some time, both as a convenient outlet for his own nonfiction (which, as an *Asahi* employee, he felt uneasy about publishing in other newspapers) and as a source of income for struggling young writers and critics who frequented his home. When one such disciple, Morita Sōhei (1881–1949), became a virtual

social outcast after a scandalous love affair with the femi-
nine-rights activist Hiratsuka Raichō (1886–1971), Sōseki
arranged for him to publish his novelization of the affair
in the *Asahi* from January to April 1909, under the title of
Baien (Sooty smoke), and convinced the editors to institute
a literary column (*"Bungeiran"*) with himself as nominal
head while Morita did the actual day-to-day editing (at
home, since the company refused to employ him formally
and, in fact, paid his Y50 editor's fee indirectly to Sōseki!).
The arrangement was an open secret, however, as mentioned in the literary gossip column (*"Bungei zatsuji"*) of
the conservative journal *Nihon oyobi Nihonjin*, edited by
Miyake Setsurei.[35]

The literary column made its debut on 25 November
1909 carrying Sōseki's preface to the first volume of *Baien*,
which was being republished, somewhat expurgated, in
book form.[36] After that, the column appeared on page 3
virtually every day, featuring essays on literature, art, and
music written by a brilliant array of critics, scholars, and
novelists.[37] Several important Sōseki pieces appeared in the
column, but Sōseki was ill much of the time, and the
impetuous Morita abused the free hand this gave him,
publishing opinions that proved embarrassing for Sōseki.[38]
Eventually, Morita's handling of the column led to its
demise in November 1911—much to Sōseki's relief, no
doubt.[39]

One consistent target of the *Asahi* literary column was
the literature of the naturalists, but under Morita's direction the column also became embroiled in a rather low-
minded altercation with *Nihon oyobi Nihonjin*. The 15 May
1910 issue (no. 533) of that bimonthly journal contained a
report in the gossip column that Morita was living with
"some suspicious woman from Hama-chō" and speculated
that there might be another *Baien* appearing soon in the

Asahi. In response, Morita himself wrote the *Asahi* column for 24 May in which he criticized gossip columns in general for printing false reports of scandal in order to attract readers, concluding with the observation: "I was quite shocked the other day to see this same sort of morally questionable material in no less a magazine than Miyake Setsurei's *Nihon oyobi Nihonjin*, which makes itself out to be such a reformer of public morals."

It was Sōseki who had to bear the brunt of Morita's rashness, for beginning with the 1 July issue (no. 536), *Nihon oyobi Nihonjin* began to run a series of attacks on Sōseki, both in the gossip column and in the supposedly more respectable critical column (*"Bungei jihyō"*) written by Mitsui Kōshi (1883–1953). Whereas the former tended to carry sheer malicious rumor (impugning Sōseki's mastery of English, for example), the latter responded to several of Sōseki's recent critical pieces with appalling hysterical outbursts, resorting on at least one occasion to deliberate misquotation. During one particularly extreme temper tantrum, Mitsui exposed Sōseki as "one of those who admires the poetry of Yosano Akiko, that woman responsible for the spreading taste for obscene fantasy, which we find utterly sick." It must have been quite a shock to Sōseki, seeing himself labeled a writer of potboilers who knew nothing about art, a haiku-writing fossil from another age, a dilettante, a superficial and irresponsible critic, and a conniver—although he might have taken some comfort in being occasionally lumped together with the likes of Mori Ōgai and Nagai Kafū.

Then suddenly, after the 1 October issue of *Nihon oyobi Nihonjin* (no. 543), the attacks ceased, doubtless because of the news that Sōseki had almost died of hemorrhaging ulcers on 24 August. The gossip column in that issue noted that Sōseki seemed to be recovering. "We are concerned that it might be stomach cancer, and we have heard that people suffering from this disease tend to criticize others . . . but we certainly wouldn't want him to die." Small wonder that Sōseki felt moved to tell his audience that the attacks "made me feel very odd."

Notes

1. This was Sōseki's fourth serious bout with stomach ulcers.

2. One version of this story, *"Meguro no Sanma,"* can be found in Imamura Nobuo, ed., *Rakugo zenshū*, 3 vols. (Kin'ensha, 1969), vol. 1, pp. 915–36. Sōseki makes his interpretation of the story abundantly—not to say painfully—clear, but for a discussion of the tale's surprisingly wide range of meanings, see Ikegami Shin'ichi, *Rakugo rinrigaku* (Tōkyō Shobōsha, 1971), pp. 252–53. In my translation, "mackerel" is a somewhat arbitrary rendering of *sanma, Cololabis saira,* or mackerel (or saury) pike, a saltwater fish which the sheltered daimyo are convinced can be found only in the woods of Meguro.

3. Ōmori Kingorō, apparently a professor of history at Gakushūin. SZ 11:679.

4. In a 1906 interview entitled *"Rakudai,"* Sōseki describes what a poor student he was until the age of nineteen, when he made up his mind to study hard "in order to gain the confidence of others." Two years later, in 1888, he graduated from Higher School with a brilliant record. SZ 16:499–504.

5. Sōseki graduated from—and entered the graduate school of—Tokyo Imperial University in July 1893 at the age of twenty-six. By August it was clear that he would not be teaching at Gakushūin, and by October he had settled on the job at the Higher Normal School, as described below. For further (sketchy) details, see Ara, pp. 148, 150–52. The man who secured the Gakushūin post, Shigemi Shūkichi, had degrees in science and medicine from Yale.

6. For a discussion of the Meiji ideal of success and the diminishing opportunities for realizing it, see R. P. Dore, "Mobility, Equality, and Individuation in Modern Japan," in Dore, ed., *Aspects of Social Change in Modern Japan* (Princeton University Press, 1967), pp. 113–50.

7. Kuhara Mitsuru (1855–1919) who had by the time of Sōseki's lecture become president of Kyoto Imperial University.

8. Kanō Jigorō, 1860–1938. Also known as a judo expert and founder of the Kōdōkan.

9. See chapter 2 of *Botchan* (1906) for similar scruples on the part of Sōseki's comic hero, SZ 2:256, or Alan Turney's translation, *Botchan* (Kodansha International, 1972).

10. This had been a period of psychological stress for Sōseki, which had included an unsuccessful attempt at Zen meditation such as that described in *Mon*. Quite suddenly, in April 1895, Sōseki left graduate school and his part-time post at the Higher Normal School for a full-time position as an English teacher in Matsuyama.

11. A conniving hypocrite, Redshirt receives a sound thrashing at the end of the novel.

12. This was in May 1900. As a teacher in a state institution of higher learning, Sōseki "really had no choice, for the offer had been more an order than an invitation." Edwin McClellan, *Two Japanese Novelists* (University of Chicago Press, 1969), p. 10.

13. Sōseki left for England in September 1900 and returned to Japan in January 1903.

14. James Main Dixon (1856–1933), a Scotsman, taught English literature at the university from 1886 to 1892. McClellan (*Two Japanese Novelists*, p. 6) notes that he was the author of *Dictionary of Idiomatic English Phrases, Specially Designed for the Use of Japanese Students*.

15. "*Mekura no kakinozoki.*" There are several such expressions for pointless activity, e.g., "*Tsunbo no tachigiki*"—a deaf man's eavesdropping.

16. *tanin hon'i.*

17. *jiko hon'i.*

18. *jiga hon'i.*

19. No longer wishing to remain bottled up in the provinces, Sōseki maneuvered his way out of the post in Kumamoto, to which he was supposed to have returned, and into these two part-time positions in Tokyo. See Etō Jun, *Sōseki to sono jidai*, 2 vols. (Shinchōsha, 1970), vol. 2, pp. 231–33.

20. Thus inauspiciously did his literary career begin in 1905 with the writing of "*Wagahai wa neko de aru*" for *Hototogisu*. In response to popular demand, the story grew into a novel.

21. On *Bungakuron* (1907), see Matsui Sakuko, *Natsume Sōseki As a Critic of English Literature* (Tokyo: Center for East Asian Cultural Studies, 1975), pp. 107–45. Professor Matsui has kindly offered several suggestions for improving the present translation.

22. "*Shijū chūgoshi ni natte yo no naka ni mago-mago shite inakereba naranai.*" For a discussion of these characteristic Sōseki expressions for anxiety and lack of direction, see my *Sanshiro* (University of Washington Press, 1977), pp. 228, 229.

23. In *Sanshirō* (1908), Professor Hirota delivers a speech on the new generation's unwillingness to live for the sake of such external entities. SZ 4:178–81, or pp. 122–25 of the translation.

24. Witnessing the eruption of Mt. Aso, Kei-san (the son of a bean-curd maker) says to his companion, "My soul is just like that. . . . an enlightened revolution . . . a bloodless revolution. . . . The enemies are power and money, all those bastards who oppress our helpless brothers!" *Nihyakutōka* (1906), in SZ 600–601.

In this section of his talk, Sōseki is being remarkably consistent with ideas expressed in some of his early writings when, as Matsuo has pointed out, Sōseki saw himself as engaged in a battle against the immoral capitalists who stay well fed while allowing others to eat "monkey fodder." (See letter of 16 August 1907 in SZ 14:626–27; Matsuo, pp. 76–77.) One particularly striking parallel can be seen in a nearly hysterical diatribe against the rich that climaxes *Nowaki* (1907):

"No one can object when a merchant uses his money to make more money. That is his profession. But when he exploits his power in human affairs rather than in business, he must look to those with greater understanding (i.e., scholars and writers)" (SZ 2:800–806).

And in *Kokoro* we read: " 'Give a gentleman money, and he will soon turn into a rogue.' Sensei's trite answer disappointed me" (SZ 6:81; McClellan translation, p. 64). At this point in the novel, Sōseki primarily wishes to assert the disturbing ease with which people change, but Sensei's "trite" answer is, in fact, one of Sōseki's most persistent themes.

25. "Henchmen" here is the usual underworld term for an underling, *"ko-bun"*—literally, "having the characteristics of a child." Sōseki is sardonically pointing to the familial organization shared by underworld gangs, intellectual cliques, and most other groups in Japan, despite the use of such egalitarian-sounding terms as *"dōjin"* (same-[aspiration]-people), translated here as "col-league."

26. Further details about this affair are given in the Appendix, pp. 315–18, below.

27. Abe Jirō's critique of *Sore kara* (1909) occupied the column for three issues on 18, 20, and 21 June 1910. Although the review paid due respect to the richness of the novel's philosophical content and praised Sōseki as the only novelist of his day capable of handling such grandiose themes, the essay pointed out an unwelcome artificiality and abstractness that marred crucial events in the novel, and it lamented that the portrayal of the central love relationship was particularly unsatisfactory for this reason. Sōseki wrote a highly appreciative note to Abe praising his critical acumen. SZ 14:835.

28. Morita Sōhei, *Natsume Sōseki* (Kōchō Shorin, 1942), p. 90: "What made me feel close to [Sōseki] Sensei was that it was possible to speak one's mind freely in his presence."

29. Not all of Sōseki's contemporaries would have agreed with him. The socialist pacifist Kinoshita Naoe (1869–1937) wrote in 1904, just after the beginning of hostilities with Russia, that freedom of speech is necessary in peacetime and all the more so in time of war, for that is when people are called on to take the greatest risks and make the greatest sacrifices. Paraphrased in Yanagida Izumi, *Nihon kakumei no yogensha Kinoshita Naoe* (Shunjūsha, 1961), p. 145, from *"Gunkoku jidai no genron"* in *Mainichi Shimbun* (25 March 1904). Admirable as this may sound, Sōseki's grudging recognition of reality remains as true as ever.

30. The club was probably the one known as the Dōtoku-kai (Moral society),

described by Sōseki's friend and classmate, Masaoka Shiki (1867–1902). It was founded in 1889 amid the new wave of intense nationalism styled *"kokusuishugi"* that had been marked by such events as the assassination of the Minister of Education, Mori Arinori, on 11 February 1889 for supposed offenses against the national gods, and the founding, in 1888, of Miyake Setsurei's new magazine, *Nihonjin* (later, *Nihon oyobi Nihonjin*), devoted to the preservation of the "national essence" (*kokusui*). Shiki reports that Sōseki criticized the Dōtoku-kai for presuming to reform morals despite the nonexistence of any absolute standards. See Etō, *Sōseki to sono jidai*, vol. 1, pp. 141–43.

31. Kinoshita Hirotsugu (1851–1910), later president of Seoul Imperial University.

32. For a discussion of Sōseki's theme of "possession" of the individual by external entities, see my *Sanshiro*, pp. 229–30.

33. See Yoshino Sakuzō *"Kokka-chūshin-shugi kojin-chūshin-shugi ni-shichō no tairitsu—shōtotsu—chōwa,"* *Chūō Kōron* (August 1916), p. 58: "No doubt, as the commentators tell us, Japan faces some extremely difficult times ahead. But surely we will not be so hard pressed in comparison with other powers and in comparison with our own situation until now that we will be unable to consider the problem of individual fulfillment."

Like Sōseki, Yoshino argues that attacks on individualism are based on misunderstanding, that individualism and nationalism are reconcilable, and that extremes in either direction are dangerous, concluding, "We must not, in fear of some apparition of foreign oppression, concentrate solely on a superficial show of national organization to the neglect of individual-centered policies [*kojin hon'i no seisaku*]" (p. 60).

Yoshino makes no mention of *"Watakushi no kojinshugi"* or Sōseki; perhaps, significantly, he does suggest at one point that most writers are socially unconscious decadents (p. 44).

34. In *Garasudo no uchi*, Sōseki tells of three young men who came to see him shortly after the lecture. One of them did indeed ask for further clarification, but the other two had specific domestic difficulties and asked how they might apply Sōseki's ideas to these practical problems. One of the Gakushūin students who helped arrange the lecture claimed to have known four or five students who visited Sōseki seeking clarification.

Sōseki tells another anecdote with regard to the lecture, elsewhere in *Garasudo no uchi*. He was annoyed and embarrassed when a Y10 honorarium was sent to him from the school despite his having given the talk out of sheer goodwill. His objections show him to have been anything but an absolutist in such matters, however: had the amount been more commensurate with his intellectual riches, he says in effect, he might not have felt so constrained to donate it to charity as he did, but, "If it's an insult to give ten yen to an Iwasaki or a Mitsui, it's an insult to give ten yen to me!" See Ara, p. 788, n. 53, and SZ 8:446–48, 493–96.

35. See issue no. 522 (1 December 1909), p. 79. On Miyake Setsurei (1860–1945), see Kenneth B. Pyle, *The New Generation in Meiji Japan* (Stanford University Press, 1969).

36. See " *'Baien' dai ikkan jo,"* in SZ 11:568–70.

37. Including Mori Ōgai, Nagai Kafū, and also a bright, young Russian student named Serge Elisséeff, who contributed introductory pieces on Russian novelists for the columns of 21, 22 December 1909; 14, 15 March, 30 July, and 27 September 1910; 9 February and 30 March 1911, before becoming the first foreign graduate of Tokyo Imperial University in 1912. See Ara, pp. 578–700, and E. O. Reischauer, "Serge Elisséeff," *Harvard Journal of Asiatic Studies,* vol. 20, nos. 1–2, p. 15.

38. See *"Sōhei-shi no ronbun ni tsuite"* (18 March 1910), in SZ 11:234–36.

39. Komiya 3:124–40.